THE CROSSING

A Terrorist Plot Against the United States

THE CROSSING

A Terrorist Plot Against the United States

By

C. Ed Traylor

Oak Tree Press  Hanford, CA

Oak Tree Press
Publishers Since 1998

For information, address Oak Tree Press, 1820 W. Lacey Boulevard, Suite 220, Hanford, CA 93230.

Oak Tree Press books may be purchased for educational, business, or sales promotional purposes. Contact Publisher for quantity discounts.

First Edition, September 2015

ISBN 978-1-61009-207-4
LCCN 2015914383

To my wife, Pat, and my daughters

ACKNOWLEDGMENTS

The author wishes to extend his grateful appreciation for help in the creation of this work to Taylor Pensoneau; Jane Primose; Mary Pat Corder; his wife, Pat; and his daughters, Angela and Lori. The author also recognizes the encouragement of the late Becky Austwick.

PROLOGUE

From their base in Kabul, American intelligence forces sweep the region, searching for terrorists in any number of surrounding countries. The depth of their surveillance exceeds anything that American users of Google experience from their laptops on lunch breaks. Their information entails not only the most miniscule physical locations, but reams of paperwork and stacks of CDs on millions of people of interest.

Their watch also sweeps the northwest territories of Pakistan, including Seidu, a hotbed of anti-American threat. The tribes are known to shield terrorists, and the dusty backlots are established training bases for radical Muslims seeking higher places in death.

Air strikes are designed to eradicate terrorism in a variety of ways. Some strike directly at bases of terror, eliminating the threat by death. Others are intended as "shock-and-awe," to show the terrorists that American military might means business, and they may be next in line.

The former was the reasoning behind the identification of one home in Seidu. From the outside, it appeared as the typical slab home that shelters millions of Pakistanis. But this particular dwelling harbored several individuals whose anti-American leanings have made them conscious threats. A drone was sent from Kabul to blast the house and its inhabitants.

Racing across the open sky, the drone flew directly above its target in Seidu and fired its missile. The townspeople, watching from below, had only seconds to scramble for cover. An orange fireball erupted in the targeted home, with a report that rattled windows and nerves.

The impact of the blast decimated the structure, blowing the walls outward in shreds and collapsing the roof. Shards of glass became shrapnel, while bits of slab were thrown for hundreds of yards.

Inside, the militants were annihilated almost instantly. The force of the blast sent deadly shockwaves through their bodies, snapping their heads backward, twisting in midair as they were hurled from their chairs and beds. Chunks of debris crushed their bones and sliced through them as knives. Limbs were ripped off and tossed through the air, landing amid the rubble and strewn about the yard.

Under the smoldering pile of stone lay the blood-splattered, mangled remains of four young extremists, their threat to America neutralized in the blink of an eye. Neighbors, dazed at the spectacle, emerged from their basements and bunkers and roamed the streets, comforting the crying and spewing anger at their western enemies.

Some staggered to the demolished terror haven and struggled to lift the still-warm rubble from the now-cooling bodies. As they shoved aside beams and heaved blocks of crumbling stone, they uncovered the first ravaged corpse, causing screams of horror from the rescuers. Within reach of his outstretched, pallid hand was a blackened copy of the *Koran*.

Omar Ul-Bashar, a tribal leader and bomb maker, walked from his nearby home to the site of the drone strike. His coal-black eyes flared as he surveyed the devastation and carnage. Simmering with rage, he returned to his cramped, gray stone abode and reached for his phone to call his son in Karachi.

CHAPTER I

The waves from the Arabian Sea crashed against the dark sand as Mahammed Ul-Bashar watched from the picture window in his home in Karachi. The sky was hazy on this April afternoon, less the result of the seasonal ninety-degree heat and more the polluted air that entrapped the city, the largest in Pakistan and home to some 13 million.

Still, life was much better here than elsewhere in a nation that ranks among the poorest in the world. Per-capita incomes in Pakistan are a paltry $2,500 a year, and many of Pakistan's 187 million people struggle for necessities such as food and shelter.

The impoverished dot Karachi by the millions, but the elite are born rich and stay that way. Karachi is a hub of business, political, and intellectual pursuits for both Pakistani nationals and the city's international community, and the city is one of the most recognizable to those in all hemispheres.

The desire for something better brought Mahammed from the city of Seidu from his native lands in the northwestern territories. Karachi is over a thousand miles from these lands, and the distance is measured not only in miles but in personal safety and economic opportunity. In Karachi, Mahammed saw a place to advance among the elite. His father, Omar, saw no need for such ambition.

A man whose Muslim faith ruled every aspect of his thinking, Omar was now in his seventies, his face pocked with scars partially camouflaged by his salt-and-pepper, flowing beard. His eyes emitted a glare that melted men of lesser intensity. His wife, Sabhila, had passed away fifteen years before, and without her soothing influence, Omar became increasingly bitter, driven even more by a burning dislike of the West.

He had always made bombs and now with more time on his hands, there was no reason to stop. He whiled away the hours in a twelve-by-twelve stone block shack behind his residence, producing bomb vests used by suicide bombers. A steady stream of customers frequented his home, most never to return. The neighbors noticed, but never seemed to care. The tribes of northern Pakistan share a radical Muslim devotion and a hatred of all things Western, and when Omar spoke, he was speaking for most in the neighborhood.

Mahammed could certainly sympathize. He hated Israel as much as the others, and deplored the American aggression into their neighboring peoples. Many of his friends had given their lives in the name of Allah. But life in Karachi meant cars, computers, cleaner streets. The dusty one-lane alleys and dilapidated stone huts of Seidu held little promise for a promising young man who sought better things in life.

Mahammed's new wife shared those desires. Yalina was the daughter of another warlord, and Mahammed knew her well. They had grown up together, were classmates in school, and played games on the crumbling backstreets of Seidu as youngsters. She also knew there was life outside Seidu. Their fathers were allied in the tribes and quickly approved the union, which was born more of mutual respect than shared passion.

They were married in 1982 and Yalina soon bore him two children, Solomon and Sasha. In early 1986, Mahammed was accepted into medical school in Karachi, and the young family quickly relocated. The following year, a second son, Racheed, was born.

Mahammed progressed well in medical school and showed much promise. He was also not wedded to the old ways. In Karachi, he had access to American cable television, British newspapers, and western radio. He learned how those parts of the world thought and felt, and how they viewed Pakistanis. His views of Americans did not change, though he harbored less anger than his father. He saw no reason to avoid their foods, their electronics, their clothes. In time, he dressed in western apparel as often as in traditional garb, though his head dress remained a fixture.

Like most third-world countries, Pakistan suffers from a severe chasm in economic equity. While the multitudes languish in tent cities and mud-caked shantytowns, the rich barely bat an eye as they drive to and from their well-paying government, university, and medical jobs. From their comfortable homes on hilltops and in secluded neighborhoods, their children enjoy educational privilege, their wives shop in the finest fairs and western department stores, and their men fret over money and peer respect.

Mahammed was one of the elite. He quickly established himself as a star in medical school, rising to the top of his class with hard work and an eye for detail. Some viewed him as humorless, but his closest friends saw a focused young man with a drive to succeed, even in rare lighter moments over dinner or in front of the television.

Upon graduation, he became a doctor at a neighborhood clinic, where he treated some of the same people whose filthy neighborhoods he passed in his black Mercedes every morning. Mostly, though, his patients were of the same social set as himself. Mahammed shared none of the worries of the lowest peoples, and saw little reason to care. As a doctor in government employ, he could rely on a cushy salary to support his wife, family, and lavish lifestyle.

As he enjoyed a day off at his home near the sea, Mahammed could reflect on his journey. Now in his late fifties, he roamed the thirteen rooms, following their free and airy flow, sometimes stopping to gaze at his glassware collections and native-made furniture that was the envy of neighbors. Looking over thick, dark-rimmed spectacles that sat comfortably against his dull white head dress, Mahammed's eyes met Yalina's as she strode by, clutching the copy of the *Koran* she had cherished since her youth.

This self-assured couple could also take pride in their three children. Solomon, now thirty, had attended the finest schools in Karachi and resembled his father's erect, well-groomed persona. He also reflected his father's quiet devotion, not only to religion, but also to country. Solomon craved military glory, and successfully applied to the Kakul Military Academy in Abbottabad, far to the north.

He graduated with high honors and was accepted into the Pakistani army's branch of military intelligence. In his role, he could keep an eye not only on threatening neighbors such as India, but also global enemies like the United States. Stationed in the Pakistani capital of Islamabad, Solomon proved well-suited for his assignment. Dignified yet unassuming, his upright carriage masked the two hundred pounds he carried on his five-foot-ten-inch frame. Stoic and unflappable, he handled the most sensitive matters with speed and competence, earning the trust of high commanders and slicing through the corruption that held back peers.

Twenty-eight-year-old Sasha had not been quite as easy on her parents. As a teenager, she showed none of Solomon's scholarship and jeopardized family respect by donning short dresses, miniskirts, and western footwear. Her beauty made her the envy of her girlfriends and the object of the rich boys' crushes, and she showed little inclination for the oppressive values of her parents. Still, her family doted on her, particularly Solomon, who relished the role of protective big brother despite her errant ways.

College in the major city of Lahore followed, and there Sasha finally began to mature, her grades improving with every passing year, her wildness mellowing into covering dress and burquas. Like some of her friends, she did not share the fiery hatred of the west and became acquainted with the American and British businessmen, envoys, and students who worked in the big cities of Pakistan.

Sasha's behavior was surprising, but Racheed's was far harder to comprehend. He was a brooding sort, content to hole up in his room with his computer and his thoughts. Standing five-feet-nine and weighing barely 160 pounds, Racheed bore little resemblance to Solomon, four years his senior. Rather, the younger man was built for athletics, and he did not disappoint. In field hockey, he had played on the junior national team against India and other fierce rivals, and was mentioned as an Olympic possibility. Darkly handsome, he could have had his pick of the neighborhood girls, who filled his inbox and cell phone with inviting messages.

But Racheed wanted the world on *his* terms, not someone else's. He stared out the window for what seemed like hours, stoking his beard and lost in solitude. He was an outstanding student, proficient at every subject he ever studied, particularly engineering. That brightened his future. In many third world countries, skilled, wealthy students have their pick of opportunity, and engineering was a sought-after profession.

In Racheed, Mahammed saw elements of his own father. The intense personality, the inability to relax, the innate hatred of America were all reminiscent of Omar. Mahammed had chosen a different path for himself; he did not want to emulate Omar, steeped in tradition and burning with vengeance. Mahammed feared those traits now simmered in his own son.

He approached Racheed, lost in himself on a sofa in the parlor. “Have you thought more about university?” he quizzed.

Racheed's brow tightened. “Yes, Father, certainly. I heard from Punjab earlier today. They have accepted me.”

“Very good. It is a fine school,” nodded Mahammed approvingly. “What about others?”

“I now have four other applications in other universities,” replied Racheed. “Many in Pakistan have engineering programs of high quality.”

“Yes,” said Mahammed, stiffening. “But what about America?”

Racheed swiftly jerked his head, staring Mahammed directly in the eye. His voice turned frosty. “You know I do not want to study in America. I cannot accept their ways. We have discussed this before.”

"We have," said Mahammed sharply. "But university in America offers much promise. Their schools are full of the world's best and brightest. You are a fool if you ignore that."

Racheed sprang from his seat. "I am no fool!" he snapped. "Americans are the fools, not I. They try to run the world, when we don't want them. They think their ways are the only ways. Their people are arrogant. Their beliefs are deceitful. They hate us for our way of life."

"Not all of them," said Mahammed, raising his finger for effect. "I know many Americans who are good people. I've met many more than you." He sauntered about the room, turning his back on his son. "I disapprove much of their culture and their ways. I know their actions have resulted in the suffering of our people. But their universities are the greatest in the world. You will also be safe there, safer than in our own nation."

He ceremoniously raised his index finger and turned to face Racheed. "Many of our people have studied there. I have told you this before, and you do not honor your father's wishes. You must consider American university."

Racheed bowed his head and clenched his lips. Resignedly, he said, "I have been accepted into several American schools."

"Why did you not tell me?"

"You knew I was applying to them. It was your idea all along."

Mahammed struggled to hide a smile. "What ones want you?"

"Michigan was the first to accept me," said Racheed, his voice trailing. "There was also California, Minnesota, Texas A & M, Purdue, and Columbia."

Now Mahammed made no effort to suppress his pleasure. "What of the school in Boston? How should you say, M.I.T.?"

Racheed stared at the floor in shame. "They denied me," he said. "My application was received too late."

"No bother," said Mahammed. "Your efforts have been successful. What about Texas A & M?"

"That's the last one on my list," said Racheed, shaking his head intensely. "They are not as highly rated as some others. And why would I want to live in the middle of that cowboy land?"

Mahammed waved his left hand in dismissal. "Texas A & M has a fine engineering program," he declared. "Our friend Abdul sent his son there. He has told me how much he has gained. Several other of our friends have sent children there. You will know people there. You will not at other universities."

"That is a bad thing?" said Racheed, voice rising in disgust. "I do not care for our friends in Texas."

"*Silence!*" roared Mahammed. "It is best for you to go there. Besides, it is my money that will send you. Honor your father. Respond that you accept their offer."

"Very well, Father," sighed Racheed. "I will consider it. We will talk later." Having won the argument, Mahammed smugly dropped into his favorite chair and reached for the newspaper.

CHAPTER II

Mahammed hung up the phone and turned toward the dinner table. He assumed his seat at the head and after a brief reflection, began to speak.

"That was my father," said Mahammed, grimly. "There was another drone strike in Seidu this afternoon."

"Our family?" Yalina inquired.

"No. None to which we are related," replied Mahammed, watching his wife and children exhale.

Sasha was still concerned. "But our friends?"

"Some," said Mahammed. "Some of our neighbors' families from back home. Father blames the Americans. It was their strike, and their responsibility. He is enraged at the loss. So many of the tribesmen have been lost over the years."

"He is right," said Racheed, eyes flaring. "Strikes with drones are cowardly and unjustified. They only kill the innocent women and children. The Americans have no right to inflict this upon us."

Mahammed saw the boiling anger in his son. "That is true," said he in a trailing voice. "It is nothing new. I have never seen Father so angry. He demands retribution for all who have been lost. I could not reason with him."

"*Reason?*" The usual monotone in Racheed's voice evolved into a shout. "There is no reason for what they have done. I cannot accept it." His glare zeroed in on his father. "You want me to attend their university. I cannot, and will not. I *cannot* study among the evil. *I cannot live among those who want our people to die!*"

He jumped from his chair and briskly strode outside to the deck. Mahammed and Yalina looked at each other, then looked at Solomon, searching for answers. Solomon, though, had none. "I will try and talk to him," said Solomon, who deliberately put his hands flat on the table and pushed himself away.

Turning toward the sliding glass door, Solomon saw Racheed pacing across the deck like a caged lion. The weather had turned sour and the waves violently crashed below. The latch of the door jingled and Racheed offered a glance.

"What is it, my brother?" inquired Solomon, trying to muster a soothing voice.

"You know very well. Father wants me to attend Texas A & M. I cannot do it. I cannot go to university in America. You see what kind of people they are."

"I am aware," said Solomon. "My job brings me to that every day. I more than you know the damage that America has done to us, our neighbors, our faith."

"They are such a greedy people," mused Racheed. "Always wanting more. Their buildings the shiniest in the world, their streets cleaner than ours, their lands enormous. Such economic power, yet such evil. No respect for Islam. If we had such power, we would use it to serve Allah. They would sooner destroy us than shake our hand."

"But that is really not the issue," responded Solomon, struggling to break the train of thought. "American university is the issue. You must follow Father's wishes."

Racheed clutched the deck railing and bowed his head. "I know," he murmured. "I cannot disobey Father. I must go. I *hate* the thought. Still, I must."

"Yes, my brother," said Solomon, patting Racheed on the right shoulder. "It is for the best. You will learn much there, and you will be successful. There are other reasons you must go as well."

"Like what?"

"We need Pakistanis to be in the United States. If we should declare war on America, we must know the territories, and have people within their borders who are familiar."

Racheed raised his head and peered over his shoulder. "Are we considering war?"

"We always have to. Against America and any others of distrust."

"You want me to be a spy?

"Not a spy," said Solomon, raising his right hand to stop Racheed's thoughts. "But men as you can help us. You may travel freely in the United States. That will be our benefit. As you do, you will learn of military installations and other defenses. You will also know the transportation hubs and their infrastructure. You will see the sites that we may strike them at, and inflict the most damage."

"Everyone knows where the American military bases are," scoffed Racheed. "You don't need me for that."

"But we must know more. We need to know where all military are stationed, where the National Guard posts are, where equipment and weapons are stored. We must have as much information as possible if we are to attack."

Racheed pondered Solomon's words. As seconds passed, his posture straightened and a hint of a smile crept across his face. "Yes, yes. Who would I report to?"

"Me, of course. We will be in contact, as only brothers could be. You may send me e-mails or texts with the information you have, and I will tell you what I need."

"But they will know," said Racheed, brow furrowed. "The United States has a massive intelligence network, and they are spying on their own people. How will they not find out what we are doing?"

"They will not," reassured Solomon. "I will give you secure websites and our own network. It will be difficult for them to know what we are doing. Besides, you will send messages in such a way that they will not easily understand."

Racheed seemed convinced by Solomon's explanation. He concluded his persuasion. "You must do this. You must attend university there, as Father wants. As we need."

He turned on his heel and returned inside. Racheed gazed at the sea for a while, contemplating his brother's words. The thought of Texas repulsed him, but a larger issue was at stake. He knew he could no longer defy his father, nor his brother.

*****

College Station is a city of 72,000 in southeastern Texas whose claim to fame is Texas A & M, founded in 1876 as the agricultural and mechanical institution that gives the school its popular acronym. With over 49,000 students, it is one of the largest schools in the United States, though its football teams are far better known than its academic virtues. It is also home to the Presidential library of the elder George Bush, who remains a revered figure in this part of the world, over twenty years after leaving office.

Unlike many university towns, College Station is rather isolated, and in an expansive state such as Texas, it takes a long time to get anywhere. Driving distances are routinely measured in the hundreds of miles, though on Saturdays in the fall, the football fans of "Aggieland" flock in droves. The entire city of College Station would easily fit inside the school's football stadium.

Racheed arrived for the summer term in June and quickly went about securing housing and a car. Succeeding in that, he soon found his new home distasteful. Certainly, plenty of internationals dotted the student body, as in most large American universities. He managed to look up his family friends and spent a little time with them, praying and exchanging news from home. His apartment was in university housing near other Pakistanis, though, as he had told Mahammed, he had little use of these acquaintances.

College Station represented everything Racheed disliked in America. The oilmen were obnoxious, the cars big, the buildings sprawling and the people snooty. As he motored around in his Honda

Civic, his back tightened when he was passed by a bulky sport utility vehicle. There was no need for such a show of power, he thought. This is why they want our neighbors' oil. This is why they pay any price. This is why they kill for it.

Whenever possible, he avoided Bush Street and the Bush library. That only reminded him of the war on Islam. He had heard the stories of Khomeni and the hostages he had taken in Iran before his birth, and he knew that Israel had been a source of contention for decades. But it heightened under Bush. As a boy, he remembered the Gulf War and the patriotism that had swept America. It was all for oil, for aggression, for dominance. Clinton followed, bombing whenever his sinful womanizing called for a deflection. Then the younger Bush. Racheed could barely think his name. He lived not far from here, only twenty miles away.

As summer turned to fall, Racheed became more settled, his hostility tempered by concern for his studies. As in Pakistan, he proved an excellent student, proficient in computer graphics, architecture, and physics, which he especially enjoyed. He took particular interest in chemical reactions and how structures held, examining their strong and weak points.

By his sophomore year, Racheed sported a GPA of 3.8 and was being encouraged by professors to consider graduate school. Few worked more diligently. His life consisted mainly of class, brief trips to the grocery store, and study in his three-room university apartment. Every so often, he took in a varsity soccer game, or perhaps a volleyball match. He shied away from the football stadium, believing the sport barbaric.

Several years older than his classmates, he found their laughter and carousing immature. He had come halfway around the world to be here, he thought, and here they were, mere miles from home, drinking beer and sleeping around. They did not care about education or bettering themselves, he believed. Even his roommate, Ahmed, strayed. A Muslim from Faisalabad who was studying mathematics, Ahmed kept beer in their refrigerator and smoked an occasional joint.

"Why do you live this way?" Racheed once asked. "You know it violates our faith. We are to abstain from such things."

"Oh, Racheed," laughed Ahmed, waving his hand in dismissal. "Who am I harming? My parents will never know, and I want to have a little fun. I pray every night, just as you do. But really, Racheed, who cares?" Much to Racheed's chagrin, others agreed with Ahmed.

Their apartment was a frequent site for prayer. Twice a day, several other Muslims ventured there, colorful prayer rugs in hand, to conduct their worship. Muslim prayer is far more grueling than that of Christians. The exercise takes several minutes, requires deep concentration and recitations, and is done on one's knees, often leaning face forward to the floor. Shoes are removed during the prayer, conducted on the cloth mats.

Those who have never experienced a Muslim prayer often do not know how to react. Most watch in silent awe. Others, though, feel threatened. The campus mosque held a steady stream of devotees, and afternoon prayer sometimes attracted hundreds, particularly during Ramadan. It was also a gathering spot for racists. Sometimes, they would hide outside, dash inside to grab a handful of the Muslims' shoes, and toss them in a nearby fountain.

Most Americans accepted the Muslims and tried to welcome them, but not all. They were subject to taunts and threatening gestures, such as the extended middle finger and screams of "Paki go home," "USA!" and "9-11." In the cafeteria lines, snickers sometimes arose when Muslims declined beef or burgers, adhering to the sacred cow of Islam. Those same yahoos referred to Muslims by stereotypical names like "Akbar" and "Muhammed" and bumped shoulders or poked them.

Once, Racheed broke up a fistfight between a fellow Muslim and an American. Sitting at the police station, Racheed corroborated the Muslim's version. His opponent's story apparently held up better. No charges were filed.

Many internationals mixed with Americans in the same circles of friends, dating and hanging out. But those from the host nation were rarely drawn to Racheed. When conversation with Americans arose,

Racheed invariably stiffened and offered basic courtesies, if at all. He frequently sat alone in class, empty seats between him and the nearest person. With the exception of a couple eclectics, many gave up on Racheed after one or two tries.

“What's the matter with you?” chided Ahmed. “Americans have their problems, but a lot of them are all right. What's your problem?”

“They're my problem,” retorted Racheed. “I'm here to study, not make nice with them.”

“Devout Muslim,” scoffed Ahmed. “Millions of our people seek peace. It is the heart of Islam. And you call yourself a son of Allah.”

“Shit.” Racheed wadded up a piece of paper and tossed it at a trash can. “This from one who uses. The heart of Islam, you say.”

Ahmed shook his head. “You need to look for a new roommate next semester.”

The short list of Racheed's friends was reduced by one.

CHAPTER III

When the spring semester dawned, Racheed was living alone in a two-room apartment in an eight-story brick unit a half-mile from campus. Rather than start the Honda for a few blocks' drive, he bought a used bicycle for ten dollars, and it became his primary mode of transport. His landlady was an older sort, and smiled whenever he passed by or brought the rent check.

He declined the chance to return home at Christmas, choosing to spend the holidays in California with a couple of Islamic friends. Christmas meant nothing to them, as their faith dictated a different path. But few college students ignore a four-week break, and Racheed was no different.

Fellowship, though, took a back seat to practicality, and Solomon's words were heeded. He spent ample time noticing the gates of military bases and any sign that identified a government installation. He also noted the centers of transportation in the cities he visited. Information was passed back to Solomon in coded e-mails or voice messages.

The first day of the semester brought a new schedule, including a course in computer drafting held in the school's gleaming addition to the engineering hall. This class was a requirement, one that Racheed welcomed. He was the best among peers in computer technology, so this challenge struck no fear. As usual, he came in just before the start of the lecture and had his pick of seats, since only a handful of students were scattered across the dozens of seats.

Near the middle was a young Hispanic woman, a stranger to Racheed. Her beauty immediately drew his gaze, and she detected his attention. She smiled and looked down at her desk, but quickly lifted her eyes to meet his glance once more. Normally, Racheed sat by himself. Today, the loner wanted company.

He slid into a seat two down from her chair, leaving a space in between. Racheed knew how to conduct himself around women, though he usually paid little attention beyond flirtation. Back in Karachi, he was in high demand among the neighborhood girls, and he would toy with them, coming on, smiling, then backing away.

Racheed and the young woman exchanged a pleasant "hello" and the lecture began. Friends and faculty all knew Racheed for his intense concentration during lectures, but today his focus was her. He kept turning his head, watching her shift her petite frame, twirl her flowing dark hair with her finger, check her watch. Her dark red Texas A & M sweatshirt and light gray jeans accentuated her slender build and butterscotch skin. She realized his glances and smiled coyly, hoping that he had not seen her own stares. As his head turned, she had a moment to admire his slender, athletic build and dark, piercing eyes.

Class finally ended, and Racheed, nervous as never before, quickly rose. "Are you...are you a new student here?" he stammered.

"No." she said, her voice soft and cool. "I am a sophomore."

"I am, too," he said, beginning to catch his breath. "My name is Racheed."

"I am Maria," she said, extending her hand. Her delicate wrists and fingers melted into Racheed's larger palm.

"Where are you from?"

"Pakistan," he replied, quickly thinking of something to impress her. “My father is a doctor in Karachi. And you?”

“I am from Mexico City,” she said. “My father is a general in the military.”

“Then you are not far from home,” he noted. “I am many miles from my home.”

“I am sorry,” said Maria sympathetically. “Do you like it here?”

“It is all right,” said Racheed, masking his true feelings. “The school has a fine engineering program, which is why I came here.”

“I have a political science major, but I minor in engineering,” said Maria. “It is funny that I have not seen you before.”

As they spoke, students from the next class began to trickle in. “Maybe we should leave,” said Racheed. “Where is your next class?”

“I do not have one until eleven. I was going to the library in between.”

“So was I,” said Racheed, forgetting a need to stop at the bookstore. “Let's walk together.”

As they did, he learned more of this fragile, winsome beauty whose face his eyes fixated on. She was Maria-Therese Santos, a product of the finest finishing schools in Mexico. Her parents, Carlos and Miragel, were a union of two of Mexico City's most politically powerful families. Miragel's father was a former member of the Mexican cabinet, while Carlos, from an old line of aristocrats, was in charge of Mexican military intelligence.

The lovely Maria had led a sheltered life, protected by a doting father who made sure his daughter only worried about what dress to wear at the latest parties. Their home in the hills of Mexico City was gated, and she knew little of the crime and poverty running rampant on the streets. For long periods, she never left the safety of the hills, as her private Catholic school was nearby and most of her friends were neighbors. Carlos knew well the dangers his little girl faced on the mean streets of Mexico City. Standing five-foot-two and barely weighing one hundred and ten pounds, she would have been no match for the gangs who despised the establishment and ruled the night.

The walk to the library took an hour, rather than the usual ten minutes. For Racheed and Maria, it seemed like seconds. By the time they separated inside the lobby, they had exchanged e-mail addresses and cell phone numbers.

*****

The innocent flirtation of that first day in class blossomed into a white-hot affair. Many evenings were spent in Maria's apartment in intense lovemaking, the sort of interludes others only fantasize of.

Maria was intoxicated by him. To be sure, there were plenty of beaus in the upper circle at home, and she allowed some to touch and kiss her. A couple had taken her further, unbeknownst to her father, to her delight. But she had never experienced a love such as this.

Those boys were cultured gentlemen, meeting her parents' approval and feeding her boredom. Racheed, though, was rougher around the edges. She had never known someone from that part of the world, and there was nothing subtle about him. He was not one to hold doors and rise when she walked into a room. In their most intimate moments, nothing was gentle in his touch.

His anger both intrigued and scared her. He disliked America with ferocity, while she admired the American ways, freedoms, lifestyles. It became a subject that they could barely discuss. When she looked into his soul-less coal-black eyes, she saw a coldness that sometimes frightened her. But when they made love, she only felt the masculine features of a man she longed for.

He was devout in his faith, as she to hers. She loved that in him; his relentless devotion to Allah was like nothing she had ever seen. She was irresistibly drawn to the air of mystery that projected from him at every turn. Sometimes she felt he was a stranger. Other times, as his body was pressed against hers and she ran her hands through his combed, dark hair, she knew him as no other.

She wanted to know every thought, every fear, every passion in his mind that she could never seem to penetrate. But when she was near him, a fire consumed her entire being.

She was certainly different than any of the girls Racheed knew back in Karachi. Her delicate features, soft curves, and buttery skin were far different, more desirable than the women who had thrown themselves at him over the years. She never minded being subservient, more than willing to go with Racheed to wherever and whatever he wanted.

He was far less interested in the long walks, sipping coffee at the downtown bistros, or cuddling on park benches that she craved. He was a man, with a man's wants and desires. He deserved to have a woman like this, beautiful and sophisticated, who worshiped his body and wanted to please every part of it.

He lusted for her more as every hour of the day passed, as he sat through classes, studied in the library, stopped by the store. Then evening finally came and he could let his body go, savoring every instant of pleasure she gave him. He could hardly stop thinking about how she would stimulate him in their moments alone, and the look on her face when she touched, kissed, held him.

As their relationship intensified, Racheed expressed a desire to learn Maria's native tongue. "I want to speak Spanish" he declared one morning as he prepared to leave for class.

"Really?" Maria was startled at Racheed's statement. He was already proficient in English as well as several native dialects. "You are going to take classes?"

"No. I want to learn from you. You can teach me."

Maria assumed that his desire to learn Spanish stemmed from their closeness. She threw her arms around him and kissed him passionately. "Oh, Racheed, my darling. Yes, Yes. I'll be happy to teach you."

Racheed could not understand her emotional reaction. "Yes. I think I could really benefit from fluency in Spanish."

Maria fantasized about their future. "I think so, too. If we're living in Mexico, it will really help you."

"Yes," said Racheed, his air of mystery again protruding. "That's possible."

For the next several months, Maria acted as a tutor to Racheed, teaching him all the nuances of the Spanish language, its vocabulary, greetings and common phrases, and the dreaded rolling "r" sound.

He studied with his usual intensity, the same traits that alarmed and enthralled her.

Still, she loved every moment of their time, and looked forward to their sessions. She was gentle and laughed when he made an innocent mistake. Racheed, though, rarely laughed at anything. In time, he became remarkably proficient, able to hold his own among native Spanish speakers.

He was able to put his fluency to the test on their trips to Mexico City to visit her family. Several times over the next two years, they flew the thousand miles from nearby Houston to the Mexican capital on spring break, the Christmas holiday, and during summers. Maria anxiously awaited the trips and cherished every moment she had with Racheed, and she filled the hours with chatter of each other's families, likes and dislikes, and goals in life. Once arrived, they would stop at points of interest, and she would help him learn of Mexican geography, landmarks, and history.

"Your nation was at war with the United States," said Racheed once. "Over 150 years ago."

"Yes, but our nations are friends now. That was a long time ago."

"No, it is not." Racheed's hatred for America again flared. "They provoked a war over land. They were a much stronger nation than you. They were the aggressors, just as they are now."

"Oh, Racheed," Maria said playfully. "That is in the past. They are our friends now. My father always says so."

Racheed offered no response. Despite her father's tolerance of the Americans, Racheed found him fascinating. Carlos Santos was in his mid-fifties, mustached and balding, with a slight paunch protruding from his solid frame. He was immaculately dressed in his dull green and white Mexican military uniform, which he had proudly worn for over thirty years.

As a son of the elite, Santos was welcomed into the best Mexican military schools. He worked his way through the officer corps, and for the last twelve years, wore the decor of a general in Mexican intelligence. As he progressed, his personal wealth zoomed, and he now enjoyed life with his wife and Maria in a sixteen-room stucco villa surrounded by a three-acre floral garden that was the envy of his affluent neighborhood.

Unlike most of his compatriots, Carlos' name was free of the stain of corruption, and presented a genteel front. He trusted others almost to a fault, and seemed to have difficulty seeing the worst in people despite his position, which required analytical thought.

His success allowed his wife to devote time to her own pursuits. Miragel was little interested in her husband's work and rarely cared to discuss it at the dinner table. Rather, she devoted herself to the arts, a loyal patron to the best museums in the city. She spent frequent evenings in the theater, taking in the sights and sounds of the music and dance that attracted high-end tourists the world over. One look at her striking physique showed where Maria had acquired her beauty. Though several inches taller than her daughter, and nearly as tall as her husband, Miragel naturally attracted attention with the bright-colored sarapes and scarves that fit her form perfectly, complementing her jet-black eyes and short, styled hair.

Unlike the general, Racheed had little difficulty in finding the worst in people. But he found no such fault in General Santos, and they became good friends. The general was thrilled that his little girl had found someone of such character that she cared for so deeply, and was impressed by her lover's focus and determination. Often, the general and Racheed would stroll through the sprawling villa or the flower gardens, discussing world politics and economic issues.

They often discussed the drug cartels in Mexico. For the last several decades, Mexican society has been littered with drug lords, who rake in massive amounts of money in the narcotics trade that often spills across the American border. Thousands of Mexicans and many Americans have lost their lives at the hands of these ruthless criminals with little regard for human life, backed by strong organization, plenty of funding, and seemingly unending supplies of heroin, cocaine, marijuana, and meth.

Racheed listened intently, familiar with similar troubles back home in Pakistan. He said little as the general explained his country's dilemma in the greatest of detail. Their conversations sometimes lasted hours, and Maria, like her mother, had little taste for the dullness of such issues.

On the flight back to Texas after one visit, Maria chided Racheed. “My boyfriend,” she scoffed. “I almost think you love my father as much as me.”

Racheed simply smiled and stared at the rolling Mexican landscape as it zipped below his window seat.

CHAPTER IV

Racheed maintained his high grades throughout his final two years at Texas A & M and routinely carried a heavy course load, collecting enough credits to graduate a semester early. But his commencement came both slowly, and much too soon. He could barely wait to escape what he thought of the cowboy world of south Texas, the epitome of the American arrogance he despised. But he also remembered the nights in Maria's apartment, and hoped there would be no break in their flaming passion. He also hoped he would be able to maintain his close relationship with her father.

As Racheed prepared to graduate that December, sister Sasha had plans of her own. She wanted to make a quick trip to Seidu, to visit her grandfather Omar.

"Can you not wait?" asked Yalina. "Racheed's commencement is in only two weeks. Why do you not wait until after then?"

"Oh, mother," sighed Sasha. "I have not seen Grandfather for months. He has been asking that I come."

Yalina shook her head. "You can wait a while longer. After we return from Texas, you may go then."

"No!" Sasha was always impetuous, and this time was no exception. She also never shied from annoying her mother. "I will be gone only a few days. I will return in plenty of time to go with you."

Yalina rolled her eyes. She suspected that Sasha wished to deflect attention from Racheed's big day. But she also knew that her husband would support his little girl's wish. "Very well. But you cannot travel alone."

"All right," said Sasha, excitedly. "I will go with Hassan."

"No, you most certainly will not," snapped Yalina. "Your father and I have no use for him. He is not from a good family. I will call Khalid. His parents live near Omar, and he is trustworthy."

Sasha saw she could not have her way entirely. "Khalid is so dull. But, if that is what you wish."

"It is," said Yalina, knowing she had salvaged at least part of the argument.

Khalid, an accountant, managed to secure a few days off, and was more than willing to escort Sasha on the twenty-hour trip to Seidu. Like many of the best young men in Karachi, he had a crush on her, though he could not break off with his girlfriend, thirty pounds heavier than Sasha with far less intoxicating eyes and smile. He told his date that he had to make a quick trip home, neglecting to mention his travel partner.

Sasha cared little for Khalid and pouted for most of the drive, longing for the daring Hassan. Still, she adored her grandfather, despite the obvious differences in personality. Her cosmopolitan interests conflicted with his old ways, and she harbored far less of his Western hatred. His rigid exterior also contrasted with the vivacious, fiery young woman only partially masked by burqas. Nonetheless, Omar held a fondness for Sasha that did not extend to her brothers.

She arrived after a day and a half drive, dismissed Khalid and settled herself at her grandfather's residence, a slab house that, while dreary, was one of the largest in the neighborhood. The bomb trade provided Omar more income than most, and he could afford such luxury. Other leaders lived well, too, though the vast majority lived in two- and three-room abodes, some of which surrounded Omar's property.

Of little concern to Sasha, and everyone else in the vicinity, was one small structure, just next door, that was home to terrorists. These extremists were common to the region, as much a part of everyday life as the sunrise. The terrorists were sons of the tribe, friends to all in the neighborhood. They rarely ventured outside, but when they did, they were greeted as any other.

The forgiving neighbors took little interest, but American intelligence was practically obsessed. From their base near Kabul, intelligence officers kept a near-constant surveillance on the home, aided by moles who had infiltrated the tribes. This home was the base of a sect whose threats on American embassies was well-established. Though living in simplicity, they had ample money, explosives, organization and above all, motive, to make good on their threats.

Once again, a drone was launched from Kabul. The drone soared high over the mountains of Afghanistan, and once the target was identified, the missile was launched. It pierced across the skies, headed east across the border, and was over Pakistan within minutes. With little warning, the drone completed its flight to Seidu.

The missile crashed through the home, triggering a massive explosion that instantly destroyed its occupants. The sweeping blast spread next door, blowing the gray stone walls of Omar's dwelling inward. A towering fireball followed, consuming the structure and allowing no escape. The bodies of Omar and Sasha, mangled and barely recognizable, were found buried beneath the rubble.

*****

Around 3 a.m., Racheed's telephone rang in College Station.

“Hello?” said Racheed, sleepily.

“Racheed. It is your father,” said the voice on the other end. “I have news I must discuss.”

“What is it, Father?” replied Racheed, mustering an abnormally respectful tone.

“I have just received news. There was another bombing in

Seidu.....” His voice trailed into silence.

Racheed became nervous. “Father?” No response. “Father?”

“A drone struck a house next to Omar's. The strength of the bomb was too great.” He paused again. “His home was destroyed.”

Racheed gulped. “Then he is dead?”

“Yes.”

A long pause resulted. On the other end, Mahammed collected himself to deliver more sorrowful news.

“He is not the only one,” said Mahammed in a whisper.

“What do you mean?”

“Sasha had wanted to visit her grandfather. We did not want her to go....”

Racheed's blood ran even colder. “She was there?”

“Yes, my son.”

Her location perplexed Racheed. “What was she doing there? She knew my graduation was coming.”

“Her mother tried to talk her out of it. But you know Sasha. You could never say no to her.”

Racheed fell silent, expecting what was coming next. Still, he had to ask. “And she is dead, too?

A longer pause came from the other end. “She too, my son.”

Racheed's hand slid with the receiver as he looked at the ceiling. “It cannot be. It cannot be.” Realizing his father could not hear him, he put the phone back to his ear. “No. No. No. When?”

“A few hours before. Khalid's mother called just a moment ago.” Racheed offered no response.

Mahammed barely offered one himself. “We are leaving now for the burial.”

Racheed recognized the Muslim tradition of burying the dead as soon as possible. “There is no way I can return in time. It takes nearly a day and a half in flight alone.”

“I know,” said Mahammed sympathetically. “Solomon will meet us there, and we will have other family. too. Just return as soon as you can.”

With graduation impending, Racheed hesitated. Then he

remembered his high class standing. “I will speak to my professors. I think I can work a way to come, with no loss of study.”

“Very well. I will see you soon, my son.”

As Racheed hung up the phone, his sadness proved fleeting. He now felt the seeds of anger, which only grew as the days passed.

CHAPTER V

Since Racheed was such an excellent student, his professors understood his need to leave, and offered him an extension for outstanding coursework and exams. Missing the winter graduation ceremony was no loss, as he was little interested in such pomp. He vowed to return at the earliest possible time in the summer, complete his coursework, and finish his time in College Station.

He then contacted Maria, who wept at her lover's loss and offered her support. He promised to keep in touch via e-mail, text message, and cell phone.

A grueling trip followed. Racheed drove the two hours to Houston, left his Honda at the airport, and flew to New York City. A six-hour layover at LaGuardia ensued before he boarded an Airbus to London, a six-hour flight. After another four-hour layover at Heathrow, he finally caught a direct 767 for the remaining four thousand miles to Karachi. He landed, caught a taxi home, and piled his luggage into the silver Toyota that his father had bought new for him six years ago. Next came the remaining 850 miles to Seidu, and he arrived exhausted, three days after his sister's and grandfather's deaths.

The time in the air gave Racheed an opportunity to think, and his mind was far from forgiving. He had long opposed the drone strikes, believing them unjust and evil. Before, though, he had lost only friends and distant relatives. Now Sasha and Omar had been taken. By the time he landed in Karachi, his anger had turned to controlled rage.

The family stayed in Seidu for a couple of days, visiting relatives and old friends as they came to grips with their loss. Many offered their sympathy, as Omar was a prominent resident, respected by all. The loss of Sasha, an innocent victim and so young, also troubled them.

Racheed, though, shed few tears and spent only limited time with his family. Most of his hours were spent walking the streets, examining the damage to Omar's home, and brooding. Before, he felt powerless to help those lost in the barbaric drone strikes. Now, he must seize the power.

After a few days, the Ul-Bashar family was prepared to leave. Racheed, however, expressed a desire not to join them, but he had to devise a viable excuse.

"I want to stay here for a few days," he informed his father.

Mahammed was startled, as Racheed seldom showed interest in his ancestral lands. He also knew his son had responsibilities back in Texas. "Oh? For what reason, my son?"

"I would like to visit my other set of grandparents," replied Racheed. "Besides, I would just feel better if I remained. This has been such a shock to all of us. I think I would like to take a little more time, to reflect."

"That is wise," said Mahammed assuredly. "I wish I could take more time myself. But my practice is waiting, and I must return."

"I understand, Father," responded Racheed, feigning sympathy. "I will not be long, though. I will come home in a few days." Satisfied, Mahammed and Yalina offered their goodbyes and departed.

Though few spoke directly of it, there were pockets of Taliban throughout the area. Western television anchors told their viewers that the Taliban was weakened in the "war on terror," almost to the point of extinction. The locals knew better. They were still strong in number and potent in force, and everyone knew who they were. Some offered their help in hiding these young warriors in basements, dugouts, and caves.

Not a resident of Seidu, Racheed needed a little assistance in finding Taliban men, but that proved simple. He arranged for a meeting in a backyard bunker near the charred rubble of Omar's dwelling.

In a dimly lit, 12 X 12 enclave, Racheed faced six men in khaki green suits and pants, each wearing white head dress. The dirt floor and stone walls contrasted with the computers that were set up around the room, as well as wireless telephone equipment and surveillance materials. In one corner was a gray cloth bag from which thousands of rupees, the Pakistani currency, were spilling. The room was uncomfortably warm, trapping the outdoor temperatures that hovered around seventy degrees, even on this late December afternoon.

“What is it you want?” inquired the leader of the enclave, named Ashish, a middle-aged man with sunken eyes and humped back.

“I come here about the drone strikes,” said Racheed. “They cannot continue.”

“We know that. We are angry as well.”

“What are you doing about it? What does the Taliban want done?”

Ashish waved his hand. “That is for us to know.”

Racheed was unintimidated. “I want to help. What may I do?”

Quizzically, Ashish glared at Racheed. “How may you serve us?”

“America must pay for their actions. So many of our people have died. They must pay for their evil.”

“We agree. That is why we are dedicated. We fight in the name of Allah against those who wish us harm.”

Racheed bowed respectfully. “I am aware. Israel and its allies must be conquered. America is the backbone. They must suffer as we have.”

Ashish began to loosen. “Their Bush inflicted terrible suffering on us. It has continued under Obama. His people say he is a Muslim.

But no Muslim may cause such suffering on his own people."

"I seek revenge on them," declared Racheed loudly. "They have killed my sister and grandfather, and many of my friends. They have hurt our economy, and prevented us from serving Allah. I will not stop until they have paid."

"What do you wish?" said Ashish with businesslike tone.

"I wish to create a plan," mused Racheed. "I want as many of them to suffer as possible. I want them to pay many times over for Seidu."

"Very good," replied Ashish with a wry smile. "But I ask you again, my son. What is your plan?"

"I am still contemplating," said Racheed, knowing his position was weakening. "My brother is in the military in our capital. I wish to talk to him. He will help me."

"No!" snapped Ashish. "You will tell of us. We cannot be found!"

"Do not worry. You are my friends," said Racheed presumptively. "I honor your wish. You will not be bothered."

Men such as Ashish are naturally distrustful, and Racheed's vagueness did little to ease his mind. But Ashish knew Omar well, and was a frequent customer of his explosives. Omar was a revered citizen, and Ashish's admiration for him swayed his opinion.

He surveyed the other five men around him, then made his decision. "I take you at your word, my son."

Racheed stifled a sigh of relief. "How shall I contact you?"

"You will not," replied Ashish. "You will only contact Salaam." He pointed at the youngest man in the room, who nodded in introduction. "He will pass your message to me. Do not contact anyone other."

"I pledge," said Racheed, bowing again.

"In the name of Allah," said Ashish, raising and lowering his right hand. Racheed turned and slowly departed.

*****

Racheed walked to the cottage where he had stayed with his family. Now without the hindrance of his parents, he took the opportunity to call Maria. After graduation, she moved back to

Mexico City, into a one-bedroom luxury apartment overlooking the downtown business district near her father's office. Rather than land a job, Maria chose to take a year off, as wealthy young college students are wont to do.

They had not spoken in over a week, and she was ecstatic at the sound of his voice. “Racheed!,” she exclaimed. “I'm so happy you called. I miss you so. How are you?”

“I am fine,” he said with decidedly less enthusiasm, though she could hardly have cared. “It's good to talk to you, too. How are you doing?”

“I'm well!” she responded amid giggles. “You just caught me. I just got out of the shower.”

Racheed smiled at the thought of Maria naked, as she hoped he would. “I'm so glad that finals are over. I did well on them, all A's and B's.”

“Congratulations,” replied Racheed. “How was graduation?”

“Boring,” laughed Maria. “But my parents came for it, and we had a nice weekend.”

“How is your father?” asked Racheed, with more interest in his voice.

“He is well,” she sighed, recalling her lover's infatuation with her father. “He sends his best to you, as always.”

“And the same,” he offered. “I wanted to let you know that I'm coming back to visit.”

“Oh, Racheed! I'm so happy,” Maria's voice was almost a shout. “When? How long?”

“I'm flying in a couple of days,” Racheed said. “I must visit my brother in Islamabad first. Then I leave.”

“I cannot wait,” said Maria. Then her voice turned seductive. “My bed is so lonely.”

Racheed smiled on the other end. “I've missed you, too.”

“We can spend the whole day making love when you get here,” mused Maria. “And the day after that, and the day after that.”

“Yes,” said Racheed. “And I'll want to visit your father, too.”

“Of course,” said Maria. Her sultry tone was now tinged with sarcasm. “You and my father are so close, after all.”

“I respect him greatly,” replied Racheed defiantly. “As I do his daughter. I'll see you later this week. I'll call from the airport.”

“I'll be waiting. I love you.”

“Me, too.” Racheed hung up the phone, brooding as usual, thinking about plenty of things other than the desirable young Maria.

CHAPTER VI

The next day, Racheed bid farewell to his parents, whom he had spent relatively little time with in either Karachi or Seidu. Never particularly close to begin with, neither Racheed nor his parents spent much emotion in their goodbyes. They had never met Maria, and did not seem especially inclined to. Racheed only mentioned her in passing, and Mahammed and Yalina knew little of the intensity of their son's love affair. Racheed then drove his Toyota to the capital of Islamabad to speak with Solomon, who had earlier returned with the family.

Racheed arrived in the capital and drove straight to Solomon's office, located in a modern steel office complex teeming with security. However, the front guard was also from Karachi, and knew Racheed's family. He let him pass with no check.

Solomon was expecting Racheed, so other guard posts were notified, and Racheed passed with no effort. He rode the elevator to Solomon's fourth-floor office and knocked on the door. "Hello, my brother," said Racheed.

"Hello to you as well," said Solomon, embracing Racheed. His uniform was neatly pressed as usual, his carriage upright. "I am sorry I could not stay longer in Seidu."

"No one expected you to," replied Racheed. "I know Sasha's loss was very difficult for you."

"Yes," said Solomon, eyes welling. "I still cannot believe it."

"Nor I" replied Racheed, eyes dry.

"Why did you wish to see me?" inquired Solomon, collecting himself from his momentary lapse.

Racheed's eyes now flared. "They must pay for what they have done."

"What?"

"America. The drone strikes have harmed us so much. Now they have taken our family."

Solomon turned away. "I am well aware of that. Every day, I deal with the threat of violence against our people."

"Then you understand," insisted Racheed. "They must pay."

Solomon stepped toward the window and gazed at the city skyline. "Why did you come?"

"I wish a favor from you."

Solomon dreaded what that would be, but showed nothing outside. He trudged toward his desk and sat down. "What?"

"I would like you to provide false documents to me."

"What are you talking about?" Solomon's body stiffened as he looked across his desk.

"I want documents that identify me as Pakistani intelligence."

"Out of the question," dismissed Solomon. "You are not a member of our military."

"I am well aware of that." Racheed tried his best to keep his composure, and his voice monotone.

"Why do you need such documents?"

Racheed drew a breath. "It is part of my plan."

"What plan?" Solomon stared straight into his brother's face.

"I must avenge Sasha and Omar."

"You already said that. Now tell me. *What do you mean*?"

Racheed never especially trusted Solomon, though knew he must trust him now. "I am formulating a plan to avenge their deaths. I want to inflict punishment on Americans."

"In what way?"

"I am not clear on that. I have ideas and I want to pursue them." He breached his confidence from his warrior friends in Seidu. "I have spoken with the Taliban."

Goosebumps swept across Solomon's body. "Tell me you did not."

"It is true. I have explained my desire to them."

Solomon's analytical nature percolated. "Did you speak to the sect near Omar's home?"

Racheed was surprised that Solomon knew of the six warriors. "You are aware of them?"

"*Of course I am aware of them!*" snapped Solomon. "*That is what I do for a living, you fool!* I am supposed to keep track of threats to us and those within our borders!" He paused to settle himself. "How will you use the documents?"

"Do you remember my girlfriend, Maria?"

"Maria? What about her?"

"Her father is a general in the Mexican army, in charge of intelligence," explained Racheed. "Remember how I described him to you?"

"Yes?"

"If I can present myself to him as Pakistani intelligence, he will give me access to his information."

Solomon failed to understand the logic. "Why do you need his information?"

"I think I can work a plan that will use the drug cartels of Mexico to help me. They will give me what I need for my attack."

"On American soil?"

"Yes." Racheed struggled to bury a smile.

The creases in Solomon's forehead deepened. "You must not care for Maria. I thought you did."

"Of course I care for her," replied Racheed. "Why do you say such a thing?"

"You're lying to her," said Solomon, matter-of-factly. "You will pose as a false officer to gain information from her father. That is a brave plan."

"We must be brave," replied Racheed, snapping his body to the side. "The time for cowardice is over. The Americans are cowards for what they have done. We will not be."

"So you will use the woman you say you love?" shot back Solomon. He turned in his swivel chair to face away from his brother. "And why should I believe this is done in Sasha and Omar's name? I was much closer to Sasha than you were, my brother. I have not seen you weep yet for either of them."

"I am aware," said Racheed coolly. "But we must avenge their deaths. We must do so in the name of Allah. The time for weeping is over. We must act."

"And these Taliban warriors you spoke of? They will help?"

"I hope so."

Solomon paused for several seconds. "You know that I am breaking my code if I supply you with false documents. You know what my punishment may be?"

Racheed knew all too well. "You will be expelled."

"If I am lucky," said Solomon. "You know how our military officers sometimes disappear?"

Racheed had not wanted to say it in words. "I know what I am asking of you."

Solomon was not about to let Racheed off so easily. "I am very proud of my service to my country. I am very proud to wear this uniform, and serve our people." Racheed silence indicated Solomon had achieved the desired effect.

Solomon drew a deep breath and blew a stream of air between his lips. Another pause of seconds followed. "I will give you what you want."

"Thank you," said Racheed, quickly adding, "When may I receive them from you?"

"It will be at least two days," said Solomon. "I will have to work in secrecy, and alone. I will not be able to finish these documents until then. Do not ask before two days."

“I will wait to hear from you,” said Racheed. “I am indebted to you, my brother.” He bowed his head in respect.

“Do not bow,” scoffed Solomon. “Bow only if we fail.”

“I will not,” responded Racheed, ignoring the risk to Solomon. “I will do Allah proud.”

Solomon was unmoved. “You had better.”

Racheed offered no embrace this time, choosing to quickly leave the room.

*****

Two days later, Racheed's phone rang at his Islamabad hotel. Solomon was on the other end, in a less than cordial tone.

“I have what you need,” said Solomon, not bothering with “hello.”

Racheed was startled at his brother's brusque response. “Oh! Ah, thank you. I am in your debt, my brother.”

“You said that before. Do not say it again.”

“Do you want me to come back to your office?”

“*No, you idiot!*” snapped Solomon. He then lowered his voice to protect against eavesdroppers. “That is the *last* place you should come. If anyone sees this, I am in trouble for certain. You have no idea what you have asked of me.”

Even in this delicate moment, Racheed could not let it pass. “Yes, I do, my brother. I know exactly what I have requested.”

Solomon doubted his brother's attempt at sincerity. “Whatever. I will come to your room in half an hour.”

He broke the connection before Racheed could respond. Less than thirty minutes later, a rapping was heard at the door.

As Racheed opened, Solomon barged past, eager to escape the hallway. He set a black briefcase on the bed and nervously pried open the latches. He reached inside and withdrew a manilla file folder.

“Here are your papers,” he said, shoving the folder at Racheed. “These identify you as an intelligence officer.”

Everything about the papers looked official, from their wording below the letterhead to the seals and signatures. “Very good,” said Racheed. “These will do just fine.”

His jocular response annoyed Solomon. “I am glad you approve. You have asked me to risk my career and life, after all.”

Now that he had what he needed, Racheed saw less reason to soothe his brother. “As you have said. I will use these wisely, and do what I must.”

“Then I do not need to remind you of what will happen to all of us should you fail.”

Racheed shook his head and clutched the file to his chest with both arms, as if embracing it. “No, you do not. Because I will not fail.”

Solomon slammed his briefcase shut, snapped the latches, and strode quickly from the room, brushing past Racheed's offer of an extended palm as he went.

CHAPTER VII

Several days later, Racheed finally arrived in Mexico City. He was later than planned, much to the dismay of Maria, who was waiting at the airport when his flight arrived at 7 a.m on this New Year's Eve.

"Where have you been?" asked Maria after a long hug and deep kiss. "I have been waiting for you!"

"I am sorry," said Racheed. "I had expected to be here sooner."

"Well, you are here now," said Maria, swaying her curvaceous body to show off her dress, a sheer brown slip-style number offering plenty of leg and cleavage and a bit warm for the climate, when temperatures reach only seventy that time of year. "What do you think?"

Like any other man, Racheed could barely look away. "I love it."

"I wore it just for you," said Maria, flirtingly. "But I don't plan to wear it for long..."

The car trip to her apartment, only two miles away, seemingly took forever. Maria's skimpy attire left much to the imagination.

The increasing heat of the moment about to cool. Maria was so taken by the sight of Racheed that she forgot to inquire of Racheed's family, and finally remembered after several blocks."I am so sorry for what happened to you," she blurted.

"Thank you," he replied. "It has been difficult for my entire family."

"I can only imagine, my darling." A wave of sympathy permeated through Maria's dramatic personality.

Racheed's anger at the drone strikes oozed as well. "These drone strikes are needless and barbaric," he said icily. "My grandfather and sister were innocent victims, like the others." He turned his head and gazed blankly out the window. "They must be stopped."

Maria tried to soothe his anger. "Were you close to your sister?"

Racheed covered well. "I loved her, and my grandfather as well. They did not deserve to die like this."

Fearing she had ruined their reunion, Maria let the subject drop. After a moment or two, Racheed turned his attention back to the beautiful Maria and her barely-covering dress.

Walking to the front door and through the lobby, Racheed worried that others were staring as Maria clung to him, but she did not care. Though it was early in the morning, her desire was never higher. As they reached her door, she could wait no longer, and began yanking the clothes from his body. It was their first time together in weeks, and she had fantasized of their reunion. She kissed and caressed every part of him, and he could only relax and enjoy every touch.

During their passionate encounter, the clock passed midnight, though neither Racheed or Maria seemed to notice that a new year in their lives had dawned. Following a long afterglow, the lovers, still tangled in each other's arms in her white canopy bed, began to murmur a few words. In minutes, a conversation developed.

Maria had urged Racheed to find an engineering job in America or Mexico, and was still hopeful. Knowing what it would mean to his daughter, her father had even offered to help Racheed land a job in the Mexican capital. "Have you found a position yet?" she asked, somewhat nervously.

"Not yet," said Racheed, not noticing Maria's small exhale.

"Why don't you take time off?" she mused. "I have been relaxing for several weeks, just unwinding. I've had a lot of fun, doing things I've always wanted."

Her body shifted as her excitement grew. "We could spend the year together! Oh, yes, Racheed! We could travel the world, go to London, Paris! Or we could visit your family!"

"I cannot," said Racheed, rather firmly. "I have other things I must do."

Maria was disappointed. "Like what?"

Racheed dropped it the news. "I am in the military."

Maria sat up and held the snow white sheet to her breast. She turned her head slightly over her bare shoulders. "What did you say?"

"The military. I am in intelligence in the Pakistani army."

The shock still had not worn off Maria's face. "When did you decide this?"

"My brother arranged a position for me," said Racheed, selling out Solomon. "He is also in intelligence..."

"I know, you said," Maria interrupted with a wave of her hand. "So what does this mean?"

Racheed also sat up. "I felt I needed to serve my country before I went into engineering. Many others in our country serve, and I wished too as well."

"Oh. Hmm," she sniffed. "You never said anything about it until now." Maria snapped her head in anger, and looked away.

"It never really came up." Racheed grasped for excuses. "I felt it was my duty." He lay back and stared at the ceiling.

He touched a nerve, as duty was a buzzword in the Santos family. "I see," she said coolly. "Will you be in any danger?"

"No. None at all. I will only gather information, not fight with guns."

Maria again exhaled. "Then you must do what you think is right." She settled back and lay against Racheed, her hand sliding up and down his body. "Will this keep us apart?"

"No more than now," said Racheed. "I am actually supposed to be here for a while. I would like to interview your father."

"Why?"

"A military matter. When my brother found I was coming here, he asked me to speak with your father."

Maria was beginning to tire of Racheed's interest in her father. "Now I understand why you found my father so interesting. He is in intelligence, as you are now."

"I have always found your father interesting. But now, I am in an official capacity. There are things we must discuss."

"Very well," dismissed Maria. "We will go tomorrow." She stared into Racheed's eyes, and her anger melted. "Now, no more talk of this. I have waited weeks for you, and no more talk."

Her passion had been building for weeks, and one encounter could not fulfill it. She pulled Racheed closer and within seconds, another intense lovemaking session was flowering.

*****

This morning for Greg Foster was like any other as he sat in his spartan office in the United States Embassy in Mexico City. As an employee of the Central Intelligence Agency, Foster had served around the world. For the last six years, this beige-walled, barely-furnished cubicle in Mexico City was his home for twelve hours a day. The other twelve were spent in his one-bedroom apartment in a brown brick walk-up where he lived alone, three blocks from work.

As the sun ascended above his window on this early January day, the glare lessened and Foster poured himself another cup of bitter coffee. Now forty-five, he had given much to the CIA. His marriage dissolved seven years ago when his wife finally tired of the bizarre hours, the never-ending pressure, and the secrecy that affected even basic conversations.

She also had outgrown the youthful excitement of living in one foreign country, then another. The appeal of global travel also drew Greg into the agency just out of Vanderbilt. Two decades later, it consumed his life, but he knew little else. The transfer to Mexico was a route to leave his failed marriage behind, and get a fresh start – or so he thought. As it was, life in Mexico City was the same as it had been in the three states and nine foreign countries of his previous assignments.

Among Foster's duties was to review the flight manifest of the names of people flying into Mexico from the Mideast, including the hot spot nations of Afghanistan and Pakistan. He would then compare the names with the list of known terrorists, or associates of terror organizations. The work was tedious, the lists lengthy. But he knew any slip could allow a terror cell to get a foothold in Mexico, and the results to the U.S. and their southern neighbors could be catastrophic.

On this day, one name on a manifest printout was Racheed Ul-Bashar. That was a new one to Foster. As was protocol, all new names had to be ran through the CIA network database, as well as those of Homeland Security and the FBI, to see if a threat was emerging. Foster clicked in his passwords, then entered Racheed's name into the database.

Nothing derogatory was found on Racheed. The database revealed that Racheed lived in the United States, and had attended Texas A & M. It also found that he had crossed the border into Mexico on multiple occasions. Foster raised his eyebrows and took off his glasses as he read. *Why would a Pakistani national make that many trips into Mexico?*

Foster was on friendly terms with General Santos, and he picked up the phone to call him. Santos was often Foster's first contact in Mexican government, and a well-placed source of information. Unlike many others in the notoriously corrupt Mexican government, Santos could be trusted.

As a senior member of American intelligence, Foster had the number of Santos' direct line. Within seconds, the general's voice was heard. “Buenos dias.”

“General Santos? This is Greg Foster, at the U.S. Embassy.”

“Oh yes, Senor Foster, my friend. How are you this morning?”

“I am well, General. And yourself?”

“Fine, fine. It is good to talk to you again. What may I do for you?”

Foster flipped through his printouts while continuing the niceties.

His diplomatic skills were known throughout the agency office in Mexico, though he wasted few words otherwise. "General, I appreciate your time this morning, and I hope I may trouble you for a few minutes."

"Not at all. How may I help you?"

"I was reviewing manifests from flights that originated in the Middle East this morning."

"Oh?" Santos feigned surprise, though he knew full well that was part of Foster's job. "Is there some problem, senor?"

"I don't know. I am hoping you may be able to answer that for me."

Santos dropped the ruse. "What is the name?"

Foster also became more direct. "I've got a Pakistani national who lives in Texas, and went to Texas A & M. He's been into Mexico a bunch of times, and that seems unusual to me."

Santos perked up and repeated himself. "I see. What is this person's name?"

"Racheed Ul-Bashar."

The general emitted a hearty chuckle. "Oh, Senor Foster. You need not worry about that man."

"Why not?" asked Foster, puzzled.

"Because I know him well. You see, Racheed is the love interest of my daughter."

"Oh?"

"Si, senor. Maria met him when she was also a student at Texas A & M. They have been, how should you say? Dating for over two years."

"So *that* explains it," mused Foster. "You know this man well, then."

"Oh, si. He has been a visitor in my home many times. I know him *very* well."

Trained in turning over rocks, Foster could not let it drop. "What about his family?"

"His father is a doctor. He has a brother in the Pakistani army. He is also in intelligence."

"Hmmm," Foster pondered. "Interesting. Do you know his name?"

Santos hesitated, the memory of a middle-aged man slower than the past. "I believe his name is Solomon Ul-Bashar."

"Ul-Bashar?" Foster asked quizzically. "The same last name as Racheed."

"Yes."

"That's unusual," replied Foster. "People of those cultures don't always share the same names."

"You are right," said the general. "But there is no problem. I know Racheed well, and he means well. He is no threat to you."

Some of Santos' words failed to ring true with Foster, particularly the sharing of a surname. Still, Foster trusted Santos implicitly. If the general *said* there was no problem, then there must be no problem. "Then I am sorry to have bothered you. How is your daughter, sir? I have not seen her in a while."

"Not since before she left for university," said Santos, remembering a reception at his home five years before that Foster had attended. "She is a beautiful girl, and did very well at university. She is taking some time off, as you Americans say. You know how young people are."

"Yes. I have two sons myself," reminded Foster, realizing that he had shown the general photos of his own teenage boys at that same reception.

"And how are they?" Santos continued the pleasantries.

"They are well," said Foster. "But, unfortunately, I don't see them much."

"I am sorry," offered Santos, sympathetically. "Is there anything else I may do for you, my friend?"

"No, that is all," replied Foster. "When you see Racheed, please do not mention that I have inquired about him."

"Of course not," said the general. "There is no need to say a word."

"Then, I thank you for your time, General. Have a good day, sir."

"And the same to you, my friend. Buenos dias."

Foster hung up the phone. As was standard procedure, he entered

Racheed's name and information into the network databases of the CIA and Homeland Security. But Santos offered no reason for concern, and Foster had no reason to doubt the gentleman. There were plenty of other threats to address, and Foster poured himself another cup of coffee to face the rest of the day.

CHAPTER VIII

Maria actually had no intention of taking Racheed to see her father the next day. She wanted to stay in bed with her lover, and exhaust the desire that raged in his absence. Their first full day together was consumed with more passion, in her bed, the shower, the sofa. Racheed did little to resist, though as the day wore on, his mind was increasingly distracted by thoughts of Maria's father.

She had no such distractions, but petulantly noticed his interest seemed to be waning as afternoon turned to evening. "Are you tired of me?"

"Of course not. But I thought we were to see your father today. I must speak to him about important matters."

"Oh, Racheed," Maria got out of bed in a mild tantrum. "You just got here."

"Yesterday," he said. "There are things my brother says I must do." Racheed was able to successfully fib his way through the conversation. "We will have many days together."

She slowly walked to the bathroom to shower, letting out a loud, sarcastic sigh. "I will call him and tell him we are coming tomorrow."

He rose as well. “Thank you.”

Maria showered and called her father to inform him of Racheed's arrival. He was pleased to hear that his daughter was bringing her boyfriend for a visit. He added that Mirgael, his wife and Maria's mother, would also be eager to see Racheed. The next day was a Saturday, and the general would be at home. Racheed tried to get a few hours sleep that night, though Maria's inner fire was still burning, and bedtime came late. After a quick breakfast the next morning, they strolled downstairs to Maria's white Lexus.

“I will drive,” said Racheed.

“What, I cannot?” demanded Maria.

“Of course you can. I just prefer to drive,” said Racheed, mustering reassurance.

“Very well.” Maria rolled her eyes and threw her hands in the air. The traffic was lighter than usual, and within minutes, they were at the Santos villa. By then, Maria had calmed, again lost in thoughts of the man she desired.

The doorkeeper welcomed Maria and Racheed, and went into the general's study. In seconds, he emerged, wearing white shirtsleeves and dark, pinstriped dress pants. He embraced Maria, then clasped Racheed's hand. Miragel then followed with her own hug for Maria, and smiled pleasantly at Racheed.

“Racheed, it is good to see you again,” the general exclaimed, clasping Racheed's hand with both of his. “I have missed you, and I know my daughter has as well.” He turned to Maria and smiled at the look of love on her face. “You are glowing, my child.”

“I have missed you as well, sir,” said Racheed, not noticing Maria's face. “It has been a while, has it not?”

“Indeed, it has.” His expression turned sympathetic. “I am sorry to hear of your sister and grandfather.”

“Thank you. It was very difficult on my family.”

“As it would be,” said the general, nodding soothingly. “If there is anything I may do...”

“Yes, please let us know,” echoed Miragel.

“Nothing, thank you.” Racheed quickly turned to another topic. “I have news for you. When I was home, I joined the military."

Santos' eyes brightened and a toothy smile flashed. "The military! In your home country?"

"Yes," said Maria. "It was a surprise to me as well." Seeing her father's happiness, she forgot her own reservations and looked up at Racheed, adoringly.

"My brother arranged a position for me," said Racheed, again invoking Solomon. "He is in intelligence, and that is the department I am in as well." He displayed his counterfeit credentials to the general.

Santos laughed heartily. "How interesting. I can certainly relate to that, my son."

Racheed mustered a laugh in reaction to the general's irony. "I actually come to you on official business, in addition to our friendship."

"Oh? And what business is that?"

"If you may grant me some time, I will explain."

"Very well. How about in my study?"

"That is fine." Racheed turned to follow the general, while Maria moved in unison. He saw her and extended an open palm, to halt her.

"I am sorry," he said. "I cannot allow you to hear."

Maria was miffed at his secrecy. "Why not?"

"It is a question of national security. Solomon told me that I must not share my conversations with ones other than military."

"I will not tell anyone. You know that."

"Still, I cannot let you...."

Santos jumped in. "He is right, my daughter. You know how the intelligence community must act."

His words finally swayed her. "All right," she said resignedly. "I will go speak with Mother, then."

"And we will join you when we are finished," soothed the general. Miragel and Maria then headed for the outdoor garden for a cool drink and idle chatter in the bright sunshine. General Santos turned to Racheed. "Then, shall we?"

The two men sauntered into Santos' lavish study, decorated with traditional Mexican artwork and colorful artifacts that contrasted with the off-white stucco walls. Santos sat at his oversized mahogany desk, while Racheed settled into a cushy brown leather rolling chair across from him. The general reached for his cigar case. “Would you like one? They are made specially for me.”

Each cigar was banded by a paper strip that read “For Senor Carlos Santos.” Racheed shook his head. Santos then helped himself to one, struck a long match, and lit his smoke. “Now, then. What is it you wish to speak of?”

“I wish to talk about the drug cartels you face in Mexico. Do you recall, when we discussed them when we first met?”

“Ah, yes.” Santos leaned back and stared over Racheed's head, lost in thought. “I remember those days with you and Maria very well. It is still a grave problem. We face few problems larger than the cartels.”

“We also face serious problems with them,” countered Racheed. “The cartels have immense power in Pakistan and our neighbors. They are violent, and do not care who they hurt.”

“No, they do not. They spread terror, and cause much crime. Many Mexicans have died at the hands of the cartels. Our American neighbors have also lost because of them.”

“We have each lost because of them,” responded Racheed, ignoring the Americans. “We are a poor country, and much of our money is in their hands. The real problem, though is heroin.”

“What of it?

“Many Pakistanis suffer because of heroin. It is highly addictive, and we have poor treatment for those who are addicted.” Racheed rose from his chair and turned his back to the general. He shifted his eyes and stared at the floor, feigning real emotion. “Our people can barely afford to feed themselves, let alone purchase drugs. But there are many who do, and it destroys them. It destroys their homes. It destroys their families.”

“As it does here,” replied Santos. “Our nation is always in turmoil, it seems. But heroin seems to be a constant. Many do not care what it does, only if money is earned from it.”

"Many of our nations produce it," continued Racheed. "It is a cash crop, as you say. But the less fortunate see little of that cash. The Tailban warlords use the money to make even more, and it is an endless cycle. So many are caught up in it, and many have died from it."

Racheed then turned his conversation to corruption. "Heroin also brings with it severe social issues. The money it generates is often used to bribe public officials in my country. Even men who do not use heroin are affected, for they take payoffs from the drug lords and shape policy accordingly. Usually those policies have dire consequences for the growth and safety of our people. The effects of heroin in my country are endless, and all negative."

Santos lightly tapped his fingertips together, pondering Racheed's words. "What is it you need from me?"

"I reflected on our conversations about the cartels, and described them to my brother. He said you may want to help us." Racheed turned once again and faced the general, standing erectly and now looking him squarely in the eye. "I would like to review your procedures for handling the drug cartels. You seem to be having more success than we are. I have been sent to investigate how you do it."

Santos was surprised, for rarely is Mexico complimented for its handling of the drug cartels. The neighboring United States is among its most vocal critics, frequently pressuring Mexico to crack down on border violence. He seemed pleased at Racheed's declaration. "We do our best. Here in Mexico, we believe we are making progress."

"We would like to see how you do it," said Racheed. "We are interested in studying your ways. We must improve our procedures. The stability of our country depends on it."

Again, Santos was startled at Racheed's words. Surely, Pakistan had other troubles than merely the cartels. But Racheed knew his own country's problems better than he, and his sincerity struck the general. "How may I help?"

"I would like to examine everything you have. Any information could help me," said Racheed, quickly adding, "And help Pakistan."

"I am happy to help," replied Santos. "I will make everything I have available to you. Please come by my office on Monday morning, when my staff is there. They will be at your disposal."

"I am grateful," said Racheed, breaking into a smile and grasping the general's hand. "The Pakistani government is indebted to you."

"Think nothing of it," said the general. "I am happy to be of service to Pakistan, and help my future son-in-law."

Racheed smiled down his chest. "We will see about the latter."

"Maria may have something to say about that," poked the general, playfully. "She is wild about you. I have never seen her this way with a man."

"She is a beautiful girl," said Racheed, his mind flashing to the previous two days in Maria's bedroom. "I enjoy being with her," he added cryptically.

"Then, are we done here?"

"Yes. Let's enjoy the rest of the morning."

The two men strode from the study and into the den, where Maria and her mother were now waiting. A sumptuous lunch followed, and the rest of the day was spent in laughter and light conversation.

*****

On Monday morning, Maria enjoyed breakfast with Racheed at a modern downtown cantina and dropped him off at her father's headquarters. Racheed displayed his false documents to one guardpost, then another, and made his way to the general's office, armed with a laptop and an empty black briefcase.

"Good morning, Racheed!" greeted the general, smiling as usual. His office was dark-walled and commodious, a showplace of military decoration that offered visitors a glance at his many honors. A portrait of Santa Anna hung within view of the mammoth black cherry desk. "Allow me to introduce you to my staff."

Santos warmly introduced his Pakistani visitor to all of his workers in the foyer, describing him as an officer of Pakistani intelligence. He also added a caveat of "future son-in-law, I hope," which drew chuckles from all but the straight-faced Racheed.

"You are to see to his every request," directed Santos. "I have placed all of you at his disposal. See to his every need."

Santos turned to Racheed, grabbed his extended hand, and returned to his office. Racheed quickly requested all operational procedures of Mexican intelligence against the cartels, as well as lists of names and any relevant files to the drug trade in Mexico. He also requested all available information on drug trafficking near the American border.

Within twenty minutes, he was supplied with a mountain of boxes and stacks of file folders, manuals, and reports. Needing a place to review them in peace, he requested and was sent to an isolated conference room, where a long faux-wood table was surrounded by twelve brown leather swivel chairs. The staffers carried the information into the room, asked if they were needed further, and closed the door behind them.

By now, it was nearly ten o'clock. Racheed spent the rest of the morning sorting through the mounds of papers to find the information he needed. He was interested in the cartel leaders, and he wanted names. He swiftly typed them into his laptop and sometimes pulled out a small digital camera, taking quick pictures of images of known cartel leaders and their underlings. He also made some Xerox copies on a sprawling Bizhub machine in the corner.

Around noon, General Santos strode through the door. Lost in thought, Racheed was startled at his entrance and the fact that two hours had passed. "Racheed, may I interest you in lunch? We have a fine serving room downstairs, if you may permit me to escort you."

Racheed could barely think of food. "No sir, thank you. I am not hungry. I think it is best for me to spend more time here."

"Very well," said Santos. "I trust my staff has taken care of your needs. Please come to my office when you are finished."

"Thank you." Santos left, and Racheed reached for a sandwich he had stuffed in his briefcase. He gulped it down and returned to his research.

Now armed with names, Racheed began to cross-reference. He reached for files that had more personal information, some devoted solely to individual drug lords. He wanted every bit of information available, such as the cars they drove, the bars and restaurants they hung out in, the names of lower-ranking cartel members. Addresses, locations of operations, family members and their personal data, everything was of interest.

Photocopies were slipped into the briefcase, as was the laptop. Finally, Racheed looked up at a clock. To his surprise, it was nearly four twenty. The headquarters would soon be closing, and Racheed knew an exit was in order. He rose stiffly from his chair, his body in knots from hours in a sitting position. His blood flow changed and rushed from his head.

He walked down the hall to Santos' office. The general was sitting on his young secretary's desk, joking with her. “Racheed! I thought we had lost you!,” he exclaimed. “Did you find all that you needed?

“I certainly did,” replied Racheed. “This will help me a great deal.”

“I am glad we could be of service. Please join Maria's mother and I tomorrow night. We are having a dinner party, and I should love to introduce you to our friends.”

“I will tell Maria,” said Racheed, thinking if the friends may be as influential as the general. “Thank you again for your assistance. The Pakistani government is in your debt.”

He left the headquarters and called Maria from his cellphone. Minutes later, she picked him up, dressed only in a midriff and shorts from a session with her personal trainer. Now feeling a high from his success in the conference room, he slid his hand along Maria's bare thigh on the drive to her apartment. He needed no such hint, as Maria's desire for Racheed knew no bounds. The rest of the evening, and much of the night, was spent in one searing interlude after another.

*****

The next morning, Racheed awoke with hunger pangs, having eaten only the one sandwich since the previous morning. He climbed out of bed, pulled on his pants, and silently walked to the kitchen, where he poured himself a large bowl of corn flakes.

He had just added milk when he saw Maria standing in the doorway, wearing his dress shirt that went with the pants. She had left the top buttons open, and she stood with one leg bent, foot pressed against the doorframe.

"Good morning," she cooed.

"And to you." He raised his bowl. "I was hungry."

"You were hungry all of last night," she giggled. "I was too. Hungry for you." She slid toward him and sensuously kissed his lips.

Racheed's need for sustenance was all he could consider. He gulped down a couple of spoonfuls. "I forgot to mention something last night."

Maria pulled herself up to sit on the breakfast bar next to him. His shirt barely covered her lower half. "What?"

"Your father invited us to dinner tonight. He is having a party for friends."

"Oh." Maria's interest was tepid. "He always has parties."

Racheed was more concerned with the guest list than the party itself. "Who will be there? Are they other generals, or members of the parliament?"

"Probably neither," scoffed Maria. "It's Tuesday night, so it will be just the neighbors."

"Oh." Racheed managed to mask his disappointment. "The people from the haciendas around yours?"

"Yes. They're businessmen and social leaders. They'll probably bring their children." Maria crossed her legs and shifted her body, angling for jealousy. "Some of my ex-boyfriends."

Racheed did not take the bait. "How do you feel about that?"

"I'd rather spend the evening in bed," said Maria, lightly brushing Racheed's arm with her fingertips.

He smiled. "I have some things I must do today. I must call Solomon, for further orders."

She sighed in resignation. "I have things to do as well. I have another appointment with my trainer. Before that, coffee with the girls."

"Tough day," smiled Racheed. Finished, he set his bowl in the sink. “I had better get going.”

“I'll meet you in the shower,” she mused.

“I'd better not,” he replied. “I need to get moving.”

“Oh, all right!.” She jumped down from the breakfast bar in a snit and reached for the cereal box. Racheed headed for the bathroom and quickly showered. She then followed, taking much longer. In the other room, Racheed took the opportunity to open his laptop and review some of his findings from the day before.

Maria emerged, wearing another dark midriff and clingy shorts. She rubbed past Racheed on her way out the door, and he could not help but respond to her flirtations. But the moment was fleeting, and his focus quickly resumed.

He spent the next several hours reviewing the information he had obtained from General Santos. Much of his effort was consumed in studying the drug cartels along the border, and he made meticulous notes on their leaders and smuggling routes.

Around noon, Maria returned. Her hair was windblown, and small beads of sweat covered her body from her workout. She tossed her gym bag aside and turned to Racheed. “You're still here,” she smiled. “Let's go have lunch.”

Her eyes shifted to the corner of the room, where she spied his two suitcases, packed and upright.

His eyes turned with hers to the suitcases. “I cannot,” he said firmly. “We must talk.”

“Racheed?” Maria was surprised at his coolness.

“I spoke to my brother while you were gone. He says I must return immediately.”

Her face fell. “What? Why?”

“Important matters have arisen. My presence is needed at headquarters. I can stay no longer.”

“Oh, Racheed!” Maria began to cry. “But you just got here!”

“I know.” Racheed's face softened at the sight of her tears. “I wish I could stay as well. But I have no choice. I must go back.”

She threw her arms around his neck and rested her head on his shoulder. “Oh, darling. I know it is not your choice. I have just missed you so. These days have been beautiful for me." She pulled her head back, and looked longingly into his face. "When will you return?"

"In a month. It should take no longer. I will be back then."

Maria sighed. "I guess I have no choice, then." Her tears began to dry, and her mind began to fantasize. Her eyes took on the seductive look he loved. "We can catch up then, as we have now."

"Yes" smiled Racheed. "I will look forward to it."

They shared several kisses before he was able to pull himself away. He had called for a taxi, much to her chagrin, as she wanted to drive him to the airport and savor a few more minutes with him. From the taxi, he called General Santos and wished him well. Like his daughter, the general was sad at his departure.

A 747 was waiting at the airport to fly Racheed to London, and from there, on to Karachi. Racheed spent the hours in-flight contemplating his next move, and who could help him the most.

*****

Racheed spent a few days with his family, a visit reminiscent of his boyhood days. Always distant with his parents and siblings, he was now even more withdrawn, spending most of his hours in his room. As a boy, he whiled away the hours on the computer. Now, he continually reviewed notes from his day in General Santos' office.

Mahammed had long seen the similarities between Racheed and his grandfather, and feared that hate would ruin his son, as it had Omar. Now, Racheed was in his late twenties, and the shared traits began to manifest.

One afternoon, Mahammed could stand it no longer. He approached as Racheed emerged from his room and headed for the refrigerator. "We must talk, Racheed."

Racheed never broke stride. "About what, father?"

"I am concerned about your views on America. They are so strong."

"And why wouldn't they be?" shot back Racheed, stopping suddenly. "They have killed your father and my sister. They have killed many of our friends. You can stand there and ask me that?"

"I know what they have done," replied Mahammed, trying to calm his son. "But you cannot carry such deep hatred. Remember Allah. Remember our mission of peace."

"I remember Allah in everything I do," bristled Racheed. "Their actions are attacks on Him. I serve Allah every day of my life."

"But you cannot do it in this way," said Mahammed, his voice nervously excited. "Remember our cleric. Recall what he says."

"That old man is no friend of Allah. He is a silly old fool."

"Racheed!" Mahammed called down his son as if a wayward child. "Do not speak of our cleric in that way again. I will not have that in my home, from my son."

Admonished, Racheed offered no response. Mahammed turned away and took several seconds to collect himself. Finally, in a deliberate voice, he said, "I spoke to Solomon yesterday."

Racheed tried to hide his alarm. "What did he say?"

"He was like me. He was concerned about your hatred."

That hardly answered Racheed's question. "What else did he say?"

The inquiry sounded more like a order, and startled Mahammed. "What do you mean?"

"Be specific, father. What did Solomon say?"

"Only a few words." Mahammed could not understand Racheed's concern. "He only said that you had visited him, and your views frightened him. As they do me."

Racheed stifled a deep exhale, realizing that Solomon would incriminate himself if he told the whole story, and that was not likely to happen. "Oh. Yes, I spoke to him. I was surprised he told you."

"Racheed, you must listen to me." Mahammed placed his hands on his son's shoulders, and looked him squarely in the eye. "This hatred will destroy you. Do not let it. We have suffered much sadness. Do not let the hatred take you as well."

Racheed stared at the floor and uttered a controlled response. "Very well, father."

It was not the ringing agreement Mahammed had hoped for, but better than nothing. He drew a deep breath of his own. "Just remember, my son. Just remember."

Racheed turned away, heeding his father's words in a literal sense. But his remembrances were hardly the same.

CHAPTER IX

The next several days were much the same in the Ul-Bashar household, as Racheed and his parents went their separate ways. He then left for Seidu, to visit other relatives and pay homage to the graves of Omar and Sasha.

As he stood at the foot of their graves, a cool breeze blew in a dreary rain, but he was oblivious, his mind was consumed less with sadness than rage. He made cursory visits to some uncles and cousins, but was little interested in their idle conversation. A few moments were spent in each household before Racheed made excuses to leave, usually that he had many others to visit, and little time to do so.

After making the rounds, he turned his attention to what mattered most. He looked up Salaam, the youngest of the Tailban sect that he had contacted in his previous visit to Seidu.

A day passed, and Racheed was allowed back into the enclave with Salaam, his friends, and Ashish, the local leader. Racheed was to the point. "I have made progress in my plans, and wish to proceed. I have information that I obtained in Mexico that will help me, but I need support from our elders. I would like to see Ali Sighn," he told the six men, who reacted with surprise.

Ali Sighn was a Taliban warlord who ruled Seidu and the surrounding villages. A man of over sixty, Ali was rarely seen, but always heard. When in public, he wore the off-white robes and headdress normal for Pakistani men of his age. Occasionally, he visited Seidu, and most locals were familiar with him, though few seemed to know when he may appear. He was invariably polite to others, though highly distant. His glaring eyes and lengthy, peppered beard dominated his face, and when he spoke, others were expected to listen. Those who did not usually met an unsightly end.

"Very well," said Ashish. He turned to the three men at his immediate left. "You will escort this man to Ali."

Usually, men were not referred to Ali so quickly, but Ashish, normally methodical, could resist no more. He still simmered over Omar's death, and his need for revenge colored his thoughts. The three rose almost in unison. For the first time, they addressed Racheed. "You will come with us. Do as we tell you, and do nothing to attract interest. We will leave at sundown. Be here then."

Racheed bowed to his hosts and left, only to return in a matter of hours. As the sun set, the men left the enclave and silently piled into a Jeep parked in the rear of the bunker. They drove north out of Seidu, toward the Afghan border. A potholed ride followed before they pulled into Peshawar, on the border of the two countries.

Peshawar is a hotbed for terrorists such as Ali Sighn, which Racheed knew well. The city is a high security risk for Western visitors and even for Pakistanis themselves, and many choose not to go there. Racheed, though, was barely nervous. A sweeping relaxation came over his body and mind, a comfort level that he never seemed to feel elsewhere. He felt invigorated, and anxious to see the great Ali.

The Jeep approached a dilapidated, gray slab building, surrounded by barbed-wire fencing, that appeared to be a large warehouse. Racheed, though, quickly noticed that several men were posted outside, some concealing semi-automatic rifles under their native robes. The Jeep approached the gate, and the driver told the guard, “We have been sent to see Ali.” Clearly, the guard knew the men, and only that simple utterance was needed to pass. The Jeep proceeded inside, parking at a large double door.

Racheed watched as the men climbed out, and knew that he should follow. By now, it was almost midnight, and the compound was cloaked in darkness. The eldest of the three men knocked five times on the door, and another guard answered. Again, he was told that the party was sent to see Ali. They proceeded inside, where Racheed was frisked and searched by a burly young guard armed with pistols and machetes. Racheed and his escort then passed through three rooms before reaching Ali, seated on the floor at the front of the chamber with crossed legs. He was surrounded by four men, each with emotionless expression.

Ali cocked his head, sized Racheed up and down with a piercing gaze, and offered no greeting. “Who is this person?” demanded Ali.

“This is Racheed Ul-Bashar,” replied one of the three men. “He has asked to speak with you.”

Ali refused to address Racheed directly. “Why is he here?”

“His grandfather and sister were lost in the last drone strike on Seidu. He seeks revenge, my lord.”

Ali again chose not to recognize Racheed. “We all seek revenge. He is no different than anyone else. Why is he special?”

“He has a plan to attack America.”

Ali's face brightened at the mere thought. Finally, he turned to Racheed. “What is your plan?”

“I want to punish America for what they have done. I have prayed and contemplated. I am creating a plan of attack.”

“Attack?” Ali was unimpressed with such vague talk. “I spend my days planning attacks. My people do the same. Why should you bother me?”

“I believe I can inflict great harm on America. I have spent much time in planning already. I have made high-level contacts that we may use.”

“We? How do you mean?” Ali had little use for Racheed's

indirectness. "Speak now!"

Racheed realized he should remain on point. "Are you familiar with Carlos Santos?"

"No. Why should I be?"

"He is a general of intelligence in the Mexican army and a personal friend of mine. I know him well."

Ali was bored and still skeptical. "How do you know him?"

"I have a close relationship with his daughter, Maria. I met her while I was in university in America. I studied engineering at Texas A & M."

"Oh?" Ali smiled slightly at the hint of Racheed's "close relationship." He rephrased his original question. "And you have come to know her father?"

"Yes. I have spent much time with him. I have been in his office and gained much information that will help us."

Ali finally began to display some interest. "Tell me. What is your plan?"

Racheed began to relax. "I want to smuggle men across the Mexican border into the United States. Once we have, there are selected targets I want to bomb."

His interest further piqued, Ali sat more erectly. "Tell me more."

The countless hours Racheed had spent in reflection formulated a deadly plan. "I want to send three teams of men into the United States. One will head to Las Vegas."

A frown bore across Ali's face. "The gambling capital? Heathenish. So many sins, so many misdeeds. They deserve to pay."

"You've heard of Caesar's Palace?" inquired Racheed. Ali, who had extensive knowledge of the United States not only from his own intelligence network but also from American cable news, nodded.

"I want to bomb that. I will also send a team to Mount Rushmore, to bomb the visitor's center."

"Ah, yes," pondered Ali, breaking into a broad smile. "That is a landmark to the Americans. A strike there will damage their psyche. It will also strike at their history."

"I am glad you approve," agreed Racheed. "The third team will travel to Nashville and bomb Broadway. That is their tourist center, where the heart of their music they call `country' is...."

"I know what it is," interrupted Ali, waving his open palm to stifle the words. "I cannot stand that music. It sounds as banshee screams."

His bristle only lasted seconds. Then, Ali's smile widened even further, nearly reaching his ears. Seeing their leader's pleasure, his men also nodded in self-satisfaction.

"Yes, yes!" exclaimed Ali. "So much to be gained from that. Our attacks on the World Trade Center had such an impact, but a strike on their heartland may have even more effect. They will have a false sense of security, and will not think they could be hit there. Their country music is so dear to them, and it will affect a significant part of their culture. Every time the name of `Nashville' is mentioned, it will be a never-ending reminder to them. Yes. Yes...."

Ali's voice trailed off, lost in anticipation. He stroked his beard and made eye contact with each of his men. As he did, each nodded their approval. Though a man such as Ali Sighn needs no such approval, it was clear that all in the room were now on Racheed's side. Now Ali wanted more details. "I want to know how you will enter the United States. It will take planning and organization for such a plan."

Racheed's confidence soared. "The information I mentioned. It is names of the leaders of the large Mexican drug cartels and their members. They operate along the border of Mexico and the United States, and are very powerful."

"I am aware. What will they do for you?"

"They have routes to smuggle their own men and drugs, and American authorities cannot catch them. They could help me smuggle my men and equipment across in the same way."

"Go on."

"The cartels will have the equipment I need. They will have weapons, vehicles, and explosives for an attack. They use those type of things for their own trade. They will certainly have them available for my use."

"Yes, they would. But why would they help you?"

Racheed was becoming nervous again, though he stood steadfast. "I think I have an idea to help them gain a supply of drugs."

Ali brushed his hand in the air. "That is not something I deal with directly. Continue with your plan, though."

Racheed had suspected Ali would disassociate himself with the drug trade, though he had plenty of contacts. "I need at least five men to carry out my plan. I hope that you may be able to help me with that."

"In what way?"

"I need five men who are trained in bomb making. They must be the kind of men who serve Allah as others have. They must be committed totally, and be willing to martyr themselves."

"*All* of us are willing to martyr ourselves," snapped Ali. "That is what we must do. We must serve Allah, and reap our reward."

"I know, I know," Racheed countered, trying to calm him. "But I want to make sure that the best men are available."

"Of course," replied Ali, now understanding Racheed's words. "I recruit only the best men. They must be willing to make the ultimate sacrifice for our interests."

"I also need them to be trained to speak Spanish. They also need to be fluent in English."

"Yes," pondered Ali. "That is necessary, to blend in and communicate with others there. Most of our men are fluent in English, as they have studied it for years. But few of the men speak any sort of Spanish."

Racheed's disappointment was only momentary. "If they are able to speak a little of that language, I can train them further," he said. "Maria has trained me well enough to function in that tongue, and I think I can pass my knowledge on."

"Very well." Ali expected the next question. "And you need money for this?"

Racheed was taken aback at Ali's perceptiveness. "Yes. I must cover travel expenses. I need money for air fare, travel, food. Prices are so high, so it will not be a small sum."

"How much money do you mean?"

Racheed swallowed a gulp of anxiety. "Maybe $120,000. I must have something to be able to offer the cartel. If I have little or nothing, they will go no further to help me. I think that $100,000 for them would be enough. The rest will be for my expenses."

Even to a man with access to millions, the sum seemed high to Ali. His startled eyes looked in either direction as Racheed spoke. "You do not have money of your own? What is it that you do for a living?"

"I have a degree in engineering, as I told you. But I do not have a job. I must carry out my plan first."

Ali kept pressing. "You went to school in America. Your family must be wealthy, then."

"Yes. My father is a doctor." Racheed saw no reason to hide the truth, knowing Ali had plenty of opportunity to check on him. "But if I take money from them, they will know something is going on. I cannot take that risk."

"No, you cannot." Ali was never one who showed his cards, and he would not now, either. "I must discuss this plan with other members. We will decide if we wish to help you."

Racheed expected such a noncommittal answer. "When should I contact you again?"

"We will contact *you*," said Ali forcefully. "Return to Seidu, and we will find you."

"My thanks to you. When should I expect to hear from you?"

Ali offered nothing. "When we are ready."

Racheed bowed respectfully to Ali, then turned and offered respect to the others. His three escorts stepped forward, and led Racheed to the door. They quickly made their way outside, loaded into the Jeep, and returned to Seidu at daybreak.

*****

Anxiously, Racheed spent the days in Seidu, waiting for word from Ali. Engrossed in his wait and his planning, he made no attempt to contact his parents, Solomon, Maria, or anyone else. Two days passed, then three, then four. Finally, after a full week, one of the local Taliban men pounded on Racheed's door.

“I have word from Ali,” he said brusquely. “He has provided the money you need.” He pulled a manila envelope from his jacket that was stuffed with rupees.

Racheed stifled a smile. “What else does he want of me?”

“You will contact one of the cartel leaders. Determine if a crossing into America is possible, and what the price will be.”

“Is there anything else?”

“Fly to Mexico immediately and see what must be done.”

“Please express my thanks to him. Also, please tell him that I do this for Allah.”

“He knows that.” Racheed bowed to his visitor, who offered no reply. He turned quickly and left the room.

He was no sooner gone than Racheed was logged on to his laptop, checking on flights to Mexico. One connection was leaving in three days, and Racheed would have time to be on it. In a matter of hours, he was packed and on the road back to Karachi to catch a flight to Paris, where a plane to Mexico awaited.

Racheed's final flight destination was Ciudad Juarez, in northern Mexico, and he would have another connection to make in Mexico City. While other passengers slept on the long flight to the Mexican capital, Racheed chose to forego rest, reviewing his laptop notes and thinking about which cartel leader could best help him.

As he mulled over his plan, CIA agent Greg Foster sat in his cramped office in Mexico City, on his daily business of reviewing the flight manifests for passengers from nations of high security risk. He again noticed Racheed's name on the manifest, and wondered why Racheed was flying into Juarez.

But Foster recalled his conversation with General Santos on

Racheed, and there were plenty of other pressing matters. He nonchalantly typed Racheed's name into the CIA, Homeland Security, and FBI computer systems with the date and destination of his flight, poured himself another cup of coffee, and thought no more of it.

CHAPTER X

Racheed arrived in Mexico City and had a three-hour layover until his connecting flight to Juarez. He kept out of sight in the airport, worried that Maria, her father, or someone else familiar may see him. The 1,100-mile flight to Juarez took just under two hours, less time than the layover.

Ciudad Juarez is a city of 1.2 million just across the Rio Grande from El Paso, Texas. Though a popular destination for Americans crossing the border from Texas and New Mexico, it has become a haven for crime, much of it from the drug trade. It has also become a source of contention for its neighbors across the river, as polluted emissions from Juarez have tainted the air and water of El Paso. Like most Mexican cities, poverty is rampant in Juarez, much to the dismay of El Paso residents, who are hardly affluent but much more so than their Mexican counterparts.

Once in Juarez, Racheed first found a bank that would exchange rupees for American dollars. He then rented a room in an economy hotel, and after his long trek over six cities in two countries in different hemispheres, took some time to rest. After only a few hours, though, he returned to action.

Two blocks from the hotel was a cantina that Racheed's information revealed was a meeting place for members of a drug cartel. Though nearing dark and with security on the streets lax, Racheed was unintimidated and walked down to the cantina, where he ordered dinner.

After he finished, Racheed strode to the bar to pay his tab. A bartender was standing at the end of the bar, washing out a glass as his eyes followed the Pakistani visitor. Racheed noticed and approached the bartender, a portly man in his thirties with combed black hair, dressed in white shirt and pants.

"Buenos noches," offered Racheed.

"Buenos noches," replied the bartender, barely looking up from his work.

"I am looking for a man named Juan Rodrequs. I would like to meet with him."

The bartender's eyebrows raised and his lips clenched, the reaction picked up by the perceptive Racheed. "Did you say Juan Rodrequs, senor?"

"Yes."

The bartender barely let Racheed respond. "I know no one by that name."

Racheed detected the nervousness of the bartender. "I see."

"I do not know that name," The bartender repeated, almost for effect.

Now Racheed suspected the bartender knew more than he was letting on. "I am staying in the hotel down the street," he began, though the bartender's eyes never rose from his dishwashing. "I am in Room 211. Have Senor Rodrequs or one of his men contact me. I wish to discuss a business matter with him."

The bartender uttered a quick, "si, senor," never turning to look Racheed in the face. Racheed paid his bill and started to leave. As he turned, he noticed that several men at the bar were also paying close attention to him.

Racheed walked briskly back to his room in the cool night, and the wait began. The night passed uneventfully, as did the entire next day. He had meals delivered, fearful of being gone when word came. By seven on the second evening, the wait continued. Now, he wondered if the bartender was right – that he knew no one by the name of Juan Rodrequs. Or, if Rodrequs was not interested.

He left the hotel and walked back to the cantina with a dual purpose. One, simply, was to get dinner. Two, he wanted to see if there was anything he could learn from the bartender or any other men that frequented the place.

Racheed walked through the hotel door for the two-block walk in the twilight of the early evening. He was only seconds out when a black van pulled up along side, brakes screeching. The sliding door of the van flew open and two Mexicans, dressed in black clothes and stocking caps, jumped out. Instantly, they grabbed Racheed and forced him into the van, which then sped away.

Once inside, one Mexican held Racheed in place while the other searched him. The harsh slaps up and down his body stung, but revealed no weapons. Racheed's head was then covered with a black hood, and he was handcuffed behind his back. He heard one of the Mexicans say something to the driver, though the exchange was muffled by the hood.

The van did not drive in a straight line, turning at multiple corners. After a few minutes, it became clear to Racheed, laying on the floor unable to see or move freely, that the driver was trying to confuse him. A myriad of thoughts raced through Racheed's head. *Had the bartender sold me out? Did the Mexicans watching me at the bar know something? Were the cartels nervous about something?*

He thought of Maria, of General Santos, of his family. But most of his mind was devoted to his plans, to avenge Omar and Sasha. *I cannot die now*, he thought. *America had not been punished. Allah could not want it this way. I must have the chance to act, to make Americans suffer the way I have. This could not be the end.*

*****

The van motored around for a half-hour, an eternity to the bound, blinded Racheed. Finally, the vehicle suddenly braked to a stop. Racheed could hear what sounded like the whirring of an electric door. The van jerked to a roll once again, this time driving slowly. Racheed could hear a distinct echo, which indicated the van was now inside a building. The sound of the ignition clicking off was audible, followed by the sounds of sliding the side door.

Still hooded and handcuffed, Racheed was pulled out of the van and shoved into another part of the building. Hearing the sound of a door, he deducted that he was entering another room. Here, his handcuffs were removed, relieving him of aching muscles from his arms forced in one position for so long. His hood was also yanked off. Racheed's dark eyes struggled to adjust to the newfound light, and he blinked repeatedly until his eyes were adjusted.

The room appeared to be some type of suboffice, a small space with some file cabinets and a couple of chairs. No sounds were heard; it was clear that the building was not highly occupied. The two Mexicans offered no sounds, either. Their force did their talking for them. Racheed still had no idea what was going on, or what would happen next. Again, he thought of his plans, and how it could not end this way. His life could end in minutes, he feared, but he had no way of knowing otherwise.

A third man, armed with a semiautomatic rifle, entered the room from a door on the opposite wall. He appeared to be some type of guard, dressed in military-style camouflage resembling a guerrilla. He motioned to the other two, and one moved toward Racheed. “Take off your clothes,” he demanded in a gruff voice.

The two Mexicans strip-searched him, checking every part of his body for concealed weapons. Finding none, the men backed off and barked, “Put your clothes back on.”

He quickly dressed, and accompanied the armed guard through the far door. On the other side was a large office, lit by two bright table lamps on either side of a sprawling desk. The contrast of the lamps to the darkness nearly blinded him, leaving him unable to discern the figure that he saw sitting at the desk.

As he approached, the face of the man at the desk became clearer. Racheed immediately recognized the man, flashing back to grainy photos in the files of information from General Santos' office. The man was the subject of thick files, and clearly of great interest to the Mexican authorities. In an instant, Racheed knew why he had been brought here. The shadowy figure was none other than Juan Rodrequs, leader of one of the largest drug cartels in the country.

By simply looking at Rodrequs, there was nothing friendly about him. Six feet tall and a hulking two hundred and forty pounds, he was dressed in a khaki safari-style jacket and matching pants that had clearly seen better days. He looked far older than his forty-six years, the product of a lifestyle that had made him fabulously wealthy, though always looking over his shoulder.

Orphaned at age eight when both parents were killed in a robbery, he had grown up a street urchin, one of many who slip through the cracks in third-world Mexico. As a teenager, he found a home in the cartel, and moved in with one of its mid-level leaders. As he ran messages back-and-forth to the power brokers in the dark of the Mexican nights, he was exposed to violence at an early age, and saw many men die bloody deaths. As he worked his way up the ranks, he caused many of those same violent deaths, and hardly batted an eyelash at any of them.

Five years ago, he had assassinated the leader of the cartel in a power coup. Though the dead man had taken Rodrequs under his wing as a youth, Rodrequs only saw the opportunity for more power and greater riches. Now he was one of the most feared men in both Mexico and the border towns in the United States. He was also one of the richest, the leader of a drug trade netting hundreds of millions of dollars every year.

He kept a low profile, however, and few had actually seen him. Given the opportunity, they would have shuddered at the sight. His bushy mustache partially hid a long, curving scar, and he was missing a couple of fingers, the result of the firefights that his cartel was known for.

A pistol lay on the desk in front of Rodrequs, facing toward any visitor and setting the tone for the encounter. Sitting in a chair to Rodrequs' right, facing outward, was Diego Garcia, his trustworthy assistant. A semi-automatic pistol was stuck in Garcia's pants, ready for quick use.

Garcia had grown up with Rodrequs and had also worked his way up in the cartel. At six-two and 180 pounds, he was taller and thinner than his boss, and without the fearsome persona. Though uneducated, some members considered him smarter than Rodrequs, though he hardly shared his superior's ambition. Happily married, he was also more of a family man than Rodrequs, who only sought the company of the finest Mexican prostitutes. His personality had less of an edge, but he had gained Rodrequs' trust like no other, and they spent countless hours together.

Rodrequs could have driven a hole through Racheed with an icy glare. “I understand you want to discuss business with me.”

Racheed nodded. “Yes. I have been looking for you.”

“I know your name is Racheed. What do you want?”

“I am a Pakistani national. I understand that you have the resources to smuggle men and goods across the border into the United States.”

Rodrequs had learned in his decades of dirty dealing to reveal nothing. He sized up Racheed with a frigid stare. “Why do you want to know?

“If it is true, I would like to hire you for that purpose.”

Rodrequs leaned back in his swivel chair and drummed his fingers together. “I may be able to help. But I need more details.”

Racheed turned and looked at Garcia. “I was hoping to speak privately with you.”

Garcia in turn looked at Rodrequs, who shook his head angrily. “No. Diego is my good friend and trusted confidant. He is also my second-in-command. Anything you say may be heard by him.”

Racheed knew the name of Garcia from his extensive review of the Santos files. He saw no reason to argue, and began. He told Rodrequs the story of Omar and Sasha's deaths, and of his relationship with Maria. He then explained his dealings with General Santos, and how he had been able to identify Rodrequs and his location.

"Santos is a fool," scoffed Rodrequs, interrupting Racheed. "A stupid, stupid man. It does not surprise me that he would let you have this information. He claims he is after us, but never comes close. He is too weak to threaten us."

Racheed pondered Rodrequs' words but disagreed, still having a measure of respect for Santos and his uniform. But he knew better than challenge the cartel leader with a pistol pointed in his direction. Rodrequs continued his condescension. "I will give Santos this, though. He is a fool, but an honest fool. He cannot be swayed by money. Many others in the army and the government can be." Flippantly, he then asked, "Why do you think I operate untouched as I do?"

Finished with his braggadocio, Rodrequs returned to the task at hand. "What did you say to get inside Santos' office?" he questioned.

"I obtained false military documents from the Pakistani army," responded Racheed. "They identify me as an intelligence officer."

Unimpressed with Racheed's scheming, Rodrequs curtly told him to proceed with his plan. Racheed then explained how he and others in Pakistan wanted to avenge the deaths of Omar, Sasha, and the others who had died in drone strikes. He then came to the big question.

"America must pay for what they have done, and I know how to do that. I have been in contact with the Taliban, and they are supporting me." Racheed paused, then calmly reached the climax. "I need a way to smuggle myself and five other Pakistanis across the border. Is that something that you could do for me?"

The question was far too vague for a man like Rodrequs. "What do you plan to do with the five men once they are across?"

"They will be in three teams of two men each, including myself. One team will travel to Las Vegas and bomb Caesar's Palace. Another team will head north to Mount Rushmore and bomb the visitor center. The third team will go to Nashville and bomb the heart of their country music district, on Broadway."

"I see. Hmmh. That will result in a large loss of life. And great psychological damage."

"Yes, it will," replied Racheed. "But it must be done." He returned to his original question. "Are you able to help me move the men across the border?"

Rodrequs also paused in turn and sat back in his chair. He glanced over at Garcia, then swung his eyes back to Racheed. "Yes. That would be no problem. But...."

A large qualifier was coming, and Racheed knew it. He waited for Rodrequs to continue. "What is in it for me?"

Weeks of planning had prepared Racheed for this moment. "There are several ways that you may gain from this."

"Such as?"

Racheed coolly offered terms he had not explicitly discussed with Ali Sighn. "If you can provide the smuggling routes, I can put you in contact with people who can supply you with large amounts of heroin. The Taliban profit from a heavy drug trade. Or if you prefer, I can get access to a large amount of money, an amount we could both agree upon. Or both."

Rodrequs was not one to waste words, or seconds, on someone he knew little about. "I need details. How would this money come to me?"

"I can have it wired to a Swiss bank account or an offshore account. That would protect your security."

Skepticism permeated Rodrequs' gravelly voice. "And you are sure you can do this? Do not waste my time otherwise."

Racheed again stretched the truth to close the deal. "I have close contacts with Taliban leaders. They know what I want to do, and support me fully."

"I see." Rodrequs reflected on the proposal for several seconds, staring at the back wall behind Racheed. "What, specifically, do you need from me?"

"I need weapons, some C-4 explosives. I also need to purchase three vehicles that would be parked across the border in the United States. I must also have communication equipment."

Rodrequs and Garcia exchanged another glance. Garcia's eyes

shifted slightly to the door as if to indicate that Racheed was to be escorted out. “I need to think about this for a few days,” said Rodrequs. “I will contact you at your hotel.”

He then summoned the armed guard. “Return this man to his hotel.”

Racheed was led back into the suboffice, and his two captors again placed the black hood over his head. The van again drove a circular route, to confuse Racheed on his whereabouts. After a half hour, the van stopped, and Racheed's hood was removed. Through bleary eyes, he saw that he was in front of his hotel, and the men shoved him out the sliding door. Woozy from the wild drive and his eyes still reaching focus, Racheed stumbled inside the lobby, made his way up the elevator, and back to his room.

CHAPTER XI

As Racheed was being driven away, Rodrequs asked Garcia what he thought of the plan. Garcia had seemed anxious to be rid of Racheed, and he had a reason for that.

"I do not like it," said Garcia. "I am opposed for several reasons."

Diego Garcia was one of the few people who could disagree with Juan Rodrequs and get away with it. Rodrequs was always eager to hear what his number-two man had to say. "What are you thinking?"

"If this plan fails, we will have trouble," said Garcia, his bushy brow furrowed. "If the United States authorities ever find that the cartel helped terrorists cross the border, the border will be closed. There will be no way for us to get our drugs across."

Rodrequs' eyes widened in shock. "*You believe that the United States could close that entire border?*"

"They would find a way if they thought terrorists were coming across to attack them. They have been lazy in protecting the border until now, and that has helped us. But if they saw the border as an avenue for terrorists, they will take action."

Rodrequs pondered Garcia's words. "And we could not find a way around that? We always have."

"Not this time, I fear. Our drug trade will be damaged, if not destroyed. The fact that the border is not heavily guarded has been key for us. If it is closed, we will have no way to move our products across."

"You are right," replied Rodrequs. "But this Racheed has a plan that could help us. A steady supply of heroin from Pakistan would be worth a fortune. That is a high-grade product, and has a high street value."

"Yes, it does," said Garcia, nodding in agreement. "What are you getting at?"

"Every day, we face risk," said Rodrequs. "How is this plan any different? We have evaded authorities in both nations before. And the rewards are great in this case."

"The money?"

"Yes. Heroin from Pakistan will ensure our cash flow continues. And, if this Racheed can obtain two or three million dollars for us, it is certainly worth the risk."

Garcia could not help but agree with his boss, but still had reservations. "I think the risk is greater this time. The United States government never seems to crack down on the drug trade, and our government does not seem to care. But if terrorism is involved, it changes everything. The Americans will demand answers, and they will force Mexico to go along with them. Mexico will have to respond the way the Americans tell them to."

"But how would they find out?" chided Rodrequs. "You are worrying too much, my friend. You are assuming that Racheed and his men will be caught, and talk. Terrorists on their level are much too smart for that. They know how to evade capture." He then broke into a chuckle. "And who knows? They may all be dead before anyone can investigate!"

Garcia knew Rodrequs was right, since terrorists are often willing to sacrifice themselves for their cause. He shook his head and tugged nervously on his pant leg. "I don't know. I just don't know."

"There is such a remote possibility that we would be connected to the plan," said Rodrequs, in a reassuring manner that was unusual for him. "Do not worry, my friend. We will not be found out."

The discussion continued for nearly an hour. Then, Rodrequs pulled rank and made his decision. If a heroin route from Pakistan could be established and a payment of two or three million dollars was made, the cartel would help the terrorists move across the border.

He rose from his swivel chair and opened a small refrigerator on the far wall that held a small cache of the finest Mexican beers. He offered one to Garcia, and they spent the rest of the night laughing and recalling their youthful days on the streets of Ciudad Juarez.

*****

Men like Juan Rodrequs never act quickly, and love to make others squirm. Though he had decided to help Racheed within hours of their meeting, he chose to let Racheed sweat it out for a while. After two days, he sent his men back to the hotel. Again Racheed was accosted on the front sidewalk, hooded, and shoved into the van for a second meeting with Rodrequs.

The cartel leader still saw no reason to completely trust Racheed, so the Pakistani visitor was again strip-searched and treated roughly. He was led back into Rodrequs' office, where the conversation was limited.

"Hello again," said Rodrequs with a hint of sarcasm. "I will tell you what I want, and you will answer my questions."

"Very well," said Racheed, blinking away the bright light from the table lamps.

"If a heroin route from Pakistan into Mexico can be established," he began, "and three million dollars can be wired into a Swiss bank account, I will help you."

"I am glad to hear that. My thanks to you."

"Do not thank me yet." Rodrequs shot back sarcastically. He stiffened his back and sat at attention, hands folded on his desk with eyes fixated piercingly. "How will this be done?"

Racheed was no expert on the Pakistani drug trade, but he was well aware of how the Taliban operated. “I believe that the Taliban have a smuggling route in place to France. The Russian mafia handles it for them.”

“I have heard that as well,” replied Rodrequs, who *was* an expert on the worldwide trade. “How does that help me?”

“I will put you in contact with the Russian smugglers. Then you can work out a deal with them.”

The Russian mafia is one of the world's most dangerous crime organizations, and Racheed knew it. Rodrequs, though, was scared of no one. “And you know them well?”

“I have some contacts,” said Racheed, concealing the fact that his contacts were sketchy. “You can negotiate the specifics of the smuggling operation, and the payment, with them.”

“And what is in it for you?”

Racheed shook his head. “Nothing. I am not involved in heroin operations. I can only put them in contact with you.”

Ever the businessman, Rodrequs was skeptical. “No money for you, then?”

“I have no use of it,” said Racheed sharply. “I am only interested in getting my men across the border. The drug trade does not interest me.”

Rodrequs looked at Garcia, taken aback by Racheed's determination. He was also surprised at Racheed's refusal of profit, something Juan Rodrequs never turned down.

“Very well, my friend. You are not a man of money, but I am. Now.” A phony smile painted his face. “When do I get it?”

Now Racheed gambled on promises once again. His discussions with Ali Sighn were rather vague, and there were no assurances of high funding levels. “Half of the money will be wired into the Swiss bank account, as you mentioned. I will discuss it when I meet with the Taliban again.”

Rodrequs demanded to know when that would be, and Racheed told him as soon as he returned from Pakistan. That satisfied half of the cartel leader's demands, but not all. “What about the other half of the money?”

This time, Racheed had some leverage. "You will get it on the day that my men and I cross the border."

Both men were driving hard bargains, the only type of negotiation that Juan Rodrequs knew. He admired Racheed's focus, and he recognized that Racheed was not intimidated by him, unlike so many others. For the first time, he let his satisfaction show, and a toothy grin spread across his face.. "I am pleased, my friend. I will expect to hear from you when you return from Pakistan, then."

He motioned for his men to escort Racheed out of the office. Again, he was hooded, driven a false route, and dropped off at his hotel. As he lay on the floor of the van, Racheed's blood was rushing through his veins, and he could barely contain himself. His plan was taking shape, and his goals were coming into view.

*****

No sleep came that night, as Racheed was too excited to close his eyes. As before, his manly desires overcame him, and he called Maria early the next morning.

"Racheed?" Maria was a late riser, and nearly asleep at the sound of her boyfriend's call.

"Yes. I am coming for a visit."

That was all Maria needed to fully awaken. "Oh, darling! When? Soon?"

"Late this evening. My flight lands around nine."

Always emotional, Maria was practically shouting. "Where are you? Are you on the plane?"

Racheed then knew he had overstepped, and a delicate moment was coming. "Actually, I am in Ciudad Juarez."

Her elation cooled rapidly. "Ciudad Juarez? You are in Mexico?"

"Yes?"

The old saying of "hell hath no fury" applied to Maria at that moment. "*And just how long have you been there?*"

"A few days. I had business to attend to?"

She was hardly soothed. "Your military? Do not play me for a fool. What on earth would you have had to do in Juarez?"

"My brother sent me here." Racheed had sold out Solomon many times before, and once more was of little concern. "That is all I can tell you."

"Pfft," Maria blew air between her lips. But Racheed again struck a chord, and she remembered that her own father had to be secretive as well. "There were no other girls?"

"What do you mean?"

"Were you there alone?"

"Of course I was," Racheed had not expected such a question. "Why would you ask that?"

His startled tone reassured his jealous girlfriend, and she retreated. "Of course there would be no other girls. Oh, darling, I am sorry I doubted you. I just wish you had called me. I would have flown up to meet you."

"I know you would have. But there was nothing I could do."

"Of course there was not. Oh, Racheed. I am so happy you are coming. I cannot wait. I will see you this evening, my love."

"Yes. Pick me up at the airport."

Racheed hung up the phone, packed, and by daybreak was on the road to the Juarez airport in his rental car. The moderate drive passed quickly, mainly because Racheed was lost in thought the entire time, contemplating his meeting with the Taliban. In rare moments that his train of thought was broken, he fantasized about the next few days in Maria's arms. His preoccupation affected his driving, and more than once drew honks and gestures from frustrated passersby.

He arrived only minutes ahead of his flight, and two hours in the air did nothing to temper his desire. While airborne, he called Maria once again, to advise her of his flight number and scheduled time of landing. She sensuously described what she planned to do once she had undressed him, further wetting his appetite.

He had just stepped inside the terminal at Aeropuerto Internationale Benito Juarez when someone jumped him from the side. It was Maria, who could not wait to say hello. She threw her arms around him and kissed him deeply, moving so quickly that

Racheed barely realized what was going on.

As she pulled away, he finally got his first look at her, and a fire consumed his body. She was dressed all in white, with a sheer, short skirt and a strapless top that flattered her supple back and shoulders. Her eyes met his, and he was tempted to pull her into any spot that offered a little privacy, to have her then and there. But even his masculine desires were no match for his emotional control. He could wait until they were in private.

They walked to her car, Maria hanging all over him, nudging as close as she could. Once in the privacy of her white Lexus, though, she could be even closer. She never bothered to put the keys in the ignition, throwing herself at him in the passenger seat and tearing open his shirt. She had waited for weeks, and even a few seconds more was too much. He was now powerless to resist, and they reconnected in the front seat, bodies tangled with each other.

The excitement was heightened by the thought that a passerby might peer into the car and see them, as the overhead parking lights illuminated the lot as if at midday. But no interruptions were forthcoming. After several minutes of sweaty passion, they sat up, moaning and gasping for breath. They pulled on just enough clothes to not attract attention on the thoroughfare, and drove to her apartment.

Once inside, there were no such boundaries, and their clothes fell off just steps from the door. The rest of the night was spent in unbridled passion, and when the sun rose, they were locked in each other's arms, resting until another moment of desire arose.

CHAPTER XII

Even as Racheed was being driven back to his hotel in Juarez, Rodrequs and Garcia were discussing the Pakistani's plan. As before, Garcia was adamantly opposed.

"*I still do not like it*," said Garcia. "There is far too much risk."

"You worry too much, my friend," Rodrequs chuckled. "What is your problem now?"

"The same as before. If the United States authorities learn that we are helping a terrorist group, our entire business is in jeopardy. There will be no way that we will be able to move drugs across the border."

"How will they learn?" Rodrequs had a cavalier streak in him that was not about to change. "We have been doing this for years. They have not stopped us before."

"But this is different. The Americans have cracked down on terrorists since their attacks they call 9/11."

"And where has that gotten them?" sniffed Rodrequs. "Their border with us is still porous in many places. Crazy-ass Americans. They don't know what they are doing!"

He had a point, though Garcia remained unconvinced. "If their trail leads back to us..."

"It will not!" Rodrequs barked. "The risk is too small! *And the rewards, my friend*! The rewards!" He pressed his upright fingers and rubbed them together, to indicate money.

Garcia knew a constant supply of heroin from Pakistan would be a boon to their business, and the three million dollars would pad their fat bank accounts. He also knew that a failure of Racheed's plan meant the end of their lavish lifestyles, and would lead to years in prison – if they were lucky.

Still, he had to try to convince his boss. Rodrequs would hear none of it. A heated exchange ensued between the two men that lasted for over an hour. Rodrequs normally welcomed his friend's opinion, but as the pitch grew, he again pulled rank.

"That's enough!" He pounded his fist on his desk with such force that an echo rang through the office. "We are doing this. I work myself to death to supply heroin, and a flow of cheap product from Pakistan is what we need. I will also not turn away from that amount of money. We can afford a little risk. And that is it. *We are doing this!*"

Knowing where he stood, Garcia knew when to shut up. "Very well. I will do as you say."

Rodrequs also knew where the power lay. "Yes. You will." Garcia then saluted his boss and left the room, as any other soldier.

*****

Racheed spent the next week with Maria, much of it in the same fashion as the interlude in her car at the airport. Still, there were episodes of innocence. Racheed was Maria's first real love, and she cherished the light moments she spent with him. Whenever she could pull herself out of bed with him, Maria persuaded Racheed to take walks with her, and they enjoyed the best that Ciudad de Mexico had to offer, the finest cantinas, the street fairs, the streetcorner mariachi bands.

She loved holding hands or cuddling against him as they sat on benches, strolled the streets, and toured the city's many museums and cultural attractions. She detected that he was less enthralled with such affection, but she did not seem to care. She chalked his reticence up to male pride, since men are normally less excited about romance.

One day, they made the four-hour drive to Acapulco and spent the afternoon on the beach. Maria's tiny black bikini, wet and clingy against her caramel skin, was too much for Racheed, and he spent the afternoon admiring her soft curves and shapely form as she splashed in the water and lay in the sun.

Racheed had limited himself to a week with Maria, however, and when it was up, he was ready to move on. "Oh, Racheed," she whined. "You just got here. Why can you not stay longer?"

"I must return home," he said, rather bluntly. He then silenced her. "My military duties call for it."

"But..." Maria was like a pouty child, though she knew she could not argue with him. "Oh, all right. I know you must do what you have to."

"Yes. It is for my country." Racheed was becoming increasingly skilled at telling the truth as he saw it. He also knew that a sense of duty appealed to Maria. "I will be leaving late this afternoon."

That gave Maria a few hours to say her goodbyes. After the second one, Racheed was finding it increasingly difficult to depart, but his version of a "sense of duty" was paramount. He showered, dressed in his finest clothes, and had Maria drive him to the airport. There he boarded a flight back to London, where he caught a connection to Karachi.

Solomon was on a three-day furlough, and was waiting for his brother's plane. He met Racheed in the terminal, and only the most basic of greetings were exchanged. The drive to their parents' home was largely silent.

Racheed had never been particularly close to his parents, and the gap was only growing. Mahammed was the first to notice it, but he was still willing to make the effort. "Hello, my son," he said, placing his hands on Racheed's face. "We are glad to see you."

"As am I, father," replied Racheed. He then turned to his mother and quickly kissed her left cheek.

"My son," she said, reciprocating the greeting on both of his cheeks. "How long will you be visiting?"

"I will be here for a few days. I wish to see family, and consider my job prospects."

Mahammed's face lit. "Very good. You should not waste your fine education."

Racheed bristled, remembering his father's wish that he attend Texas A & M. "I know, father, and do not plan to. I have also looked at work in Mexico and the United States." Solomon simply turned away, unnoticed by his parents.

"And where have you been these last weeks? We have not heard from you" chided Mahammed.

"I have been in Mexico," said Racheed. "Visiting Maria."

"Ah, yes," said his father. "We look forward to meeting this young woman. She must be very special to you."

"She is," replied Racheed, cryptically recalling the hours of mind-blowing passion in Maria's bed. "I enjoy spending time with her."

"You must," replied Mahammed. "You have been gone for weeks."

Ever conscious of social standing, Yalina chimed in. "And you said her father is a general in the Mexican army?"

"Yes. He is in intelligence. Her mother's father is a former member of the Mexican cabinet."

"Very good. She comes from a fine family," Yalina nodded in approval. Ever socially conscious, she now expressed her desire to meet her son's partner.

Racheed was tiring of the niceties. "You will someday. But I must excuse myself. My flight was very long, and I would like to rest."

"Of course, my son," Yalina's maternal instincts took over. "Your room is waiting for you."

Racheed bowed to both of his parents and headed for his room. He lay on his old bed, remembering his childhood and how he had never liked America. But he was a man now, and his old feelings seemed boyish and shallow. He had a duty, and it must be fulfilled.

*****

Conversation with his parents over the next few days was polite, but distant. Mahammed, not wanting to rock the boat, did not broach his prior discussions with his son on his anti-American fanaticism. Yalina, managed to enjoy a few pleasant moments with Racheed, something that his normally dour personality prevented. For his part, Racheed stayed in his room for much of the time, and mere minutes each day were spent conversing with either parent.

Before Solomon's furlough was up, though, Racheed took a moment to speak with him. The two were the only ones at home, as Mahammed was at work and Yalina was on her daily shopping excursion. “You know how I told our parents that I was visiting Maria?”

“Yes?”

“That was only partly true. I was only with her for a week.”

Solomon dreaded what was coming next. “And where were you the rest of the time?”

“In Ciudad Juarez.”

“That city on the border? Why?”

“Do you know a man named Juan Rodrequs?”

“No. Should I?”

Racheed was proud that he knew someone as important as Rodrequs, and his brother did not. “He is the leader of one of the largest drug cartels in Mexico.”

Solomon still did not know where this was going. “So?”

“I met with him to see if he could help me smuggle men across the border.”

The penny had dropped. “So you are going ahead with your plan.”

“Of course I am. America must pay.”

“You have told me that time and time again. But I had hoped you would not follow through.”

Racheed bristled at the insinuation of commitment. “I am more committed than ever. It is my duty to Allah to see this to completion.”

Goosebumps spread under Solomon's white dress shirt. Racheed was oblivious to his brother's concern.

"What do you want to do?" inquired Solomon.

"Rodrequs will help me move men across the border. In return, I will put him in contact with the Taliban to organize a supply of heroin into Mexico."

Though he did not know Rodrequs by name, Solomon, as a member of intelligence, was certainly familiar with the international drug trade, since much of it originated from the region. He also knew how men like Rodrequs operated. "He will not do that for nothing. What else is in it for him?"

Racheed was as brash as ever. "The Taliban will supply me with three million dollars."

"They have promised you this?"

Racheed could not lie as well to his brother as others. "Yes" he offered in an unconvincing tone.

The two men stared at each other for several seconds. Solomon broke the silence with a chuckle and a roll of his eyes. His monotone stifled his anger. "You know what you are getting yourself into?"

"Of course I do."

Solomon's rage rose with his monotone. "And do you also know what you have gotten *me* into?" Racheed offered no response.

"What do you plan to do once the men are in America?"

Racheed was cornered. "We have not made a final decision on that."

An unflappable personality and a calm demeanor had opened doors for Solomon in the Pakistani military. Few had seen him react to any crisis. But he was no longer behind the closed doors of army headquarters. His career was in jeopardy, and his brother was about to commit unspeakable crimes. He exploded on Racheed.

"*You fool! You stupid, stupid man!*" Racheed had never heard his brother yell so loudly, and he hoped the neighbors could not hear. "You have risked *everything!* You stupid bastard!"

Solomon could not hold back any longer. "*You are in legion with the Taliban!* They are our enemies from inside! They will do more to harm this country than any enemy. And now you are one of them!"

"No, not really," Racheed quietly replied, hoping to settle his brother. "I only talk with them..."

"*Shut up!*" Solomon refused his brother's patronization and slammed his fist on the dining room table. "You are in business with them! But of course, you have not even told them all of your plans, have you?"

Racheed remained silent, but Solomon kept screaming. "Of course you haven't! You *hope* they will go along with you. And your plans aren't even final yet! You stupid, stupid fool! *They will kill you!*"

"If that is true, then it must be done. I stand ready to die for Allah."

"*I don't want to hear it!* Islam is a religion of *peace!* I read the *Koran* all the time too, you idiot!"

Racheed strongly disagreed with that statement and Solomon's audacity at challenging his devotion to Allah. "I must do this for our sister and grandfather. Our friends who have also died. I cannot turn my back on my family."

"*Stop it!*" Solomon would not be appeased. The furor in his voice was even more pronounced. "You hypocrite! Turn your back on family! You almost never saw Omar! I was close to Sasha, but you sure as hell were not! You barely spoke to her!"

Solomon spied a pile of Racheed's notes on the table and swept them away with an angry brush of his hand. He moved toward Racheed, who walked backwards around the table, hoping for some space . "And if the Taliban doesn't kill you, your friend Rodrequs will! Do you know the type of people you are dealing with? *Of course you don't!*"

Racheed was unmoved. "They hate America as I do. We agree that death must be brought to them."

"*We all hate the Americans!* You think you are the only one? Pfft," Solomon's scoff was as forceful as his voice. "I hate them too, you dumb ass! But I am able to control myself. I don't run around trying to bomb them all the time! That would be devastating to our country!"

He kept walking toward Racheed, who began to fear his brother would strike him. "And do you know what you are doing to me?" Solomon's voice had now dropped to a loud monotone. "*My career is at stake!* You have put me in jeopardy as well! I gave you fake documents. *That is reason for dismissal!* They could execute me for this! Do this for your family, you say! *You miserable son-of-a...*"

His voice broke and he turned away in disgust. Then he appealed to whatever sense of guilt he hoped his brother had left. Finally his voice lowered to a icy coldness that belied his ferocity.

"You were not raised this way. The people in Seidu, maybe. But not you. You have everything, money, education, looks, a good family, a beautiful woman." His voice then rose with each word. "*And you are such a fool!*"

Solomon reached for the table and pounded it. "Do not count on me for anything else. I have given you too much already. I do not care if you are my brother. But from now on, I am no longer yours."

He stomped from the room and out the front door, slamming it with such force that Yalina's china cabinets tinkled. Racheed was distracted only for a moment. He then gathered his notes off the floor, retired to his room, and spent the rest of the afternoon contemplating his plan.

CHAPTER XIII

Racheed stayed at his parents' home for four more days, and never heard from Solomon again during that time. At first, Racheed feared that Solomon would tell their parents of the attack plans, but then realized that Solomon's hands were tied. Any mention incriminated Solomon as well, and his military career was too important to him.

On the fifth day, Racheed informed his parents that he was leaving. “Why so soon?” said Mahammed, disappointingly.

“I want to go to Seidu,” replied Racheed. “I'd like to see our family there, my other grandparents.”

Racheed had actually been around Yalina's parents sparingly during his adolescence, and his wish to see them surprised both Mahammed and Yalina. Still, family is of the utmost in such cultures, and they were only too happy to see Racheed take an interest in any family matter. “Very well, my son,” said Mahammed. “When will you return?”

“I will let you know,” said Racheed evasively. “I will be in Seidu for a few days. I will call you.”

"So you will be coming back here?" Yalina inquired. "Let us know. We have dinner parties scheduled for all next week, and we will expect you at them."

Racheed was neither a social animal nor a social climber. He skirted his mother's order as best he could. "I know, mother. Like I said, I will call you."

The parents and the son exchanged their goodbyes, and Racheed piled his luggage into his Toyota. The car was much nicer than most Pakistanis could afford—if they could have one at all—but Racheed, ever the egotist, felt he deserved better. Solomon's words sank through on one point–Racheed had it all, and thought he deserved it. *A man such as I needs something better*, he thought. *Something more luxurious than an outdated Toyota. My father should have realized that and given me a Mercedes or Lexus, like Maria's father had for her.*

Still, the Toyota was here, and needed. He made the long drive to Seidu and paid cursory visits to his maternal grandparents and other relatives. That way, they could rightly tell Mahammed and Yalina that Racheed had spoken with them. But his real interest was finding Salaam, the young member of the local Taliban sect, and telling him that he wanted to see his leader.

Salaam was fairly easy to find, and within hours, Racheed was again in the backyard bunker, talking with Ashish, the local Taliban leader. It was in the early evening. "I want to see Ali Sighn again," Racheed said.

"I know you saw him before," said Ashish, who was obviously in the loop. "He told me of your plans. He will be expecting you."

The same three men were summoned, and with darkness approaching, they escorted Racheed to the Jeep and headed out on the bumpy, dusty road to Peshawar. They drove to the same dilapidated warehouse, gained entrance, and passed through the multitude of guard checks into the room where Ali Sighn held court.

"You have returned," said Ali Sighn in a commanding voice.

"Yes," said Racheed, thrusting his chest forward with pride. "I have news from Mexico."

"Tell me, my son." Ali Sighn respected Racheed's diligence, something that did not go unnoticed by the visitor.

"Are you familiar with a man named Juan Rodrequs?"

"Did you say Juan Rodrequs?" Ali pondered the name, and turned to his subordinates. Each man subtly shook his head. "No, I do not know that name. Why do you bring it up?"

"He is the leader of one of the largest drug cartels in Mexico, a rich man with many connections. He is located in Ciudad Juarez, just across the border from Texas."

"Texas?" Ali straightened at the mention, and waved his hand in disgust. "Where that cowboy Bush was from?"

"It is," said Racheed, knowing he had touched a nerve. He probably hated Bush as much as Ali did, but now was not the time to stoke the old man's fires. "But that is not the point, my father. Rodrequs has the ability to smuggle men across the border. He does it all the time with his drug trade."

Ali stroked his long, flowing beard with his wrinkled right hand. "Yes, he would." He paused and again ran his fingers through his whiskers. "And he will help you?"

"Yes."

"But a man such as this must want something in return. What is it he wants?"

The moment of truth was at hand for Racheed, a swashbuckler up to this point. "He is interested in heroin. He knows of the Taliban profits from the drug trade, and that the Taliban is in business with the Russian mafia."

Ali nodded. "He is a perceptive man. We *are* partners with our friends from Russia." Ali turned to his compatriots before shifting his gaze back to Racheed. "And Rodrequs wants *you* to broker a deal with the Russians?"

"I cannot do that. I am not interested in the drug trade. I only want to finish my plan. I told Rodrequs that I could put him in contact with the Russians, but nothing more."

"And you want no money, then?" Ali still was unconvinced of Racheed's motives. It was a rare man indeed that stood before Ali not looking for riches.

"No. I have told you that before, my father. I only want men."

Again Ali stroked his beard and shrugged in surprise. "Very good," he said. "What else does Rodrequs want?"

Racheed collected himself momentarily. "He wants three million dollars. Half of it should be wired into a Swiss bank account. The rest will be paid on the day my men cross into America."

Ali did not know that Rodrequs' "demands" were, at least in part, formulated by Racheed himself. The Taliban warlord looked each of his men in the eye. None offered dissent.

"That, we can do," said Ali with an almost royal air. He then smiled in approval. "You have created a good plan, my son."

"Thank you, my father. I am humbled by your praise."

"And may we both praise Allah."

"Yes." Ali motioned to Racheed to step forward to a prayer rug. The next several minutes were then spent by all present in Muslim prayer.

After the prayer concluded, Ali again addressed Racheed. "We will obtain the money for you. As Rodrequs indicated, we will sell our heroin to the Russian mafia. That will more than cover the cost of what is needed."

The next question is what concerned Racheed the most. "May we start training men for the attack?"

A broad smile stretched across Ali's face. Like Racheed, the time for talking had passed. "Yes, my son. I will send word for you to return here. We will select the best men for the task at hand."

"Thank you. Is there any other way I may serve you, my father?"

"No, my son. You will report any developments to me. My men will be in touch with you."

Racheed bowed deeply to Ali Sighn and was escorted by the three local Taliban to the Jeep. The long drive over the bumps and potholes back to Seidu took several hours, and Racheed arrived at his grandparents' home around daybreak. Like a wayward teenager, he crept into the house, fearful that he may awaken someone. When the sun rose, he joined the family for the morning meal as if he had been there all night long.

*****

At 9 a.m. that morning, Racheed called his father in Karachi. After the usual greetings, Racheed told Mahammed that he planned to stay in Seidu for another month to visit family.

"Why so long?" Mahammed inquired, startled because Racheed had never maintained close family ties.

"I have not seen many of our relatives for so long," offered Racheed. "I have never taken the time to know them very well. I have enjoyed my days here greatly, and I wish to know more of our people."

Mahammed still wondered why Racheed would want to stay in Seidu. He also worried that Racheed's anti-American obsession would be fed in the hills and bunkers of the countryside. Still, he wanted Racheed to be respectful of relatives.

"Very well, my son," he said. "Will this affect your job search at all?"

"No, father," said Racheed, who had not thought of the search in days. "I am in contact with several employers. I hope to hear from them soon."

"Good. Then enjoy your stay, and keep in touch with your mother and me."

Racheed broke the connection, completely unconcerned with any of his father's words. He asked his maternal grandparents if he could continue to stay with them, knowing full well what the answer would be. Many such cultures are loathe to turn relatives away, and his grandparents were not about to reject their grandson. Unlike many others in Seidu, the home of Yalina's parents was spacious and modern, and there was plenty of room and many amenities.

He was little interested in those, however. Two days later, Ali sent word for him through Ashish, and he was soon back on the dusty road to Peshawar. He anticipated this meeting as never before, as Ali indicated he wanted to recruit men for the attack on America.

Racheed arrived to find Ali surrounded by several men unfamiliar to him. Dressed in a flowing off-white robe with matching headdress and clutching a long walking stick, Ali greeted Racheed with a warm smile. "You have never met these men," said Ali. "These men are some of my finest. I trust them with my life, and they trust their lives to Allah."

Ali turned to the strangers. "This is Racheed. He is the mastermind of the attack on America I have discussed with you." The men, in unison, bowed to Racheed. Struck at their subservience and prideful of his newfound authority, Racheed returned their courtesy.

"These are some of my leaders," said Ali by way of introduction. "It is my wish that these men be present when we choose our soldiers. They are my most trusted warriors, and they may be of assistance to us."

He addressed his subordinates directly. "Today we select the best men for this task. We want men of youth, ones who are the fittest. But we also need men with intelligence and mental strength. They must be able to move fast, to think quickly, to face danger." He hesitated for effect. "They must also be willing to die for Allah."

He turned to Racheed. "We need men like you, my son. The description I just gave is for a man like you." He then turned to the other Taliban. "We need men like Racheed."

All nodded in unison. "Then let us go outside," said Ali.

In single file, all in the room walked outside, where three Jeeps were waiting for a ten-minute drive to another outskirt of Peshawar. They arrived at a field that resembled a crude athletic complex. Waiting for them were three dozen more men, all in their twenties and thirties and each with the appearance of an athlete. They were dressed in a variety of khakis, but most wearing traditional headdress. They stood at attention as if soldiers when Ali and the other leaders approached.

"Praise to Allah," said Ali to the crowd, who repeated the mantra. Ali then turned to Racheed and the leaders. "We will select five men from this group," he said. "We will watch them, and find the fittest. We will also speak to them, and learn of their commitment."

Racheed found little reason to do any of the talking, since Ali was virtually reading his mind. For the next hour, they observed the men run sprints, climb poles and rope ladders, and navigate obstacle courses, as if in basic training for a national army. The men conducted their workout with quiet diligence and great stamina, and it was not easy to differentiate among them. Eventually, though, the fastest, strongest, and most agile rose to the top.

Next, Ali and Racheed spoke to the men individually, asking a battery of questions. Each bowed deeply to Racheed, who relished the respect. Racheed considered each man's intelligence and gauged their dislike for the West. Ali, who viewed himself as something of a sage, pondered each man's commitment to Allah. Racheed kept notes on a clipboard, while Ali relayed his thoughts to an aide, who wrote them down. The men were not advised of any details concerning Racheed's plan of attack.

As he viewed the proceedings, a bolt of energy rocketed through Racheed's body. The excitement building in him for weeks, and it had burst through in his meetings with Rodrequs and Ali Sighn. Today, though, the high was different, searing, intense. The months of planning were now coming to fruition. His plan was nearing its goal, and as he watched the men work out and interrogated them, Racheed experienced inner power as never before.

After four hours, the men were dismissed, and they walked back to a gray block building on the rear of the compound lot. Racheed, Ali, and the others were driven back to the compound.

A discussion ensued, though Racheed and Ali Sighn were the only ones who spoke. In comparing their notes, both written and mental, and found they were in near-complete agreement. Five men were chosen for the attack, and the Taliban leaders nodded in their approval.

Though the discussion was quiet, there was a charge in the room. Normally stoic, they could hardly stifle their smiles. This was what they lived for, and spent their days planning and organizing for. They had watched their comrades die for the cause while taking thousands of other lives with them, on 9/11 in America, on 3/11 in Spain, on 7/7 in London. Now more would suffer.

When it was over, Racheed rose first, and all but Ali Sighn bowed to him. Racheed, in turn, bowed at Ali Sighn, the elder, who placed his hands on Racheed's face as if a son. "You will stay with me while the men are trained," said Ali, who turned to a subordinate. "Take him to my home, and show him his quarters."

The man bowed respectfully to Ali and extended his arm toward the door, as if to point Racheed where to go. Racheed was escorted to a dark gray Humvee and chauffered to Ali's compound, encircled by walls that enclosed a twelve-room house and a large courtyard. He was given a large corner room on the second floor that overlooked the courtyard and offered all the luxuries and technological advancements that one would not expect in this region of desolation.
*****

Training began the next day, and lasted for a month. Each day, Racheed and Ali would arrive at the compound lot, where the five men were put through rigorous exercises. Racheed joined them, and his athletic inclinations served him well amidst the chin-ups, obstacle courses, swinging ropes, and endurance races that were the order of each morning session. Racheed remembered seeing his brother Solomon in basic training for the Pakistani army, and believed he and his men were enduring an even more demanding regimen.

The grueling routine was enhanced by the searing heat that builds in Peshawar in the spring. Temperatures normally reach the high nineties by the end of the season, and June brings three-digit highs. The terrorists seemed to ignore the pounding heat, and their physical stamina and emotional determination pushed them through even the most challenging conditions.

Afternoons were spent in building necessary skills. The men were trained in bomb making, a practice in which Racheed had some experience. A couple of times as a youth, he had snuck into Omar's workshop and watched his grandfather construct bombs for suicide missions. Even at such a tender age, Racheed retained the knowledge from these boyhood secrets.

His rudimentary knowledge, though, was far supplanted by Ali's top men, who oversaw the bomb-making courses and sternly induced each man to attend to the smallest details. Like the others, Racheed was an eager student and a quick learner. He found every second of instruction stimulating.

The equipment and parts needed to make bombs were easy to collect. In his compound, Ali had a virtual arsenal, with everything that was needed to construct powerful explosives. On the rare occasions that Ali did not have a part, he simply called one of the other Taliban leaders, who was sure to have it available.

Weaponry also received the utmost precision. Racheed and the five men drilled incessantly in weaponry practice and if they were not already, became expert marksmen. Deadly firearms ranging from pistols and automatic weapons were practiced, using state-of-the-art equipment. Again, Ali supplied the most expert weaponry instructors the Taliban had to offer.

In the evenings, the men were led in prayer by Racheed, Ali, or another Taliban leader. Hours were spent reading the *Koran,* and devotion to Allah and the cause were constantly preached. In between, Racheed taught the men words and phrases in Spanish. Since some time was to be spent in Mexico, it was prudent that the men learn basic communication skills. One criteria for selection had been fluency in English, and each of Racheed's men spoke and understood that language masterfully.

The rigor and structure of the training was arduous, but none of the men asked questions. Mostly, they worked in stoic silence. Racheed was struck by their commitment. He and Ali were confident that they had chosen the proper men. It took mere days for their confidence to be justified.

Back in Karachi, Racheed felt isolated in his anti-Western hatred and his interpretation of the *Koran.* That was one reason that he enjoyed visits to Seidu, where he found some common ground. Now, he was surrounded by those who completely shared his views. Here, he was not alone in his devotion, his commitment, his raging desire to make Americans suffer.

When the month was over, the training was complete. As he sized them up and down, Racheed had rarely seen men of such athletic prowess and marksmanship. He also had never been around such expertise in bombs and weaponry, and he could converse in basic Spanish with each of them. The rush in his veins grew with each day, and despite the grueling schedule, he could barely sleep at night.

Finally, a discussion was held with the five men to detail them on Racheed's plan. Until now, they only knew they were being recruited for an attack; they had no idea how, when, or where. On this day, they found out, and they shared in Racheed's enthusiasm. These were men whose sole purpose in life seemed to revolve around death to Americans, and they stood ready to avenge their fallen comrades. Each man was given a passport, and told that explosives and weapons would be provided later on. They were then told to wait for further instructions.

CHAPTER XIV

When the training was complete, Racheed drove back to Karachi. He had kept only minimal contact with his parents while he was away, but their concern, like his, was only cursory. The gap between Racheed and his parents was nearly a chasm. Racheed was never particularly close to either parent, and Mahammed found he shared little with his radical son. Yalina was usually too preoccupied with dinner parties and social outings to notice, and when she did, she disdained the fact that Racheed had not yet found a proper job.

So the few days he spent at home were mostly silent ones. Neither parent was home much, which that allowed Racheed the quiet time that he savored. He did not dare use his parents' landline telephone to make calls to Seidu and Peshawar, but his cell phone and handheld device were invaluable.

He did, however, use the landline to call Solomon. The conversation was predictably subdued, though Solomon's demeanor was considerably more restrained. Racheed wondered if that was due to Solomon's normal self-control or the fact that Solomon was on duty at the time.

"Hello, my brother," Racheed attempted to greet Solomon more warmly than usual.

"Hello" was the response.

"I want to let you know what I have been doing in Seidu."

Solomon's voice never rose. "I can already guess."

Racheed, as usual, was unfazed by his brother's coldness. "I spent the last month training five men for my plan. I am most pleased with their progress."

Ever the military man, Solomon just had to ask. "What did you train them in?"

"Bomb making, weapons usage. I taught them some Spanish phrases as well."

"Hmm. Well, you covered everything, didn't you?"

"Yes. Our training was extremely difficult. It was even harder than your basic training."

Unabashedly proud of his military career, Solomon recognized the potshot, but offered no comeback. "When do you plan to do this?"

"Soon. I will be flying back to Mexico to meet with Juan Rodrequs."

"I guess that the Taliban have approved your plans with him."

Racheed swelled with pride, which Solomon detected on the other end. "Yes. Ali Sighn was impressed. I am a leader among them now."

Sibling rivalry had never been a problem between them, since they were never that close. Now, though, Racheed had the upper hand. A few weeks before, Solomon screamed that Racheed's plan was not approved by everyone, and would not work. Now it *was* working, and Racheed took every subtle opportunity to rub Solomon's face in it. His self-control was back in evidence, though, and he refused to take the bait. "Why did you call?"

"I just wanted to talk to you. We left on bad terms the last time."

"I told you then that I would be of no more help to you."

Again, Racheed could not resist. "I do not need your help. Everything is going as I want."

Solomon saw no reason to continue the conversation. "Well, then. I guess there is nothing more to say."

Since their last encounter, Racheed experienced an occasional pang of guilt for what he was doing to Solomon, though certainly not strong enough to throw his plans away. Though he had taken every opportunity to stick it to Solomon in this conversation, a little remorse crept in.

"My brother...." Racheed began deliberately. "I know that what I have asked of you is great."

He was met with no response, so he continued. "The false documents that you obtained for me. I do not need them anymore. I was able to get the information I needed in Mexico, and I have no use of them now. I will see that you get them."

Solomon could not help but breathe a slight sigh of relief. "You will mail them to me?"

"Yes. I will send them to your apartment, so there will be no questions at headquarters. I am sure you will want to destroy them."

Solomon emitted a weak chuckle at Racheed's obvious thought. "I will do that. Thank you." He paused, hoping for more from Racheed. "Was there something else?"

"No, I guess not. Goodbye, my brother."

"And the same to you...my brother."

Solomon's hesitation spoke volumes, though Racheed was not interested in reading them. He had proven Solomon wrong on many fronts. His plan was working, and the Taliban had embraced him. Now he made preparations to meet his new friend in Mexico, Juan Rodrequs.

*****

Racheed never revealed much of himself to his parents, and was not about to start. He even chose not to tell them that he was flying to Mexico, for fear that they would ask too many questions. On his fourth day back from Seidu, he waited until after breakfast, when his father had left for work and his mother had departed for the mall. Quickly, he packed his things, scribbled a brief note that he left on the dining room table, and headed for the airport, where an Airbus to Barcelona was on the tarmac. In Spain, a one-hour layover was all that was needed to catch a 767 to Mexico City.

Before leaving, he took a moment and called Maria, who was ecstatic at the news of his return. His only thoughts of her inflight were sexual. He was a man, and had manly desires. She was a beautiful, sensual woman, one that he deserved. He remembered his friends back home, and how they worked their meaningless jobs and went home to women who were neither as pretty, passionate, or as eager to please as Maria.

Racheed's ego was also massaged by the budding success of his plan. Much of the time in the air was spent in contemplating his next meeting with Rodrequs. He also recalled the invigoration of training in Peshawar, and the physical and intellectual highs that lingered. In time, the world would feel the shock of his actions.

Maria was at the airport as usual, dressed in a sheer halter and leggy miniskirt that was begging to come off. It did back in her apartment, and stayed off for the next two days as Racheed channeled his training high into masculine desire. She was only too willing to acquiese, her body reveling in his strength and staying power. When he finally tired, he lay on his back and she took over, caressing and kissing his body as she gave herself to him, the only man that ever fully satisfied her raging desire.

On the second day, Racheed's body could take no more, and he sought sleep. Maria, though, had no need to rest, and she pulled him out of bed, steering him to the cafes and cantinas that she frequented with friends. With glowing pride, she introduced him to her cohorts, many of whom had never met the mysterious Pakistani whose mention put a sly smile on her face. They had teased her, saying that no such man existed, that she was only imagining.

Exasperated, Maria was determined to show off her boyfriend on his next visit. Racheed had little interest in Maria's friends, wishing instead to spend the time in her sensuous white canopy bed. But he went along, making small talk when called upon over cappuccino in the high-end coffeebars of Maria's daily routine.

The girlfriends were nearly as beautiful as Maria, all with flowing, dark hair, curvaceous figures, and almost as scantily clad. They were from the finest families of Mexico City society, educated in the best schools in the United States and Mexico. They provided pleasant eye candy for Racheed, who enjoyed the view amid their chatter. His boredom was alleviated by the self-assurance that he could have any of these women he wanted.

After a while, he could not overcome the dullness. "Do we have to keep doing this?" he asked as her friends excused themselves for the powder room. "I have spent the last month thinking about you."

He was a good liar, good enough that she had no clue. "Oh, Racheed," she cooed and seductively kissed his lips. Public displays of affection are the norm in such cultures, which many Americans view as sex-drenched. But here, none of the other patrons in the café seemed to notice or care as she kissed him repeatedly, with almost the same fire as in their lovemaking.

Finally, she stopped and stroked his face. "Darling, I only want to show how proud I am of you. You have never met my friends, and I have told them so much about you." Maria was clearly enthralled to be on his arm, while Racheed only wanted her arms around him. Still, he played along, not wanting to upset his radiant lady friend.

When the tortuous visits were over, they strolled back to her apartment and another long night of seduction. As they awoke in the morning, still clutching each other with bodies pressed together, she felt as complete a woman as she could possibly imagine.

CHAPTER XV

After a week, Racheed could allow himself no more of Maria's kisses. He had a job to do, and a meeting with Rodrequs awaited. He also knew that Maria would linger at the airport, and he was in no mood to divulge his plans, or destination. "I will just take a cab."

"Why?" whined Maria. "I can drive you." She threw her arms around him and pressed her face against his chest. "You're leaving so soon, and I want every minute I can get with you."

"No," said Racheed, mustering some firmness. "You have a busy day planned."

"Oh, Racheed, you're so sweet, always worrying about what I want," gasped Maria breathlessly. "*You are the perfect, perfect man.*"

Racheed saw no need for a rebuttal. "Well, it's only a few minutes, and we've had a week together. I am a grown man. I can at least get to the airport when I need to."

Maria pulled herself from him and sauntered to the window, wrapping herself playfully in a curtain. "I hate to think of you half a world away. When we're apart, it feels like even further."

She assumed he was flying home, and Racheed was not about to correct her. “I feel as you do. But I must return to Pakistan.”

“Oh, yes. Your duties, after all.”

Several minutes were spent in a series of deep goodbye kisses, which kept the taxi waiting on the street. Ali Sighn had certainly never expected that some of his money would be wasted in such an exchange, with the meter running. Finally, Racheed thrust himself away and to the door.

At the airport, he boarded a 737 for the short flight to Juarez, and upon landing, rented a car. Now, he chose to upgrade, electing to spend more of Ali's funds on the finer things. He selected a charcoal Lincoln Town Car, but checked into the same economy hotel. Contact with Rodrequs was difficult enough, and he saw no reason to compound the issue by staying in a different location than before.

He still had no idea where Rodrequs lived, since transport to their first two meetings was made in the back of the van, while hooded. Rodrequs was certainly not one to advertise his location, but he knew how to make the first move.

Later that night, he strolled down to the bar and approached the same bartender as before. He ordered a Corona Light and looked away, like any secret agent. “I am still looking for a man named Juan Rodrequs,” he said in a soft voice.

“I told you before, senor,” said the bartender, who never looked up as he wiped down the bar. “I know no one by that name.”

The bar was empty, save for two men. They were some of the same Mexicans who were in the bar the first time, and closely watched as Racheed fidgeted with his beer. He drank none of it, still wedded to his Muslim abstinence beliefs. He paid his bill and left, noticing that two sets of dark eyes were following him out the door.

Maria may not have known where her lover was, but CIA agent Greg Foster had an idea. In his daily routine of poring over the flight manifests, he noticed that Racheed had again flown into Mexico City, and subsequently flown to Juarez. Again, though, Foster saw no reason for alarm. He recorded the data into the CIA, FBI, and Homeland Security computer systems and moved on to other business.

*****

After his encounter with the bartender, Racheed went back to his room to wait. He correctly suspected that Rodrequs would not move swiftly. The next day passed in its entirety with no response until midnight the following evening.

Then, a sharp knock was heard on the door. Racheed spied through the peephole to see the two Mexicans who had hooded and cuffed him for his meetings with Rodrequs. They were attired in dark blue shirts and pants, almost as the hotel maintenance crew. Racheed opened the door a crack and peered outside.

“Senor Rodrequs wishes to see you. Come with us.”

Racheed reached for his key card on a nearby end table and left immediately, never bothering to switch off the lights. The men made no move to restrain or blindfold him, simply walking briskly past the elevator and down the steps. Once in the lobby, they slipped past the nonchalant desk clerk and outside to the same van that Racheed was familiar with.

This time, though, the men ceremoniously held the side door open for Racheed, and he climbed into a rear seat. The van sped off, though Racheed could tell it was now driving a direct route. The van rolled through downtown, past the finer homes of the town, and into an impoverished neighborhood. Even at that late hour, children were wandering the streets, and their deep-sunk, empty eyes stared at the van as it raced by.

Racheed barely noticed as he anxiously awaited the final destination. The van proceeded to the outskirts of town, down a couple of out-of-the-way streets and onto a secluded dirt road. At the end of the road was a sprawling compound, shut off from society by a ten-foot-high silver chain link fence lined with barbed wire.

The van approached the gate and pulled up to an intercom. The driver spoke only two or three words, and seconds later the gate opened automatically. In the moonlight, Racheed noticed a bevy of surveillance equipment located every few yards along the fence and on utility poles along the drive. The van stopped at a side door of the compound, a spacious tan stucco structure with a maroon terra cotta roof and long, connecting wings.

The men disembarked and courteously held the sliding van door for Racheed, who nodded his thanks. He was led through the foyer of the home and into a fine parlor, dimly lit but with enough light to display of dozens of high-priced vases and native pottery. Sitting in an oversized brown leather recliner, looking straight ahead, was Juan Rodrequs.

He turned when he heard his visitors' approach. “Buenos noches, my friend,” he said, extending his hand. For the first time, he offered a smile, showing unusually large, animal-like teeth. “It is good to see you again.”

Racheed was taken aback by the warm greeting, but quickly regained himself. “Hello to you as well,” he said. “I am happy to be in your presence again.”

“May I offer you a drink?” Rodrequs waved his hand at a butler, who was standing off in the dim shadows.

“No thank you,” said Racheed, mustering good manners unusual to his nature. He nominally recalled his vow of abstinence due to his faith. He surveyed the room. “You have a beautiful home, my friend.”

“I am glad you like it,” replied Rodrequs, grinning toothily. “I have twenty-two rooms here, as well as a large warehouse on site for my business. It is the result of my years of hard work and success.”

“You have every reason to be proud of it,” said Racheed, admiringly.

Rodrequs, as usual, was lying. He had actually gained the home when he took over the cartel. This was the former leader's residence, and when Rodrequs eliminated him, there was a clear path for the new leader to move in.

“The warehouse I mentioned is where I met with you before,” said Rodrequs. “I hope you will forgive the rough treatment my men and I gave you. But as you know, a man such as I must be careful.” There was a clear sense of pride in his voice.

Racheed nodded, then ended the niceties. “You wish to speak with me?”

Rodrequs was content to play cat-and-mouse. “Yes, but not now.

It is late, and I am sure you are tired. You will stay with me for as long as you are here."

Startled at the invitation, Racheed stammered a response. "Oh. Uh, thank you. You are too kind."

"Not at all," Rodrequs raised his hand, as if to dismiss Racheed's concern. "My men will take you back to your hotel to gather your things in the morning. Until then, good night, my friend."

The white-clad manservant stepped forth and motioned to Racheed. He was led to a commodious bedroom on the second floor, with an oversized sliding glass door leading to a balcony. The luxurious room offered the best of Mexican hospitality, including a king bed with colorful spread and sheets, topped by a pair of men's white cotton pajamas. A bookcase and flat-screen television were just inside the door, while a private bath sat off one wall.

Racheed nodded to the manservant, who turned on his heel and quickly departed. He undressed, put on the complimentary sleepwear, and sat on the edge of the bed until he felt sleepy enough to lay back.

When Racheed walked downstairs at 7 a.m, the two men from the van greeted him. They stood on either side of Rodrequs as if bodyguards. "Buenos dias, my friend," offered Rodrequs, seated in his easy chair and enjoying a huge cigar. "Did you find your room to your liking?"

"Yes, senor," replied Racheed. "Very comfortable."

"I am pleased to hear it," said Rodrequs, who turned to the two men. "Take our guest back to his hotel to get his things." He then turned to Racheed. "When you return, we will have breakfast."

Racheed was driven back to the hotel, where he packed his belongings and checked out. The men remained in the van. The three then returned to the compound, navigating their way through the early rush-hour traffic.

When they returned, the manservant led Racheed into an enormous dining room, dominated by a long mahogany table with seating for twelve. Rodrequs sat at the head of the table, with Diego Garcia to his right. A meal of spiced ham, beef, eggs, and native fruit was spread before him. “Join us in dining, my friend.”

“Thank you.” Racheed was carrying a black briefcase, which he set beside him on the floor. He had not eaten since the previous day, and helped himself to a healthy serving of eggs and fruit, foregoing the beef in respect to his Muslim beliefs.

He poured himself a glass of fruit juice from a large carafe and turned to Rodrequs. “Again, sir, you offer your guests only the finest.”

“Nothing else will do,” chuckled Rodrequs, who piled his plate with meat and eggs. Garcia did the same. Rodrequs then reached for a bottle of vodka that sat ready a small end table. He turned to Racheed and said, “I hope you do not mind.”

“Not at all,” said Racheed. “It is *your* home.” At Texas A & M, he had chided his old roommate for his indulgence. Now it seemed to matter less.

Rodrequs raised the bottle as if a toast and poured a healthy serving into his fruit juice. He then poured a smaller serving into Garcia's glass, stirred his drink with his index finger, and turned to Racheed.

“Now, my friend. What can you tell me about our plan?”

Though between mouthfuls, Racheed was only too happy to answer. “I have much to report. I have met with Ali Sighn, and we have selected five men who will serve us. They are only the best, smartest, fittest. I trust them with my life. I have spent the last month training with them. They are ready to be flown here at a moment's notice.”

“Very good,” smiled Rodrequs. “I can see you have trained with them.” He ran his eyes up and down Racheed's slender physique.

“Yes. There is not a military in the world who trains their men harder than I have mine.”

“As I see. When will you bring them here?”

“I will not bring them together. The idea of several Pakistani men flying into Mexico at once would alert authorities. They would see no other reason for them to be here but for an attack. I will send for them one by one. It may take several weeks, but it will be safer that way. There will be less reason for the Mexican or American government to be suspicious."

"I agree," Rodrequs looked at Garcia, who nodded his agreement. "We must not act in haste. The men can fly into Mexico City. Diego will then transport them here. I will provide a safe house for them."

"That is good news," said Racheed. "I am indebted to your assistance."

"No bother," replied Rodrequs. "It is what I do." He waved his open palms in a slight shrug, as if mocking humility. "I will also tell you that Diego has obtained the explosives and weapons that you requested. He has fifty pounds of C-4 explosives per vehicle, and two pounds for each bomb vest. He has worked with some Mexican federalies, and they were generous in their supply."

Racheed knew the federalies likely had no other choice, since Rodrequs wielded tremendous power and an equal capability for violence. Still the federalies and the cartel had a mutually beneficial, and usually peaceful, relationship. "You have as much of everything as I need?"

"Yes. Everything you asked for. But this effort has cost me a lot of money." Rodrequs leaned back in his chair and threw his hands up. "I am not a rich man," he said without a hint of sarcasm. "When will I be compensated for my hard work?"

Racheed reached for the briefcase, set it on the table in front of Rodrequs, and popped the latches. Inside was $100,000 in cash.

"I hope this will ease your mind," said Racheed, feigning diplomacy. "This came from my partners in Pakistan, from my meeting with the Taliban. They are putting together the rest of your money as we speak. When I return, the rest of what you are owed will be wired into your account."

"That pleases me more than you know." Rodrequs hardly had the acting ability to plead poverty, especially in such lavish surroundings. "My mind is now free from worry."

Two could play that game. "It is not my intent to trouble you," said Racheed. "I am glad you may relax. But now I must ask of you..."

"Please do, my friend. I have made other promises that I must keep."

"How do you intend to move my men across the border?"

"That is easy," Rodrequs threw his head back, puckered his lips, and waved both hands in the air to demonstrate the ease. "I have a tunnel that is under the U.S.-Mexican border. I move my men and my goods through it all the time. It has never been detected by authorities."

"They have no clue of it?"

"None at all," Rodrequs had another reason to brag. "And no one ever will. It is too well hidden."

"Is that the only route that I may use?"

"No. There are others," said Rodrequs. "The border patrol is lazy, and undermanned on both sides. Getting my products through is, how do the Americans say it? Like taking candy from a baby."

He roared at his own joke, and Garcia smiled broadly. "It is too easy, my friend," said Rodrequs, still chortling. "Besides, I have a border patrol agent on my payroll."

Racheed now joined the laughter. "I have the feeling he is not the only one in your employ."

"Of course not," said Rodrequs. "I employ many people. I am a respected businessman!" He guffawed again at the irony of his statement. "That is why no one bothers me here. I own half of the people in this town!"

He ignored the fact that he was never bothered because so many people were terrified of him. "Remember the bartender in your hotel?"

"The one who pretended not to know you when I asked him?"

"Yes. He plays stupid, doesn't he?" Rodrequs laughed once more and continued to relax. He reached for his cigar case and offered one to Garcia and Racheed. Both declined, so he helped himself, striking a long match that he tossed aside. "That bartender supplies my product to hotel guests. He is not the only one in that bar employed by me. Did you notice who else was watching you?"

"There were a couple of men in the bar who never took their eyes off me," Racheed recalled.

“That is because I pay them not to. Those men were on the streets when I hired them. Now, they support their families well.”

Racheed already knew that Rodrequs' men were all around, and was not particularly interested. “This tunnel you speak of. I would like to see it.”

“But of course.” Rodrequs summoned his butler. “Bring my car around.” After a few seconds, he rose from his chair, and Garcia and Racheed took the hint. They followed Rodrequs through the parlor to the front door.

Waiting for them out front was a black Hummer, with a driver dressed in camouflage khakis. Rodrequs and Garcia climbed into the back seat, while Racheed was left with the front. “Take us to our facility,” directed Rodrequs.

On the trip, Rodrequs became a little nosy. “So, senor,” he said, directing at Racheed. “You must really hate America to go to all this trouble.”

“Yes,” replied Racheed. “They killed my grandfather and sister, and many of my friends. I will make them suffer for that.”

“Ah, yes,” said Rodrequs, pretending to be reminded. “But I do not share this hatred of the United States. Americans are my customers. Without them, I lose much of my business.”

Racheed hesitated, fearing Rodrequs was having second thoughts. “Then why are you doing this?”

Rodrequs detected Racheed's apprehension. “Oh, do not worry, my friend. What you plan will not take my customers, or at least not many of them. The rewards I will gain will more than offset what I may lose.”

“So you say,” said Racheed. “Remember, though, we are seeking different rewards, my friend.”

CHAPTER XVI

The "facility" to which Rodrequs referred was a warehouse located ten minutes away and a mere hundred yards from the Rio Grande River. The warehouse appeared as any other, three stories of dark, dusty brick and two thousand square feet on each floor. Several battered delivery trucks surrounded the structure, which had no signage or other signifying marks save for an imposing concrete fence that enveloped the property.

The three men disembarked from the Hummer and approached a gate in the fence. Rodrequs playfully called out, "let us in, ombres!" The gate swung inward to reveal a detail of armed guards, dressed in paramilitary camouflage and carrying assault rifles. Rodrequs led his friends inside, slapping several of the guards on the buttocks and patting their faces.

Garcia raised one of several green garage doors on the building, and the three proceeded inside. Facing them were thousands of boxes and crates, most with no labeling.

"This is one of my warehouses," offered Rodrequs. "I have complete access to it." Racheed wondered what was inside the containers. Perhaps they held portions of Rodrequs' drug trade, or some of his arsenal.

He barely had time to ponder, as Garcia walked to the opposite edge of the floor, to an area rug mostly obscured by a desk and file cabinet. He pushed the furniture out of the way and pulled back the rug. Hidden underneath was a trap door with a hole on one end, large enough to stick a couple of fingers in.

Garcia thrust his index and middle digits through the hole and yanked them back, swinging the door upward with them. Visible under the door was a shaft that stretched some eighty feet downward. A set of ten steep wooden steps led a few feet down to a steel landing that was the apex of a utility elevator.

The elevator was six feet square, encased with three feet of chain link on all sides to prevent falls. It ran on a high-voltage electric cable and boasted a reinforced dark gray steel floor designed for carrying heavy quantities of cargo. The three filed into the elevator, pushed a red "down" button, and the machine whirred to life, deliberately sinking to the bottom of the tunnel.

The tunnel itself was commodious, some six feet wide and seven feet high. Planks for bracing ran the length of the tunnel to prevent cave-ins, and a line of electric light bulbs illuminated the path. A smooth path of concrete had been poured on the floor, to offset the dampness that resulted from the shallow Rio Grande above. A steady drip could be heard throughout. Still, it was sophisticated enough that men and their goods could move through unnoticed and unopposed.

"Pretty good, eh, senor?" laughed Rodrequs, slapping Racheed in the ribs. "Let us go now to America."

The tunnel was so long that the other end was not discernible. "I have the best engineers money can buy," bragged Rodrequs. "I told them to build this for me, and look what they have done!"

The men walked some five hundred yards before finally seeing a second elevator, identical to the first and pointing up a second, similar shaft. Rodrequs stroked the chain link with his open palm. "Clean as a whistle," he mused. "Just look how it sparkles!"

As they rode upward to another landing, the three crept up another short flight of stairs. Racheed watched as Garcia reached the ceiling, then knocked. After several seconds, he pushed on a door that opened and let some light through.

When he reached the top, Racheed saw the outcome. They were in a storage closet in a vehicle repair shop, four thousand square feet of grease-covered floor space. Parked inside was a tow truck and several vehicles in various states of repair. "Welcome to America!" beamed Rodrequs, his wide grin exacerbating his even wider facial scar.

Racheed stared down at the trap door, amazed at the sophistication of the tunnel and his new surroundings. Garcia edged toward the closet door, peered outside, and swung it open. Rodrequs and Racheed followed him into the main floor space.

Two mechanics of Mexican descent, wearing cadet blue coveralls with nametags, walked by the men, and Racheed nervously turned to Rodrequs. "Do not worry," said the cartel leader. "The men who work here are also on my payroll. Some of them help me move goods when I need them. The ones who need the job so badly that they say nothing. The owner of this shop is one of my best pushers. No one here will say a word."

Rodrequs turned and pointed to a mechanic, wiping his hands in the corner. "Jose Carlos," he called out playfully. "Were you the one who cleaned my elevator for me?"

"Si, senor," said Jose, laughing. "As I always do for my good friend." Rodrequs turned to Racheed, grinning. "See what I mean?"

The shop was on the outskirts of El Paso. Its gray concrete slab walls did nothing to attract attention, and it looked as any other car repair shop. The three men walked outside. A sign, "Mendez Auto Shop" hung above the door, topping a banner that offered full service oil changes for $34.95. A parking lot of cracking concrete surrounded the business. A two-lane road carried a modest stream of traffic, and as they flew by, drivers had no reason to suspect anything out of the ordinary.

Racheed took it all in, scanning his eyes over everything he could think of, finding nothing that alarmed him. After a few minutes, the three men were headed down the elevator again to the bottom, retracing their steps back into Mexico. The other elevator led them up to the warehouse, where they moved the area rug back into place, reset the desk and cabinet, and walked outside. The driver was waiting in the black Hummer, and in ten minutes, they were back at the Rodrequs compound.

Once there, Rodrequs sauntered to his easy chair in the parlor, and Garcia and Racheed found seats on a sectional. "Now, gentlemen," said Rodrequs, snapping his fingers for the manservant. "Would you care for a drink?"

Garcia nodded but Racheed declined. "Before we retire," he said, "I would like to discuss a couple of more things with you."

"Of course," Rodrequs said, pouring himself a gin and tonic. He ignited another cigar and blew a large cloud of smoke at the ceiling. "What else do you wish?"

"As you remember, I will need three vehicles," said Racheed. "I must have transportation for my men once they are across the border."

"Certainly, my friend," replied Rodrequs offhandedly. "That is no problem at all. Your vehicles will be ready for your men and parked at your disposal in the repair shop we were just in. Your vehicles will be nice, but nothing eye-catching."

He sipped his drink, set his glass down, and put his fingertips together. "I have found that if cars look too nice, particularly depending on who is driving them, then the authorities become suspicious. You will have comfortable, nice vehicles – just not too much so."

Racheed had not thought of those factors, and listened intently. "I understand what you are saying. Go on."

"Here is what I will do," explained Rodrequs between gulps of gin. "I will purchase your vehicles in El Paso, from a nice used car dealer whom I do business with. The cars will then be taken back to the auto shop you were just in. I have expert mechanics who know how to remove all forms of identification, like the, how do you say? The vehicle identification numbers.

"Those are found on the frame, motor, transmission, and the front window," continued Rodrequs. "My men will either grind those off, or pool them with a torch. They do this all the time. When they are done, there is no way that the identifications will be seen, or traced."

This satisfied Racheed only partially. "But what about license plates? That could be a problem."

"No, it won't," replied Rodrequs curtly, as if his intelligence was questioned. "I will just have someone remove some plates from an impound lot that I know of in El Paso. I can send two or three men over the fence of the lot and steal three sets of plates off the cars that are parked there. We do it all the time, it is no big deal. We will then put those plates on your cars, just like they belong there."

"Gracias," said Racheed. "But I am worried that your tunnel is the only way to get across. What if something should go wrong?"

"That is not a concern. The border is very porous, and is largely unguarded. You can cross anywhere from here to Nogales."

Nogales, Mexico is a city of over 150,000, some sixty-five miles south of Tucson, Arizona. It is also nearly three hundred miles from Juarez. "That is a wide area," said Racheed increduously. "I can cross anywhere?"

"Oh yes," reassured Rodrequs. "I send my men and drugs across in that region all the time. Rarely do I ever lose one of them."

"Very good," said Racheed. "The crossing will be the easiest part of what I am doing."

"That is certain." Rodrequs had finished his drink and now poured himself another one. He also lit a second cigar from the first. "But once you are across, you are on your own. I can do nothing else for you."

"I understand. You are taking a great risk as it is."

Still concerned of that risk, Garcia looked over at Rodrequs, who met his glance. His icy black eyes, though, convinced Garcia to stay quiet.

Racheed also wondered how he would communicate with Rodrequs in the interim. But all the hours spent in contemplation were not in vain. "I have an idea how we may stay in touch."

"What is it?"

"I will send you coded letters via the mail. I presume you do not have a mailing address?"

Rodrequs chuckled. "No, senor. Very few people have even been to this hacienda. The mail does not deliver here. It could never get inside the front gate if it tried."

"I do not suppose it is wise for a man such as you to make himself known, eh?"

"No, my friend," Rodrequs uttered another snicker. "Do not mail anything here. Send it to the bartender in the hotel. He will make sure I receive it."

"What is his name?"

"Vicente Morales. Send it to him in care of the hotel. I have done this with him several times before. He will keep it discreet."

"Very good. But we need to work out some type of code."

Racheed, Rodrequs, and Garcia then spent the next half hour hammering out a secret code. Words and phrases were designed to signify different meanings. To the outsider, the letters would have simply been pleasant greetings. To the three insiders, they conveyed entirely different news.

The final order of business was for Racheed to obtain account numbers and other wire data on Rodrequs' Swiss bank account. The cartel leader was only too happy to supply such information. Racheed then advised his partner that he would leave the following day for Pakistan.

Spurning his Muslim abstinence, he joined Rodrequs and Garcia in drink, and the three toasted their upcoming good fortune. They then spent the rest of the afternoon joking about beautiful women, the finest wines, and the stupidity of Americans.

*****

The following day, Racheed headed home to Karachi via London, electing not to tell his parents of his arrival. Once there, he loaded his luggage into his Toyota and drove the thousand miles north to Seidu. He spent only enough time there to send word to Ali Sighn, requesting another meet. Salaam, the perennial messenger, promptly sent the word up the chain, and Racheed only had to wait for two hours to receive permission to proceed. This time, he needed no escort and drove himself on to Peshawar, directly to Ali Sighn's headquarters.

Ali Sighn was pleased to receive Racheed and was eager to hear of the latest meeting with Juan Rodrequs. Racheed presented the information on Rodrequs' Swiss bank account to Ali, who ordered one of his top advisors to step forward. He handed the paper to the man, who quickly left the room. Within minutes, he returned and whispered something in Ali Sighn's ear.

"It is done," said Ali. "Your friend now has his money."

"He will be most pleased," said Racheed. "What now?"

Ali waved Racheed off and turned to another of his inner circle. "Send for Adeeb Ahmad," he ordered.

Racheed immediately recognized the name. Adeeb Ahmad was the best of the five men trained for the attack, and Racheed knew that Ali was ready to move.

Forty-five minutes later, Adeeb was escorted through the door and into the chamber. He bowed to Ali and stood at attention.

"My son, the time is now," said Ali. "You will be leaving in one week. You will be transported to Karachi, and you will fly to Mexico City to begin the operation."

Adeeb nodded solemnly at Ali, who raised his hand in circular fashion. "You are serving Allah. You must be willing to die for him, and reap the rewards in the afterlife. Praise be to his name."

The young terrorist rose, bowed deeply to his elders, and left the room. A chill raced through Racheed's body, and his hairs stood on end. His plan was now on the brink.

*****

From his guest room at Ali Sighn's compound, Racheed wrote the first coded letter to Rodrequs. Under their system, proper names could not be easily deciphered. Any layperson who saw the letter would not have read the name "Adeeb."

The flight number was also buried. The letter read as if a business note, and several telephone numbers were mentioned. The second telephone number was the key. The digits of the flight number were encoded in the last three digits of the fake telephone contact. Each digit was two higher than the actual number of the flight. Since Adeeb's flight number was 361, Racheed wrote the last three digits of the fake telephone number as 583.

Racheed advised Rodrequs to have Garcia pick up Adeeb at the Mexico City airport. The flight on the 767 from London, via Karachi, landed on time, and Garcia was indeed there to meet Adeeb, as planned. Garcia approached Adeeb in subtle fashion, to not attract attention. He led Adeeb to the parking lot and one of the black sport utility vehicles of Rodrequs' personal fleet for the drive to Ciudad Juarez and Rodrequs' safe house.

In his Mexico City office, Agent Foster read through the flight manifest and noticed something new. The name of "Adeeb Ahmad" was on the flight, which Foster was unfamiliar with. In the post-9/11 era, this was enough to raise an eyebrow on any prudent CIA official.

As usual, Foster ran the name through the Homeland Security system, as well as the CIA and FBI systems, but no information turned up. He entered Adeeb into the computer system with the time and date of the flight, but this time took an extra step. He also contacted a counterpart in the CIA office in Islamabad, the Pakistani capital, and requested a name check on Adeeb Ahmad.

CHAPTER XVII

Though Rodrequs and Garcia were heavily involved in Racheed's plot, the drug business of the cartel had not slowed down. In fact, it was more profitable than ever, since American authorities were unable to keep up with the flow, and anti-drug policies remained ineffective. As a result, tons of cocaine and meth were flowing through the tunnel to the Mendez Auto Shop.

Though Rodrequs made himself hard to contact, dealers from across the continent found a way to get in touch with members of his organization. On the day after Adeeb arrived in Juarez, Rodrequs received word from a subordinate of a call from a drug dealer in Chicago with high demand and deep pockets. Rodrequs responded to the man and received a typically large order. Four hundred kilos of cocaine were requested, which carried a wholesale value of over $1.2 million.

No successful supplier does it alone, and in Rodrequs' case, having a trusty aide like Diego Garcia was invaluable. The two men had been inseparable for decades, and both were experts in moving drugs of all qualities and quantities. Rodrequs instructed Garcia to make the necessary arrangements to deliver the drugs to Chicago.

While both men were used to high-dollar amounts, the Chicago order was unusually large, so Rodrequs deviated from his usual method of simply sending his men down the tunnel to the owner of the shop. Over breakfast in the dining room, he told Garcia to deliver the drugs personally, and return with the money. Not unexpectedly, some discussion arose on the exact nature of the mission.

"How do you wish I do this?" asked Garcia, ever the loyal subordinate.

"I will move the drugs through the tunnel," replied Rodrequs. "I'll send some men to help out. But that should not be a problem."

"We certainly have the men," noted Garcia.

"Yes, I do," responded Rodrequs, correcting the "we" part. "But I need you to have a reason for being in the United States."

Garcia pondered for a moment, then his face brightened. "I know," he exclaimed. "I will take Rosa with me."

Rosa was Diego's wife of eighteen years. Like her husband, she had grown up poor, the sixth of nine children in a family of farm laborers. At fourteen, she was sent to live with an aunt and uncle in Chicago, keeping house in return for her board. Short and slight with medium-length, scraggly black hair, her angular face, dry skin, and lack of curves did little to attract the mixture of black, white, and Hispanic boys in her South Side neighborhood. At nineteen she was waiting tables in a bar in the Loop when she met Diego, a frequent customer. He was in and out of Chicago on the drug trade so frequently that he kept an apartment there.

Within two years, they were married. She was fully aware of his profession, and sometimes helped smuggle his boss's product. As he rose in the cartel, so did their lifestyle, and Rosa now dressed in clothes ordered from the finest American catalog houses. The couple's two children attended an upper middle-class private school, and had no inkling of where their tuition money came from.

"Rosa used to live in Chicago," remarked Garcia. "She has relatives there. I will take her with me, and she can visit them. If I am detained, I can say that we are simply in the United States, visiting family."

"Excellent," said Rodrequs. "She will not have a problem with this?"

He well knew the answer. The drug trade had been good to the Garcia household, and they lived much better than most in Juarez. She also had a high opinion of Juan Rodrequs, so warm that it made her husband nervous. "Of course not," said Garcia. "She has helped me with this before. It will be no problem. But what vehicle do I use?"

Rodrequs weighed the question, then made a decision. "I will have a new pickup truck waiting for you in the auto shop." The cartel leader rose from his chair and wandered around the room. "There is this one truck I own that has a special feature," he chuckled. "To the naked eye, it looks like any other truck...

Garcia finished his boss's sentence. "I know which one you speak of. Is it just like the other trucks I have driven?"

He was referring to a tried-and-true method of drug smuggling that he had used many times. The truck had a false bottom beneath the bed that was not visible to the passerby. However, the floor of the bed could be lifted to reveal a secret compartment with ample storage space. In that concealed compartment, a considerable amount of cocaine could be transported, completely out of sight.

"Yes, my friend," exclaimed Rodrequs. "We will move the product just as before. And no one will know the difference!"

Both men, now finished with their meal, were in the mood to celebrate. Rodrequs summoned his butler for two bottles of Corona, and he and Garcia drank a toast to their brilliance.

*****

Later that afternoon, Rodrequs gave the go-ahead to load the drugs. The warehouse to the tunnel housed tons of cocaine and other substances, mostly in an ancillary storage room off the main floor. The door to the storage room was concealed; the lock was tripped by a long wire, inserted into a hole in the wall. A push on this false part of the wall revealed the door, which was otherwise not noticeable.

Rodrequs was indeed correct that a small army of men was needed to move that much cocaine. Since the Chicago order was nearly nine hundred pounds, several Mexicans were required, each pushing handtrucks holding several bags each. The bags were carefully stored inside some of the hundreds of crates of narcotics in the warehouse.

Moving the drugs required physical strain, but Rodrequs' tunnel was constructed well. The elevator was constructed to carry heavy loads, and only two trips were required down the shaft.

The bags were then ferried the five hundred yards to the other end, which required no small amount of human strength, since the length of the tunnel was nearly four-tenths of a mile. As usual, Rodrequs selected only the best men for the job, the tallest, broadest men he had, hulking masses with muscles that were up for the challenge. At the end of the tunnel, the process was then repeated.

Waiting in the shop was a black Ford F-150 pickup, with the false bottom in the bed. The cocaine was carefully arranged in the secret compartment, which was completely clean and watertight. The floor of the bed was then lowered into place, making it impossible to discern that the truck was carrying over a million dollars in illegal substance.

Diego and Rosa had both grown up in Juarez, but since each had resided in Chicago for a time, they both had green cards. This allowed them to travel freely in the United States, and both had crisscrossed the country as mules for Juan Rodrequs. Though they could have crossed the border freely, they chose the tunnel route, carrying their luggage as they went. Before they left, she dropped the children off at an older cousin's home, offering a flimsy story that she and Diego had a family emergency back in Chicago. At 4 a.m., they were in the auto shop, loaded in the truck, and ready to go.

They needed the early start, since the trip to Chicago was some fifteen hundred miles in length and was expected to require twenty-five to twenty-seven hours. Speeding was not an option, as any traffic stop threatened to expose their cargo. As a result, they were content to motor along at nearly seventy miles an hour, just under the interstate speed limit and slow enough not to attract attention. Garcia made the decision to drive straight through and hoped to be in Chicago at daybreak the following morning. When he needed rest, Rosa would spell him.

The Garcias left El Paso on Interstate 10, which they traversed for two hundred miles until switching to I-20 in the west Texas plains. The midsummer heat pounded down on the black Ford even in the early morning hours, but the truck's powerful air conditioner kept the drivers comfortable.

Seven hours later came Dallas and another interchange to I-30. The broken center lines passed as if one and the telephone poles flew by, unnoticed by the Garcias. They spoke little, choosing to focus on their job at hand. Still, there was no cause for alarm, and the journey was treated as any business trip. Diego Garcia had driven this route many times before, helping his boss reap millions of dollars in profits. His cargo had been concealed in all sorts of ways, stuffed in false bottoms, sliding seats, and false dashes as well as inside fenders, bumpers, and gas tanks.

Neither Diego nor Rosa had much on their mind as they rolled across the Texas highways. At Dallas, Garcia, having been behind the wheel for over eleven hours, told Rosa to take over. They each pulled a couple of ham sandwiches from a Tupperware container and had a meal, their first since leaving El Paso. This was no pleasure excursion, so any of the myriad of fast-food joints at every exit were not a viable option.

The traffic was fairly light, and the troopers were paying little attention. Every so often, the Garcias would spy one on an overpass, holding his radar on the drivers below. But, since their speed rarely broke seventy, there was no reason for concern. They were hardly the only ones with brown skin on the Texas highways on this, or any other day.

Three hundred miles down I-30 was Little Rock, Arkansas, where Garcia spelled his wife. They had been on the road for sixteen hours, and the early evening sun further baked the truck. They had only made the minimum stops for bathrooms, and here they would make another. This time, Rosa was attracted to a Kentucky Fried Chicken sign, and after a small debate as to the propriety of such a stop, Diego gave in. They pulled in and ordered a carryout meal. Rather than leave the truck totally unattended, either husband or wife stayed with it at all times. In this case, Rosa stood by the passenger side door while Diego brought the food outside.

They gulped their chicken and headed back on the highway, this time to I-40 and the 130-mile trip to West Memphis. There, they turned north on I-55 and were now 600 miles from their destination. It was approaching nine o'clock, and they were slightly behind their goal. In the darkness, Diego sped up and made the 280 miles to St. Louis in just under four hours. Rosa slept for most of that time.

Now they were just three hundred miles away from Chicago. As they left the St. Louis interchanges behind, they pulled into an all-night convenience store across the Mississippi near Collinsville, Illinois. Exhausted, Diego pumped some gas, paid the attendant, woke up Rosa, and told her to take over. As he pumped, she stumbled inside and bought an extra-large black coffee, two Hershey bars, and a box of doughnuts.

Diego fell asleep almost instantly as she drove up the entrance ramp, and Rosa would be alone in her thoughts for the next several hours. The drive, as it had to that point, passed uneventfully. When they reached Joliet, a city of 80,000 an hour south of Chicago, Rosa was to wake her husband. There, he would take over the driving, but not before contacting the dealer to hand over the drugs and receive the $1.2 million cash payoff.

CHAPTER XVIII

By now, it was nearing four a.m. Rosa navigated the truck around the interchanges near Bloomington, Illinois, home to the international State Farm Insurance headquarters and a beneficiary of the jobs created in Normal, its twin city, the home of Illinois State University. She motored past the spurs and cutoffs and was approaching Exit 160 when she saw red flashing lights in her rearview mirror.

The flashers were on the Illinois State Police squad car of Officer Pete McCord. It appeared a normal traffic stop to McCord, a forty-something family man who had racked up thousands of miles on these Illinois prairie highways in his twenty-one years on the force.

He picked up the Garcias on the south side of Bloomington, and following procedure, radioed the state police's District 6 headquarters. “6-97. District 6 traffic stop.”

As usual, the response from headquarters was nearly immediate. “Go ahead 97.”

McCord ran a license check on the vehicle. “Traffic stop on I-55 northbound, near mile post 160. Texas registration OH 5402.”

With sophisticated equipment, these checks now take only seconds for the headquarters to run. “Plates are clear. Registered to Torres Santiago.”

“10-4.” McCord then activated his red lights and pursued the truck.

After a couple of seconds, it became obvious to Rosa that the lights were for her. An icy chill ran down her spine, and she thrust her hand out to rock her sleeping husband awake. “Wake up, Diego!” she screamed. “We are in trouble!”

Startled, he turned over, wiped his eyes, and saw the reflections of the red flashers that now filled the cabin. “Shit!” he yelled before his thoughts returned to practicality. “All right, all right,” he said excitedly. “Just pull over nice and slow. Let's see what they want.”

Both thought of their payload in the secret compartment. “What about...” started Rosa.

His response was firm. “No! Just remain calm, and answer their questions. We can get this over with, and get on our way.”

Rosa eased the Ford onto the right shoulder and turned off the ignition. Nearly a minute of uneasy silence passed before McCord walked up to the truck.

“Good evening,” he said in a businesslike manner. “How are you tonight?”

“Fine, fine,” stammered Rosa, her thick accent coming through.

“Just out for an evening drive, or something?” asked McCord.

“Yes.” Her quick reply left an awkward silence. She turned and waved her hand at her husband with a couple of jerking motions. “This is, this is my husband, Diego,” she stammered.

McCord had noticed the unidentified passenger, and now addressed him. “Good evening, sir.” His attention switched back to Rosa. “Do you know why I pulled you over?”

Rosa replied in the negative, so McCord provided his reason. “I was sitting back at the last exit, and clocked you at eighty-two miles per hour. The speed limit through here is sixty-five miles per hour.”

Rosa knew she and Diego were running a little behind schedule, and had wanted to maintain a constant speed. But, tiring from the grueling trip, her foot sank harder on the gas, and she failed to pay attention to the speedometer.

"Oh? I see." Rosa had little idea what to say. "I guess I, I guess," she stammered as her grasp of English lagged amid the moment. Large beads of sweat broke out on her forehead as the mid-summer humidity poured through her open window. "I guess I did not realize it."

"Well, you were," said McCord, who was used to such excuses. "Can I see your driver's license and registration, please?"

Now the tension built. During her years in Chicago, Rosa held an Illinois driver's license, which she had renewed on a subsequent visit. But that was years ago, and the license was now badly outdated. The registration also did not help the situation. The owner of the truck, Torres Santiago, was an El Paso resident familiar to Juan Rodrequs, but much less so to the Garcias.

McCord accepted the license from her outstretched hand and walked back to the squad car. He noticed that the driver's license had expired, and radioed headquarters.

"District 6, driver's license check."

"Go ahead 97."

"Name is Rosa Garcia. Date of birth is 11-8-75. Driver's license is G-100-9997-5987."

The verification from headquarters was swift. "Driver's license has expired."

McCord exited his squad car, methodically walked back to the truck, and informed Rosa that the license was expired. The date of the expiration, so far in the past, concerned him.

"Ma'am, did you know this license is expired?" McCord's eyebrows were raised at the years-past date, and why she would not have realized that. Still, he had to follow protocol.

"It is?" Rosa asked. "Oh, officer, I am sorry. I guess I did not realize it. I had to go back to Mexico to visit my parents, and it must have expired while I was gone."

The flimsy excuse provided nothing satisfactory to McCord. "Then I will have to ask you to step out of the truck, and come back to the squad car. You will need an explanation on bonding."

Rosa looked over at Diego, and he shifted his head backwards, signaling her to go back to the squad car. She deliberately opened the door, crept out of the truck, and walked ahead of McCord, though staying at a considerable distance. Terrified, her legs felt stiff, her stomach twisted, her feet leaden. The red flashers reflected off the dark truck and created a visible shadow of her.

When she finally reached the patrol car, she paused, collected herself, and opened the door, sitting on the seat beside the officer. The air conditioner in the squad car did little to alleviate her nervous perspiration. McCord engaged her in small talk, to gain some more information.

"Why were you driving so fast tonight?"

Rosa now offered several excuses. "Oh, officer. I did not realize how fast I was going. It's so late, and I was tired. I guess I never thought to look at, what do you call it? The speedometer."

"And your driver's license. That expired a long time ago."

She stammered her response. "Y-Y-yes. Well. Like I said, I had to go back to Mexico for my parents. It must have expired before I came back."

That excuse was just as shallow as before. "You must have been in Mexico for a long time, then," prodded McCord. "Why were you heading to Chicago tonight?"

Rosa and Diego had offhandedly discussed this beforehand, and in passing came up with an alibi if needed. "I have family in Chicago," she said, knowing that was verifiable. "We were also picking up furniture for the man who owns the truck."

"He must have really wanted that furniture," McCord said with skepticism evident.

"Oh, yes. It was a family heirloom." Rosa seemed proud that she could pull that word from her limited grasp of the English language.

McCord spied that Diego seemed to be slumping in his seat, almost as if trying to hide. "Your husband. Could I have his name and date of birth?"

She provided McCord with the name "Diego Garcia" and his date of birth. McCord wrote down the information and called back to headquarters. “District 6, wants and warrants.”

“Go ahead, 97.” As the radio conversation opened, beads of sweat broke out on Rosa's forehead, and she squirmed in her seat. McCord's eyes slid toward her, seeing the sudden uptick in her discomfort.

“Wants and warrants on husband's name, Diego Garcia. Date of birth 11-24-73.”

Again, technology provided the data within seconds. “Subject has been arrested. Served time for drug trafficking. Arrested by DEA in Texas. Served four years in federal penitentiary.”

The arrest was the only other time that Garcia had failed to complete a drug run for Rodrequs. Eleven years before, he had attempted to deliver a large load of cocaine to a dealer near Houston, only to find the dealer was actually an informant.

That was all McCord needed. “10-4. Is there a K-9 unit in the area? If so, send unit to my location.”

To his right, Rosa whimpered softly as headquarters responded. “10-4.” A few seconds of silence followed before another response. “K-9 unit 6-11 en route to your location.”

“10-4.”

Tears flowed down Rosa's weathered face. Less than ten minutes later, two patrol cars arrived on the scene. One was driven by Doug Madden, backup, while the other held Neptune, a German shepherd trained in sniffing out narcotics. Both McCord and Madden exited their cars and approached the truck once more.

Neptune briskly trotted around the vehicle. In only seconds, his body became tense, and he stretched his front paws on the back of the truck. He stared at the bed, barking and trembling.

That was all his human partners needed to know something was amiss. McCord requested that Diego get out of the truck, while Madden returned to McCord's squad car, to ask the same of Rosa. Both were handcuffed as their Miranda rights were recited. Rosa was placed in the back seat of McCord's squad car, while Diego went into Madden's squad car for the drive to District 6 headquarters of the

Illinois State Police.

Before they left, McCord radioed to headquarters for another trooper and a tow truck. He did not have to wait long, and the third officer was on the scene. McCord and Madden then drove away, prisoners secured in their respective back seats. The tow truck took a little time in coming, as the company the police employed was in downtown Bloomington. Finally, it arrived, hooked on to the abandoned black F-150, and towed it to headquarters.

Neptune's reaction and Diego's prior record were ample reasons to request a search warrant on the truck. One was swift in coming, and a team of trained officers was ordered to the holding area to pour over the vehicle. It was certainly not the first time they had searched a possible drug vehicle, as those were among their most common inspections.

As they meticulously went over the truck, they noticed what appeared to be a slot in the bed. One officer ran his fingers into the slot and noticed that the bed shifted with it. He slowly raised the bed to reveal the false bottom, stuffed with the four hundred kilograms of cocaine.

No one on the team reacted strongly, for they had seen it all before. Still, it was a sizable load, and there was more work to be done. Procedure called for the Drug Enforcement Agency to be informed, and a call went to the office of agent Tony Martinez.

CHAPTER XIX

The sun was now coming up, and Martinez was just arriving at the office. He hung up the phone, and along with fellow DEA agent Des Woodson, drove straight to District 6 headquarters.

He was sent to an interrogation room, where he found Diego Garcia sitting across from state police drug investigators. As custom, Rosa was interrogated in another room. Both had been searched upon their arrival, Rosa by a female investigator. Neither was alone in their interrogation chambers, as an investigator was stationed with them. Diego was refusing to talk and barely uttered a word when asked one of the many questions the Illinois State Police had for him.

An echo constantly bounced off the sedate off-white block walls of the room, furnished only with a table and four chairs. But the echo was produced solely by the investigators, stonewalled by the silent Garcia.

Martinez had seen it all before. He was a career agent, a veteran of twenty years service and well versed in the illegal drug trade. Forty-three years before, he was born in Texas to a Mexican-American family, and was bilingual, an advantage in situations such as the one posed by the Garcias. Martinez had spent most of his career in the Chicago suburbs, maintaining a quiet home for his wife and two children in the attractive residential suburb of Elmhurst while commuting into the inner city. The comfortable life he had carved for his family contrasted with what his job dealt with routinely. Drug dealers, pushers, meth labs, and crack houses were all in a day's work for him.

Three years ago, it all finally got to him, and he requested a transfer downstate to the Bloomington office. Though his wife was less enthused with the move, he relished the chance to get out of Chicago and into more docile surroundings. The switch also helped him encourage his children, now in their teens, to attend nearby Illinois State University in the next few years.

On this day, he was briefed by state police investigators, read the reports from the night before, and stepped into the interrogation room. He took a seat and stared across the table at Diego. An expert interrogator, Martinez had mastered a way of warming up to suspects, unlike the direct, no-nonsense drilling of Woodson and others. But he also found a way of not becoming too emotionally involved.

"Good morning," he opened. "I see that you are from Mexico. What brings you to our little neck of the woods?"

No response. Perhaps the suspect spoke poor English, and if that was the case, Martinez was ready to proceed in Spanish. "Do you speak English?" Diego nodded.

"Then, tell me. What are you doing so far from home?"

Diego sighed heavily. "We have told you before. We borrowed a truck to move furniture from Chicago to El Paso. We were driving to Chicago when we were stopped."

"I see. And were you going to trade the drugs for the furniture?"

"No, senor. We have no idea of the drugs. We do not know how they got there."

"No idea at all? That's an awful lot of drugs. Surely you had to notice the truck was sitting heavy." Martinez relaxed in chair, and began to theorize. “When a truck has an extra half-ton on it, it will accelerate slower, or sit lower. You're telling me you never noticed anything different?”

“No, senor, no.” Diego was pleading again. “There was nothing wrong with the truck. We only wanted to move furniture for the man who owns the truck.”

“Hmm. Just to move some furniture, you say.” Martinez was playing along, but had plenty of questions left. “Seems an awful long way to just pick up some tables and chairs. Who did this furniture belong to?”

“We have family. My wife's relatives. They live in Chicago.” Martinez asked for their names, wrote them down, and motioned to an agent in the hallway. The man stepped inside, and Martinez handed him the slip of paper.

“Check on this.” said Martinez. His eyes switched back to the suspect. “Was your friend, the one who owns the truck, in need of furniture that badly?”

“Oh, yes, senor. He said he really wanted this furniture.”

Martinez, though polite, kept pressing. “So he loaned you this truck to visit some relatives, and pick up furniture for him?”

“Si, si.” In his nervousness, Diego was switching back and forth from Spanish to English.

“What is it that you do? What is your occupation?”

Diego was making it up as he went along. “I do not have a job. I am looking for work.”

“Anything you can find, eh?”

“Oh, yes. I do odd jobs, some carpentry, some building work. I haul things for people, whatever I can find.”

Martinez smiled slightly at the irony of “haul things.” He continued. “There must have really been a need for furniture to drive over fifteen hundred miles like this.”

Diego squirmed as if ants were crawling up his leg. “Oh, yes. He said these were family heirlooms, and he wanted them back.”

Martinez nodded in mock agreement, then moved on to another line of questioning. “That is a very nice truck. I'd like to have one of those myself. But you say you were out of work. How were you able to afford something like that?"

"It does not belong to us. We, how do you say? Borrowed it."

"Oh yes, yes. You told us that earlier." Martinez was not letting up. "So you borrowed it from a friend? A relative?"

"Yes," replied Garcia. "A friend."

"What does this friend do?"

Torres Santiago, the owner, was a pusher for Rodrequs, and Diego had barely met him. "He owns a liquor store," said Diego. "He sells only the finest wines."

"And you know this man well?"

"Oh, yes. He is a good friend of mine, of ours."

"And he just loaned you this truck? Rent-free?"

"Yes, senor. He is a good man."

"Just so you could repay the favor by moving his furniture?"

"Si." As Diego answered, the agent from the hallway knocked, took only one step inside, and handed Martinez a sheet of paper. "Thanks," said Martinez, who then turned to the matter at hand.

Martinez slid the sheet across the table to Diego. He repeated the finding of Officer McCord on Diego the night before. "It appears you've had some drug trouble in the past."

The sheet was a court record of Diego's drug conviction in Texas. Martinez filled in some blanks with carefully chosen words. "It seems that you sold a large amount of narcotics to an informant in Houston, and did time in a federal pen for it."

Garcia's hands were now trembling, and clearly noticed by Martinez. "You seem to have a history of moving a lot of drugs."

"*No, no, no, no! I told you!*" Diego was like a cornered schoolchild, pleading innocence in the face of guilt. "I don't know where the drugs in the truck came from."

"Now, let's be serious," Martinez did not believe a word of it, and assumed a blunt manner. "You tell me you are out of work, yet you drive a big, shiny truck. You're a long ways from home just to be picking up a little furniture for some guy. And you keep telling me you don't know about the drugs, but you did time in Texas on drug charges just a few years ago."

Diego knew little of American history, but he did have some knowledge of the legal system, since his defense attorney in Texas had filled him in. "I take the Fifth," he said. "I will answer no more questions."

Martinez had heard that one before, too. "All right. Just take your time." He looked at his wristwatch. "It's still early. We have all day."

Diego and Martinez' eyes met, and Martinez saw the fear in his suspect. Diego bowed his head and stared at the table.

"Since you don't want to talk anymore, I'll just take this time to tell you what you're facing." said Martinez. "You have a prior drug conviction, and every bit of evidence points to the drugs in the truck being yours as well. You've done nothing to convince us otherwise, and no judge in this state is going to believe your story.

"So, here's what you're looking at," Martinez dropped the news. "You're probably looking at twenty-five years to life in a federal prison. You're a repeat offender, your story doesn't hold up, and when you've been caught, you're in the possession of hundreds of pounds of illegal substances. Any court is going to look harshly on you, and will send you to prison for a long, long time."

Though shaking inside, Diego Garcia still had a little of Rodrequs' brashness in him, and had never expected to be faced with such a penalty. He had only been caught once before, one of the dozens of times he had crossed the border with heavy loads of narcotics.

He thought of the children, of his now-jeopardized lifestyle, but most of all, he thought of his boss. Rodrequs. His old friend never looked kindly on failure, and had killed subordinates for far less than the trouble Diego was in now.

Martinez sensed that Diego's mind was a whirlwind. "Think about it for a while." The agent pushed himself away from the table, rose from his chair, and strolled out the door.

Now alone in the interrogation room, Diego thought of Rosa. He could not let her go to prison, and leave their children alone. He also suspected she would be loyal to Rodrequs, whom she adored, and might even risk herself for.

In her own interrogation, Rosa Garcia was even less forthright than her husband. Her grasp of English, though spotty, was not to blame. She was, every bit, a hostile suspect.

To say that the DEA agent across the table, Des Woodson, was less engaging than Tony Martinez was an understatement. Woodson had grown up on the south side of Chicago, and was all too familiar with the effects of street drugs. He had watched some of his friends gunned down in front of him over narcotics, and made a pact with himself amid the daily gunfire that riveted his neighborhood. *If I ever get out of here, he thought, I'm going to do something about it.*

The law appealed to him, and he earned a basketball scholarship to Loyola University in north Chicago. He used it as a springboard, and by his late twenties, was a rising star in the DEA. But he could never forget the bloodshed of his own neighborhood, usually the result of meth, cocaine, and crack. Sitting across from narcotics suspects like Rosa, he could never muster much patience.

Likewise, she had no patience for Woodson. She refused to answer most of his questions, demanding to be taken to her husband. When that was denied, she screamed for a lawyer. Advised that she had that right under federal law, she then chose to lambast in broken English "you Americans, for holding an innocent man and woman" who "just wanted to haul furniture from their relatives."

The mention of the drugs in the secret compartment, though, neutralized her. Her anger was then muted, and she stared down at the table, offering nothing further. When Woodson returned to questioning why the Garcias were in Illinois, her temper reignited. She barked the same response, that she and her husband were good people, only wanted furniture, and had no right to be subjected to such horrible treatment.

She was angry, frightened, humiliated. She was also fearful of Rodrequs' response. He had been good to her and Diego, and had provided a worthy lifestyle for them. Like her husband, she knew that Rodrequs killed for far less. However, she hoped that he would take kindly to her, and if Diego was forsaken, that she would at least be taken care of. The children, as well.

CHAPTER XX

Martinez and Woodson met in the hallway and compared notes. As they murmured on the other side of the wall, Diego sat alone in the interrogation chamber.

A firestorm of thoughts raced through his mind. He knew that he could not be sent to prison in America, since his prior conviction in Texas removed any chance at leniency. He could not depend on Rodrequs for any support, for any mention of his boss to the authorities could destroy the cartel, and Juan Rodrequs was not about to stick his neck out to help a buddy in this kind of trouble.

Rosa and the children were foremost in his mind. As damning as a long prison term was to him, he knew she would never survive. She was a woman who liked finer things, and would certainly struggle for daily existence inside the gray walls of a penitentiary. He feared for her safety among violent inmates, who were bigger, meaner, sexually aggressive.

He thought of his own safety in prison. When he was incarcerated in Texas, he was in medium-security, and that was misery enough. Every minute, every day, he was looking over his shoulder, wary of the gangs that ruled the prison yard. He spoke to few others, and kept out of their way. In the cafeteria, he heard tales from the inmates who had been in maximum-security, of the beatings, the rapes, the stabbings. As a repeat offender, one with such a large stash of drugs, he worried that he may be sent to the toughest lockups, where he was no match for the murderers, deviants, and street gangs he was certain to be thrown in with.

He feared for his children. They would be practically orphaned, passed around from one relative to the other. Their world was a house of cards, a comfortable lifestyle built on crime and lies, that could be shattered at any moment. There was no safety net. Rodrequs would certainly cut them loose, and make life miserable for the survivors. Perhaps his children, left without parents, would drift to the streets, where he had grown up. Maybe they would not be as lucky in life as he had been.

For the first time in two decades, serving Juan Rodrequs was no longer an issue. All that mattered was what he, *Diego,* did for his wife, his children.

He wandered about the cramped chamber. Finally, he stood facing the back wall, exhaled deeply, and looked at the ceiling. He crossed himself for guidance and moved closer to the door, tried the knob, and found it locked. He then rapped on it, to attract attention out in the hallway.

Martinez was reviewing his files with Woodson when he heard the knock, and opened the door. He attempted to greet Diego, but the suspect spoke so quickly that he was cut off. “I have something else I want to talk to you about.”

“All right,” said Martinez, who stepped from the hallway and followed Diego inside. “What is it?”

Diego returned to his chair, straightened his back, and clasped his hands on the table in front of him. “I have information that you will be interested in.”

Martinez was anxious, expecting more facts on the drug bust. “What do you have?”

“I have information on terrorists that want to cross the Mexican border. They want to bomb cities in the United States."

*****

Tony Martinez was stunned, wholly unprepared for such a bombshell. He peered over his glasses at Diego, hoping for some kind of nonverbal verification. Diego merely stared straight back at him, and Martinez knew he was on to something.

"You realize what you are saying?

Diego was firm. "Yes. I have details of a plot to kill Americans. I have sat in on meetings, and helped a man plan it."

"This was your idea?"

"No, senor. I only do what I am told."

Martinez was beginning to think Diego was telling the truth, so he pressed on. "Where did these meetings take place?"

He received no response. Diego clenched his lips and stared back across the table.

"I'll ask you again. Where did these meetings take place?"

This time, Diego responded. "I will answer no more of your questions, senor."

"Why not?"

"I will say nothing else until my conditions are met."

Martinez had an idea. "What conditions are you talking about?"

"I will give you the information, but first I want a deal."

Martinez sat back in his chair and exhaled a gulp of air through his lips. "I don't have the authority to cut a deal with you. I will have to talk to my superiors." Though he hated having to pander to an alleged criminal, he still had to ask. "Will your deal still be on the table in a little while?"

Diego knew he had no choice. "Yes. But I will answer *no other questions* until a deal is in place."

"Okay, then," Martinez replied. "Give me a little bit, and I'll make some calls." He exited the room.

Now alone again, the thoughts in Garcia's mind flew even more strenuously. Now he had taken the leap. *What have I done*, he thought. *Oh, God, oh, God. Now I have told on Juan. If he learns I have betrayed him....*

The pressure was getting to Diego, and he finally had enough. He slammed his open palm on the table, causing such a thump that he feared the officers outside would hear. The room, though, was soundproof, and they were ignorant of his frustration.

He sprang from his chair, folded his arms tightly as if cowering from the cold, and had a revelation. *I worry about Juan. But...if he were here right now, in my shoes, and I in his, would he not do the same thing?*

A sea of relief washed over Garcia's mind. The risk was enormous. But the path was right.

*****

Martinez walked down the hallway to the captain's office, looking for some privacy, and used a desk phone. The call went to his supervisor, who advised him to contact the Federal Bureau of Investigations. Martinez then dialed the number of the Springfield office of the FBI. It was now nearing noon.

“This is Tony Martinez of the DEA office in Bloomington. I need the agent-in-charge of the anti-terrorist task force to contact me immediately.”

He provided his cell number for immediate access, and did not have to wait long. Fifteen minutes later, his cell rang.

“This is Agent Jack Hudson of the FBI office in Springfield. Tony Martinez, please.”

Martinez was surprised that his request went so high on the power chart, and that Jack Hudson was in a smaller city like Springfield at the moment. The name of Jack Hudson was familiar to all law enforcement agents, not just in Illinois, but around the Midwest. Hudson was in charge of the anti-terrorist task force in the Springfield area, with close connections to the DEA and Homeland Security.

A career FBI agent, the fifty-three-year-old Hudson had been stationed across the nation, first in the Illinois capital of Springfield, then in Chicago, and on to Washington. Now he was back in the Land of Lincoln. He brought a tunnel vision to his job, and other agents marveled at his tenacity and emotional and physical stamina. Hudson had a wife and three daughters, but few of the other agents had ever met them, and it was a running joke that Hudson hadn't met them, either.

Hudson's stamina resulted not only from his mental toughness but also a maniacal workout program that helped him blow off steam in the bureau's fitness center. Though little of his dark brown hair circled his spreading bald spot, he had the build of a man twenty years younger, and was well-equipped to handle even the most demanding crisis.

His career-mindedness drove him steadily up the ladder in his three decades in government service, and now he was back in Illinois as assistant Special Agent in Charge of the Springfield office. He also headed the anti-terrorism task force for southern Illinois. The media, seemingly stuck on 9/11, always focused on terrorist impulses on Chicago high-rises like the Willis Tower, but Hudson knew better. He spread his focus across the entire state, making sure he never had to live with the consequences of a massive terror attack as some of his less-prepared colleagues had.

Though there is a natural rivalry between high-level law enforcement agencies, Martinez never had a problem dealing with other departments. Still, even he felt a little intimidation in speaking with someone as high-powered as Hudson. “This is Martinez. Thanks for calling so soon.”

Hudson never engaged in pleasantries. “What do you have for me?”

“I've got a narcotics suspect from Mexico that the ISP picked up last night. He and his wife were carrying close to a thousand pounds of drugs in a brand new F-150.”

Hudson wasted no words. “What's the status?”

“They've been arrested, and are being held at District 6 headquarters in Bloomington. He's got a prior record of trafficking in Texas. He gave us the usual bullshit story about why he was here, but then he comes back at us with a bombshell."

"What about it?"

"He says he's got information on a potential terrorist plot out of Mexico. He says they plan to bomb U.S. cities."

Hudson was trained to take all threats seriously. "What's the guy's name?"

"Diego Garcia. His first name is like `San Diego,' and the usual spelling of Garcia."

"Hold on a sec." Hudson quickly typed his name into his computer databases. He found the trafficking conviction in Texas, but nothing else. "Where's this guy from?"

"He says El Paso, but we don't believe him. He's got a green card, and so does his wife."

"Her name?"

"Rosa." Hudson entered her name, and came up with nothing. "What's he want with us?"

"He won't cooperate unless a deal is made." replied Martinez. "He's got the prior conviction, and we've got him dead to rights. He's looking at 25 years to life in a federal pen."

"And he claims to be the mastermind of this terrorist plot?" asked Hudson.

"No. He says he just sat in on the meetings. But I think he's telling the truth on that."

"All right." Hudson had worked with Martinez before, and trusted his intuition. He would have just as soon raced up to Bloomington at that moment, but he knew he had to follow the protocol.

"Fine," replied Martinez. "You want me to interrogate him further?"

"No," said Hudson. "Hold him and his wife there. I'll come up there and sit in on it."

Bloomington is little more than an hour north of downtown Springfield by car, but Hudson had no time to lose. He knew this situation was fluid, and could not wait. He ended the conversation with Martinez, then called three other agents to meet him in the parking garage. Hudson jogged down the stairs to the garage, hopped in his black Buick Regal with the three agents, and sped off.

CHAPTER XXI

As Jack Hudson rolled up the interstate, Diego and Rosa sat alone in their respective interrogation rooms. Their thoughts of each other were hardly divergent. Diego dreaded the thought of describing his deal to her, while Rosa harbored a building resentment for her husband, somehow angry that he had allowed them to be apprehended.

The drive from Springfield to Bloomington took right at sixty minutes, and Jack Hudson marched into District 6 headquarters just after the lunch hour. Martinez was gulping down a roast beef sandwich from a vending machine when he saw Hudson striding briskly down the hallway toward him, three agents in tow.

Diego and Rosa were still in their interrogation rooms, each having only been excused once to use a bathroom. He was nearly lulled into a stupor by the tepid surroundings when the door flew open.

Hudson was never one to act lightly, and the door nearly banged the side wall when he threw it open. Martinez came in on his heels and did the honors as Hudson flashed his identification. "This is Jack

Hudson of the FBI office in Springfield. He is in charge of the anti-terrorist task force for southern Illinois," said Martinez. "He's got something he wants to talk about with you."

Hudson was barely in his chair when he began. His three partners stood along the wall, for the room was short on chairs. "All right, Mr. Garcia," Hudson's words dragged coolly. "You wanted to cut a deal with us. But you are going to have to cooperate with us fully, tell us everything you know, and we have to verify that what you are saying is true."

He followed with a directive. "No funny business. If you don't do what we say, the deal's off, and you're going to prison. I'll tell you again. You need to cooperate with us completely, and tell us everything you have. Is that clear?"

"Yes, sir." Diego's voice was unusually crisp.

"Okay, then. What do you have for us?"

Diego drew a breath, and scanned his eyes at each of the five agents in the room. "There is a plot that will send terrorists across the border from Mexico. They will bomb places in the United States."

Authorities in Jack Hudson's position routinely hear of vaguely worded bomb threats. He needed much more to go on than just a simple statement. "What places are you talking about?"

"Caesar's Palace in Las Vegas. Something at Mount Rushmore, the visitor center, I think. And the country music district in Nashville."

Hudson and Martinez raised their eyes, turned their heads to one another, and exchanged a surprised glance. Neither had expected so many targets. "When is this supposed to occur?" inquired Hudson.

"Soon. I do not know the exact date, but very soon. One of the terrorists is already in Mexico."

"How many terrorists are there?"

"Five. Six, counting their commander."

Hudson moved on to the next point. "What type of explosives do they have?"

"Fifty pounds of C-4 each. I am supposed to be the one who supplies them. I get those kind of things from a federalie, who is on the outskirts of Juarez."

As Hudson listened, Martinez and the others were taking notes on Garcia's every word, some on paper, some on laptops. "Who is running this operation?"

Garcia was now beginning to relax, as if a weight had been lifted from him. He had never approved of Rodrequs' plan, and almost seemed relieved that now it would not happen. "A man named Racheed. He is from Pakistan. I have only met him briefly."

"What is his last name?"

Garcia had never been formally introduced to Racheed Ul-Bashar, and only knew him by his first name. "I do not know. No one ever told me."

Hudson raised his eyebrows in skepticism. "Then how well do you know him?"

"Not very well. I have only been around him three times or so. I know for a fact that he is planning this, though."

"How?"

"He told my boss in no uncertain terms. I was there for both of their first meetings."

Hudson suspected he had another mark. "Who's your boss?"

Diego knew that question was coming, but still felt loyalty to his longtime friend. His voice quivered. "Juan Rodrequs. He is the leader of a large drug cartel."

Hudson and Martinez looked at each other. "I know that name," said Martinez. "He's got one of the biggest cartels on the border. He runs millions' worth of drugs across all the time, and he'll shoot first and ask questions later. We've traced him to dozens of murders."

The normally stoic Martinez shuddered slightly. "Nasty, nasty guy." Diego raised his eyes and peered weakly at his accusers.

Hudson was also familiar with the name. He managed to muster a little sympathy for Garcia. "You're really sticking your neck out, then."

"Yes. Juan is my friend. I have known him since I was a little boy."

"You must be very close, then."

"Oh, yes," Garcia produced a sickly smile. "I work for him. I am the second-in-command, and his confidant. I am one of the few people he trusts."

"Is he in Juarez, still? Or has he moved on?"

"No, he is still in Juarez." Garcia then provided the location of Rodrequs' secluded compound.

The agents were getting more cooperation than they expected. "Thank you," said Martinez. "What else do you have on Rodrequs?" Garcia then offered the sites of his boss's cocaine warehouses, the names of some cartel members, and identified the federalie that supplied the C-4 explosives and weapons.

It took the agents several seconds to finish writing down and typing in all of the information. But there were hardly through. "Go back to the terrorist plot. How are they coming across the border?"

Garcia still had several cards up his sleeve. "There is a tunnel under the border. It stretches from one of Juan's warehouses to an auto shop in El Paso. It is run by a man named Mendez."

Martinez and Hudson were familiar with tunnels, since they are a usual way for illegals to get into the United States. "Under the Rio Grande? How long is this tunnel?"

"I think Juan told me it was five hundred yards. Is that the same as five hundred meters?" Garcia forced a chuckle. "We have different ways of measuring things in Mexico."

The five agents were startled at the size of the tunnel, and their heads turned, eyes meeting one another. "Tell us more about this tunnel."

"It is eighty feet deep, and has plenty of lighting. It has a full concrete floor, to keep out the mud. There's an elevator down to it."

"An elevator?" quizzed Hudson.

"Yes, senor," replied Garcia. "Oh, no, not like something you would see in a hotel," he said, emitting another nervous chuckle. "Kind of, how do you say? A work elevator. Something to carry cargo."

"I can only imagine." Hudson was still shaking his head at the size and sophistication of the tunnel.

"I presume the drugs in your truck came through the tunnel as well?"

"Yes, senor."

"And now here you are," smirked Hudson. "Where were you heading from here?"

Garcia finally came clean with his plans. "I was supposed to deliver them to a dealer in Chicago. He is one of our biggest clients."

"No surprise there," said Hudson. "They love their drugs in Chicago. Go on."

"I am supposed to meet him at a motel near Matteson, on Interstate 57. I was to call him from Joliet."

"Sounds like you've done this before."

"Oh, yes. Like I said, he has bought a lot from us before."

"Hmm," Hudson snickered at the mundane description of illegal activity. "So what was going to happen in Matteson?"

As Garcia admitted each step, his chest began to loosen, the tension ebbing from his body. His breathing became deeper and less strained. "I would leave the truck in the parking lot of the motel, and contact the dealer, to let him know what room I'm in. He gets there, and comes up to my room with the money. I hand him the keys to the truck. The dealer drives off in the truck, and unloads it at his warehouse. He then returns the truck when he is finished and leaves the keys in it."

"And after that, you're done?"

"Yes. We can leave for home." Garcia seemed to overlook the fact that he would not be heading home quite as planned.

Hudson switched focus to the other matter at hand. "And the terrorists are going to come through the tunnel?"

"Yes. Juan will have cars waiting in the auto shop for them."

"What's Rodrequs getting out of all this? He must want something."

"Racheed promised him three million dollars. He also promised a steady supply of heroin from the Taliban. He said the money would come from the Taliban, who would raise it by selling drugs to the Russian mafia."

Jack Hudson was used to terrorist threats; he received them all the time. Most were vague, with no specific time, date, or place. This one, though, was highly developed. There were named participants, details of what would happen and where, and a funding source.

Clearly, this Racheed person had his act together.

Hudson turned his attention back to Diego. “You mentioned one terrorist is already in Mexico. Where is he at?”

Diego provided the location of the safe house. “But I do not know much about that terrorist. I drove him to the safe house from the airport in Mexico City. His first name is Adeeb, but that is all I know. He never said much on the drive, and Juan never told me anything about him.”

“Go back to this Racheed person,” said Hudson. “Why does he want to do this?”

Garcia recalled the conversations in the compound and in the Hummer on the way to the tunnel. “He says he wants revenge for his grandfather and sister. They were killed in a drone strike, or something like that.”

“Go on.”

“He talks about his religion all the time. He says he must do this in the name of Allah.”

Hudson had heard that one before, since many Islamic terrorists say the same thing. “What about his partners, the terrorists he's bringing from Pakistan?”

“He says they all feel the same way. Racheed says he trained them harder than if they were in basic training. He spent a month doing it.”

Now Hudson saw a motive. “Where is this Racheed now?”

Diego was still in the dark on some details. “In Pakistan, I guess. I haven't seen him in a while.” He did, however, recall one of the dates of Racheed's flights to Mexico and gave it to Hudson, who still had more questions.

“How did this Racheed get all this information? Who else knows about this?”

“He said he obtained false military documents to identify himself as an officer of intelligence. I think he said he got them from his brother, who is in the army back home.”

“Know his name?” asked Hudson, and Diego nodded no. “Anyone else?”

“Racheed showed his false documents to General Santos in

Mexican intelligence. I don't think the general knows about the attack, though. I think Racheed just wanted information on the cartel."

"So, who all knows about the terrorist attack?"

Diego used his fingers to count off. "Racheed, of course. Then Rodrequs, and myself. No one else."

Hudson wrote down the names. "What about Rosa?"

"Oh, no. I never told her anything. She has no idea?"

Hudson seemed suspicious. "None at all?

"No. Nothing. And I do not want her to know. Please, senor. Don't tell her about the plot."

One final question arose from Hudson. "Were you on board with all this?"

"No, not really," replied Garcia. "Oh, I had to be, because I had no choice. I was ordered to do it. But I told Juan that I did not approve."

"Why not?"

Garcia knew how his response would sound, and he fidgeted, staring at the floor to his right. "Because I was worried it would put our drug trade in danger. I did not like the risk, and thought it would damage our business."

Hudson tapped his pencil on the desk, organizing his thoughts. A pause ensued, leaving everyone in the room wondering what was about to happen. Hudson finished his notes and looked directly into Martinez' face. He then turned in his chair and similarly looked at each of the agents standing behind him.

"Okay," he finally said. "We need to verify this information."

Martinez knew what he meant. Hudson muttered a quick "thank you" to Garcia and sprang from his chair, heading for the door. Martinez and the others followed.

Now alone, Diego exhaled as if he had been underwater for two minutes. His arms and legs felt as lead chains, and he was consumed with the same overpowering grief as after the death of a loved one. Physically and emotionally spent, he folded his arms on the table and lay his head on them like a tired schoolchild.

CHAPTER XXII

Hudson and Martinez walked briskly down the hallway. “What do you think?” inquired Martinez.

“I think we're on to something.” Hudson only looked straight ahead, never turning his eyes. “If what he says checks out on our systems, we could have a big deal on our hands.”

“What do you think of the guy? Do you think he's just bullshitting us?”

Hudson approached an office door, abruptly stopped, and finally turned toward Martinez. “If he is, he's the best actor I've ever seen.”

The door led to the state police computer system. There, the agents could access the Homeland Security computer system. Hudson plopped down at the desk, tore off his dark blue blazer, and tossed it on a file cabinet. He logged into the computer, entered the name “Racheed,” and waited. Martinez pulled up a folding chair beside him.

After twenty seconds or so, there was a hit on the screen. An entry of “Racheed Ul-Bashar” came up, indicating several flights into Mexico that originated from Pakistan. The data was the result of the nonchalant entries of Greg Foster in the Mexico City office of the CIA. The date that Garcia provided of one of the flights matched the information onscreen.

There were also records of Racheed's short junkets from Mexico City to Juarez. Hudson and Martinez looked at each other. "Still think Garcia's bullshitting us?" said Hudson, with a tinge of sarcasm.

He then entered the name "Adeeb" in the system. Again, there was a hit. The name Adeeb Ahmad came up, with the dates and flight numbers of his connections from Karachi to Mexico City. Garcia's story was further verified.

Hudson and Martinez both leaned back in their chairs, as if on cue. Hudson clasped his hands behind his head, while Martinez drummed his fingers on the desk. "Damn," said Hudson after a long pause. "He's got his story straight."

"Yep." Martinez was so stunned, he could say little more. He nervously flipped the end of his tie up and down.

Hudson knew it was one of the better-developed terrorist plots he had seen. Thirty years of service had desensitized him to the worst, but even now, he thought of what could have happened, the massive loss of life, the destruction of buildings, the psychological blows, if this terrorist plot had played out. He looked down at his arm and saw his hairs standing on end.

Martinez noticed as well, since he felt the same chill. Hudson acknowledged him. "You never get used to it, do you?"

Martinez shook his head subtly. "What now?"

"Well, we won't be sitting on our asses," said Hudson, snapping back to attention. "We've got a lot of work to do. I'm glad my wife understands me, because I sure as hell won't be seeing much of her for the next several weeks."

Martinez stepped out of the room as Hudson reached for the phone. Now armed with accurate information from Garcia, he was in position to make a deal. He dialed the number for Assistant U.S. Attorney C.J. Sturges, who was assigned to the task force.

He had a good relationship with that office, so getting to speak with the attorney was not a problem. Ten minutes later, he received the response he wanted. Hudson rose from his chair, opened the door, and peered around the frame, motioning to Martinez. He followed Hudson inside.

"Here's what I've got," said Hudson with his usual bluntness. "I just hung up with Sturges, the assistant U.S. attorney assigned to us. We can make a deal with Garcia under which neither he, nor his wife, will be charged with drug trafficking if, and only if, he fully cooperates with us. Sturges wasn't real happy about it, but he went along with it, since we had verified what Garcia told us."

"All right," replied Martinez, exhaling slightly. "Anything else?"

"Yeah. He insisted that we hold Mrs. Garcia in a safe house until the operation is over. He wasn't about to let her go with him."

"Bet she'll love that," said Martinez sarcastically, remembering her lack of cooperation. "Where will she be?"

"In Springfield. We've got a place down there we use." Hudson was hardly concerned with any of Rosa Garcia's complaints. His mind was a swirl of strategy and plans, of duties and concerns, of pressure and protocol, as the afternoon waned in Bloomington.

*****

Although human lives were at a premium, there were plenty of other factors to consider. Juan Rodrequs could be given no reason to suspect anything was out of the ordinary, including the delivery of his cocaine. If it was delayed or did not arrive at all, the Chicago dealer was sure to let him know. Then Diego, the newly-turned informant, would have some explaining to do, perhaps at the point of an AK-47.

Hudson asked for a private room and a telephone hookup for a conference call. He had a lot on his plate, and needed to discuss it with his superiors in Washington, the U.S. attorney's office in Springfield, and high-ranking agents of the DEA. By now it was mid-afternoon.

Almost everyone that Hudson wanted to talk with was available for the conference call, and those absent were not necessary to the task at hand. What to do with the drugs was the pressing issue, and intense discussion ensued on how to proceed.

Billions of dollars are spent every year by the American government in the war on drugs, and most trained law enforcement officials are well aware of the dangers of narcotics not only to the individuals who consume them, but to those around them. A large percentage of murders in American society are drug-related, as are a high portion of driving offenses. Jack Hudson, Tony Martinez and thousands of other professionals devote their lives to stamping out the epidemic of illegal drugs.

The idea of allowing a half-ton of cocaine to be released on the streets of Chicago was appetizing to no one. Still, the question had to be weighed; if the drugs were not delivered, would Rodrequs suspect something was amiss? Garcia was his close ally, and if the drugs were not delivered, the cartel leader may react, clean out his stores, and could go into hiding. More importantly, the terrorists could scatter, fearing capture.

As a result, the conference call became heated, as the suggestion of letting the drugs walk conflicted with personal and professional ethics. Still, there was a large enough faction to sign off on it, knowing the risks if the drugs never made it to Chicago. The decision was then made to let Diego and Rosa deliver the cocaine.

The Garcias were tiring from their long day in their interrogation rooms, and had barely eaten. Hudson, though, was a man of great energy, and as the dinner hour approached, he strode into Diego's room, with Martinez close behind.

"All right," declared Hudson in his usual authoritarian tone. "Here's what is happening. I just spoke to the assistant U.S. Attorney in Springfield, and he has approved our deal with you. You must fully cooperate with us, and if you do, neither you nor your wife will be charged with drug trafficking. Understand?"

"Yes, senor," said Diego with bleary eyes.

Hudson was little concerned with Garcia's fatigue, but repeated himself anyway. "You understand what I'm saying?"

"I said, yes, senor," replied Garcia, irritation evident.

Satisfied, Hudson moved on. "Now, for the next part. You're going to take the drugs to Chicago, as you planned."

Diego immediately revived from his drowsiness and sat up in his chair. "What did you just say?"

"I said you're going to take the drugs to Chicago. If you don't, then the drug dealer is going to think something is wrong. And then your friend Rodrequs may also think something is wrong, and we can't let that happen. We've got to make it look like everything is normal." Hudson corrected himself and looked directly into Diego's eyes. "You've got to make it look like everything is normal."

Diego had openly told the authorities of the terror plot, knew there was no way he could walk out the door and deliver the drugs "as normal." As if a hostage at gunpoint, he asked, "What do you want from me?"

"Oh, you won't be alone," said Hudson. "We'll have a DEA agent in the truck with you. You'll also be tailed by a lot of others. We'll have other agents from the task force, DEA agents, and Illinois State Police drug agents. You'll have a whole army behind you."

"Please, senor." Diego was pleading again, as he had done so often since the traffic stop. "You really expect me to be able to carry this off as normal? The dealer will be very suspicious."

"No, he won't, because he won't know we're coming along for the ride." The wheels were turning in Hudson's head. "Okay, then. You will just go to Joliet as you planned, and call the dealer. Make the arrangements, and we'll go to wherever you're supposed to meet him."

Despite his cooperation, Diego still harbored a little defiance. "And if we do not?"

"Then your deal is off. You'll go to federal prison on the trafficking charge." Hudson then paused for effect. "You will cooperate fully with us, as we asked you to before. But there's more that you need to know."

He then tilted his head and flicked his eyeballs to the side, as if pointing at Rosa down the hall. "To ensure your cooperation, we are going to hold your wife until the operation is complete, and will not release her until then. That way, you have no other choice but to go along with us. If you don't, then she stays here with us, and faces a criminal trial."

Diego sat back in his chair, stunned. When he pushed to cut a deal, he had not expected that he and Rosa would be separated. Immediately he thought of their children back home, soon to be left without their mother, at least temporarily. Hudson was piling on, and Diego's decision to cooperate was not looking as attractive as before. Still, there was no other option.

"Will she be in jail?" inquired Diego, staring down his chest as if embarrassed.

"No," said Hudson. "We're probably hold her in a safe house in Springfield or something."

Diego knew he had little choice but to go along. "Very well, senor," he said resignedly. "But there is one more thing."

Hudson bristled. "What are you talking about? I thought everything was settled and we had a deal, dammit!"

Diego was taken aback by the reaction. "We still have a deal, senor. But I do not want Rosa to know about the terrorist plot. Like I said, I have never told her anything about it. Please, senor. Don't say anything to Rosa."

Surprised, Hudson recoiled. "Oh! Ah, all right. We won't say anything to her about terrorism. She'll just think this is all about the drug issue."

This satisfied Diego's mind. "Then I will do as you say."

"Good." Hudson rose from his chair and strode down the hallway to the office of Lee Bickford, the District 6 commander. There, he informally briefed Bickford on the interrogations and investigation of the previous few hours, and described his strategy to allow Garcia to make the drug drop as planned. Bickford pledged the continued cooperation of both himself and his officers.

Hudson left the meeting and returned to Martinez. "Tell them to get the truck loaded again," he ordered.

Martinez hopped up and left the room. He called down to evidence and requested the half-ton of cocaine be loaded back in the secret compartment of the black F-150. There was a silence on the other end before Martinez reassured them that the FBI was making the request.

The drugs then came down to impound, where the truck was parked. It took several wheeled carts to haul nine hundred pounds of cocaine, and a couple of trips had to be made. The ISP drug team was summoned back, and they carefully lay the bags in the secret compartment, just as they had found them. Photos were snapped of the drugs, and samples were also withheld, to ensure there would be ample evidence to prosecute both Diego and Rosa if the drop, or their deal with Hudson, should go awry.

Martinez then conferred with Des Woodson, who was designated to accompany the Garcias in the truck. Next, Martinez called his wife and told her not to expect him home that evening. She was clearly annoyed at yet another long work day, since one of their daughters had a recital that night. Still, she told him to be careful, as she always did.

*****

Rosa was led back into the interrogation room, and Diego briefly discussed the plans for the drug drop. Her eyes exploded from exhaustion to horror upon hearing of Hudson's directive. Before she could utter a sentence, Diego cut her off. “Do not ask questions,” he said. “We must do as they say.” She remained silent, still choking back tears at their downfall.

Certainly, she would not expect the news that Diego had sold out Rodrequs, and he dreaded having to tell her. His words were deliberate and soft, hoping to ease the blow, but to no avail.

“Oh, Diego! How could you!” she shrieked. “What have you done?”

“I did the only thing I could do,” he replied, in an unusually calm tone. He reached for her hand, but she jerked away. Undaunted, he continued. “We could not face prison. I've been there, and it is a hellish, horrible place. I barely survived. You know that.”

Rosa was losing her grip on reality. “But we could get through it. We made it through before, and we could do it again.”

"Neither one of us would!" he snapped, drawing his hand back. "You know that! The agent who questioned me said what we are facing. I am a repeat offender. They will throw the book at me! I could die there!" He then remembered her own consequence. "We could both die there!"

With her limited English, Rosa was not aware of the latter phrase, and still could not understand. "But they may be easy on you. How do you say, time off for good behavior, like the last time?"

"No. NO!" Diego's nerves were frayed, and he sprang from his chair. "There is no chance of that. I am looking at twenty-five years to life! You, too!"

Rosa had been stubborn since a small child. Now, in this moment of crisis, he could not reason with her. "That will not happen! I am a woman, a mother. Surely they would not send me to jail, a woman. What kind of a country is this, land of free, home of brave?"

Diego was in no mood to taunt the Americans, and took an uncommonly angry tone with his wife. "Stop it! You are as guilty as I am. You were driving the truck, and traveling with me. Your husband is a convicted drug transporter!"

He swayed back and forth. "And don't tell me about the Americans! You have seen our own system in Mexico. They have sent many to prison, people more innocent than us, for a longer time!"

Garcia caught himself and lowered his voice, dropping wearily into his chair. He was careful not to mention the terrorist plot, since he had not told Rosa, and never planned to. Still, there was plenty to worry about with the drug rap. "They will be as harsh with you as with me. There is no way out for us."

Finally, Rosa seemed to grasp the situation. She began to imagine herself locked away in a small gray block cell, scared every moment of her existence, her beloved lifestyle, home, possessions, all gone. Large tears began streaming down her weathered face, yet she still clung to hope. "What about Juan? He has been our friend for years. He will help us. Yes. He will help us."

She recalled the mutual fondness between Juan and herself. But Diego's words were permeating her defenses, and now she seemed to be trying to convince both her husband and herself.

Diego knew his boss more intimately than Rosa. “He cannot and will not help us. He will cut us loose, and you know it. He has to protect the cartel. We threaten it, he will have no use for us.”

“But you are turning on him. How could you?” she cried. “He is our friend, and we have failed him!”

He bristled at his wife's concern, but was too preoccupied to fight it. He also knew that the agents would be back any minute. “We cannot think of Juan. He is not important.” Those last words painted a look of angst to her face. “We must think of ourselves, our children.”

“Yes,” she said, almost offhandedly. “The children.”

“That is right,” he replied. “We must always think of them, no matter what happens to us. If we go to prison, it will ruin their lives. They will end up like us, living in the street. We cannot worry about Juan now. What is done, is done. We must think of ourselves, our children, our family.”

His attempt to soothe her had little effect, and her salty tears were still flowing. He scooted his chair closer to hers and draped his arm around her shoulders. She turned and buried her face in his chest, crying desperately and whispering prayers for herself, for Juan, for her husband and children.

CHAPTER XXIII

As the Garcias endured their tortured reunion, Jack Hudson, having met with the district commander, then held an impromptu meeting with Pete McCord and the rest of officers who were involved throughout the previous several hours. The meeting lasted less than ninety seconds.

"All right," said Hudson. "You know what's happened, and what's going on. I do not want anyone here to make any reports, or notify anyone of the arrest of Diego Garcia, since this could be a Homeland Security issue.

"So don't anyone make a report, or leak anything to the media," continued Hudson. "Understand? I do not want any mention of this until you have heard from me. Nothing, nowhere." Hudson took no questions, and the officers only nodded in agreement.

A couple of sandwiches and some bottled water was brought to the Garcias for their dinner, though they were told to eat quickly. They were then taken to the impound, where Woodson, the DEA and FBI agents, and the Illinois State Police drug agents were waiting. Hudson was standing there, too.

He turned and pointed his finger out the window to two unmarked cars parked outside. "See those cars?" he asked. "Those will be the ones following you. They will be in constant contact with both the agent and with us. Maintain a normal speed, and stop in Joliet as you planned."

The Garcias silently got in the truck, and Woodson climbed into the back seat. Hudson piled into a tail car with the other agents. He was now running the show, since the FBI had taken over the operation from the DEA. Both vehicles headed out for I-55 and after nearly two hours, were on the outskirts of Joliet.

Though he had been awake for hours and had skipped a couple of meals, Diego Garcia was running on adrenaline. He was wide awake, with no inkling of tiredness. His wife, always a nervous sort, was even more fidgety than usual.

When he approached Joliet, he took the exit onto I-80 east, took the Larkin Avenue exit, and stopped at the first filling station he saw. He fumbled for his cell phone, nervous because the many eyes of his escorts that watched his every movement.

Awkwardly, he called the drug dealer, who only knew that the drugs were coming that day, with no specific time. Therefore, he was oblivious the problems that had delayed the shipment for several hours. Garcia suggested they meet at the Holiday Inn on I-57 in Matteson, a crime-ravaged suburb south of Chicago. Both were familiar with the location, since Garcia had met the dealer there before.

The Holiday Inn was some twenty-five miles from Joliet. Woodson radioed the agents in the two unmarked cars, which had parked across the street at another gas station, that the drop site was set. The cars then quickly pulled out to move forward to Matteson, to give them time to set up the surveillance at the Holiday Inn. Since the dealer had to come from the north side of Chicago, it would take him a little longer to arrive at the drop site.

Jack Hudson had given Woodson explicit instructions for the Garcias, and radioed other agents to advise them how, and where, the delivery was to be made. Diego was to arrive at the Holiday Inn, park the F-150 in the hotel lot, and rent a room. Then he was to use his cell phone to contact the dealer, advising of his arrival. The dealer would come to Garcia's hotel room, hand over the money, and take the keys. He would then drive the truck to an undisclosed location, unload the cocaine, and return the empty truck to the parking lot, leaving the keys inside.

As Diego and Rosa were renting the room, the DEA agents swiftly placed a tracking device on the truck so it could be followed once it exited the hotel. Diego paid for the room in cash, stepped away from the front desk, and went outside for a moment. He used his fingers to flash the room number, 315, to the waiting agents and left one of his two key cards on a decorative planter by the door.

The FBI task force sprang from their car, discreetly picked up the key card, and headed upstairs, actually beating Diego and Rosa to Room 315. The agents then wired the room to monitor the money exchange and any conversation.

In minutes, the dealer arrived in a dark, mid-model panel van. The agents were stationed outside in their cars, listening carefully. The dealer was a heavyset Mexican man, approximately thirty-five years old, and dressed in a black leather jacket. He briskly entered the hotel and headed for Garcia's room, where the exchange of the money and the truck keys took only a minute.

The agents then heard Jack Hudson's voice come over the radio. "Let the drugs walk," he ordered. "Tail the truck, and see where it goes. Then return to the hotel. *But do not intercept the narcotics.* Do you understand me?"

Hudson's directive had barely finished as the dealer was pulling out of the parking lot. One of the cars held DEA agents, and they pulled out behind him, keeping a safe distance but close enough that they never lost sight. The truck was followed to a warehouse in Oak Lawn, a city of some 54,000 twenty miles north of Matteson. No movement was made by the agents to intercept the truck, its driver, or its cargo.

The dealer then returned the truck to the same parking spot as before at the Holiday Inn. He left the keys in the ignition and drove off in his van.

From his hotel room, Garcia watched from the window as the van pulled out, completing the transfer. The FBI task force, Woodson, and others then came to Garcia's room, and watched as Garcia called Rodrequs from his cell phone.

No "hellos" were offered. "It's complete," said Garcia. "I've got the money, and he just left the truck in the parking lot."

Thinking of the $1.2 million exchange, Rodrequs roared with laughter. "Very good, my friend," he said. "Did you have any problems?"

"None at all," replied Garcia, mustering enough courage to lie smoothly. "We will be heading back to Juarez from here."

"I will see you then, my brother." Rodrequs only referred to Diego as "my brother" when he was extremely happy over something. "Give my best to your lovely Rosa."

Diego hung up the phone, sat down on the bed, and let out a huge sigh. The events of the past twenty-four hours finally caught up with him, and he felt exhausted as never before. The thought of turning his back on his old friend Juan still gnawed at him, though he knew he had to save himself and his family. He grabbed for Rosa's hand, and for the first time all day, she allowed his fingers to wrap around hers. He wearily raised his eyes to the agents who filled the room. "Cooperation," he muttered.

*****

The agents escorted the Garcias from the Holiday Inn, offering no explanation to the quizzical desk clerk as they strode by. The next stop was the FBI offices back in Springfield. Des Woodson was assigned to drive the F-150, while the Garcias were placed in the backseat of one of the unmarked cars. Both dozed off as the caravan sped southward to Springfield, making no stops along the way.

It was now in the early morning hours, and even the agents were starting to tire. Martinez and his associates walked deliberately into FBI headquarters and instantly poured themselves another large cup of coffee to prop themselves up. Jack Hudson, though, looked as fresh as if he had just stepped out his front door at the start of the day. His eyes wide, his posture straight, his thinning brown hair perfectly in place, there was no indication that his work day was now in its twenty-first hour.

He raised his eyes from his manila folder and saw the Garcias trudging down the hallway, surrounded by the agents from the run to Matteson. Even the hardy Hudson knew the Garcias could use a pick-me-up. “Do you want a cup of coffee?” he offered.

Diego's face assumed the look of a man lost in the desert who finds a water hole. “Yes,” he said.

“Could we also have something to eat?” added Rosa, who was never one to settle.

“Yeah,” said Hudson, who turned to one of the younger agents on duty. “Have some sandwiches and doughnuts brought in here, or something.”

The food arrived, and Hudson pointed Diego into a white-walled, spartan interrogation room, much like the one in Bloomington. Martinez and Woodson joined him, while Rosa was escorted to a another holding room, down the hall.

The group was barely seated when Hudson began. “This won't take long,” he started. “Because this case involves terrorism, I have the authority to hold both of you indefinitely. National security is at risk, and you have information we need.

“I will remind you again,” continued Hudson, staring at Diego with a piercing glare. “You have to give us your full cooperation. I can do nothing for you if you don't. Since you sat in on a terrorist plot, and have participated in transporting and supplying the suspects, you will be considered an accomplice. Our government treats cases like this very seriously, and usually hands out the maximum punishment possible.”

Hudson now slowed his voice for effect. “Think about that. The only way out for you is to cooperate with us to the fullest extent possible.”

Diego had heard it all several times over on this day, and was now committed. He was too scared to change his mind. “But like I said before. I don't want Rosa to know about the terrorist plot."

Never a patient sort, Hudson did not care to be reminded about something he had already agreed to. "And like *I* said before, we won't say anything about it."

Though put off by Hudson's sarcasm, Diego remained steadfast. "Then I give you my word."

Hudson recognized that the word of Diego Garcia, an ex-con who worked for one of the continent's most dangerous drug lords and who had assisted in a massive terrorist plot, was suspect at best. Still, he had plenty to go on, and more than enough information to foil the plot. "Very good," replied Hudson, who was adept at playing along, and playing the odds.

Diego collected himself and raised his head. A slight feeling of pride flowed through Diego's mind, and he responded as if he were addressing a business deal. He returned Hudson's gaze. "I accept your terms."

"Okay," replied Hudson condescedingly. "Now, let's go and tell your wife."

Breaking the news to Rosa was something Diego dreaded. She had been through so much on this nightmarish day, and this would only add to her despair. Hudson and the others surrounded Garcia as he walked down the hallway. A middle-aged man with reddish-blond hair, wearing a finely pressed white shirt and dark, striped tie, stood near the holding room, holding a tablet.

"You need to meet someone," said Hudson to Garcia. "This is C.J. Sturges, the assistant U.S. attorney for this district. He will be meeting with both of you to go over the terms of the deal."

"Hello," Sturges nodded, offering no handshake. "I was the one who authorized your deal to begin with. I'll be sitting in, to make sure everyone is in agreement."

They entered the room and found Rosa cowering in her chair. She looked up at Diego with exhausted, swollen eyes. The conference was brief, and Rosa was bluntly apprised of the severity of the situation. Then the worst news came. She was told that she would remain in custody until the drug investigation was complete.

She had wept periodically all day, but now her exhaustion gave way to uncontrollable sobs. She likewise had expected to remain with her husband, and horrified at the idea that she may be jailed. Rosa knew her husband had done the only thing he could do, but her horror at the thought of separation was rampant. She also feared how Rodrequs may react, particularly if he learned that Diego had sold him out.

Diego sat next to his wife and wrapped his arm around her slumping shoulders. His comfort was of little help, and she buried her face in her hands, weeping as never before.

After fifteen minutes or so, Rosa settled down, and was led from the room. Hudson, Sturges, Martinez, and the others then crowded around the table of the compact room to again brief Garcia.

"One more time," said Hudson, "we want you to go over what you told us before. We need names, exact locations, anything that is in your head." Diego then repeated all the information he knew on the terrorists, the location of their safe house in Ciudad Juarez, the tunnel from the warehouse to the repair shop, and the other details.

The agents busily took notes again, both in longhand and on laptops, and also digitally recorded the conversation. When Garcia was finished, Hudson reached for a small black leather case, set it on the tabletop, and popped the silver latches.

Inside were seven cell phones. "Here's what I'm going to do," said Hudson in his typical authoritarian manner. "I'm going to give you these phones. Give one to each of the terrorists, and keep one for yourself. I want you to use yours to keep me updated on anything new that happens, particularly when each terrorist arrives."

For the first time since he clammed up to cut a deal, Diego took a sharp tone. "How do I know these phones will work? What type are these?"

"Don't you worry about it," replied Hudson in mock reassurance. "These are the best phones that money can buy, or at least government money. We had the manufacturer test these in all parts of Mexico. The reception came in clear as a bell."

Diego was still skeptical. “Are these phones secure? The cartel has hackers everywhere. How do I know that Rodrequs won't have his men listening in?”

“That's not going to happen, because these phones don't have voice-monitoring capability. They're trackers only. Besides, these phones are completely secure. They've got a firewall like nobody's business.” Hudson frequently used the strength of the federal government to keep his suspects in check. “And they've got an extra little perk. They're equipped with teeny-tiny tracking devices. That way, we can monitor the movements of the terrorists at all times.”

“Even if the phones are turned off?”

“The tracking devices don't care if the phones are on or off. They work regardless.”

Diego still had ample doubt. “And what will happen if anyone asks me why I have these cell phones?”

Hudson could be cavalier at times, and this was about to be one of them. “They won't. You're supposed to be the guy who supplies the equipment the terrorists need, right? Won't cell phones be part of the equipment?”

He had Garcia on that point. “No one's going to be suspicious of you supplying the phones. You seem to be a tech guy, based on what you're saying. Doesn't the cartel know that?”

Diego was losing the argument. “Yes. They know.”

“Well, then. They won't have any reason to suspect otherwise if you hand them state-of-the-art phones then, will they?”

Hudson returned to the crux of the deal. “Let's go over this one more time. You need to cooperate fully with us on every point, on everything you know. If you fail to do this and the terrorists are successful, here is what will happen.”

He raised a fist and began counting off the results, starting with his right index finger. “Your wife Rosa will never see the light of day.” A second finger was raised. “You, Rodrequs, and any others who are involved will be located and arrested.” Finally, the third finger. “Then all of you will be facing a death sentence in the United States.”

Hudson closed two of his fingers and pointed his index straight at

Garcia. "You will be considered an accomplice to a deadly terror plot, and the government here does not look kindly on deadly terror plots. So, do you understand me?"

By now, Diego was getting a little tired of that question. "Yes, senor, just as before."

"Good." Hudson looked at each of the other agents in the room and offered a concession. "Take the suspect to visit his wife before he leaves."

Des Woodson had stood silently along the wall throughout this latest briefing, resting his lanky frame against the wall. Martinez motioned to him, and Woodson then stepped forward as Garcia rose from his chair. They walked back to the holding room where Rosa was held before. "You have five minutes," said Woodson.

Like most long-married couples, the tenderness in the Garcias' relationship had worn off years before. Now, they were more like partners, each having the same goals and understanding the other's thoughts. Certainly, Rosa could never be accused of selflessness. Her initial reaction to her first interrogation, when fears of lifestyle and concern for Rodrequs came before thoughts of her children, were testament to that. Still, somewhere in her tortured mind, she worried for Diego's safety, and was terrorized by the thought that she may never see him again.

It has been said that, in most couples, one loves the other more strongly than vice-versa. In the Garcia's case, Diego was the lover. Though the youthful passion he once felt for Rosa had waned, he still felt a responsibility to her, and in the worst of times, took on a protective air. Like his wife, he worried that they may never see one another again. He was more cognizant of his danger than she, knowing that any inkling that Rodrequs had meant certain execution.

Few words were spoken in their five minutes together. Careful to omit any reference to Racheed's plot, Diego reminded her that cooperation with the American authorities on the drug arrest was his only choice, and hers as well. He told her to cooperate fully with them, and act carefully. He knew she would be tempted to contact family in Mexico, perhaps to tip them off and help her try to escape.

He urged her to forget any thoughts of phoning or writing anyone back home.

Normally she would bicker with him, but not this time. Her silence may have been due to fear, or exhaustion. Finally, they heard a knock on the door. Woodson was a textbook official, and clocked the five minutes exactly. The Garcias rose from their chairs, and Diego kissed her face. Woodson led him from the room, while another agent stepped inside to escort Rosa.

Rosa was driven to the west side of Springfield, where she was placed in a safe house. Several agents were assigned to guard her and ensure that she did nothing to jeopardize their operation. Jack Hudson, like Diego, correctly suspected that Rosa may try to contact someone on the outside, and ordered his guards to watch her at all times.

Hudson then contacted the special agent-in-charge in the FBI office in El Paso, to brief him about the operation. Hudson also advised that he, three other FBI agents, and Martinez would accompany Garcia to El Paso. The SAC in El Paso promised to supply ample personnel to support the operation, which would be directed by Hudson.

Afterward, Hudson took a few minutes to run home and pack. The next couple of weeks would be grueling, but as usual, he was wholly prepared. He explained to his wife that he would be gone for an extended period, and knowing his vow of secrecy, she asked no questions. She was accustomed to his quick departures and long absences in their twenty-four years of marriage, and promised to tell the kids that their father would be gone for several weeks. He gave her a peck on the cheek and piled some clothes in a suitcase for the trip ahead.

Meanwhile, arrangements were being made for Diego's return trip to El Paso. The black Ford pickup that brought him to Illinois was now waiting for him, stripped of the illegal cargo that had created his predicament. Martinez would ride along with him, while Hudson and other agents would follow. Garcia had barely slept in the last thirty-six hours, and asked if he could rest before hitting the road.

Hudson, having returned from his sprint home, approved and directed his top aide, Gord Lindsay, and two other FBI agents to escort Diego to the Holiday Inn Express in Springfield, where a room was rented. Diego welcomed the chance at a few hours' sleep. The agents stayed awake, watching him sleep and making sure he did not contact anyone.

At four o'clock that afternoon, the agents awakened him, and Diego was on the road to El Paso. The trip home was more unnerving than the journey north, as Hudson and other agents tailed the F-150 for the entire route, filling Garcia's rearview mirror at every glance. From the seat next to Garcia, Martinez kept in close radio contact with Hudson in the tail car.

Garcia's mind was also a cyclone of thoughts. He was terrified for Rosa, anxious that he may be revealed in Juarez, and touchy about being tracked by the authorities in such an array. He was also carrying the $1.2 million from the drug deal, and as usual, was edgy about having so much cash in his possession.

Garcia drove straight through, only stopping for gas, fast food meals and bathroom breaks. Hudson and the surveillance team dutifully stopped as well, pulling in right behind Garcia, then parking close enough that Garcia was forced to notice them as he stepped away from the truck. More than once, he was tempted to step into the bathroom stalls at gas stations, whip out his cell phone, and dial Rodrequs to warn him. Juan had been his friend since boyhood, and he still felt a certain amount of loyalty. He also had sworn himself to the cartel, and had many other friends among its members. But Garcia realized that he would have no such opportunity to alert his associates, as the agents followed him into the men's rooms, and they had confiscated his cell phone, anyhow.

He felt guilty that he was ratting on his cohorts, and wondered how he would live with himself, regardless of the outcome. But he also remembered Rosa and the children, and knew that extended prison sentences – at the very best – could not be allowed to happen. He also thought of himself. Despite his often-dangerous profession, he unabashedly entertained a great fear of dying.

As the caravan approached El Paso, Garcia and Martinez pulled into a highway rest stop. Hudson's car slipped in behind, and he threw open his door, jumping outside.

"We're just about here," remarked Hudson, stretching his arms to relieve the stiffness. "Nice trip, eh? Good time and good mileage."

Garcia chose not to respond to the sarcasm, but Hudson was in no mood for chit-chat. "This is the last I'll see of you for a while, so I wanted to remind you about your cooperation," he began.

"I know, I know," interrupted Garcia. "You don't have to remind me."

"Well, I'm going to, anyway," responded Hudson mockingly, cocking his head to demonstrate additional sarcasm. "You have to cooperate with us fully, do everything we say, when we say it. If you do, you and your wife will not be charged. If you don't, then you'll face the consequences. And we've been over those, haven't we?"

"Yes, senor," sighed Garcia. "I am fully aware."

"Very good," said Hudson patronizingly. "This is where we get off. You're going into El Paso alone." He pointed to the cell phone that bulged in Garcia's pocket. "Use that thing to keep us informed of every move. And if I try to call you, you'd better answer, or have a good reason if you don't."

Garcia nodded and stepped back into the truck. Martinez climbed into the car with the FBI agents, and waited for Garcia to start the ignition. Once he did, he was allowed to travel ahead, alone, to the Mendez Auto Shop and the tunnel entrance.

So the temptations, powerful as they were, were dismissed. He knew the closer he was to Juarez, the harder it would be to warn the cartel. As a result, he was almost relieved when he pulled into the auto shop. Garcia parked the truck inside as the agents breezed by on the highway, their surveillance complete. He offered only the basic response to welcomes from the mechanics and headed down the tunnel, clutching the dark red duffel bag with Rodrequs' money.

Once he reached the warehouse at the other end of the tunnel, he phoned Rodrequs and asked to be picked up. Rodrequs sent his driver with the black Hummer that had transported Racheed to the warehouse days earlier. In minutes, Diego was sitting at the lavish dining room table in Rodrequs' compound.

"Welcome, my friend," said Rodrequs, grinning so widely that his smile erased part of his facial scar. He embraced Garcia and kissed both cheeks. Few others in the cartel, or anyone else along the border, could expect such warmth from the ruthless Rodrequs. "Do you have something for me?"

Garcia withdrew himself from the embrace and set the duffel bag on the faux wood table. He turned the bag upside down, and bundles of $100 bills came pouring out. The bag was stuffed so full that Garcia had to shake it to loosen the tightly packed stacks of bills.

"Wonderful, my brother!" Rodrequs beamed. "I hope you had no problems on your trip."

Diego was a skilled liar, or else he would have never risen so high in the cartel. Still, he was challenged at the idea of fibbing to his old friend and boss. "None at all," he said crisply. "Everything went according to our plan. No worries."

"Very good. But where your beautiful wife?" Rodrequs shared the fondness for Rosa, though she could hardly be classified as beautiful. Any of the high-end prostitutes that Rodrequs hired were far more attractive than Diego's plain wife.

"She stayed behind," responded Garcia, rationalizing to himself that the words were not exactly a lie. "She wanted to visit her relatives for a time. You remember, the ones that raised her?"

Rosa actually did visit her relatives in Chicago from time to time, so this news was not surprising to Rodrequs. "Oh. Very good for her. I hope she has a fine time. When do you expect her back?"

Diego pulled out another response. "Oh, in a month or so, I guess. She said she wanted a vacation from all of us."

His attempt at humor won over Rodrequs, who roared with laughter. "Of course! Who would not want a break from our ugly faces!" Diego smiled weakly.

Rodrequs then returned to the business at hand. "Was our friend in Chicago happy with our product?"

The veiled reference was immediately recognized by Garcia, since the dealer was a returning customer. “Oh, certainly. He was quite pleased with what we brought to him.”

“And there was no problem with the drop?” Rodrequs then answered his own question, his eyes fixated on the large pile of bills in front of him. “Of course there wasn't!”

Juan Rodrequs only had a sense of humor when he was successful at something, and this was one of those times. He relaxed in the high-backed chair at the head of the table and reached for the bottle of vodka that was a fixture on the end table beside him. “Well, this calls for a celebration!”

In seconds, the large glass of orange juice in front of Rodrequs became a screwdriver. He motioned to the manservant to bring Garcia a glass of fruit juice, and poured a healthy quantity of vodka into his drink as well. Rodrequs howled with laughter again, completely oblivious to the duplicity that his confidant had engaged in.

CHAPTER XXIV

When Jack Hudson arrived in El Paso, he hit the ground running, as usual. His first order of business was to set up a command post at the local FBI headquarters. Hudson briefed the special-agent-in-charge, Vicente Cruz, on the progress and plans of the operation. He then picked the phone and dialed Greg Foster at his CIA office in Mexico City.

Foster had met Hudson in passing on previous cases, and was familiar with him. “How are you doin', Jack? It's been a while.”

“Sure has. Got something we need to talk about. You know a Pakistani by the name of Racheed Ul-Bashar?”

Foster had seen the name on several manifests, and had questioned General Santos about it. “Yeah. He's been on several flights to Mexico. I've ran him through our computer and the Homeland Security system. Nothing came up.”

Hudson was not at all surprised that Foster had followed protocol. “Well, hold on to your ass for this one.”

“What are you talking about?”

“This Racheed person is the mastermind of a major terrorist

threat. He plans to move terrorists and explosives across the border from Mexico and bomb three cities in the U.S."

"No way." Foster was stunned, remembering how Santos eased his concerns about Racheed's motives. "Can't be possible. When I saw his name on the manifests, I called Carlos Santos to see what this guy was all about."

"Santos?" Hudson knew the name, and had heard nothing bad on him. "What'd he say about it?"

"Apparently Racheed is dating his daughter. Santos thinks the world of him."

"Damn." Hudson was putting more pieces in place. "That may explain how he got into Mexico without anyone caring about it."

Foster wondered if that was a veiled criticism of his work, but the professional in him chose to overlook it. "Well, like I said, he came up clean on our systems, and Santos vouched for him."

Hudson realized how his last comment must have sounded. "I know, I know," he said in a halfhearted effort to reassure Foster. "He slipped right in under all of us. Sleeping with the general's daughter," he said resignedly.

Foster was still wondering what was going on. "How do you know all of this?"

"We nailed one of Juan Rodrequs' top men in Bloomington, Illinois. He was hauling four hundred kilos of cocaine to Chicago."

That was no shock to Foster. Like every other law enforcement agent in the region, he knew of Rodrequs and his cartel. "Who's the guy's name?"

"Diego Garcia. He's the second-in-command. He was looking at 25 years to life because it was his second offense, and his wife was picked up with him, too. So he decided to cut a deal." Hudson's voice crackled with sarcasm. "Apparently, he sat in on meetings with Racheed and Rodrequs. Racheed wanted to smuggle his men and bombs across, and Rodrequs was only too willing to help, since he stands to get three million bucks and a big supply of Pakistani heroin for his trouble."

"Son of a bitch." Foster normally did not swear, but the magnitude of Hudson's story was overwhelming. “What's the motive?”

Hudson rolled his eyes, unbeknownst to Foster on the other end. “Garcia says that Racheed lost his grandfather and sister in one of the drone strikes in Pakistan, up north, up in the hills. He apparently talks about Allah all the time, too.”

“Doesn't surprise me,” responded Foster dismissively. “Damn near everyone who wants to bomb America always falls back on that.”

“Yep.” Hudson had heard it all before, too. He paused to sip his coffee. “This Racheed has already flown one guy in. Name is Adeeb Ahmad. You got anything on him?”

Foster remembered the name. “Yeah. He flew in to Mexico City, and disappeared.”

“Not quite,” Hudson liked having information that no one else had. “Garcia says he's in a safe house in Juarez. Drove him there himself, to a place owned by Rodrequs.”

Greg Foster took great pride in his work, and was beginning to feel as if he failed. “Right under our noses again. Dammit!” He rapped his open palm on his desk, as if to release frustration.

“Well, there's four more coming. You got any names?”

A shuffling of papers was heard on the other end. “Nothing from Pakistan,” said Foster. “That Adeeb guy is the last one I've seen in Mexico.” He remained curious. “How were they getting across the border?”

“Rodrequs has this tunnel under the Rio Grande. It originates in a warehouse outside of Juarez and comes out in an auto shop in El Paso.” Hudson fingered his handheld, scrolling down for the name. “Mendez Auto Shop.”

Foster was impressed. “That must be some kind of tunnel.”

“Concrete floor, lights, and everything, about fifteen hundred feet long. Even comes with elevators. They've got some engineers or something, don't they? You had no idea about it?”

Hudson was pricking Foster, who knew that the FBI had no idea, either. “Nope. Did you?”

Knowing he also had no answer, Hudson changed the subject.

"Send me everything you've got." He loved giving orders to people. "You've got my e-mail. And let me know if any of these other bastards come in. Garcia says they're supposed to be spaced, to throw us off."

"Will do." Foster, like everyone else, had reason to distrust Garcia. "You think Garcia's solid? That this isn't a wild goose chase?"

"Hell, I don't know. I think he is," replied Hudson argumentatively. "But what else do we do? If he's telling the truth and we sit back, we could lose thousands of people. Even if he's lying, we've still got his ass. He gave us the locations of the tunnel, the warehouses, and the safe houses. Their drug trade is ours, thanks to that. We can go in whenever."

That was enough for Foster. "I'll send you what I've got. Keep me posted, and I'll do the same."

"See ya." Jack Hudson then turned his attention to the myriad of other tasks in front of him.

*****

At the embassy in Mexico City, Foster also inherited a long to-do list. First was to notify his CIA counterparts in Karachi.

Fortunately for Greg Foster, he did not have to work his way up the channels in Karachi. Answering the phone was Tom Howard, a longtime buddy who came into the agency at the same time as Foster. Both were from the mid-South and close in age, so they always had plenty to talk about.

"Hey, Greg. How's it been?" was the cheerful response on the other end.

"I've been better. Got something I need you to do."

Howard laughed. "You always do. What now?"

"I've got a credible report of a major terrorist plot. I just hung up with Jack Hudson of the FBI, and he's got an informant. The mastermind is based in Karachi."

Howard's demeanor instantly changed. "What's the name?"

"Racheed Ul-Bashar. Born in 1986 and graduated from Texas A & M. Engineering major. Says he wants revenge because his grandfather and sister were killed in a drone strike in Seidu."

"Big damn deal. What's he want to do to us?"

"He apparently wants to move five men across the border from Mexico into the U.S. and plant bombs in high-traffic areas."

Hundreds of goosebumps rose on Howard's arms. "Where is he now?"

"He flew back to Pakistan, but that's all we know. He could be back in Karachi. I'd seen his name on flight manifests, and nothing came up in our system or Homeland Security. So I called Carlos Santos, and asked what was going on."

"Yeah?" Tom Howard was normally an easygoing guy, but his sense of alarm was rising.

"I guess our man Racheed is dating the general's daughter, and Santos was completely oblivious. Racheed managed to get in touch with Juan Rodrequs, one of the big cartel leaders, and offered him three million in cash and an endless supply of heroin if he could move the men and the bombs across."

"Wow." Howard could think of nothing else to say. As Foster talked, he was typing Racheed's name into the agency computer system, to also see the information. "I've got his address." He also ran the name through a different database. "His dad is a doctor. I also see he's got a brother named Solomon. I know him, he's in Pakistani intelligence."

"Damn, that's right," Foster snapped back in his swivel chair, remembering that fact from his conversation with Santos. "That may be a link."

"Could be," pondered Howard, nervously tapping his pencil on his desk, "though I've never heard anything bad on the guy."

"Yeah, well, I never heard anything bad on Racheed until ten minutes ago." pointed out Foster. "Tape the phones of every family member you can find. Also find any other information you can get on Racheed and anyone else in the family."

"You want surveillance, right?" CIA agents are trained to ask these questions, and a seasoned vet like Howard knew what to do.

"Absolutely," replied Foster. "Put them under 24 hour watch. Also put a cover on their mail, everything going in and coming out."

"I'm on it." Howard also thought ahead. "You said there were five terrorists coming over. Where are they?"

"One's already here. Name is Adeeb Ahmad. He flew into Mexico City, and was taken to a cartel safe house in Juarez. The informant drove him there."

"Got it. I'll get anything I can on him. Who's the informant?"

"Rodrequs' second-in-command, a guy named Diego Garcia. He was nailed in Illinois on trafficking, and wanted to cut a deal."

Howard was impressed. "They got someone that high up? Lucky bastards. Wish I could get informants like that."

"Yeah, and a whole lot of Americans will be glad, too," said Foster, thinking of the extreme casualty rate if Racheed were successful. "Get back to me whenever you have something."

*****

As the sun set over the mountains surrounding El Paso that evening, Jack Hudson was too busy to notice. He was sitting in a black van within sight of the Mendez Auto Shop, impatiently waiting for nightfall.

With him were two FBI agents from the El Paso office, carefully eyeing the shop from their concealed location behind a derelict mobile home, five hundred feet away. The agents were some of the best tech guys the FBI had in Texas, and they eagerly watched as the overhead lights in the shop flicked off, one by one.

They then watched as a hand reached for the red-and-white "Open" sign and turned it around to "Closed." Mendez and several workers walked lazily outside, piled into a couple of beat-up older-model pickups, and headed for the nearest bar.

Hudson and his colleagues watched as they drove down the highway, out of sight. Then the van lurched forward, rolling slowly toward the shop, still parking out of view. It was now completely dark, and the moderate flow of traffic from mid-day had slowed to a trickle. Few drivers noticed the van pulling near the shop, and none had any reason to suspect anything.

The tech agents meticulously surveyed the building until 1 a.m.

They then departed the van and walked past the auto shop, trying to locate any surveillance equipment placed by the management. Seeing none, they proceeded toward the building.

One of the men was an expert locksmith, and had little trouble with the aging front door of the shop. Seconds later, two were inside, while Hudson remained in the van. They then conducted a "black bag job" in the garage. Taps were placed on phones, and other listening devices were scattered in concealed locations around the shop. The devices were so tiny that they could be easily attached to equipment, door frames, and inside cracks and crevices, and attract no attention.

Minuscule video cameras were also placed around the shop. The cameras were barely the size of a pack of gum, easily able to slide in wall cracks, on seldom-used high shelves, and among the piles of junk that sat pell-mell around the shop. They also pried open the storage closet door and inspected the entrance to the tunnel. A camera was squeezed into a transom in the closet door, to focus on the entrance. Other cameras were set to face the closet door.

The operation took less than ninety minutes. More cameras were placed outside the shop, on nearby telephone and electric poles. None of the sporadic drivers on the road out front spotted them, as the agents' dark jackets and stocking caps camouflaged with the black of night. The men then returned to the van and sped off.

*****

Greg Foster's tip led the CIA office in Karachi right to Racheed, who was back home for a brief visit, or so he wanted it to appear. He was quickly identified by agents and placed under twenty-four hour surveillance. Unbeknownst to him, vehicles with agents were stationed outside his every hangout, including his parents' residence. Some of the agents were darker in complexion and less likely to stand out to the native passersby. A tracking device was also placed on Racheed's silver Toyota.

On the first day of the watch, Racheed was observed departing the his parents' residence. He was tailed to a local computer store, where he spent a half-hour before leaving. Agents subsequently entered the shop and engaged in a search, but could not determine who Racheed had contacted. The agents found his movement peculiar, since Garcia had informed them that Racheed carried much of his information on a personal laptop. They suspected that Racheed was trying to conceal his location and make it harder for his laptop to be traced.

Two days later, an unidentified young Pakistani man was spotted arriving at the Ul-Bashar home. He knocked on the door around 9 a.m., after agents had watched both of Racheed's parents leave in separate cars. Around 1 p.m., Racheed and the unknown man left the residence.

The surveillance team followed the Toyota to the airport while another team monitored the car's route on a computer screen. Both teams kept in close contact, in case the surveillance team lost sight. Tom Howard was monitoring the situation from his office, and he frequently called Foster in Mexico City. Foster, in turn, relayed the information to Jack Hudson in El Paso.

Hudson put down his phone and turned to his subordinates. “Here comes another one of the bastards,” he said gruffly.

The Toyota headed in the direction of the airport, and in a few minutes turned into the entrance gate. This news was relayed to Howard, Foster, Hudson, and the others on the watch. Howard did not need to remind his guys what to do, but did anyway. “Get inside and see where the flight is going.”

The agents kept a careful distance from the two Pakistanis and found a seat on a sofa that allowed a full view of the main terminal. The unidentified Pakistani joined a line for a flight scheduled for Paris. From there, agents knew Mexico City. The agents used earpiece microphones to advise the teams offsite of this development, and snapped photos of the Pakistanis with concealed cameras.

The young Pakistani then joined Racheed on a couple of cushy white chairs to wait for his flight. Both men were relaxed and joking, unaware their every move was being watched. As they made small talk, Racheed reminded the terrorist that Diego Garcia would meet him at the Mexico City airport. Finally, the call for Flight 901, to

Paris, echoed throughout the terminal. In the French capital, a five-hour layover would ensue before the departure of Flight 131, an Airbus to Mexico City.

Almost on cue, both Pakistanis stood up. Racheed placed his hands on either side of the young man's face and looked into his eyes, and the man stepped back and bowed respectfully. He then grabbed a large carry-on bag and briskly strode out the door and down the hallway to the tarmac.

Racheed then strode off, walking erectly with a self-satisfied look on his face. He repeatedly walked within five feet of the surveillance team, unaware of the strangers whose eyes had been fixed on him in the terminal for the last hour. After several seconds, the agents also stood and followed him into the parking lot. He piled into his Toyota and drove off, with the surveillance team not far behind.

CHAPTER XXV

Greg Foster could be equally blunt, and that's just the way Jack Hudson liked it. "We've got another one on the way," he said with his usual bluntness. "Our man Racheed just drove him to his flight in Karachi, and he's coming your way."

"Flight number?"

"901 to Paris. Then we presume Flight 131 to Mexico City."

"Got a name?"

"Nope. Looks like a regular, devout young guy from Pakistan. Wearing a dark shirt and khaki pants, like some kind of college student."

"I'm on it." Hudson then called his agents together and informed them of this latest development. The flight was scheduled to arrive in 24 to 26 hours, and there was plenty of time for Foster to get a surveillance team in motion.

Meanwhile, Howard's men in Karachi requested a list of passengers on both Flight 901 and 131. That allowed them to find the suspected terrorist's name. It was run through the CIA and Homeland Security computer systems, and nothing came up. This information was then called in to Foster's office. Foster quickly relayed it to Hudson.

"Stay on it. Don't let the guy out of your sight," barked Hudson.

"Do we have a choice?" said Foster sarcastically. But he knew what Hudson meant, and the only thing to do now was wait.

"Just do it," scoffed Hudson as he broke the connection.

The next twenty-four hours passed with morbid slowness. Agents spent much of their time in the embassy office staring at the second-hand as it circled the clock on the wall. As the landing time neared, no one had to say anything, and three agents rose almost in unison. It was time to head to the airport.

Waiting there was Diego Garcia. As had Foster, Garcia had also called Hudson, to inform him of the impending arrival of the terrorist. The agents, all dressed in sport coats and dress pants to emulate visiting businessmen and pulling wheeled luggage carts, were expecting him and had a fairly good idea of what he looked like, since they had seen the mug shots of him.

Then, Garcia rose, extended his arms over his head as if stretching, and headed toward the airport bar. The three agents nonchalantly followed. Garcia was standing at the bar, drinking a ginger ale. He had been instructed not to drink alcohol or ingest illegal drugs while the operation was in process.

The flight was only twelve minutes behind schedule. Little time had elapsed when a young Pakistani, dressed in black and khaki, meekly entered the door from the tarmac. The agents, stationed on a dark brown bench on one side of the terminal, watched as Garcia rose from his chair and motioned to the man. They exchanged a brief word before the Pakistani clasped Garcia's hand in a shake. He bowed to his new Mexican friend, and proceeded with him toward the main entrance.

Garcia was new to this game, and unpolished. Though he knew he shouldn't, his anxiety could not prevent his eyes from shifting toward the agents. His wandering gaze went unnoticed by the terrorist, and they walked side by side, as if old friends. The agents watched intently, climbed to their feet, and walked some two hundred feet behind them.

One agent quickly pulled out his cellphone. “They're coming out,” he said. Foster had called for a drone to tail Garcia, who headed for a black Hummer, one of several in Rodrequs' fleet, and hit the remote to unlock the door. He and the terrorist climbed inside, and drove off.

Normally, Garcia would have driven much faster, but suspecting he was being tailed, he drove at a moderate speed. The drone flew just high enough to stay out of sight and at an angle that could not be easily seen from inside the vehicle, and had no trouble keeping the Hummer in its sights. If the drone lost Garcia, there was a back up plan. Garcia had supplied the make and license number of the car he would be driving, and the chase team had put a tracking device on the Hummer when they arrived.

From his command post, Hudson's eyes bounced back and forth between several monitors. One kept tabs on the tracking device on the Hummer, while another fed data back from the drone. “Got `em from every angle,” said Hudson proudly, to no one in particular.

*****

A great deal of time in surveillance operations is spent in waiting, and the men and women involved come to expect it. Still, it drives them crazy. Professional law enforcement officials want to do their jobs, and they know that any time they spend idle keeps other criminals at large, particularly the ones they are watching.

The next several days were spent waiting for more terrorists to arrive. For a go-getter like Jack Hudson, the delay was intolerable. “The bastards are keeping us waiting, aren't they?” he said one day to his subordinates. “I wish to hell they'd hurry up and get here. I'd like to end this once and for all.”

But there was plenty to do. For starters, Hudson wanted surveillance equipment to be placed around the safe house and Rodrequs' compound. But since those locales were across the border, he had no authority.

He picked up the phone and dialed Greg Foster once again. “This is getting to be a habit," said Foster snidely as he heard Hudson's voice.

"Yeah, yeah," replied Hudson impatiently. "We need to have surveillance equipment around Rodrequs and Racheed. The compound, the safe house, the warehouse, all of it. We need to watch their every move."

Foster knew exactly what he was implying. "So you're asking me to get on it?"

Hudson was not used to being tweaked, and annoyed that Foster did not snap to his order. "Yeah. Can you do that?"

"Of course I can do that." Foster got a charge out of holding the cards over the FBI. "Give me a day or so, and we'll have it done." Following protocol, he contacted one of the highest-ranking Mexican military authorities that he had access to, and described what needed to be done. The brass made no effort to stand in the Americans' way.

Foster sent agents posing as Mexican nationals who were familiar with the countryside in and around Juarez, including the remote locations of the safe house and compound. Some managed to slip down the alley toward the safe house, while others made their way up the muddy road to the compound. They crawled through wooded areas as if in combat, using the darkness of the night to further conceal their presence. Once near the compound, they crept through secluded spaces where lights were not turned on. Though the warehouse was heavily guarded, agents managed to get close enough under the cover of darkness to go unnoticed.

Entering each site was not an option, but getting within viewing distance was certainly attainable. Once close enough, the agents installed cameras and listening devices across the compound, and around the warehouse and safe house. Cameras resembling electric transformers were installed on poles, while other devices were placed around both sites in trees and on signs.

Hudson and the other agents could then monitor the feedback from the monitoring equipment at the command post. Not only could they track the movements of the terrorist plot, but also gained tips on Rodrequs as high-ranking cartel members came and went from the compound.

Still, there was no movement of terrorists at either the compound nor the safe house. The agents in Karachi were equally stymied. They followed Racheed to and from his parents' residence to the gym, the coffeebars, and the computer shop. The phone taps revealed the terrorist plot was still alive and well, and that more terrorists would soon fly to Mexico. But few other details were offered. Possibly, he was speaking in code with those in Seidu and elsewhere. It was almost as if Racheed knew others were listening, and did not want to give away information.

Racheed's e-mail account and cell phone were surveyed as well. The e-mail offered the agents far more than the house phones in the residence. It is a common misperception in the United States that the Taliban are backwards, and unsophisticated. Nothing could be further from the truth. To carry out their elaborate plans, they need top-notch organization and planning, including state-of-the-art electronics and computers. Even the most primitive Taliban hideouts often have the latest in computer equipment.

The terrorists had the latest cell phones and text devices, and Racheed was clearly still in touch with them. He frequently texted and e-mailed them with bits of information on news and plans. The messages were usually brief and to the point, but left little doubt that he was still the mastermind of a major terrorist undertaking.

*****

Finally, after two weeks, a phone tap on the Ul-Bashar residence revealed that the next terrorists were on the way. In a conversation between Racheed and an unidentified male that lasted only twenty-five seconds, Racheed indicated that he would be waiting at the airport. That was all the agents needed, and Tom Howard again dispatched surveillance teams. Photos were taken of the terrorists, including Racheed.

Again, agents with Pakistani backgrounds were stationed around the airport, and their dark complexions and native dress did nothing to alert the ruse. Armed with cell phones, they watched Racheed meet not one, but two unidentified young males, both in their twenties with dark hair, thick beards, and dressed in brown semi-casual jackets with black pants.

Howard sat at his Karachi headquarters, while Jack Hudson in El Paso and Greg Foster in Mexico City were also listening in. The agents relayed information on the young men, since they appeared much as the last terrorist seen, and seemed to attract Racheed's attention. "What do you have?" demanded Hudson.

The plants at the airport described the suspects in as much detail as possible. "Now, where are they headed?" asked Foster.

Racheed walked with the men to a sofa near a decorative tree. They exchanged small talk, laughing and joking amongst themselves. Finally, the last boarding call was sounded for Flight 113 to Paris, where a connection to Mexico City awaited. The CIA agents watched intently as the two men rose and bowed to Racheed, who clasped his hands around their cheeks. The terrorists grabbed small carry-on bags and headed for the flight.

Foster advised his agents to be ready for a surveillance in Mexico City. He had barely hung up when he received a call from Hudson, with news from Diego Garcia. Using one of the government cell phones, Garcia informed Hudson that he had just heard from Juan Rodrequs, with an order to pick up the terrorists in Mexico City.

While Racheed was normally well-organized, in this case he gave Garcia very little time, as he would barely be able to get from Juarez to Mexico City in time to meet the flight. Fortunately, a 737 was scheduled to depart in short order from the Juarez airport for the two-hour junket to the capital.

Garcia summoned another black Hummer from Rodrequs' fleet and was on the road to the Juarez airport. Before he left, he called ahead to one of Rodrequs' men in Mexico City and ordered a vehicle to be waiting for him at that airport. Garcia startled the man by pressing to find out the make, color, and model of the vehicle, but not so much that any questions were raised. As it was, a dark gray Honda SUV was sent, and Garcia dutifully informed Hudson of the description.

The plane from Paris landed a half-hour late, much to the angst of the surveillance team, itching to get a look at their latest suspects. Garcia was sitting in the airport bar, on a stool that afforded a panorama of the terminal. When the dark-clad young men appeared, Garcia rose and exited the bar, quickly approaching them with their ride. The men shook hands and briskly walked out of the terminal, heading for the gray Honda.

The agents in the terminal punched their speed dial and called Foster, who authorized another drone to follow Garcia and the newcomers in the drive around Juarez. The SUV traversed the crowded streets of Juarez before reaching the backstreets leading to the safe house, where the incoming terrorists joined their counterparts.

Back in Karachi, Tom Howard and his men continued their investigation of the last three terrorists. All they had were their names from flight manifests, and none were connected to any files in the CIA or Homeland Security computer systems. Within hours, it was determined that each terrorist on the flights to Mexico City hailed from the Seidu and Peshawar areas in northwestern Pakistan. This came as no surprise to the CIA agents, as that region is a known hotbed for would-be terrorists.

When he cut his deal, Diego Garcia had informed Hudson that Racheed's motive was revenge for the deaths of his grandfather and sister in the recent deadly drone strike on Seidu. That finding had to be confirmed, and since death records in drone strikes are often scattered and inconsistent, that was not an easy task. Hudson forwarded the information to Howard in the Karachi CIA office, which was eventually able to verify the casualties.

That was not all they learned. The American government knew that bomb vests were being made somewhere in the region, but did not know by whom, or where. The CIA then turned to their moles, informants among the Taliban who were sometimes dual citizens, but always dual agents. The moles advised Howard's men that Omar was a bomb maker, and his wares were in demand among Taliban fighters.

“Sounds like Grandpa was not so innocent after all, huh?” Hudson scoffed as he read the news at his command post in El Paso.

“That's what we have drone strikes for,” replied Greg Foster, reading the same report in his Mexico City office. “Now we gotta nail his grandson, too.” His eyes were fixed as he kept reviewing the report, and a brief silence fell on the line. “The motive, the plot, the people Racheed's around. It's all falling into place now, isn't it?”

“Sure is,” snapped Hudson. “Mystery solved. Sounds like a chip off the old block. The old man sits around in his hut making bomb vests to kill us filthy Americans. Now the grandson's smuggling bombs across the border to blow us up, too.”

After two weeks, word was received that the last two terrorists were on their way. Just as before, they were followed by agents at every turn, bade farewell in Karachi by Racheed, and welcomed in Mexico City by Garcia, who drove them to the safe house in Juarez.

As before, Racheed mailed coded letters to Rodrequs in care of the bartender at the hotel in Juarez. The letters included the flight numbers, the names of the men, and other relevant information. CIA agents had placed a mail cover on the Ul-Bashar household, and were able to intercept these letters. Copies were made, the contents carefully re-sealed, and replaced in the mail with such skill that the bartender had no reason to suspect any tampering.

With all five terrorists now in Juarez, Hudson, Foster, and the rest knew that any attempt to move across the border was nearing. Dozens of agents in El Paso, Juarez, and Mexico City were running on adrenaline, with bad food, little sleep and no family contact, anxiously awaiting the terrorists' next move.

*****

A few days after the last of the terrorists landed in Mexico City, Racheed decided it was time to join them. The phone and computer taps alerted the CIA to his plans, and agents in all three countries were put on high alert. The mastermind of this sophisticated terrorist plot, which jeopardized the lives of thousands of Americans, was again on the move

At the Ul-Bashar residence, however, everything seemed normal. Racheed had stayed with his parents for an unusually long time, though neither Mahammed nor Yalina seemed to mind. He had been more respectful than before, and engaged in a little more conversation around the dinner table. He spoke less of his American hatred, much to Mahammed's relief. Much to his parents' delight, he had also made several contacts at prime engineering jobs in Karachi and elsewhere in Pakistan.

Of course, the job searches were feints. Racheed knew he had to throw his parents off, so he played along in the job interviews, presenting himself as a budding young professional from a fine family whose education and technical skills would be an asset to any employer. He had actually been offered jobs in both Islamabad and Lahore, but had not responded and never planned to. His parents were typically oblivious to his ruse, and were about to be again.

At the breakfast table one morning, Racheed delivered the news. “I will be leaving early this afternoon,” he said. “I am going to Mexico City, to visit Maria.”

“Your lady friend?” asked Yalina. “We have been hoping to meet her. Why do you not bring her here?”

“She would very much like to come,” replied Racheed, “but she is very busy. I do not know if she could get away for that long.” His label of “busy” was a devious adjective for Maria's cushy schedule of workouts, coffee with the girls, and browsing at the mall.

“Too bad,” said Yalina with evident disappointment. “I would love to meet her, and her family. They sound like the finest people of Mexico. She would make a good wife for you.”

Her social-climbing never ceased, and Racheed cared little for any other questions. Still, there was one more, from Mahammed. “How long will you be gone?”

“A few weeks. I have not seen her in a while, and want to spend some time.”

“How will that affect your job search?” inquired Mahammed. While his wife fancied social standing, he concerned himself with professional advancement.

"It will not. Most of my interviewers have told me they will take a while to decide. I have applied for every open position I have found. There is nothing to do now, but wait."

"Very well," said Mahammed, spying the clock on the wall. "I must be to the office. Let me say my farewell to you now."

"I must be going as well," Yalina chimed in. "I have an engagement with my sister and her friends. We are meeting at the downtown club at nine."

Yalina's sister was the wife of a government official, and Racheed knew his mother could think of little else but her meeting. His parents quickly said their goodbyes and left in their separate luxury sedans.

A few minutes after they departed, Racheed called Maria in her Mexico City apartment. Not only was he unaware that his own phones were being tapped, Maria's were as well. Garcia's plea deal had brought up Maria's name, and she became a person of interest for surveillance. As she left for one of her long shopping excursions, CIA men entered her apartment, tapping her phone, setting up tiny cameras, and placing listening devices. Outside, a surveillance was set up around her building, and she was also tailed wherever she went.

Like Hudson, Foster expected Racheed to be in touch with his lover at some point, and the Americans were covering all their bases. The surveillance team certainly did not mind watching the lovely Maria go about her daily business in her apartment, or follow her to aerobics. But their purpose was far greater than voyeurism.

All this was unbeknownst to Racheed, who had not seen her in weeks, and had not been particularly diligent in returning her texts and phone messages. He thought he should take a moment to call, so she would not keep contacting him, particularly when there were other things to attend to. As he dialed her number, he wondered if she would be angry at his distance.

Her reaction, then, came as little surprise. "Hello, my boyfriend," she said coolly. "Or should I call you that anymore?"

"Of course you should. What do you mean?"

Even though the conversation had just started, her voice was a shriek. *"Why do you not return my calls? I call you all the time, and never hear from you!"*

Racheed, though normally selfish, tried to soothe her. "That's not true. I call you."

"*Not often enough!*" she shouted. "*We're supposed to be in love!*" In her distress, she began to stammer. "Now, now you tell me, Racheed. Tell me, tell me right now. *Is there someone else?*"

She had demanded this of Racheed before, and somewhere within, he kind of enjoyed her jealousy. He had a high opinion of himself, and could certainly understand why women would want him. "No, of course not. Why would you say that?"

"*What else would I think?*" Maria's heaving sobs were audible on the other end. "I cry myself to sleep at night, missing you, and you don't even care! *Damn you, damn you, damn you!*"

Maria had never spoken with such venom before, and Racheed knew he was in trouble. He played the one card that would appeal to her. "The reason I could not call you is because I was on assignment. I was instructed not to have contact with anyone. Not even family and friends."

"This military thing? Not that again!" Her voice was slightly calmer, and Racheed was an expert in reading people's reactions. He knew he touched a nerve. "You've told me that so many times before! And besides that, we are more than friends! *I love you, Racheed!* And you tell me it's all about your duty again?"

"Yes, because it's true." He was also a skilled liar. "I've been on assignment, just like before. Your father is in intelligence. You know how it is."

Actually, she didn't, because General Santos had engaged in secret missions years before, when she was a small child. She could not remember his secrecy, though her mother told plenty of stories. Now as a general, he was rarely in harm's way. She knew plenty of his subordinates, though, and had a pretty good idea of their responsibilities.

Racheed was gaining ground. She could not argue with his claim of assignment, though she could not bring herself to forgive him – yet. He began to play the victim. “I would think you could understand this. I could not tell anyone where I was, or what I was doing. I was told not to have any contact with anyone I knew. My superiors have been impressed with my work, and now entrust me with matters of national security. I cannot let them down.”

Maria's sobs grew quieter, and he pressed on. “If anyone would understand what I was going through, I would think it would be you. Your whole life has been spent with men in intelligence, and I thought you would understand me.”

An expert manipulator, he had succeeded once again. Her fierce anger melted into a sea of guilt. “Oh, my darling, my darling,” she groveled. “Please forgive me, forgive me. I know you have no choice. You would have called me if you could have.”

“Of course I would have,” he said, knowing full well he had barely tried. “I just want you to understand.”

“I do, I do. I am so sorry.” Maria was practically bent over at the waist, begging his forgiveness, though he could not see her. “I just love you so much, and I cannot bear to be apart from you.”

“Neither can I. But there are things I must do as a man, and as a citizen.” He stifled a smirk at the irony of the statement.

“And that's one of the reasons I love you so much,” she pleaded. “Please allow me to make this up to you when we see each other again.”

Racheed knew exactly what that meant. “It is no problem now. You understand. Even now, my clearance is not as restricted, but I still I cannot tell you where I am. I just wanted to hear the sound of your voice.”

She swooned at his feigning romance. “Oh, Racheed! You are such a wonderful, sweet man!”

“But I should be done with it all soon. I will call you as soon as I can.”

“Oh yes, oh yes,” she exclaimed. “Please be safe, and take care of yourself. I will be waiting for you.”

The CIA agents on the tap heard the connection break. “Dammit!

snapped Greg Foster, who was hanging on Racheed's every word. "I thought he was going to tell her something we didn't already know."

Foster's nerves were fraying, though his subordinates could not understand his exasperation. They had decoded the letters, and the flight number was right in front of them. "Come on, Greg," said one of them. "We've got it right here," pointing to the flight number and time of arrival. "He's coming in tomorrow."

Foster realized he needed no other proof. All the information was at hand, and the mastermind was flying in tomorrow. He turned to his agents with a grim look on his face. "Then this could be it. His other five guys are here, and they're probably going to move."

In his twenty-plus years in the agency, Foster had dealt with a myriad of security issues, but none with such ramifications. This plot imperiled tens of thousands of American lives. Foster, Hudson, and their men had to stop it, and failure was not an option.

CHAPTER XXVI

There were still plenty of calls for Jack Hudson to make. Next, he dialed the number of his counterpart in Mexico City, the head of Mexican investigations. “Senor Gonzalez,” he said with unusual politeness. “Jack Hudson of the U.S. FBI here. We have a major terrorist plot on our hands, and we need your assistance.”

Jorge Gonzalez was, in many ways, the American equal of Jack Hudson. A twenty-six year member of Mexican law enforcement, the tall, rangy Gonzalez was the consummate professional, an oasis of integrity amid the corruption of the Mexican government. He worked ridiculous hours to earn his money, at the cost of his marriage. His wife consoled her loneliness with multiple lovers, some of which Gonzalez was aware of, and strived to keep discreet.

Hudson briefed Gonzalez on the situation and all participants, including Juan Rodrequs. Gonzalez listened patiently and spoke the words that Hudson wanted to hear, “what do you need from us?”

“I would like you to find about a hundred federalies. Only the best you can find, men that can be trusted. We will need them to raid Rodrequs' properties, his compound, the warehouse, the safe house, everything."

Gonzalez was only too happy to help. He had been tracking Rodrequs for years, but the cartel leader was always a little too slippery, and government bureaucracy only hampered the issue. "That will not be a problem. Where do you wish them to be stationed at?"

"Put them about fifty miles outside of Juarez. I may call you later, and have you move them closer."

"But of course. It will be my pleasure to assist you."

"Gracias," replied Hudson. "I will keep you advised."

"Buenos dias, my friend. Or should I say buenos noches?" laughed Gonzalez. "Many times, we are so busy that the days run into nights. Such is our lives."

"You're telling me," chuckled Hudson as he hit the "End" button on his phone.

*****

As he calculated his plot, Racheed knew he would have to sacrifice his life for it. However, as he stood on the cusp, he chose not to think of that possibility. His radical Islamic devotion led him to believe he was destined for a higher place in the afterlife, regardless of the outcome. As he hung up with Maria, he barely thought that it may be the last time he would ever speak to her.

Likewise, as he locked the door to his family home, walked to the garage, and hopped in his Toyota, it never occurred to him that he may never do those things again. He was too preoccupied with his plan, and anxious to get underway.

His focus nearly caused an accident on the way to the airport. Lost in thought, he came dangerously close to clipping a bicyclist on the crowded avenues of Karachi. The man on the cycle shouted a profanity, but his cursing was lost in the din of the city, and Racheed's mind was too busy to notice. He also did not notice the sedan in his rearview mirror that carried three CIA agents.

Finally, he reached the airport, checked in for his flight, and headed to the airport bar. Once a teetotaler, Racheed now indulged whenever he felt like it. He set up his laptop on the bar table, never spying the three agents who appeared to be Pakistani nationals watching his every move. He swiftly headed for the tarmac, and his flight left exactly on time.

One of the agents dialed Foster on his cell phone. “He's on the plane.”

“All right,” replied Foster. He held the phone to his chest to muffle his voice and turned to his subordinates, scattered around the office. “He just boarded a flight to London. Probably heading toward Mexico City,” he told them as he called Jack Hudson, who already had an idea, since Garcia had also called him with the news.

The cell phones of the CIA and FBI were buzzing. Hudson was notified in El Paso, and the American law enforcement and intelligence network across the continent began receiving word. In Washington, the top administrators at FBI headquarters were updated on their earlier briefings from Hudson, while in the CIA offices, efforts were made to ensure coordination among their agents in both the United States and Mexico.

Jack Hudson and Greg Foster, directing the efforts from their bases on both sides of the border, were two of the best their respective agencies had to offer. Their high levels of competence made the brass in Washington feel somewhat better. Both kept their superiors well-informed and followed procedure at every turn, so there was nothing left for the striped suits in the capital to do but wait.

Homeland Security was also in the loop, and their officials pledged their assistance whenever needed. Since the plot was so comprehensive, word also filtered up to the White House, where the President's top security advisors briefed the commander-in-chief of the threat, and the steps to address it.

Of the over 300 million citizens of the United States, only a small handful are ever aware of terrorist plots. It is no different in cases that are infiltrated, as Racheed's. As a result, on this late summer day, millions of Americans, including those near Racheed's targets, went about their daily business, going to work, taking their kids to school, and chit-chatting around the water cooler.

While there was no cause for concern for the average citizen, there was plenty of reason for officials to worry. Though Hudson and Foster kept their men on top of the situation, and personnel in several cities were on alert, there were no guarantees. All it took was for one terrorist to slip through the cracks with an explosive, and scores of innocent people could be lost. Even if the defenses held up in most places, any weakness in one could be catastrophic. The authorities had done their best to ensure the safety of the American people, but as they had seen in the past, nothing was a sure bet.

*****

It was not unusual for Racheed Ul-Bashar to be lost in thought while in-flight. He was normally a sullen individual, within himself at nearly all times. As his plane streaked through the skies over the oceans toward Mexico on this September 4, though, he could hardly distract himself from his thoughts of his plan.

It was now over nine months since Omar and Sasha's deaths, early last December. As he recalled each step of his efforts since then, his self-assurance grew. Part of him was proud that he had concocted such an elaborate, sophisticated operation that spanned several countries and required such intricate planning. But he also remembered his grandfather and sister. *Their losses must be avenged*, he thought. *All of the suffering I am about to inflict. Americans will pay in blood.* The mere image of those hated infidels, lying on the streets and in the rubble, brought a smile to his face.

Bit by bit, piece by piece, he reviewed each step, mentally confirming the details of what would happen, where and who, down to the last second. His plot was months in the making, and had required immense emotional effort. Most days, his plans were the first thing he thought of when he awoke and the last thing before he slept. For most men, it would have exacted a tremendous toll, but Racheed was hardly worn. He was invigorated, stronger than ever, more focused. His body and mind could barely shut down at night, waiting for the morrow and the next steps toward his goal.

Now, mere days from the bombings, he could not keep from smiling. That in itself was unusual, as Racheed's family and friends all spoke of how seldom his face carried a smile. A British businessman, sitting in the seat across the aisle, turned and asked, "what's so funny?"

Racheed simply shook his head. "I don't think you would understand."

"Try me," chuckled the man. "I could use a good laugh."

Racheed smiled once more and turned his head toward the window. The clouds raced by underneath, giving way to a brilliant blue, streaked with white sunlight. He knew these may be his last days on Earth, but he did not care. His eyes fixated on the blinding light punctuated by the bluest of blues, and for a moment, just a moment, he thought he saw a higher place. *I am headed there*, he thought, *this place of peace, this highest of callings. Allah would be served, and I will reap my greatest reward in the afterlife*.

The Airbus could not reach Mexico City fast enough, and while most passengers curled up as best they could, Racheed had no interest in sleep. Twice, a stewardess offered him a pillow, and twice he declined. The approach call to fasten seat belts came in the middle of the night, and the attendants went from seat to seat, gently jostling the occupants to awaken and tend to their belts. Racheed needed no such prodding.

Fortunately for Racheed, there would be only a one-hour layover, as an early-morning flight to Cuidad Juarez was about to depart. Gazing blankly at the terminal walls, he never noticed three CIA agents, dressed as businessmen in dark sport coats and Armani slacks, who were keeping an eye on him.

The layover gave him just enough time to visit the airport bar for a sandwich and a drink. Once again, he saw no reason to avoid the hard stuff. He recalled his old college roommate, Ahmed, with whom he had argued the virtues of Muslim abstinence. Now, he called for a whiskey and raised his glass.

"Here's to you, Ahmed," he said out loud, to no one in particular. "Stupid bastard."

The bartender turned and looked at him, thinking he had either served a drunk or a lunatic. “Sorry,” said Racheed. “Just a little tired, I guess.”

“No problem,” said the bartender. “I get people in here a lot crazier than you.”

Racheed bristled and looked down at his glass. He saw the bartender was wearing a cross necklace, and his rage simmered. *Another Christian,* thought Racheed. *Someone who sees himself as better than us. If he's so damned great, then why's he tending bar in some airport?*

He's just the type that must pay, pondered Racheed. *This is the kind, someone who looks down his nose at me, just because his God tells him to.* Racheed clutched his glass tighter and tighter as the resentment flowed through his head. *Dumb ass bartender probably loves Americans, just like the rest of Mexicans do. He'd probably laugh at Omar and Sasha. Too bad he won't be visiting the U.S. in a couple of days. He could suffer like the rest of them.*

Racheed banged his glass down on the table, tempted to pick a fistfight with the bartender. But his restraint prevailed, knowing that if he were arrested now, the plot would fail before it even started. He also knew that any trouble could arouse suspicion, and he wanted to get to Juarez as quickly and quietly as possible.

He then realized he should not have slammed his glass. He glanced over his shoulder at the bartender, who was nowhere to be found. Finally, he reappeared from a back storeroom, oblivious to Racheed's tantrum. “Have a good day, senor,” he chirped.

“Yeah,” replied Racheed brusquely. Seconds later, the final call for his flight sounded. It was Flight 93. Racheed smiled at the irony, remembering the flight of the same name that crashed in Pennsylvania on September 11. The grin spread across his face, and stayed there as he boarded the DC-9 for the short junket.

Two hours later, he was on the ground in Ciudad Juarez, where he checked into a luxury hotel. Usually, his visits to Juarez were spent in a economy lodging, but a man of his stature deserved only the best, and that meant the nicest accommodations. After all, it was Ali

Sighn's money, not his.

He would not get much time in his room for his money, but that was unimportant. There were bigger things to deal with. Finally, he took a few hours for sleep, drifting off with the same self-assured grin.

Around noon, he was jarred from sleep by the telephone. It was Diego Garcia, about to arrive with a ride to the safe house. Since Racheed had not taken the time to unpack, there was no effort in getting ready to leave. He was standing at the door when Garcia knocked, and the two men exchanged an embrace. Racheed clasped his hands on Diego's face and offered a warm greeting of friendship. Garcia, burdened by his deceit, managed only a smile in return.

Waiting outside was one of Rodrequs' black Hummers. Garcia got behind the wheel, though Racheed noticed he seemed a little more edgy than normal. He was also sweating heavily, as perspiration soaked his polo shirt. Racheed, though, chalked it up to the ninety-degree heat and the same adrenaline flowing through his own veins.

CHAPTER XXVII

As they drove to the safe house, few words were exchanged. Racheed was his usual introverted self, while Garcia stared straight through the windshield, fearing any little slip-up. To have reached the highest levels of the cartel, Diego Garcia had to be proficient at lying. But now his life, and Rosa's, depended on it. He chose to remain silent and answer only when spoken to.

Racheed thought nothing of it, since he was not particularly interested in anything Garcia had to say, anyway. He was content within himself, thoughts focused on the coming days. Finally, they arrived at the safe house, a single-story, brown slab structure down a dead-end street in a secluded area of Juarez. Few, if any, cars made it down this street, and there were no signs of neighbors. Two men slouched against a broken lamp post, downward faces masked by oversized floppy hats.

Since Racheed was distrusting by nature and this was his first time in seeing the safe house, the sight of the two derelicts elicited alarm. He turned to Garcia, who responded before he even heard the question. “They are Rodrequs' men,” he said. “They are posted as undercover guards, to protect the safe house. To the untrained eye, they are just a couple of locals. But they each carry two pistols and a ten-inch knife, and are not afraid to use them."

Racheed sat back, knowing that Rodrequs meant business when he called it a "safe house." The guards each nodded at Garcia as he drove by, then turned their faces downward once more. Garcia drove the Hummer around to the rear of the safe house and parked. The men exited the vehicle, and Garcia rapped on the back door in cadence, as if to signal. Adeeb, the first of the terrorists to arrive in Mexico, welcomed Garcia and Racheed inside.

As Racheed entered, each terrorist bowed deeply to him, then stepped forward to place their hands on his face, as if Racheed were a visiting deity. He relished his newfound stature. "Now our time is near," he solemnly declared. "You each know what you must do. I have trained you for this purpose, and you have accepted our mission. You know that a higher place awaits those who sacrifice. But it must be done, for ourselves, for our people, for Allah."

He then positioned himself on a colorful mat in the center of the room. "We must pray," he said, dropping to his knees. The next several minutes were spent in the traditional honoring of Allah, each man chanting and gesturing with unusual intensity. Though he had witnessed Muslim prayer before, Garcia stood in a corner, awestruck at the spectacle. He knew this would be one of the final times he would see his new friends, but they never seemed to care. They had accepted their fate, whatever it may be.

Moments after the prayers were concluded, Racheed heard the sound of another Hummer approaching. Spying a pistol on a table by the door, he clutched it and stood ready. He cautiously peered out an adjacent window, then exhaled a deep sigh of relief. The vehicle carried Juan Rodrequs, who sprang from the side door, teeth surrounding a huge cigar.

Racheed let Rodrequs execute the signal knock, then opened the door himself. "Hello, my friend," roared Rodrequs, who saw the pistol in Racheed's hand, now pointing downward. He screamed in laughter and pointed to Racheed, as if to mock him to everyone in the room. "Our friend is nervous!" he shouted between gulps of laughter. "Do you always greet your guests this way?"

Other men may have been humiliated at the scene, but Racheed quickly collected himself. "As you know, my friend," he replied. "You can never be too careful. Besides, what if you had been a half-ass American drug agent?"

"Half-ass American? That's the only kind!" Rodrequs' laughter was so loud that it echoed off the walls. He then calmed, his toothy grin dominating his pockmarked face. "It is good to see you, my friend," he said, clutching Racheed's shoulders with oversized hands and dirty fingernails. "I see that you had a safe flight?"

"Yes, my friend," said Racheed. "It was like any other." As usual, his mind then returned to the task at hand. "Is our plan still in order?"

"Very much so," replied Rodrequs. "Nothing has changed. We are ready to go!"

"Then I am glad," said Racheed. "But I have a favor to ask of you first."

"Name it. Anything you wish, anything at all. You know I have the means to make it happen!" Rodrequs seized any and every opportunity to brag.

Racheed slowly turned his neck as if on a swivel, eyeing each of his men one-by-one. He was on an emotional high, his normally sullen persona pushed aside. "I would like to arrange a party for all of us," he declared. "We have all worked very hard, and for the last few weeks, our lives have been barren. We have had little contact with friends, family, anyone."

He brushed his hand, to draw attention to the young terrorists ringing the room. "These men need to relax, have some fun. Our task is nearly at hand. But I see no reason why we cannot take a few hours and enjoy life."

"Nor do I," said Rodrequs, again howling in laughter. "We should all have a little fun. God knows I am one who likes the pleasures." He slid his open palms up and down by each side of his body, as if his pudgy appearance was that of one virile and handsome. "I am only a man, after all."

Racheed smiled, and the terrorists giggled like schoolboys. "Then will you give us what we need?" He had asked such questions in his initial meetings with Rodrequs, in reference to deadly weapons. Now, his "need" was of an earthy nature.

Rodrequs saw the irony, and his toothy grin became a smirk. Never one to decline a good time, he said the words Racheed wanted to hear. "I will send for my best women." He motioned to Garcia to make the call. "I will also share some of my best drinks, beer that was made personally for me," he said, voice rising to a yell with hands waving, "for all of my good friends!"

The men cheered their host, and within an hour, a black van was pulling up to the back door. Two men jumped out, carrying twelve cases of the finest Mexican beer, in clear bottles and ice cold. The cases were barely on the floor when the men pounced on them like children with free candy.

A few minutes later, another van was heard outside. Racheed went to the window and saw nine young Mexican women tumble out, barely clothed. Some were wearing halters and short, skin-tight skirts, while others were dressed in long, clingy T-shirts and torn jeans. All had dark, flowing hair with heavy makeup. Several had glassy, hollow eyes.

Rodrequs stood by Racheed, clearly enjoying the view, and met them at the door. "Buenos dias, ladies!" he screamed. "My friends and I want to have a good time!" He turned toward the most scantily clad of the group. "Juanita!" he summoned.

As Juanita stepped forth, Rodrequs found a recliner and sat back, clutching his beer. Juanita positioned herself on his lap. "The rest of you," exclaimed Rodrequs to the other ladies, "see to it that our guests are taken care of!" He turned to Diego and cooed, "We've got one for you, too!"

Still a happily married man, Garcia simply shook his head. "Very well, my friend," laughed Rodrequs. "*That makes two for me!*" Another of the women sauntered toward Rodrequs, stood behind his chair, and ran her fingers through his hair. Juanita swayed on his lap and ran her hand down and inside his camouflage trousers.

Each of the terrorists joined up with a woman and slipped into various corners of the room. Their normally dour personalities melted into the alcohol, and they laughed with each giggle and caress of their new partners. Their wandering hands returned the favor and flirtations gave way to clutches and squeezes. Eventually, the women led them into the bedrooms, and they were not seen again for the rest of the evening. While the rest succumbed to primal desires, Garcia sat in a corner, nursing his beer, spurning the advances of the amorous visitors.

Racheed was never one to party, but tonight there was no reason to refrain. The previous months had been a trial, though one that he had enjoyed to the utmost. Now, as his dreams were on the cusp, he let himself go. A sultry escort named Vendela planted herself on Racheed's lap, stroking his face and chest. She giggled at his jokes, and smiled at his every turn. As the drinks piled up, she gave him a lap dance.

He had not been with a woman in weeks, since his last night with Maria. Now, aroused by his new acquaintance, thoughts of her kisses were barely in his mind. He was a man, and had desires. Maria was not here, and he owed her nothing, anyway.

As Vendela rose, she took his hand and pulled him toward a bedroom. Once inside, she pushed him onto the bed, stretched across him, and unbuttoned his shirt. He offered no resistance as she ran her lips down his body to his belt.

She sensuously unbuckled him and removed the rest of his clothing. He laid back, watching with visual pleasure as she pulled off her halter and shorts. She then threw herself on him, kissing and stroking every part of him as only a woman of her vocation could. Racheed relished every moment, every fondle, every thrust, and when it was over, felt nothing but the afterglow. The pinnacle of his life was only days away, and there was every reason to feel like a man.

CHAPTER XXVIII

The safe house was quiet well into the morning of September 6, as the effects of heavy drink and heated interludes were too much to overcome by daybreak. Eventually, Racheed and his men untangled themselves from their newfound partners, got themselves dressed, and heated black coffee on the stove. The ladies pulled on their slinky attire, and some withdrew from their purses a little clear plastic bag with a white, powder-like substance. They quickly shook a little onto the dressers, grabbed straws, and snorted. They threw their heads back, and rolled their eyes.

Rodrequs was standing at the door as they filed out, each planting a juicy kiss on their top client. He handed each of them a large wad of bills, and they giggled as schoolgirls as they headed to the van. The cartel leader then addressed the terrorists, standing around holding plastic cups of coffee with bloodshot eyes. "Ah, my men. You look like a pile of garbage!" he laughed. "You must have had a very good night. *I know I did!*"

He strolled over to Racheed and whispered something in his ear. Racheed, half-awake as the rest, nodded. Rodrequs then turned back to the men. “Refresh yourselves. I will be back this afternoon at four, to discuss the final plans with you.”

By now, it was nearly ten o'clock. Rodrequs, who naturally had partaken more than the others, stumbled out the door and into his waiting Hummer. The terrorists sank into the easy chairs that were now strewn about, scooted out of place in their drunken escapades. One reached for the television remote, and they spent the next couple of hours easing their throbbing heads by watching a soccer match.

Their constitutions improved over the next six hours, helped by a hearty lunch of sandwiches and curry that Racheed whipped up in the kitchenette. By early afternoon, they were their old selves, and their focus had returned. They pulled on fresh clothes, their favorite Nike and Tommy Hilfiger casual wear. The wild night was just a memory, and they had a job ahead of them. They became introverted, reflective, ready for the ultimate sacrifice, if that is what Allah wished.

The chimes on the wall clock bonged four times and Rodrequs' vehicle was heard outside. After the signal knocks, he burst through the door with his usual bravado. Garcia meekly followed, several steps behind. “Buenos dias, my friends!” Rodrequs exclaimed. “You look as if you have recovered well from last night. You looked like hell when I left you!”

He roared with laughter, always seeing the hilarity in his jokes. The terrorists, however, only mustered a chuckle. Unless he was supplying them like last night, they saw little humor in Juan Rodrequs. He was merely their bank, their source of cash and materials. Rodrequs, though, was too self-absorbed to notice or care.

“Welcome, my friend,” said Racheed, who made no secret of his attachment to Rodrequs. He embraced the cartel leader as a brother, patting his scarred cheeks. “It is finally our time.”

“That it is,” responded Rodrequs, a wide grin exploding off his face. He bowed slightly and extended his arm, mocking a stage introduction. “I turn it over to you, my man.”

The terrorists formed a semi-circle around Racheed, dropping to the floor with legs crossed in front of them. “First,” said Racheed, "we must pray."

The Pakistanis then passed the next several minutes in their usual intense devotion. Rodrequs, who never spent a day in church, turned to Garcia several times, grinning condescendingly. He threw his portly frame into an easy chair in the corner and fired up a Cuban. Garcia, whose Christianity had revived since his arrest, offered no expression and grasped a cross necklace that he had pulled from his dresser. He curled up on the floor, next to his boss, to listen for anything to relay to Jack Hudson.

*****

As their prayers concluded, each man had a sense of inner peace, in contrast to the violence they were about to discuss. "My men," Racheed opened. "Our finest moment is now at hand. It is the time that we will serve our families, our people, our Allah."

Each man stared intently as Racheed, standing erectly as if he was actually a military man. Dressed in camouflage and holding a tablet, he looked the part of a warrior, ready for combat. The terrorists sat in awe of their new friend, hanging on his every utterance. Each had a laptop, with which to take notes.

"Now, we must review our plans. Our friends, Juan and Diego will supply us with what we need. There will be weapons, materials to make bombs, and vehicles ready and waiting for us once we cross the border." Since the terrorists had not yet seen the tunnel or the auto repair shop, he provided a little background.

"There is a tunnel that will take us from Mexico, underneath the Rio Grande River, into the United States. The tunnel is completely safe, well-lighted, and able to handle our needs. We enter the tunnel in one of Juan's warehouses, and it will take us into a shop where automobiles are repaired. There is no reason for any of us to fear. The tunnel is secret, and secure. We have no enemies in the warehouse, or the repair shop. They are all our friends."

Each man busily typed the information into his laptop. Racheed divulged more of his plan. "We will work in two-man teams," he continued. "Since there are six of us, that means there will be three teams. I will assign them as such."

Racheed turned and looked at the two men to his immediate left. "You are one team. We will call you Team One," He then turned to the two at his right. "You are Team Two." Adeeb was sitting in the middle. "And you will be my partner. We are Team Three." Each man nodded solemnly to Racheed, then to each other. "Your partner is your brother," remarked Racheed. "You will do whatever is necessary to protect him."

He explained that, once the crossing was complete, bomb vests would be placed under the rear seat of each vehicle. Each terrorist was responsible for making his own bomb vest.

"The vests and the explosives for them are in the warehouse, where you will go later on," explained Racheed. "However, I will not wear one of those." He reached into a box on the floor behind him and withdrew a well-worn man's cool-weather vest, khaki in color.

"Instead, I will wear this one," he said. "This was one of the vests my grandfather made in his shop back home. I was able to save this one from the rubble of his property. I will wear this in his honor as I carry out our mission, and enjoy my reward." Each man bowed reverently.

"Now, let us discuss the timing of our attack." Racheed eyeballed each man, analyzing their attentiveness. As he saw their focus, their commitment, he reaffirmed in his mind his complete control as their leader. "It is now September 6. We are just about to approach an important date..."

His words were interrupted by a loud gasp of collective excitement as cheers erupted in the room. "September 11 is approaching," said Racheed, bursting into an uncharacteristic smile. "That is a time of reverence for our people. Now, we will honor that date with our own attack."

The terrorists looked at each other as boys at a circus. Their eyes were wide, faces radiant, mouths agape. As the moment sunk in, their laughter erupted, and some jumped to their feet, clapping and pumping their fists. They were anxious for the attack, but had not expected to make their move at such a crucial time. Now, elation overwhelmed their senses.

Racheed was even caught in the tide and high-fived Adeeb and a couple of the others. But his focus quickly returned, and he directed the others to quiet down. Like obedient schoolchildren, they closed their mouths and dropped to the floor, reaching for their laptops.

"Let us continue with our discussion," said Racheed, sharpness permeating his voice. "We will cross the border at midnight on September 9. That will give us ample time to reach our destinations."

He turned to his left, at Team One. "Once you are across the border, you will travel to Las Vegas. Your goal is to bomb Caesar's Palace. You are aware of what that is?"

The two men of Team One were certainly aware, as was everyone else in the room. Racheed had drilled the significance of Las Vegas into their collective memory during training, and they were well aware of the virtues, or lack thereof, of the aptly named Sin City from CNN and the Internet.

"Caesar's Palace is the symbol, representing heinous capitalism and filthy vice," derided Racheed. "Gambling, sex, drinking, adultery, waste of money, destruction of family, all are wrapped up in that city. Their motto is `what happens in Las Vegas, stays in Las Vegas.' Now, I ask you, my brothers. What type of society, what type of country, is proud of such a slogan? What infidels! It will be a pleasure to blow it up and take its worshippers with it."

From his easy chair, Rodrequs turned to Garcia and cocked his head with a mocking smile. As a man who had no issues with gambling, sex, and drinking, he saw the irony in the discussion. Garcia responded with a quick smile and turned away.

Racheed's hatred was beginning to color his stoicism, and he forced a stifling of his feelings. "Las Vegas is 750 miles away," he said. "It will take approximately fifteen hours to reach. You will want to share the driving, and rest while your partner is behind the wheel. You must be fresh and ready for your mission once it is time."

He turned and reached into the box. "Here is a GPS device," he said, handing it to Team One. "That will help you find the most direct route. And if that does not work..."

He reached back into the box and pulled out a road map. “This simple paper will help you.” Each man chuckled at the wry joke and the thought of using a map, like some backward Americans still did.

Racheed did not join the snickering, instead relaying information on lodging. “You have a room waiting for you at the Vegas Motor Inn. Here is the name you will use to check in.” He handed the terrorists several forms of false identification. The hours spent in solitude on his laptop were serving Racheed well. He had learned how to create fake documents and identification cards, and his best work would now be shown to unsuspecting Americans.

“While in Las Vegas, prepare yourselves as best you can for the attack,” directed Racheed. “Scout around, study the surrounding areas, acclimate yourselves with the area. I have made these plans with the utmost precision. But you will need to be familiar with the areas once you are there as well.

“You will use your cell phones to keep in touch with me at all times,” Racheed said, nodding toward Garcia as he would supply the phones, with a secret little attachment from Jack Hudson. He rifled through a sheaf of papers on his clipboard to reach a computer printout with an aerial view of the blocks surrounding Caesar's Palace. “I have analyzed the area around the target,” he mused. “Here is what I have found.”

Racheed summoned the terrorists to stand and crowd around him, so they could see the clipboard. He pointed to the front entrance to the casino. “Here is your target. Park your vehicle as close to the front entrance as you can. If you think you can leave the car in the drop-off circle right outside the door, by all means do so.

“There will be a large bomb in the rear seat. You will make the bomb yourself, using the skills that were taught to you in our training session back home. We will review those later today. The bomb is large, with enough power to inflict incredible damage. Only fifty pounds of these C-4 explosives are needed.”

He paused with a condescending chuckle. “It does not sound like much, to be sure. But this type of bomb is stronger than many of the explosives used by the armies of the world, capable of devastating effect."

He looked straight at the two men of Team One. "Use your remote devices to make the vehicle bomb explode. The strength of this bomb will wreak destruction like Las Vegas has never seen before," he said in rising tone. "The power of this bomb will demolish nearly half of the facade of the building. People standing in their windows on the tenth floor will be blown back across their beds."

"The concussion will annihilate the front doors and kill people standing at the back of the lobby. A huge fireball will burn everything that is close. The falling debris will be blown for hundreds, thousands of yards. Vehicles in the parking lot will be blazing. The debris field will make it difficult for rescue trucks to approach. I am talking about thousands of lives lost, thousands more injured and suffering."

His body trembled with enthusiasm. "Prior to the detonation, here is what I want," he continued. He reached back into the box and withdrew a large glass dish, similar to a salad bowl. "You will fill this bin with nails, screws, jagged metal pieces, ball bearings, broken glass, anything that is sharp, or heavy. I have assembled a large collection of sharp instruments that I will provide to you later on.

"When the bomb explodes, shrapnel will be thrown in every direction, and will maim and injure countless more bodies. People will be cut, bleeding, blinded, with severed limbs, shattered bones. The shrapnel will have a devastating impact, in addition to the inferno."

Now breathless, he paused to inhale. As he did, Rodrequs raised two fists in the air and opened his palms with a flourish, as if to imitate explosions. He threw his head back, mouth opened in a silent roar of laughter. Nothing in the discussion disturbed him, a man who lived by violence. Garcia pretended not to notice his antics.

Neither did Racheed, who continued to look Team One in their eyes. Their returning gaze was wide, adoring, enchanted. "Use your explosives wisely, so the blast causes as much damage and terror as possible. As the panic ensues, position yourselves somewhere nearby, in a casino next door, or someplace like that."

A devilish grin spread across Racheed's face. "People will likely be running to find shelter nearby, so find the place that holds the most people. Then, detonate your bomb vests. That will cause a second explosion that will kill many more Americans. Pack your vests with shrapnel as well, to cause even more damage."

He finally paused. "You know that you will not return from this mission. But know that as you give your lives, you may be certain of your higher place in the afterlife. As you prepare to leave this world, accept my thanks and deepest gratitude, knowing that you have given your lives to our Father."

"For Allah. For Allah," the men chanted in unison. "Praise be his name."

"Very well. Please be seated, my friends," said Racheed, mustering good manners unusual to his persona. He ordered Team One to download the same photographs of Caesar's Palace to maintain on their laptops, for future reference. He handed one team member an envelope containing cash for travel expenses such as lodging and gas.

"One other thing," added Racheed. "Be sure to dress like Americans at all times. Wear sweatshirts, T-shirts, those pants they call jeans, or even shorts. Your vests are just like any regular clothing, and will not attract attention. Do not wear our native dress. We want to become part of the crowds, not stand out among them."

He finally stopped. "My brothers. Do you have any questions?" They shook their heads and bowed at Racheed, who offered a solemn wish. "Then may Allah be with you." From his corner, Juan Rodrequs pressed his upright hands together and bowed his head in mock prayer. Diego Garcia again clutched the cross dangling from his necklace.

*****

"Now, for the second part of our mission." Racheed's eyes met those of Team Two, eagerly awaiting his instructions. Those team members leaned forward as far as they could over their crossed legs, anxious as if schoolchildren waiting for the bell.

He nodded respectfully to them. "You will travel to South Dakota, to the place they call Mount Rushmore. "I presume that you know the significance of the mountain to Americans?" Both nodded, as they were certainly familiar. Their childhood schooling of other nations of the world, a topic of study in many other countries but rarely broached by Americans, had introduced them to the four Presidents whose likenesses were carved in the mountain. Continued exposure to western cable television and the web further instilled the meaning.

Then, he veered a little. "I saw Mount Rushmore once, when I was in college. It was nothing but a pile of rocks, ugly rocks, bearing the faces of men who built America. Men who are revered by Americans, and for what? It was their vision that created American power, arrogance, evil. It will give me immense pleasure to see that site desecrated."

In his corner, Rodrequs drew his cigar from his mouth and blew a large puff of smoke through his lips. He then waved bye-bye to no one in particular as Racheed settled himself. "I know that we will not inflict the great damage at Rushmore that we will in Las Vegas. There are fewer people, and fewer buildings. But it will be a psychological blow to them. We will strike at their history, their shrines, and forever tarnish them."

The terrorists shook with enthusiasm. "It is twelve hundred miles away," said Racheed. "That is around a twenty-four-hour drive. You will arrive early in the morning of September 10. You must take turns driving, as you must be completely rested for your mission. Do not fail to be fresh for your moment." He handed each of them false identifications as well. "I have rented a room for you at the Presidents Motor Hotel. Use your identifications as you check in, and once there, become familiar with the area that you will attack," he said. The terrorists guffawed at the irony of the name of the inn. They also received their GPS devices, road maps, and cash for travel.

Again, Racheed flipped through his clipboard to find an aerial photo of the Mount Rushmore visitor center. He again summoned the terrorists to encircle him. "Here is your target. You will strike the visitor center. We will do this in the same fashion as in Las Vegas."

Racheed slid his finger across the photo to the parking spaces nearest the center. "You will park your vehicle here, as close to the visitor center as you can. By doing so, the vehicle bomb will detonate in a spot that will inflict the most chaos.

"That bomb is the same strength that we will use in Las Vegas," boasted Racheed. "but the visitor center is a much smaller building than Caesar's Palace. The explosion will have so much power that most of the center will be reduced to glass and rubble. Anyone sitting or standing near the entrance will die or be maimed by shrapnel, which you will also use."

He paused. "As I said, this will have a damaging effect on American morale. Mount Rushmore is cherished to them, and will have a tremendous negative impact. I think even more so than Las Vegas." He permitted himself another smile. "I only wish I could make a bomb large enough to blow those faces off the mountain."

The terrorists giggled in unison. As usual, Racheed's lapses were momentary. "You will do as your brothers at Las Vegas will. As in Las Vegas, your bombs should be constructed well enough, and you must be far enough away when you detonate, that you will have time to move away safely.

"Then, move to another area of the property, to wherever the panicked Americans are congregating." he continued. "There, you will set off your bomb vests. You must make sure that you are positioned in a crowd of people, as I have told your brothers in Las Vegas to do. Pack your pockets with shrapnel, to add to the destruction."

His voice then slowed. "Those will be your final moments on Earth. You leave with my greatest respect and appreciation for your sacrifice, because you do so for our Father, to serve Him."

The instructions were now complete for two of the attacks. "Do you have any questions, my brothers?" Racheed asked of Team Two. As before, they nodded negatively, and received their bosses' blessing. "Then may Allah be with you."

"Praise be to Allah," they chanted. "Praise to his name." Rodrequs pretended to play the violin in tongue-in-cheek, mauldin protest, failing to notice Garcia's stone face.

*****

“And now,” Racheed declared, “here is what Adeeb and I will do,” The members of Team Two backed away, and offered their respect to Adeeb as he deliberately rose and stood next to Racheed.

Racheed turned his head, acknowledged Adeeb, and briefly embraced him. Sliding his arms away from Adeeb's body, he resumed the discussion. “We will travel to Nashville, and attack their downtown, on the street they call Broadway. It is my belief that this will be the largest, and most difficult, part of our plan.

“For one thing, we have the farthest distance. It is 1,300 miles away, and will take us nearly twenty-six hours of driving to arrive. So we must be physically and mentally fit. We must take turns driving, since we will not stop, as you will not.” Racheed was customarily exaggerating his own importance. The distance to Nashville was no greater than that of the other targets.

The starstruck terrorists offered no reprise of their leader. “I have chosen Adeeb because I am impressed with his focus, his determination, his desire. He is a model for the rest of you to follow.” Adeeb shifted his body to stand straight at Racheed and bowed deeply upon the compliment from his leader. The other terrorists rose and in turn bowed to Adeeb, as if annoited by Racheed.

As in the previous weeks, a surge flowed through Racheed's veins at the respect from his subordinates. He shuffled his papers to find an aerial security photo of the Broadway district in Nashville, which he had hacked from an online police file. The photo had considerably more detail than a mere Google Earth search. The terrorists, still standing, again crowded around the clipboard.

“Allow me to explain the significance of this attack on Nashville,” Racheed mused. “Nashville is in the heartland, in the mid-South region of the U.S. You may wonder why I did not choose New York City, the largest and most important of their cities, as our martyred brothers did. It is because that is where an attack would be most expected, especially on September 11, this most honored of dates.

“There will be less emphasis on Nashville,” continued Racheed. “It is a city in the heartland, where security is looser. And the psychological impact will be greater, if the Americans suffer a massive attack on their midsection."

He ran his fingers up and down the photo of Broadway, across the buildings on either side. "You have heard of country music?" inquired Racheed. The terrorists winced, remembering the twang and right-wing message. "This is the center of it. This is Broadway, where many of their musicians train. This stretch is full of taverns, clubs, and, what do you call them? Honky-tonks." Again, the terrorists giggled as teenagers.

"I am as you. I loathe that music," declared Racheed. "When I was in university in Texas, that is all those people played. It was on every radio, in every store, in every restaurant. It is the sound of America to me, a sound of evil. So I want to strike at its very core, to remind Americans every time they turn on their radios and hear that damned sound, that we have hit them."

As they had all afternoon, the terrorists shook with anticipation, eagerly waiting the next part of the discussion. Racheed had not disappointed them yet.

"So here is what I will do," he said. "I will park the vehicle in the busiest part of the street, nearest the most crowded bars. I will then detonate my vehicle bomb. This will be the most powerful of our bombs. It will spread a massive fireball, enough to level rows of buildings, and will throw jagged, flaming debris for nearly a half-mile. Like you, I will enhance my bomb with piles of shrapnel, to cut, burn, maim many more."

Racheed's dramatic diction was not only motivating his men, but also himself. "Anyone standing within several hundred feet of the vehicle will be at risk, as will those inside the clubs and taverns. There will be no way for them to escape, and those that do not die instantly will do so painfully. The street will be so cluttered with rubble and remains that emergency vehicles will not be able to reach the wounded. I can only imagine the destruction that I will create."

He continually omitted the "we" part, speaking only in the first person. His partner, Adeeb, stood at his side, no trace of emotion on his face.

"My grandfather gave his life for our Father, and I as well," he said, equally lacking emotion. "We will position ourselves in the most crowded building that we may find, among the most panic and the most chaos. I will then set off my grandfather's vest in his memory, the last thing that I shall do on this Earth." He hesitated in reflection of his self-admiration, then awkwardly added, "Adeeb will do the same. Our bomb vests will create the same death, the destruction, devastation as you in your respective missions."

He lowered his head for effect and made direct eye contact with each of his soldiers. "My brothers. Do you have any questions?" None arose. Now on his third Cuban in his easy chair, Rodrequs whipped a cell phone from his pocket, barked an order, and hung up.

The discussion shifted to the timing of the blasts. "Like every other aspect of our plan, I have given this a great deal of thought," Racheed pondered. "It is my strong desire to coordinate these blasts at a set time. That will have the same effect as the attacks on 9/11, when our brothers struck their World Trade Center and the Pentagon at virtually the same moment. I want our plan to throw the nation into chaos. The Americans will barely have learned of one attack when news of another, and still another, is received. They will be confused, and terrified. They will not know what is going on, or if something worse is coming.

His words were delivered with a reverent tone, both for the image of September 11 and for his own plan. He continued, his audience riveted to his every word as he paced back and forth. "I cannot stress enough to you the importance of coordination. We must make sure the bombs detonate around the same time. That will ensure maximum effect for the damage we wish to inflict. If we fail in that, our entire efforts will fail as well." He stopped abruptly, shot a menacing glare at his soldiers, and spoke in a cool tone. "And let me remind you, my brothers. Failure is not an option."

The men nodded, their message clear. "There is a two-hour time difference between our points of attack, but that is not the primary concern. What *is* a concern is the time of day that each site will have the most traffic. Caesar's Palace is busiest at night, as is Broadway in

Nashville. But the Mount Rushmore site will be closed by then, and none but the park workers will be there.

"So I have decided on a time of day that will cause the most harm," he continued. "I want to strike at 4 p.m. in the Central Time Zone, which includes Nashville. It would then be 3 p.m. at Mount Rushmore and 2 p.m. at Caesar's Palace. I concede to you, my brothers, that is not the optimal time to strike in Las Vegas. But it will be more favorable in the other two cities.

"Also, I think this could add an element of fear to Americans across the nation. News of the strikes will be received as people are leaving work, and they will be frightened as they drive home. Their children may be at home alone, waiting for them, and will be very frightened at hearing of a terror attack without their parents' comfort. It is my hope that the shock of the news will be intensified as people are alone in their cars, or surrounded by strangers on buses. They will be more apprehensive, fearful of what we are doing."

Racheed's monotone rose with each sentence, and as he concluded, he had taken his own breath away. He took several seconds not only for effect, but to draw some air. "Are there any questions?" None arose from the terrorists, whose awestruck eyes widened at the comprehensive brilliance of their leader. "Then let us pray once more." When prayer was over, the terrorists remained in their semicircle on the floor.

The moment was broken by the sound of two vehicles outside. Almost instantly, Racheed grabbed a machete and threw himself against the wall, peering out the window.

Rodrequs erupted in laughter. "Do not worry, my friend," he said, barely able to speak through his guffaws. "It is only our ride. I just called for it a minute ago."

Racheed exhaled deeply and shook his head, to remove the tension. He set the machete on a nearby table and returned to the moment at hand.

"Our friends will now take us to their weapons arsenal," he said. "There, they will distribute our personal arms and the explosives." Two vans resembling delivery vehicles were parked behind the safe house. Racheed recognized one of them as the van that had taken him, bound and gagged, to his first meetings with Rodrequs.

"I have had the weapons sent to my warehouse on the river," said Rodrequs. "Now, they are near the tunnel. That will save us time, rather than having to bring them from elsewhere. After all, time is money!"

He threw his head back and belched an animalistic roar, again impressed with his humor. The men lined up single file, as any military, and strode outside, surrounding either side of each van like soldiers. They boarded, and were chauffeured to the warehouse housing the entrance of the tunnel.

CHAPTER XXIX

Upon entering the warehouse, Racheed's typically observant tendencies spied something new. There was a carefully placed stack of wooden crates against the far wall. The crates were marked "supplies," and Rodrequs headed in that direction. "Here is what you need," he said, slowly extending his arm as if showing off something. "Diego will take care of the rest."

Like a puppy, Garcia followed almost on Rodrequs' heels. He set the top crate on the floor, grabbed a crowbar and pried it open. Inside were 9-millimeter pistols.

"Each of you will carry one of these," he said, providing one for each of the six terrorists. The men scrutinized their weapons, inspecting the barrels and triggers. Some pointed the guns at the wall, to mimic the act of shooting. Racheed smiled at their interest, and recalled the intensive weapons training he had subjected them to in Pakistan.

"These are some of my finest weapons!" chirped Rodrequs. "My men use these all the time, and they do the job *very* well!"

Garcia pulled another crate off the pile and opened it. Amid the clumps of shredded paper for cushioning were the six cell phones, each with tracking devices, that Jack Hudson had supplied.

Racheed chimed in. “These are your phones,” he explained. “They are highly secure, and state-of-the-art. You will use these to communicate once you are inside the United States. These are to be used only for this mission, and for nothing else. Do not call home or talk to anyone other than your brothers in your mission.”

Again, each man inspected the phones, turning them back and forth in their hands and glaring at the key pads. Garcia watched anxiously, hoping that no traces of the tracking devices would be detected. After several seconds, the men, one after the other, slid the phones into their pockets, never detecting any extra hardware.

Finally, Garcia motioned for the men to come forth to the remaining crates, which dwarfed the previous two. He pried one open to uncover a cache of C-4 explosives, used in the creation of weapons of destruction.

Racheed peered into the box with widened eyes. He had not yet seen the explosives that would be used in the attacks, and was eager for a glance. His comrades crowded around his shoulders, hoping for a peek as well. After several seconds, the men stepped back, an afterglow of awe on their faces. Then giddiness overcame them, and they high-fived one another, whooping and yelling.

The sight of the explosives overwhelmed Racheed's usual focus, and he was again caught in the moment, slapping hands and hugging his men. He then realized that a leader should not act in such an undignified manner, and stiffened his body at attention.

“All right!” he snapped. “You see the type of explosives we will be dealing with. We will use these to make bomb vests, and to build the vehicle bombs. You will remember the training given to you at home. Later, we will haul these explosives through the tunnel to the repair shop, where our vehicles should be waiting.”

He then turned to Rodrequs for confirmation. “Oh, yes,” said the cartel boss. “Your vehicles are ready and at your disposal. They are black sport-utility vehicles, older models so as not to attract attention. But they will do the job nicely. Made in the good old

U.S.A!" Now the terrorists found his humor funny, and laughed heartily.

"The vehicles are full of gas," continued Rodrequs. "and ready for you whenever you want them, and will take you wherever you desire." He flashed a devious grin. "And one more thing. There is no trace of identification on any of those vehicles. I have had my men grind off the identification numbers from the transmission, engine, and dashboards. Should something go wrong, your vehicles cannot be traced."

"Thank you, my friend," said Racheed, putting his hand on Rodrequs' beefy shoulder. "First, let us make the bomb vests."

That activity required only minimal time, as the Taliban had trained the men expertly for the task. Vests were pulled from a smaller crate set off to the side, and the men again lined up single-file, as waiting for a bank teller. They each withdrew a vest from the crate, and resembling an assembly line, returned to the storage unit of explosives.

Each man deliberately reached for the components and slipped them into the sides of the vest along with pieces of shrapnel, creating a bulge not discernible to the naked eye. They then grabbed needle-nosed pliers to deal with the wiring, and grasped the electronic devices that served as timers and detonators. Two pounds of C-4 explosives were packed into each vest, which provided ample strength to blow up crowds of people.

Save for a few comments, Racheed had nothing to do but watch his men at work. As he did, a myriad of thoughts raced through his mind. He felt a rushing sense of satisfaction at his mission, and how his men embraced their tasks with skill and enthusiasm. He also thought of the time spent as a boy in Omar's workshop, covertly watching him construct his wares. The fiery blast that claimed Omar and Sasha fleeted through him as well, followed by the images of Americans, mangled and bloody, screaming and wailing, the result of his mission.

Finally, the work was complete. The men each donned their vests and proudly modeled them for one another. "They fit well," remarked

Adeeb. "Very comfortable."

"Very good," replied Racheed. "Now, let us proceed through the tunnel. We must build the vehicle bombs. Each of you, grab some of the explosives."

Though Racheed and Rodrequs had described the tunnel in detail to the terrorists, this was the first time they had actually seen it, and were quite excited at the notion. They each lifted an armload of explosives from the crates and stepped gingerly to the tunnel entrance.

Each batch of material was carefully lowered to the walkway, where Adeeb was waiting to remove the load. One by one, they shimmied down the steps to the elevator and reached the floor, carefully holding their cargo all the way. They then briskly walked the length to the Mendez Auto Shop. It was now approaching eight o'clock, and the shop workers had departed for home.

As they entered the shop for the first time, their eyes immediately spied the black, older-model Ford SUVs, and they darted over to them. Some of the terrorists admiringly stroked the sideboards, while others simply walked in circles around them, admiring them as if the used cars were dream machines on a dealer's lot.

Racheed had recognized that only the fittest men would suffice for his mission, and this was one example. Though the components were bulky and heavy, and the distance from end to end in the tunnel was considerable, the men made their trips without complaint or rest breaks. Though only fifty pounds of C-4 explosives and a hundred pounds of shrapnel were going into each vehicle, a couple of round trips were required to carry such delicate material, and nearly an hour was consumed in the transfer. It had been a long afternoon and evening, yet stamina was hardly a concern as the men moved machine-like, staring straight ahead.

One in the party, though, asked for relief. Garcia had remained in the warehouse with Rodrequs, sitting on folding chairs and smoking a huge Cuban, at a safe distance from the flammable bomb components. As the terrorists made their final round through the tunnel, Garcia turned to his boss. "Do you need me for anything else?"

"No. Why? Are you in a hurry, or something?"

Garcia chuckled. "No, of course not. But I had promised Rosa I would call her this evening, and it's getting late. I want to speak to her before she goes to bed."

Rodrequs nodded in approval. "Of course, my friend. She is more important than any of this shit. Go on, and give my best to her."

"Thank you." Garcia leaned over and patted his friend's hand. He quickly rose from his chair and walked for the door as Rodrequs reached for his cell phone once more. Flush with the excitement of the evening, he called for one of his prostitutes to meet him at his compound. Bedtime was nearing, and there was always time for a little relaxation until then.

*****

As darkness fell over the desolate landscape, the terrorists completed their installation of the bombs in the vehicles. The fifty-pound car bombs, with enough power to demolish half of a large building, were placed in the storage compartments of the Ford SUVs and covered with gray foam, to appear as part of the covering. The work took another hour or so, but the focus of the terrorists helped them go about their business in robotic fashion.

They then scampered down the steps from the auto shop and to the elevator for the final time. They laughed and chanted as they walked back down the tunnel, hanging over each other's shoulders and slapping each other's backs. They were feeling same rush that Racheed had felt for weeks, and the day, if it was to be one of their last, was one to leave the world on.

For the first time, they had seen the tunnel, their vehicles, and the explosives that would inflict blood and suffering on the hated Americans. This moment was months in coming, and they were relishing every second as they strolled the length of the tunnel, cracking silly jokes and teasing one another.

Racheed walked behind, sharing none of the hijinks. He was again lost in himself, reflecting on the losses of his grandfather and his sister. Images of the devastation to come also rolled in his mind, and he could not pull himself away from thinking of the lasting pain that would come to those who were to lose loved ones. They would now feel as him, as if something had been taken from them. Without an iota of sympathy, he thought of the widows, the grieving parents, the motherless children he was about to create, and a smug smile pursed his lips.

As the terrorists continued merrily along underground, Diego Garcia was unlocking the door to his residence, welcomed by a cousin who was handling the babysitting chores. Both of the kids were asleep, having dozed off in front of their X-box. The babysitter prodded them, and they sleepily trudged to their rooms, not bothering to wash themselves.

Garcia tipped the cousin, who climbed on her bicycle and pedaled into the night. He peered into his children's rooms to find them in sound slumber. He then crept to the parlor, turning off all but one lamp. That was all the light he needed as he pulled out his special cell phone.

"Hudson here" was the voice on the other end.

Garcia paused, not expecting an answer this late at night. "This is Diego Garcia. Uh...I was not expecting to hear your voice."

"Why not?"

"It is late, and I thought you would be in bed."

"I haven't slept in days. What do you have for me?"

Jack Hudson's unyielding stamina was serving him well, at least physically. Twenty-hour days had followed his deal with Garcia, and he was in no mood to waste precious seconds. "Come on," he ordered. "What do you have?"

"I had a meeting at the safe house today...."

"*I know that!*" While Hudson's body was holding up, his nerves were fraying with each hour of lost sleep, and the high stakes of this major terrorist threat were obsessing in his mind. The security of thousands of his countrymen was on the line, and he knew it. "We've got it under surveillance! And you didn't just come from there. You went to the tunnel and the Mendez shop as well." He could not resist a little jab. “You look good on camera.”

Diego was put off by Hudson's combativeness. “I was getting to that.” he said, anger simmering.

Hudson realized he had offended his mole, and recoiled. “All right. What happened?”

“We had a meeting at the safe house. Racheed plans to attack on September 11.”

Even the gruff Jack Hudson shuddered at that thought. Like any other American, that date was burned in his mind. “Dammit,” he muttered. “Should have seen that one coming. He wants to be a hero, doesn't he?”

“Yes. His men loved the idea, and were very happy. They celebrated and yelled.”

“Pfft.” Hudson blew air through his lips in disgust. “What else? When do they come across?”

“Do you mean the border, senor?” Diego knew, but wanted to tweak Hudson a little.

“*Of course that's what I mean! Where the hell else would I be talking about?*”

Diego had little reason to smile in the last few days, but that gave him an occasion. “The crossing will be at midnight on September 9.”

“All right. Down the tunnel and through the auto shop?”

“Yes. There are three teams.” Garcia then gave Hudson the names of each man on their respective teams, as well as where each was headed.

Hudson quickly scribbled each detail on a yellow legal pad. Later, he would type it into the agency computer systems. “Then you all went to the warehouse. What'd you do there?”

“We distributed the explosives. They are very powerful, senor. They want to make car bombs that will cause much death and suffering.”

“Give me what you know on those.” Garcia proceeded to describe the nuances of the explosive devices. He also described the vehicles that would carry the bombs, including color, make, model, and license plates. He added the information on where the terrorists would be lodging, the false identifications, and repeated where the vehicles would be parked with the bombs at each of the three attack sites, Caesar's Palace, Mount Rushmore, and Music Row.

"The terrorists will also wear bomb vests," he added. "They will detonate the car bombs from a distance. They will then enter someplace that is crowded with scared people, and blow themselves up."

"Did they make those themselves?"

"Si, senor. And they put together the vehicle bombs themselves. They are smart and well-trained." An element of admiration was evident in Garcia's voice. "Racheed must have trained them well. There are many men in our cartel that could not work with explosives that well."

Hudson kept writing. "They have the cell phones I gave you already. We can tell, since we are tracking them."

"Si. They looked them over, and could find nothing of your tracking devices. They know nothing."

"And we are sure as hell are going to keep it that way. So they've got everything over in the auto shop?"

Diego replied affirmatively. "All the vehicles are there, and all of their explosives. The vests are also in their vehicles. I think that Racheed told the men to leave the detonators in the vehicles, in the auto shop. I do not know this for sure, but I think that's what he said. He was worried that there may be an accident in the tunnel, and they would activate them."

"Too bad that didn't happen," barked Hudson. "That would have made our jobs a lot easier."

"I should mention one other thing, senor," offered Garcia. "Racheed says he will wear one of his grandfather's bomb vests. He wants to honor him."

Hudson rolled his eyes on the other end. "What an asshole. Wants to blow people up in his grandfather's memory."

Garcia offered no response to Hudson's criticism and switched to a more personal subject. "How is my wife?"

"Huh? Oh, she's fine. We're keeping her safe, and feeding her well." Hudson's indifference was painfully obvious.

"I presume you will keep your end of the deal, senor? When the attack is stopped and I am done here, my wife will be released?"

"Yeah, yeah. Don't worry about that. Just do what you're told."

Garcia was ready to break it off. "Is there anything else?"

"Nope. Call me if anything else happens."

Hudson hung up, foregoing any semblance of a polite goodbye. He hit the speed-dial to a conference call with other FBI and CIA agents, to advise them of his findings. He also called Jorge Gonzalez, his Mexican counterpart, to request that the federalies move from fifty miles out to the outskirts of Ciudad Juarez. Back at his hacienda, Garcia set down his phone and stretched out on the couch, hoping for a little sleep to escape the pressure.

CHAPTER XXX

For days, Jack Hudson had been anxious for the specifics of the attack, and now he had them. With four days to go, his existence was a whirlwind of activity. Call after call was made to the agents in the command post, who were meticulously monitoring the surveillance cameras from each of Rodrequs' locations, including his compound, the safe house, the warehouse, and the auto shop. The cell phones were not used, per Racheed's instructions, and they hardly moved from the terrorists's nightstands to their pockets. Clearly, nothing was overlooked. The least little movements aroused concern, and numerous false alarms were raised by the agents, who had learned never to take anything for granted.

As Hudson and the agents under his watch worked feverishly to protect their domain on this September 7, Racheed and his band of five terrorists relaxed in the safe house, watching English soccer on the satellite television and playing with their personal smartphones. A couple of the men flipped through past issues of Penthouse that were laying around the living room, courtesy of their host, Juan Rodrequs. Though their lives were to end in a few days, there was no sign of resignation. Prayer sessions interrupted the relaxation, and a serene peacefulness permeated the house and its occupants.

The eighth of September was the final day before the plan commenced. A late start and periodic naps ruled the morning and afternoon, along with frequent readings of the Koran. Unlike the calm of the seventh, the eighth simmered with anticipation. Racheed was the most anxious, though with no fear that anything would go wrong. Rather, his excitement was the culmination of months of training, study, preparation, coordination.

He had painstakingly covered every step, every moment, every action. Over the course of the last year, he had sacrificed his family, few friends, his sparse interests, and finally, the pleasures of a beautiful girlfriend. Now his life would follow, and if this was to be his last moment, it would be his finest. As the United States trembled with each bomb blast, everyone would feel his power, his vengeance, his wrath.

Racheed ordered all of the terrorists to be in the safe house at 5 p.m., though his directive was more of his domineering influence than anything else. The attackers had barely left the house since returning from their errand of bomb making at the auto shop, so there was little need for such a demand.

From their posts in El Paso, American agents watched obsessively, seeing no sign of movement from the terrorists. They did, however, spy a black Hummer approach the house from the battered road and pull around the back. Rodrequs and Garcia had arrived to join the party.

On this warm late summer evening, their moods seemed to be in unison. Rodrequs burst into the house and plopped into the cushiest recliner in the room. Dressed in his usual khaki safari-style jacket and camouflage pants, his pockmarked face alternated between a icy facade and a toothy grin. By now, Garcia was learning to play the part, smiling and chatting as if nothing was amiss.

Shortly after 5 p.m., Racheed strolled up to Rodrequs, whose burly frame was spread across his chair. "I would like to speak privately with you, my friend," he said.

"But of course," replied Rodrequs. "Let us retire to the other room."

Garcia heard the exchange and, ever the loyal second, rose to join them. The hours spent with Jack Hudson were hammered in his mind, and he was looking for every opportunity to gain information. This time, though, Rodrequs saw no need. "You stay here," he ordered. "Remain with the others. I will be out shortly."

Taken aback, Garcia retreated like a dog from an angry master. He was startled at the response, which was rare for Rodrequs; usually, Garcia was privy to the most delicate of conversations. Fear rocked his mind like a thunderbolt. Was Rodrequs on to the ruse? Did he have reason to suspect something?

Slowly, Diego sank back into his chair, hopeful that his boss was still clueless to his deception. He anxiously looked at the clock, seeing that mere hours remained. Soon, his boss would either be in American custody – or dead. He recalled their years spent together on the crime-infested Mexican streets, and of happier times in the Rodrequs compound. He could not overcome his guilt, and knew as tomorrow dawned he would be wracked with emotion, mourning his boyhood chum between deep sighs of relief.

As Diego wrestled with himself, Racheed and Rodrequs settled into the next room. Rodrequs planted himself on a table, while Racheed stood close by, to prevent loud conversing that would be detected by the others.

"I have something for you," offered Racheed, withdrawing a slip of paper from the pocket of his black Adidas t-shirt. "It is the contact information for the Russian mafia. This is a secret number, but you should be able to get through to the leaders as you desire."

"Ah, yes," replied Rodrequs. "I have been waiting for this. And there is something else I have waited for, my friend."

Racheed smiled and took his personal cell phone from the pocket of his jeans. He dialed the private number of Ali Sighn, back in Peshawar.

"Hello!" Ali answered gruffly, and with an obvious sense of distrust. "Who is this? Speak!"

"It is Racheed, my Father," was the soothing response. "I hope I have not disturbed you."

"Racheed, my son! Think nothing of it." Ali had a fondness for his young comrade that he displayed to few others, and his voice softened almost to a coo. "I hope this call finds you well."

"Yes. Bless you, Father." The warmth then gave way to practicality. "I am in Juarez with our friend, Juan Rodrequs. He would like to receive the second half of his payment, the $1.5 million."

"Ah, yes. It will be sent to his account in Switzerland." Ali said offhandedly, less concerned with money than the attack. "Is your plan coming as we had hoped?"

"There is no worry," replied Racheed, chest swelling with pride. Rodrequs noticed, and his eerie grin reappeared. "We are leaving at midnight. In two days, we will deliver our blow."

"Very well, my son. You are doing your people, and your Father, a great service. May Allah be with you now and in your calling. Bless you, my son."

"And my thanks and blessing to you, my Father. Praise be Allah and his name." Racheed then broke the connection. He then turned to Rodrequs. "It is done."

Rodrequs' steely eyes twinkled, and his teeth nearly bit off his cigar. "Very good. Very good!"

Even though Racheed had kept his promises, he acted as if he had done Rodrequs a favor. "And now, there is something I would like to ask of you."

"Name it. As you can see, I can make anything happen!"

"I would like for you to provide transportation for Adeeb and myself across the border."

Rodrequs' brow tightened, and a puzzled glance came across him. "But I have already done that. There is a vehicle for you at the auto shop."

"No. I would like to have a vehicle to take us across at some other place. Somewhere in El Paso. And I would like to do this without anyone else knowing it. Not my other men, not even Garcia."

The phony manners of Rodrequs peeled away. “Why do you want to do this? I have done everything you have asked of me. Why this change, and why now?”

Racheed had not expected the cool reception. “Because I do not want to risk everything, if something should go wrong. I want to have a backup plan, so we may fulfill at least part of the mission. I do not want to, how do you say? Put all my apples in one basket.”

Rodrequs noticed the slip, and chuckled. He playfully put his hands on Racheed's shoulders. “Apples in one basket! I think you mean eggs, my friend.”

Racheed was never playful, and certainly not at this late date. “Whatever you say. But I do not want anything to go wrong.”

“Oh, do not worry, my friend.” Rodrequs was hardly the coddling type, but made his best effort to reassure his Pakistani partner. “Nothing will go wrong. Everything is ready to go at the auto shop, and you have created a wise plan. What could possibly happen?”

“There are plenty of things. I just want to be sure.”

“Oh, Racheed. You worry too much, and life is too short!” exclaimed Rodrequs, forgetting the irony, since the terrorists' lives were numbered in days. “What do you think could happen? No one knows about this, and the authorities certainly do not. I have beaten those dumb asses for years! They are not a worry to you!”

Racheed held his ground. “Still, I would like another method of transport across the border. As I have told my men, failure is not an option. But if the other two teams do not make it, I want to be certain that I do.”

Rodrequs threw his hands in the air and bowed his head, finally giving in. “Very well, my friend,” he said, stifling a chuckle of frustration. “You win.” He tapped his fingers on the tabletop for a few seconds, thinking of how to accommodate the request.

A man such as Juan Rodrequs has plenty of options, so his consideration did not take long. “I will call my border agent,” he said. “Remember the one I have on my payroll? I will call him, to see what he can do for us.”

“Thank you,” said Racheed. “I just want to make sure nothing goes wrong."

Rodrequs slapped him on the back. "I will see when this man is scheduled to work. I'll let you know."

Racheed briskly strode back to the living room, where Garcia anxiously awaited. Five minutes later, Rodrequs peered through the doorway and motioned to Racheed. Most of the terrorists were napping, so the covert actions went unnoticed by everyone except Garcia, who strained to hear the conversation through the walls.

Unfortunately for Diego, Racheed closed the door behind him. "What do you have?"

"I have good news for you, my friend," said Rodrequs. "My border agent will be working tonight at midnight. I just talked to him, and his shift begins at eleven."

"I am grateful," said Racheed, who rarely expressed that emotion. "Where is his post?"

"He is off the main bridge into El Paso. Go past Chamizal Park, and you will find it. He is posted at the check-in that is the second from the right. It is lane number four. His name is Ochoa."

"And he will let me pass without incident?"

"Oh, he may pretend to check your vehicle. But he will not halt you. Just let him go about his business for a few seconds, and you will be on your way."

Racheed was pleased at Rodrequs' accommodation, but wanted more. "May I request another vehicle from you, then?"

Rodrequs was growing impatient at the demands. "Yes," he said, rolling his eyes upward slightly. "I will have another one for you."

"Thank you," said Racheed, detecting the reaction. He made a half-hearted attempt to smooth it over. "I hope you know how much I appreciate what you have done for me. You have been a great friend."

"Think nothing of it." The cartel leader's tone then turned sarcastic. "I am almost scared to ask. Is there anything else you want from me?"

Few but Racheed Ul-Bashar had the nerve to press Juan Rodrequs further. "Yes. Please do not tell anyone of our change in plans. I do not want anyone to know about this. Not my men, not even Garcia."

Rodrequs' ire was starting to simmer. "I cannot tell Garcia? My trusted friend and ally? Why should I not do this?"

"As I said. I do not want anything to go wrong. And, I do not want to give my men any reason to think badly. If they think I have changed plans, they may become alarmed, and abort."

There was logic in Racheed's words that even Rodrequs could not dispute. "Very well. I will speak to no one about this." He stared at Racheed and drummed the tips of his fingers together. "Where do you want your new vehicle?"

"Send it here. I will have Adeeb plant the explosives in it. Park it around the back, along the north wall, where the house has no windows. I will instruct him not to tell the others, and to meet me outside."

"Very well. But what about Garcia? Will he not think something is going on?"

"Well, ah, could you send him on an errand or something, so he will not be around? That will give us time to prepare the vehicle. And I must request more explosives to make a vehicle bomb and bomb vests."

Rodrequs was not used to being asked so many favors, and glanced at Racheed with a shocked expression. "Alllllright...." he said, unable to overcome the startle. "You have a lot of balls, my friend."

Racheed smiled at the compliment. "Well, I hope so. If I did not, I would not be doing this."

All Juan Rodrequs could do was shake his head.

*****

Despite his misgivings, Rodrequs set about complying with Racheed's demands. He called back to the compound, and a fourth black, older model Ford SUV was sent to the safe house, with the necessary explosives. He then checked with his border agent again, to confirm the details.

Once through, he strolled back into the living room and approached Garcia. "I do not need you here right now," he said. "Go home, and get some rest."

Garcia was stunned at the sudden dismissal. "But...there is so much going on. You do not need me for anything?"

"Just one thing. Get me the number of our man who removed the vehicle identification number on the three SUVs in the auto shop."

The request came completely unexpected to Garcia. "What do you need him for?"

"I've got another need for his services. Just give me his number." Diego remembered it by heart, and recited it to Rodrequs, who grabbed a nearby scrap of paper and wrote it down.

He then turned his attention back to Garcia. "Go back home and call Rosa. I will call you if you are needed."

Diego used the first lie that popped into his head. "I have already called Rosa," he said. "While you and Racheed were talking, I spoke to her."

"Oh?" Rodrequs had not expected that response. "Then, how is she?"

"She is well." Garcia then pulled another lie, though one less savory to his sensibilities. "She sends her best to you."

"She is a fine woman. You are lucky to have her," responded the boss. "Still, there is no reason for you to be here. Go home, and come back later on."

"Oh." Garcia struggled to hide his dejection. "What time do you want me to return?"

"Ah, 11:30 or so. You may as well be at home, rather than sitting here on your ass."

Garcia was puzzled at the switch, and again hoped that Rodrequs was not suspicious. His fears were eased when Rodrequs placed both palms on his cheeks as he rose. "Very well, my friend. I will see you later on."

"Yes. Later this evening."

Garcia exited and climbed into his gray Silverado with a mix of emotions. He was relieved that Rodrequs was still in the dark on his deceit, but worried that he would not be present if more information was divulged. But there was nothing that could be done now. He hurried home, and called Jack Hudson.

As usual, Hudson offered no greeting. “What do you have?”

“I just came from the safe house. There's something going on, but I could not get close enough to find out.”

“What `something' is it?”

“Racheed and Rodrequs had several private conversations, but did not let me in on them. Then Juan came out and sent me home. He wants me to return at 11:30.”

Hudson had learned to expect the unexpected in his career, but this late change worried him. “Dammit! And you don't know what's going on?”

“No, senor. I tried, but they would not let me in the room. Then Juan sent me home.”

Hudson's initial reaction was the same as Garcia's had been earlier. “Do you think they are on to you?”

“I do not think so. He seemed friendlier than usual as I left. But he had a strange request. He asked me for the number of the man that altered the VIN numbers on each of the vehicles at the auto shop.”

“What the hell was that about?”

“I do not know, senor. He just told me he needed the man's services again.”

It only took a moment for Hudson to figure out why. “Probably going to remove the VINs off of a new vehicle. All right. We'll see what shows up on our surveillance. Is everything else on schedule, though?”

“As far as I know, senor. I do not think anything else has changed.”

“Hmmh,” scoffed Hudson. Though he was never predisposed to human compassion, Hudson was about to have a rare moment. “You will be taking the terrorists into the auto shop, won't you?”

“Yes.”

“After you deliver the terrorists, get back in the tunnel and stay there.”

Diego was startled at the directive. “What?”

“I said, get back into the tunnel. We're sending in the raiding teams on both the warehouse and the auto shop."

Garcia had expected such force, but he still trembled at the thought. "When will that happen?"

Hudson had neither the time nor patience for details. "Don't ask questions! Just get in the damn tunnel! When it's over, I'll send a SWAT team member down for you. And don't do anything else until you hear from me!"

By now, Garcia was becoming used to taking orders from Hudson. "Very well, senor."

"Keep us posted, then." Hudson hung up without a goodbye, leaving Garcia staring at a silent receiver.

CHAPTER XXXI

As Hudson and Garcia had their testy exchange, Racheed summoned Adeeb for a meeting in the other room.

"I have made a change in plans," said Racheed. "You and I will take a different route across the border." He then explained his desire that nothing go wrong, and that another vehicle was being sent to the safe house.

Adeeb was starstruck by his leader and listened in silence, nodding periodically. He also accepted Racheed's instructions that he say nothing to the other terrorists or Garcia. Minutes later, they heard the sound of a car at the back, and the crunch of wheels slowly turning toward the north side of the house. Racheed peered into the living room, hoping the noise had not awakened the others. To his relief, they were still deep in slumber.

The agents at the command center watched the fourth Ford SUV pull into place at the safe house. "What's *that* doing there?" Hudson asked as he pointed to the screen.

"I have no idea," said Tony Martinez, equally perplexed.

Then followed the sound of a second vehicle, with the audible whine of a motor that decreased as it pulled away. The command center could not see it, as it was idling just out of sight of their cameras. Racheed looked out the window, and recognized its occupants as two of Rodrequs' men, sent to deliver the black SUV.

As he watched, a battered brown van drove up behind the SUV, carrying a third man wearing soiled white coveralls and carrying a toolbox. Racheed suspected he knew his purpose, which was verified when the man pulled out a grinder. Unbeknownst to Racheed, he was the same mechanic who had ground away the vehicle identification numbers on the SUVs in the shop.

Sparks flew as he ground off the VIN numbers on the frame, motor, and transmission of the fourth SUV. The identification number on the dash was also removed. After forty-five minutes of work, the man then slid the van doors open to reveal a portable welder, which completed the job. All three men then piled into the van and sped off.

Racheed turned to Adeeb. "Go outside. Build the vehicle bomb in the new car, and two more bomb vests." he ordered. "Be as silent as possible, so not to awaken the others."

Adeeb crept outside and within the hour had constructed another powerful vehicle bomb, enough to inflict horrifying devastation on its target. He also made two more bomb vests.

His work was oblivious to the surveillance agents, as he was standing almost squarely behind the vehicle, out of camera range. "What is he doing there? I can't see a damn thing," barked Hudson. "Anyone else see anything?"

"Nope," said another agent. "He's positioned just right."

"Jeez," said Hudson. "Hope he hasn't figured out where the cameras are."

By now, it was nearly 9 p.m. Finished, Adeeb sauntered back inside, to find his comrades only starting to wake up from their naps. Each stumbled off their chairs and couches and headed for the house's two bathrooms, to shower. They dried themselves and dressed in the same style of clothes they had worn for days. Some pulled on Old Navy t-shirts and cargo pants, while another sported a polo shirt and Dockers. Two chose the apparel of Pittsburgh sports teams. They stuffed a couple of days' worth of clothing and some toiletries into black duffel bags, traveling light for the days ahead.

Though their skin identified them as internationals, nothing else in their persona raised suspicion. They looked like part of the crowd, wearing the clothes that the gamblers of Las Vegas, the tourists of Mount Rushmore, and the music fans of Nashville would hardly notice.

*****

The attack was about to go into motion, and the American agents had to be ready for it. The tension percolated at the command center with each passing day, for no one wanted to be the person who let something slide by. Defending America and its citizens was their job, not their hope.

As Racheed and his band relaxed at the safe house in the final hours before midnight, Jack Hudson was a freight train in motion. Weeks earlier, he had recognized the need for bomb experts, and for the last several weeks, a team of the best bomb men he could find were stationed in El Paso, waiting for the word.

Now was that moment. The phone only needed to ring once before the leader of the bomb squad answered. "Get to the auto shop tonight and disarm all of those bombs," Hudson barked on the other end.

As the workers lazily trudged away from the Mendez Auto Shop, none of them noticed a battered white side-panel van parked behind a clump of scrub bushes a few hundred feet away. Darkness was setting in, and the occupants of the van watched intently as the lights of the shop flickered off and the last man exited.

His truck was less than a minute down the road when the van nondescriptly pulled back onto the roadway and into the parking lot of the shop. The four men that climbed out were dressed in dark blue coveralls, some wearing sewn-in nametags, each carrying toolboxes. To the motorists whizzing by in the dusk, they looked as any other auto worker, probably coming for a late shift.

One sauntered toward the front door as the others clustered

around, offering quick glances at the surrounding area. Hudson and his cohorts watched on the feed from the surveillance cameras, ready to radio to a backup team of armed security if something went awry.

Once inside, the men opened their toolboxes to reveal the latest in state-of-the-art electronic equipment, designed to disable even the most sophisticated explosives. The black SUVs were locked, so a few seconds were required to pick the door locks. That barrier removed, the agents poured over the vehicles, easily finding the bulky vehicle bombs and the bomb vests hidden under the seats. In a matter of minutes, each bomb was defused.

Jack Hudson and Tony Martinez watched it all from their command center, nervously sipping their last cups of coffee from their third pot of the day. Though there was no reason to expect anything to go wrong, they still sat back and exhaled slightly when the last of the bomb team disappeared out the door, undetected once again.

Hudson could not resist a jab at the terrorists and turned to Martinez, wearing a smirk. “Like to see the looks on their faces when they find their toys don’t work,” he chortled.

CHAPTER XXXII

Diego Garcia's disappointing evening was continuing at his hacienda. His youngest son was suffering from the sniffles and called for his father, ignoring the babysitter that Diego had called back to the house. Like most sick children, sleep is not always easy, and the youngster was having trouble soothing his stuffy head. As the short hand of the clock passed eleven, Diego was far less concerned with the boy's congestion. With the minutes ticking away, he was afraid he may not make it back to the safe house at the bottom of the hour.

Finally, at 11:15, Garcia persuaded the boy to drift off and slipped the sitter a few extra dollars to stay longer. Then he ran for his Silverado, threw it into gear, and sped off, hoping that the Juarez police patrols were either not in the area or indifferent to his speed. The last thing he needed was another moving violation, since the last one in Illinois had changed everything.

The chimes on the half-hour from a distant church pierced the nighttime quiet as he shut off the ignition in back of the safe house. He rapped the special knock, and his boss answered.

"Where have you been?" Rodrequs demanded, though Garcia was

actually right on time.

“My boy was sick,” explained Garcia. “I had to stay with him a while longer.”

“Huh.” Rodrequs was unconcerned with such family drivel. He turned and pointed to four of the terrorists, Teams One and Two. “Take these men to the warehouse. It's getting close to midnight.”

“In my truck, or in one of your cars?”

Rodrequs threw his thumb over his shoulder in the direction of the backyard. “Take the Hummer in back. Here are the keys.” He tossed them in a straight line at Garcia, who gingerly caught them.

Garcia turned toward Racheed. “What about him?”

“Not him,” replied Rodrequs. “Racheed and Adeeb are going to ride with me.”

The news was not welcomed by the nervous Garcia. Now he knew there had been a major change in plans. He wondered if this was the result of the covert conversations of Racheed and Rodrequs earlier in the evening. He worried what he may have missed in his three hours at home, and wished there was some way to get word to Hudson.

Again, his facial expression did not give way to his mental anguish. “As you say,” he said to Rodrequs. “I will see you there.”

The four men each bowed respectfully to Racheed, who clearly relished the moment. They strode single-file out the back door and piled into the Hummer. As he drove away, Garcia noticed that Rodrequs' vehicle was not behind him.

“They're pulling out,” yelled an FBI agent watching the surveillance feed at the command center.

“How many vehicles?” asked another.

“One” was the reply.

“How many guys?” interrupted Hudson, who overheard the exchange.

“Four. Garcia's the driver. Racheed's not with him.”

“Keep watching,” ordered Hudson. “He's got to be coming out sometime.”

As the Hummer motored toward the warehouse, the terrorists remained silent, some gazing at the streetlights and houses as they raced by their windows. Garcia kept glancing at his rearview, hoping for a pair of headlights that looked like Rodrequs' car. He only saw darkness.

At the command center, the agents were reading the signals off the tracking devices on the terrorists' cell phones. As a result, their entire route was being observed. It did not take long to see where they were going.

"They're heading for the warehouse," exclaimed one agent.

"Straight for the border," remarked Hudson. "Down the tunnel, and straight across. But what the hell is going on with Racheed?"

Garcia approached the warehouse, hoping that Rodrequs had taken another route. He stopped at the gate, and two heavily armed guards allowed him to enter the property. But the isolated building was shrouded in the dark, and no other vehicles were around. Fears raced through his mind. He hoped that Rodrequs had not learned of his deception. Juan had a way of finding even the most intimate of details, and he prayed that was not the case. He fantasized that Rodrequs had changed the plans to save himself, and was cutting Garcia and the four terrorists loose. Garcia had seen him do far less in their decades together.

As he turned the key and gently swung the front door open, he was relieved to find no one else inside. Garcia was hesitant to turn any lights on, so he and the terrorists moved about with flashlights. That hardly pleased the agents watching the surveillance feed at the command center, who wanted as much light as possible, even with their infrared equipment.

"Dammit! Turn the frickin' lights on!" snapped Martinez.

"How many of them do you see there?" demanded Hudson.

Several agents crowded around the monitor, trying to count. "There's four, no five...wait, that's Garcia," one said. "There's another...no, wait, we just saw him." Finally, all agreed that four terrorists were in the building.

"What the hell is going on? We're still short two of them!" exclaimed Hudson. He whirled in his chair and looked down the line, at the agents watching the monitors with the feeds from the safe house, the compound, and the auto shop. "We don't have two of them! Somebody find where those bastards are going, and I mean now!"

A few feet away, an agent was monitoring Racheed's cell phone, and he had an immediate answer. "They're still at the safe house. They haven't left."

"What the hell...." responded Hudson, perplexed at the change of events.

A dusty clock on a forlorn wall of the warehouse ticked toward midnight. There was still no sign of any movement from Rodrequs or Racheed. Adhering strictly to the time schedule, Garcia drew his cell phone from his pocket and called Rodrequs.

"Yeah?" was the greeting on the other end.

"Where are you?" inquired Garcia. "We've been here for fifteen minutes. It's almost midnight."

"Don't worry about it," said Rodrequs. "Don't wait for Racheed. Go ahead and take the other men through the tunnel."

His response surprised Garcia. "You want me to go on without Racheed?"

"Yes! That's what I said!" barked Rodrequs. "Get the others across, and we'll be along shortly."

None of that sounded right to Garcia, but he was in no position to argue. "All right," he dutifully replied. He led the men toward the side wall, scooted the desk, and pulled back the rug to expose the trap door. Each of the terrorists shimmied down the steps to the elevator and headed for the United States.

Jack Hudson glared at the computer screen monitoring the tracking devices on the terrorists' phones. "Four of `em are going across," he called out. But the question of the other two still lingered. Since Rodrequs' phone had no tracking device, Hudson had to rely on the surveillance to determine his location. He yelled across the room to the agent in front of the safe house feed. "Where's he at?"

"Still hasn't left the safe house" was the response.

"Dammit! It's almost midnight." Hudson snapped. He yanked the headphones off, and shook his head. "Shit! What in the hell are they doing?"

*****

Hudson did not have to wait long. Seconds later, the agent on safe house surveillance shouted down the line.

"They're leaving," he reported. Hudson sprang from his chair and parked himself in front of the safe house monitor. He observed that Racheed and Adeeb were leaving in one SUV, while Rodrequs left in another vehicle.

"They're going separately," he said. He wheeled around and yelled at the agents in charge of the cell phone tracking devices. "Watch those phones. Watch those phones!"

The agents complied, though they hardly needed to be told. Shortly, they called Hudson to their screens, brows furrowed.

"Rodrequs is heading back to the compound," the agents said. "But Racheed and the other guy are heading for the border." They turned and pointed at the screen. "Look. They're going straight through downtown Juarez. Right for the free-access bridge into El Paso."

"No!" shouted Hudson as he drew back from the screen. "They've screwed us!"

This latest turn rocked the command center, and each agent shared the same thoughts. No one knew where Racheed was headed, and what he was planning once he got there. A murmur rattled around the room as the agents tried to talk it out amongst themselves.

Hudson snatched the nearest phone. "Get me the SWAT team."

The answer was nearly instant. "Hudson here. Surround the auto shop and contain the terrorists. Do not let them out of there. They're in the tunnel, and should be arriving up top in a couple of minutes. Get there!"

Immediately, the SWAT team was parked down the road from the Mendez Auto Shop in two oversized black vans, ready to pursue or whatever else was ordered. The agent in the passenger seat snapped his phone shut. "Let's go," he said, and the others knew exactly what he meant. The vehicle pulled out, quickly followed by the other van.

They sped down the few hundred yards of highway at breakneck speed and pulled into the auto shop parking lot. The vans had barely stopped when the doors flew open and the men jumped out, spreading across the lot in an eyelash and finding cover behind barrels, dumpsters, and derelict cars on all sides of the shop.

As they swung into position, Hudson was making other calls. One went to the border patrol. “This is Jack Hudson of the FBI. I've got an unidentified vehicle carrying two male terrorist suspects and explosives that is heading toward the border.

“We're tracking them to the bridge in Juarez near Chamizal Park. They should be there in a few minutes. The vehicle is a black four-door SUV, license unknown. Be on the lookout.” He then repeated the information, for clarity. He hung up and immediately ordered another SWAT team to the border crossing area.

CHAPTER XXIII

Unfortunately for Jack Hudson, he was a little too late. Events were moving faster than anyone had expected, and the advantage now lay with Racheed Ul-Bashar. While Hudson's world was in chaos, Racheed's plan was unfolding as he intended. His environment was one of serene silence, as he was completely unaware that he was a targeted man, and was lost in thought, as usual. The car radio was turned off, and at the wheel, Adeeb remained silent, speaking only if spoken to. The devastation of the coming days contrasted with the peaceful quiet permeating the cabin of the black Ford SUV as Racheed and his partner rode to the crossing.

They rolled over the bridge across the Rio Grande and slowed on the opposite side, approaching the border patrol checkpoints. There were five of them, lined up in a continuous row and so many that the pavement had to be widened to accommodate all of them. Each booth had a uniformed officer, whose duty it was to record all pertinent information, including data on each passenger, drivers' license numbers, and purpose of visit.

Often, a physical inspection of vehicles and their contents was conducted, though not with the scrutiny that many Americans desire. Overwhelmed and understaffed, border patrol agents hurriedly, and sometimes lackadaisically, go about their chores and frequently let vehicles with questionable cargo or maintenance issues pass.

In these first minutes of September 9, the booths were mostly open, and the wait at any of them would have been brief. Racheed, though, knew right where to head. "It's lane four," he said to Adeeb. "Get in that one."

The border patrol officer in that lane was Hector Ochoa, a Tex-Mex man of forty-six who had worked at this crossing for fifteen years. The hours were poor, but the money was decent. He supplemented his income by moonlighting for Juan Rodrequs, looking the other way as large quantities of narcotics from Juarez slipped by. Save for the tunnel, this was Rodrequs' favorite way to move drugs across the border. He loved to push his product right under the noses of the authorities.

Hector also made money in his off-hours as a part-time pusher for the cartel, making sure that friends and family who used, received only the best products that money could buy. As a result, his income from Rodrequs was doubled that of his patrol earnings. His co-workers wondered why, as they were struggling to make ends meet, Hector could afford a twenty-foot boat, a roomy ranch house, and a new pickup every other year.

As he was driving to work on this stiflingly warm evening, he had stopped off at his brother-in-law's house to deliver two kilos of high-grade cocaine. While there, he had received a call on his cell phone from Rodrequs, telling him that a friend would be arriving at the crossing in a black Ford around midnight.

Hector was only too happy to help. As the Ford approached, he offered no pretense. He simply waved the vehicle through, and the crossing was made. Now Racheed was in the United States, one step closer to his deadly goal.

*****

"What the hell just happened here?"

Jack Hudson was listening in on the agents who were monitoring the tracking devices on the cell phones tucked safely away in the pockets of Racheed and Adeeb. He watched incredulously as the signals kept moving away from the bridge, never even coming to a stop.

"Don't we have a border patrol there?" Hudson asked an obvious question, knowing full well that the United States was supposed to patrol each organized crossing. "Then what the hell was he doing?"

He knocked his empty coffee cup off the table in disgust. "Dammit to hell. I know we've got some sorry border patrolmen, but that one takes the cake. That sonofabitch didn't even bother to check!"

Hudson grabbed his cell phone with such venom that the other agents thought he was attacking it. In seconds, he had the border headquarters on the line. "Yeah. Hudson here. Find out who is working lane number four at the crossing in El Paso near Chamizal Park. He just let an SUV with two known terrorist suspects through. Didn't even have them stop, just let them on through. That SUV may be carrying enough bombs to blow up several city blocks. I want that guy's name. And I want to fire his ass!"

He jabbed the hang-up button and rammed the phone back in his shirt pocket. He then forewent his anger to the task at hand and spun around in his chair, back to the screen tracking the phones in Racheed's vehicle. "Where are they now?"

"They're in the United States. Proceeding eastbound on I-10."

Hudson looked straight at Tony Martinez, then directly into the faces of some of his other agents. He had expected to intercept Racheed at the auto shop, or somewhere nearby. When the plans had changed, he reasonably expected some cooperation at the crossing.

Now Racheed was on the loose in west Texas, with no assurance that he was still going to Nashville. The last-minute switch and new site for the crossing cast a doubt on everything. The defusion of the bombs in the auto shop did little to reassure Hudson.

"He could be headed anywhere," muttered Hudson. "New York, Washington, Dallas, Houston, God-knows where. To do God-knows-what."

CHAPTER XXXIV

In the Mendez Auto Shop, the four terrorists were making their final checks of their vehicles and bombs before they hit the road. Everything was according to plan, except for an unsettling new development; Racheed, their leader, was not with them.

As they rode with Garcia, they had assumed that Racheed and Adeeb were following in another vehicle. But as they parked at the warehouse and opened their doors, they found no vehicle in sight. They immediately turned to Garcia and inquired on the whereabouts of their leader, but Garcia simply responded, “He's coming along in a little bit. Just go ahead through the tunnel.”

They complied, but were a bit anxious as they followed Garcia down the tunnel and under the river. But, they had a job to do, and that was foremost on their minds. Besides, when they left the auto shop, they would be alone with their partners, away from Racheed as well. In their minds, they overlooked their boss' absence, and went about their business as if nothing was amiss.

Once they reached the shop, Garcia advised them that he was going to return to the warehouse, to guard the tunnel entrance. It was a sensible idea, and no one questioned it. Garcia exchanged some well-wishes with the terrorists, then headed back for the trap door to the tunnel. He scurried down the steps, and in moments was riding the elevator to the tunnel floor to wait for word from the Americans.

The terrorists then silently went about their last-second preparations, ignoring the crushing heat trapped inside the unventilated shop. Repeatedly, they glanced around to make sure they were alone in the building. Then they unlocked their two vehicles, taking a moment to eyeball their vehicle bombs in the back of each Ford. They also peered at the bomb vests, to ensure they were still in place. Then they stepped up on the running boards on either side of the vehicles and boarded.

They slipped the keys into the ignition. Before turning, the occupants in each vehicle paused and looked directly into each other's eyes. Their training had brought them to this moment, and their journey was at hand. "For Allah," they spoke, almost in unison with their partner in the other seat. Then both drivers reached for their respective keys, grasping it in their fingers and rotating their wrists to start the engines. One of the terrorists opened one of the garage doors to the shop, then jumped back in the vehicle.

From their position across the street, the SWAT team vehicle turned its overhead lights on the scene, illuminating the parking lot. In the shop, the terrorists snapped to attention, fearful and unsure of the bright light shining in their direction. The SWAT team van screeched to a stop and rolled up to the doors in an instant, pulling up to block an exit from the garage doors.

Inside the shop burst the SWAT team, wearing bulletproof vests, helmets, and goggles with guns drawn. "*Freeze! FBI!*" they screamed as they stormed through the door and fanned across the shop, covering every angle. Their screams echoed off the block walls of the shop, their shadowy figures barely seen in moonlight through the windows that provided the only illumination.

The terrorists were taken completely by surprise, and a chill raced through their bodies as they confronted the screaming enemy, heavily armed and ready to fire. Their training had not prepared them for this. As thoughts flamed through their heads like an inferno, they remembered Racheed's instructions, but no emergency plan for a moment like this was ever mentioned. Unsure of what to do and in need of a split-second decision, the driver of the first vehicle accelerated, hoping to run past the agents.

The leader of the SWAT team saw the black Ford jerk as it began to move, and immediately fired three rounds into the driver's side of the windshield. The shots did their job, shattering the glass and smashing into the left side of the driver's face. The velocity caused his head to snap violently and he slumped toward the middle of the seat, blood and bone flying from the impact.

Though the driver barely had time to move the Ford before the shots, the vehicle was still in gear, and rolled a few feet toward the garage bay. Out of control, it veered off to one side, nearly clipping two agents as it rolled. The Ford finally bumped the frame of the main garage bay door and came to a stop at a slight angle, almost directly in front of the door. The escape lane for the second vehicle was now completely blocked.

In the disabled front vehicle, the passenger threw himself over the front seat into the back, throwing back the blanket and fumbling for the bomb and its detonator. The SWAT team saw the movement and reacted as trained, as if the terrorist was reaching for weapons of his own. They responded with a barrage of fire, which missed as the terrorist sprawled in the back seat, below the line of the windows now reduced to flying shards of glass. Feverishly, he tried to detonate the bomb, to no avail. Hudson's "black bag" job had rendered it useless, and repeated efforts to detonate were of no consequence.

The SWAT team continued to scream their instructions, but the thought of surrender was not in any terrorist's mind. They clutched their 9-millimeter handguns and threw open the doors of the vehicles, determined to fight their way out.

Rapid gunfire ricocheted off the walls and flashed a bright white light that cast a deadly shadow on those on the triggers. The SWAT team crouched behind any cover they could find, barrels, crates, and other parked cars, firing in the direction of the terrorists, who knelt behind the open doors of the Fords and against the side panels. The report of the guns, the shattering of the windows and headlights, and the penetration of the steel panels of the Fords created a deafening echo as a two-way hail of deadly gunfire rendered the auto shop a killing zone.

Though prepared with as much protective clothing as possible, the SWAT team's bulletproof vests, shields, and helmets could not offer a guarantee of survival. Parts of their faces were exposed under their goggles, and the terrorists, well versed in the weakness of their enemies, knew exactly what to shoot for. One agent, then another, were struck directly in the face by the high-impact ammunition of the 9-millimeters, and fell to the ground, mortally wounded. Seconds later, their wives became widows and their children fatherless. As with most in law enforcement, their loss further motivated the survivors of the SWAT team and stiffened their resistance, fighting in those fateful seconds not for their own survival but redemption for their fallen partners.

Outnumbered and surrounded on all sides of the shop, the terrorists began to fall, one by one, and the din of the firefight began to diminish. Finally the last one dropped, twisting in agony as he fell against the concrete floor, dead before he hit. Several seconds of eerie silence followed as the surviving SWAT team fighters reacted to the moment.

Slowly, gradually, the agents emerged from their cover, standing erect with their guns pointed downward, clothing soaked with sweat from the gripping minutes inside the sweltering garage. Their eyes scanned the gruesome scene. Instantly, some ran to their fallen friends, turning their bodies over to find no hope. Others examined the terrorists, to also find them limp and lifeless.

With grim faces and steely glares, the agents stood in the dim light, reflecting on the devastation that had lasted no more than sixty seconds. Two of their own had been lost, so there was no cause for celebration. But they knew that amid the flashing firefight in that dark and dingy auto repair shop, thousands of their countrymen had been saved.

CHAPTER XXXV

Seconds later, the leader of the SWAT team pulled his cell phone from inside his bulletproof vest. The call went to Jack Hudson in the command center.

"We got them all," he reported. "All four are dead, along with two of ours. They got us in a firefight, one of the worst I've seen in a long time."

"Hmm," said Hudson, torn as whether to feel relief that some of the terrorist threat was eliminated, or mourn the loss of fellow lawmen. "Which ones did we lose?"

"Lee and Peters. Looks like both were killed instantly."

Hudson was silent for a moment. "When I get a chance, I'll call their wives." He sighed heavily. "Worst part of the job, but you do what you have to do. Is the area secure?"

"Yes. We'll stay until help arrives."

"All right. Thanks." Hudson rarely thanked anyone, but felt the need now. He was the one who had sent them into the firefight, and they had risked their lives. Two had lost theirs.

He broke the connection, looked down at the tabletop, and sighed.

He shifted his glance to the other agents, crowded anxiously around him for the news. "They got them," he said of the terrorists. "All dead."

The agents knew there was more to the story. "How many of ours?" asked one.

"Two." Hudson stood up and stalked across the room. He folded his arms and threw his head back, eyes to the ceiling. "Never gets any easier, does it?"

The discipline of the agents, though, refused to let them wallow in the moment. Now that the crossing from the tunnel was thwarted, Hudson called his Mexican counterpart, Jorge Gonzalez, who had expected the call. Now nothing was standing in his way to nail Juan Rodrequs, and he could not hit his phone buttons fast enough. The Mexican federalies in Juarez were waiting, and their leader was speaking with Greg Foster when the call came in. "Si," was his only reply, and he ordered his men to don their battle gear. They piled into camouflage armored vehicles and rolled toward the Rodrequs compound, warehouse, and safe house.

It had been a long night for Rodrequs, but a thrilling one. A man who relished bloody violence, having spread so much of it along both sides of the border over the decades, he grinned at the thought of the killing and maiming his friend Racheed was about to wreak. But today there was other business at hand. He would summon his inner circle for a discussion later that day on how to manage the influx of Pakistani heroin that would flow his way.

As he watched the moonlight shine through his picture windows, he shifted the handle on his favorite recliner and drew a match to light an oversized cigar. He then poured himself a glass of straight vodka as he unwound from the previous few hours. He also dialed the cell phone of Diego Garcia.

Garcia was down in the tunnel, his mind tortured at images of the events of the last few hours. His thoughts were obsessed with what was happening in the Mendez Auto Shop. The damp, clammy air of the tunnel provided little respite from the heat above. His solitude was broken by the approach of two SWAT team members, still in battle gear.

"Garcia?" they asked. "You're free to come up. Everything is secure in the auto shop." The SWAT team walked briskly back to the elevator, Garcia trailing slowly behind. Following a silent ride on the elevator, they entered the auto shop.

The four bodies of the terrorists, bloodied and mangled, still lay on the floor, awaiting another team for further investigation and removal. Garcia was hardly a stranger to dead bodies. He had seen dozens of them in his years with the cartel, usually more gruesome than what lay before him now. But the sight of the dead terrorists was too much this time, and he glanced away.

As he stared at a wall, his cell phone buzzed. He answered to hear his boss on the other end and put his index finger to his lips, indicating the agents to be silent. He then stepped toward an empty corner of the shop, hoping for a shred of privacy.

"Diego, my brother!" chirped Rodrequs. "Where are you?"

Diego could tell Juan was in a good mood. He felt a biting pang of guilt, knowing that Rodrequs was a happy man on this morning after.

"I uh...I am at home." Diego covered his stutter with an emotional plea. "Rosa was supposed to call me, and I am waiting for her."

"Oh? Is everything all right?"

"Si, my friend. I had talked to her last night, and she sounded upset. One of her aunts is ill, and she was supposed to call me back."

Rodrequs had a never-ending soft spot for Diego's otherwise homely wife. "I see. I was going to tell you to get over here, to help me plan a meeting with our people. But if Rosa needs you, then by all means, my brother, stay there for her."

"Gracias." It then occurred to Diego that this may be the last time he would ever talk to his boss and longtime friend. Hudson had told him that Rodrequs would either be arrested or killed when the terrorist plot was thwarted, and he knew Juan's hours were numbered.

"I will be by as soon as I can," said Diego. He paused, "Juan?"

"Yes?"

"I just...I was just thinking a while ago about how we got to where we are. It was not that many years ago that we were on the streets."

Rodrequs smiled at the memory. "Ah, yes. Filthy little children just trying to get by. And now look. My products all over the continent. The best that can money buy!"

"Yes. Richer and more powerful than anyone else."

"Well, my friend, I did not do it alone," chided Rodrequs. "You have been by my side, as my brother, through good and bad."

Garcia grimaced. "Actually, I am the one who owes you. Rosa and I both."

Rodrequs was not accustomed to sentimentality, and scarcely knew how to react. "Think nothing of it. Just get here whenever you can."

The connection broke with a click. Garcia put his phone down, propped himself against the wall with an outstretched arm, and stared blankly at the stained gray concrete on the floor. Several seconds passed before an agent approached him from behind. "What'd he say?" said the official.

Garcia sighed heavily, searching for strength. "He's going to have a meeting of the cartel members today," he replied in nearly a whisper. "Nothing else."

"I'll tell Hudson," said the agent. "And, your ride is here."

An FBI vehicle was waiting out front to transport him to the command center. Diego trudged outside, climbed in the black sedan before him, and sped away, never looking back at the grimy, battered auto shop that shrank in the distance.

*****

Juan Rodrequs was, as usual, far less solemn. Before dialing Garcia, he had called for his favorite prostitute, Juanita, to provide some late-night pleasure. The night was still young, and Juanita and her lack of inhibition was not the only thought that widened his evil grin. The influx of Pakistani heroin would solidify the cartel's power and influence, as they would be the only ones with a supply of such product from Pakistan. The tens of millions of dollars generated by its sale would saturate the cartel's deep pockets, and Rodrequs' lavish lifestyle would continue indefinitely.

Within minutes, two of the six armed guards on the property escorted Juanita into the parlor. With hollow, glassy eyes and a partially buttoned white blouse that hung well below her bare shoulders, she arrived in good form, at least to her client. Juan poured her a large glass of grapefruit juice and vodka while serenading her with a mocking ditty, "Juan and Juan-i-ta, Juan and Juan-i-ta" and erupting in gutteral roars of laughter.

The two guards retired to the front entrance, and Juanita had just pulled off Rodrequs' trousers when a crash echoed in the distance. He pushed her aside and leaped to his feet to see a caravan of eleven armored vehicles, which had knocked down the front gate and were barreling down the dusty lane toward the house. The six armed guards were quickly dispatched by the federalies as they approached the house.

In an instant, Rodrequs knew the federalies were upon them. "*Those bastards! Those bastards!*" he screamed as he struggled with his pants and raced into the next room, reaching for weapons from his well-stocked arsenal.

Now armed with AK-47s and 9-millimeter handguns, Rodrequs flew to the windows, surveying the enemy as Juanita curled up in a fetal position, piercing the room with her shrieks. His six guards fanned out across the compound, heading to predetermined locations for the best possible defense.

The troops, sixty-one in number, parked their vehicles parallel to the walls of the house, and were using them for cover. The compound was now surrounded on all four sides, covering every door, window, and corner. The captain, partially crouching behind the hood of one vehicle, bellowed to the compound through a bullhorn.

"Rodrequs! We know you are in there. Come out peacefully, with your hands up."

The plea brought no response, and was repeated again. Hearing no reply, the captain started to stand up straight, only to be driven below the hood by a well-placed shot from Rodrequs.

The shot was a signal to attack, and the federalies opened fire. The compound windows shattered, the velocity blowing tiny shards into the faces of Rodrequs and his screaming whore. Rodrequs managed to return fire, and the AK-47s sprayed a deadly hailstorm of bullets into the armored vehicles. They had little effect, though, as the troops knelt on the other side of the vehicles, threatened only by flying glass from reinforced windshields that could not stand the strain.

Half of the troops made a run for the compound, dodging bullets that threw dust from the ground. Several died in the move, but over three dozen made it to the doors, kicking them open and bursting inside. Three of the armed guards were killed in the action. Rodrequs, bleeding from wounds to the left shoulder and abdomen, scrambled for protection behind sofas and cabinets, still firing.

His response took the lives of two federalies, who shook violently as they succumbed to a hail of AK-47 cartridges. But the final three armed defenders were eliminated as well, leaving only Rodrequs and his prostitute, whose shrill screams were silenced as her body vibrated from a riddle of gunfire, killing her instantly. Vases, pitchers, and bottles of Rodrequs' finest liquors disintegrated in the firestorm, the sounds of their destruction ringing off the walls and competing with the echo of bullets that ricocheted off walls and ceilings.

As he had escaped danger time and again in his life, Juan Rodrequs had made a pact with himself. Surrender was not an option, and neither was custody. As he heard the cries for surrender, he was consumed with animalistic rage.

"*Never, you bastards!*" he screamed. "*I will make you die.*"

He sprang from behind the sofa and ran toward his arsenal in the next room. Though bullets penetrated his body, he somehow made it, pursued by over fifteen invaders. As he attempted to dive behind a mahogany table in the gun room, a stream of fire rocked his body, and he writhed as the blood oozed from him. He dropped to the floor, dead before he hit.

At the American command center in El Paso, Jack Hudson felt the vibration of his phone in his pocket, and answered to hear Gonzalez' voice with news of Rodrequs's demise. “Good. Thanks,” he said. “What about the warehouse and the safe house?”

“We had no resistance at the safe house,” replied Gonzalez. “And there were only two guards at the warehouse. We took care of both of them, and did not lose a man there. We secured very large quantities of drugs, and a lot of weapons and explosives.”

“Thanks. We appreciate it.” Hudson turned to his agents. “Rodrequs is dead. The Mexican troops got him in his compound.” The men nodded in approval as Hudson gazed at the wall, repeating himself to no one in particular, “We got `em. We got `em all.” He then caught himself. “Except the one that matters most.”

CHAPTER XXXVI

One agent immediately whirled back to his screen and checked on Racheed's location. "Jack, they're still out there," he said. "They're still eastbound on I-10."

Hudson whipped his body around and strode to that screen, leaning down with his palms open on the table in front of him. "Yeah. They're already forty-eight miles out. Dammit! How fast is he going?"

The agent switched to a different computer program, which calculated the speed. "He's only going around 65. But there's nothing out there but open road. What else is he going to do?"

"Yeah, and if he decides to hide, he'll have plenty of places out in that nowhere land. Thank God we've got that device on his phone. Else, we'd never find him," replied Hudson, who reached for his own cell once again. He dialed it and spoke with his customary brusqueness. "We've got the terrorists eastbound on I-10. It's a black Ford SUV, just passed mile marker 48. Get a plane up there, to track him."

Sitting at a landing strip outside of El Paso was an unmarked high-wing Cessna, nose pointed to the runway. Three darkly-dressed men, an FBI pilot, a radio operator, and a third man for backup, stood outside the fuselage as they had for hours, expecting a call to take off on surveillance. The pilot's name was Johnny Wistert, a veteran of the Gulf War who had racked up thousands of hours in the air, much of it in fighter jets. The buzz of a cellphone in Wistert's pocket pierced the quiet.

"Yeah?" answered Wistert. He heard the instructions. "Right. We're on it." He slapped the phone shut and turned to the other two. "Black Ford SUV eastbound on I-10. Mile marker 48 a couple of minutes ago. Doing about 65."

The men scurried inside the plane, and instantly the motor caught, the propeller whirling. The Cessna taxied down the runway and within minutes was darting through the night sky, trying to locate the Ford. The agents were armed with the same tracking mechanisms Hudson had in the command center, so they knew precisely where Racheed's vehicle was.

Wistert chose a flight path that aligned with I-10, and with little effort, they caught up with Racheed. Hudson was on the plane's radio, and his authoritative bellow reverberated through the plane. "Stay with them, *stay with them,*" he barked. "Keep back far enough that they don't see or hear you. But keep that vehicle in your sights at all times. Understand? At *all* times."

Heeding his words, Wistert lifted and the plane rose to a height where its running lights were less noticeable. With the rise went the familiar whirr of the motor. Unbeknownst to the nervous agents running around at the command center, Racheed was hardly paying attention to anything around him. In the drivers' seat, Adeeb barely looked anywhere but straight ahead, worried more about his speed than anything else.

Finally, he let on his concerns. "We're going about 70. Do you think that's a little too fast?"

Racheed did not care to be bothered. "Why do you say that?"

"I don't want to get anywhere over the speed limit. What if we are stopped?"

"Don't worry about it," snapped Racheed. "Just keep driving.

Besides, we are in the middle of nowhere. Who in the hell is going to care?" Not caring to argue with his leader, Adeeb shut his mouth and stared ahead once again.

Racheed's annoyance lasted only a few seconds, as he realized that he should try and contact the other two teams. "I'm going to call them," he said to Adeeb. "They should be well into New Mexico by now."

He took his cell phone from his pocket. At the command center, the agent in charge of the tracking device on the phone motioned to Hudson. "He's trying to call someone," the agent said.

The call went to the phone of the passenger in the SUV of the Las Vegas team. Racheed heard no rings; instead, the answering system immediately came on. "Why doesn't he have his phone on?" asked Racheed, clearly irked. "He knows damn well he's supposed to." Racheed left a brief message, demanding the terrorist call him immediately.

Next, he dialed the passenger of the SUV heading to Mount Rushmore. "He's trying someone again," said the agent at the command center.

Once more, the answering system picked up. "What is going on here?" snapped Racheed. "Why don't they answer?" He left another quick message ordering a callback.

Racheed slipped his phone back in his pocket. "*What is the deal with this?*" he demanded, as if Adeeb would have the solution. "Our brothers knew damn well to turn their phones on. They don't listen to a word I say." His exaggeration turned elsewhere. "Garcia told us these phones were the best of the best. And I can't call shit on them."

"Maybe we are in a dead zone," pondered Adeeb. "It is so isolated here. Maybe reception is impossible."

"I don't know," said Racheed dismissively. "These phones were supposed to be worth something."

In a huff, he looked out the window and for the first time, wondered if there were chinks in his plan. *The other four were supposed to be better than this*, he thought. *Didn't I train them better*? In a few seconds, though, Adeeb's suggestion began to work its way through his mind. *It's probably just a technical issue*, he mused. *I will try again when we get near civilization.* His mind drifted again as he gazed at the treeless, sprawling west Texas plains that flew by the window, pockmarked by mountains visible only in shadows from the light of the moon and the stars.

*****

After a little more than sixty minutes on the road, Racheed startled Adeeb with another change in plans.

"Get off at the next exit," he said.

Adeeb's neck jerked toward Racheed, his eyes widened. "Why?"

"I want to see if I can get better cell reception somewhere else. I need to talk to our brothers as soon as possible."

That did not satisfy Adeeb. "But Racheed. Do you not want to stay on the interstate?"

"Yes, of course! But if we turn north, it will bring us a little closer to El Paso, and maybe Carlsbad Caverns. Maybe that will improve my reception."

Adeeb was still unconvinced, but his adoration for Racheed let him go no further. In a couple of miles, the signs for Sierra Blanca, an isolated village of some five hundred, came into view. Adeeb steered the Ford onto the ramp of Exit 107 and turned north onto State Route 1111, off the interstate.

Despite its small size, Sierra Blanca is the county seat of Hudspeth County, which scatters only 3,300 residents over its hundreds of square miles. It is among the least populated areas in Texas, and at least an hour's drive from any key city or landmark.

In the Cessna above, Wistert radioed Hudson. "He's turning off the interstate."

Racheed's change of direction not only threw Adeeb, but rattled Jack Hudson as well. "What? Where?"

"At Sierra Blanca. He's going north on Route 1111."

"Stay with him, stay with him!" screamed Hudson into the radio. He then put down the handset. "What the hell is he doing? Is there even anything out on Route 1111?"

"Very little," said one agent, who was from the region. "Plains and some mountains. It's practically uninhabitable."

"Then what the hell..." Hudson's voice trailed in mid-sentence. At that moment, he whirled around and saw two of his SWAT team members. "We've got Garcia here," one said. "He's in the next room."

"Get his ass in here," demanded Hudson.

In seconds, Garcia was led into the room, like an errant schoolchild before a principal. "Buenos noches," said Garcia timidly.

Hudson ignored all greetings. "Our man Racheed has just turned off I-10 and is running up Route 1111 at Sierra Blanca."

Garcia was stunned to hear that Racheed was still alive, but equally puzzled at this turn of events. "Route 1111? But why? Why would he do that?"

Hudson detected the sincerity of the response. "I was hoping you could tell me. Does Rodrequs have any warehouses or something like that out there? Anything that he stores drugs or guns in?"

"No, senor. Almost nobody even lives out there. Juan's buildings are around El Paso, not out that far. No, senor, no, no." Perplexed at the line of questioning, Garcia was repeating himself. "Juan is a smart man. It would make no sense for him to store things that far from anything else."

"Hmmh," said Hudson. "All right then." He waved a couple of fingers at the SWAT team members. "Take him back in the other room."

Before the SWAT team approached, Garcia blurted out a question. "How did Racheed get across the border? And make it so far into Texas?"

Hudson was not about to tell him. "Don't ask questions. I'm supposed to be the one doing that, remember?"

Diego heard the words, but had something else on his mind. "What about Rodrequs?"

"You'll find out later. See ya." Each SWAT team member grabbed one of Garcia's arms and led him away.

Hudson turned to his men in the command center. "Garcia doesn't have anything. Racheed is not heading for any warehouses, or arsenals, or anything like that. There's no reason he turns off on Route 1111, then. It's not going to take him anywhere that matters."

He stalked back and forth across the floor, as a tiger in a zoo. "What the hell is he doing? Out there all by himself...."

Jack Hudson was a lightning-fast thinker, and at that moment, an idea raced through his mind. In recent years, the American government had used drones to monitor the border, using tiny closed-circuit cameras that fed video back to screens viewed by federal agents. Eventually the idea of using drones for border defense came around, a concept that Homeland Security loved, though few ordinary Americans were aware of. Though light, the drones were able to carry a variety of smaller explosives that, when launched, could destroy targets upon impact.

While they were not commonly used, and certainly not as defensive shields, drones were stationed at various points along the border. Hudson wheeled in his chair and yelled down to a local FBI agent, helping monitor the screens. "You got drones in this area somewhere?"

"Sure do. We use them on border patrol. They come out of Biggs Air Field."

Hudson never bothered to reply, just reaching for his cell phone. This time the call went to Washington. "Jack Hudson here. I'm in El Paso, monitoring the situation with the terror plot."

"Yes, Hudson." was the response. The voice came from Glenn Elliott, the director of the Federal Bureau of Investigations in Washington, a veteran bureaucrat. "What do you have?"

"We have eliminated four of the six terrorists. One of our SWAT teams closed in on the auto shop, the one I described to you in my briefings. Four of the terrorists were in there, and we got `em all."

"Dead?"

"Yes. No survivors. We lost two of ours, though."

"Too bad about that," said Elliott, a trace of concern in his voice. "But good to hear otherwise. The White House will breathe a sigh of relief on that one. So will the Secretary of State. Did you get the mastermind, too?"

"No. That's what I'm calling you for." Hudson struggled to contain himself. Even after all these years in public service, he never became used to government hoops.

"Where is he?"

"He apparently changed his plans. Our informant thought he was going across with the others, but he changed his mind. He and his partner went across in downtown El Paso."

"How did that happen?" Elliott was equally perplexed at the ease of the crossing.

"We don't know. The border patrol just waved him on, we think."

Elliott instantly recognized the political risks of the breakdown. "*Dammit!* Who is in charge of that? A known terror suspect gets across, and no one stops him! What kind of horseshit is that?"

Hudson was not taking the fall on that one. "I don't know, sir. It's not my department. I'm on it, and I'll make sure someone pays for it."

"You'd better. Congress will go ape, and the press will have a field day. Heads will roll, and you know it."

Hudson knew the political aspects of his position, but tried his best to ignore them. This was one of those times. "Look, sir, I've got more important things to worry about. The mastermind, this Racheed person, and his partner are on a highway in west Texas, in a remote location. We've got a plane over him, and we're tracking him from the devices on his cells."

"Good. What else do you want?"

The moment had come. "I want the authority to send a drone with a missile after him. It's so remote, and we can blow him off the road."

Elliott paused, then his throaty voice returned. "You better make sure of this. You say no one's around? We can't have innocent bystanders blown away on this. It would be a public-relations nightmare."

His concern for the bureaucracy grated on Hudson. "Nobody who's innocent is going to die. But if this guy gets away..."

"Yeah, yeah, I know," interrupted Elliott. "Why can't you just send a state trooper out there? Do we really need to send a drone after him? I mean, come on, Jack!"

"For God's sake, sir! He's well-armed, and I am almost positive he's got a bomb in his car that could blow up half of downtown somewhere!"

Elliott picked up on the last statement. "What the hell do you mean? Didn't you defuse all those bombs?"

"Yes, I got all of them in the auto shop. But like I said, Racheed made a change in plans. They had another SUV sent over to the safe house. We think he's got a new bomb in there." Hudson wasn't entirely sure, since the surveillance cameras were just out of range of Adeeb's work.

"What do you mean, you *think* he's got a new bomb?" demanded Elliott. "Where the hell were your surveillance cameras?"

"Racheed's top guy was just out of range. He was at the back of the car for a while, and we think he was planting something there, or working on it."

"Well then, where the hell is your informant? Isn't he worth anything, or just sitting around on his ass?"

Jack Hudson was not used to being questioned, and relied on every bit of self-control he could muster. "The informant was not privy to any conversation about the fourth vehicle. He had no idea where it came from. And I guess the conversation between Racheed and Rodrequs was face-to-face. We can't hear something like that."

"I don't know, I don't know," rambled Elliott. "I don't like it. Not enough to go on. If we take a guy out who's not even carrying a bomb, I mean, God. For all we know, Racheed may have chickened out, and is just running away! "

Now Hudson exploded. He knew Elliott's people had kept him apprised of the threat, and seethed at the insinuation that it was over. "*Dammit! Don't you do that to me!* You *know* this Racheed person is dangerous. *Hell, the government's committed how many resources to taking him out!* I don't give a shit if he doesn't have a bomb! For all we know, he's heading some place to get more! Or he may have a whole pile of explosives in this new vehicle and is playing with them *as we speak!*"

"Huh," replied Elliott, not having considered that possibility.

"*And I'll tell you something else,*" raged Hudson, yelling so loud that the other agents in the command center stared, awestruck at the scene. "If we don't get him now, who knows what he's going to do? He could be going anywhere, for all we know! If not now, he's going to get us *sometime*! This Racheed guy went to all this work to kill thousands of us. He's not just going to say, `oh, well, I tried,' and drown his sorrows in a beer, dammit!"

Hudson angrily pointed his finger at the receiver, as if Elliott could see it. "And I'll tell you one more thing. I don't want to hear about the political ramifications if we hit some innocent guy out in the middle of west Texas! I worry a *hell of a lot more* about the political ramifications if we let this bastard Racheed go, and *he kills thousands of people somewhere*! I am *not* going to have another 9/11 on my hands. *And don't you expect me to!*"

Elliott had no response, knowing Hudson's logic had cost him the argument. He thought about it for several seconds. During the pause, Hudson ran his fingers through his thinning hair out of sheer nervousness. The last few weeks had worn even on him, and he wondered if he could keep it up for much longer. Finally, Elliott's voice was heard on the other end.

"All right. I need to think about it. Give me a little bit."

Hudson could barely summon the energy to respond. "How long will that take?"

"I don't know, soon," replied Elliott. "You know, I could have your ass for this."

Thirty years in service had come to this moment, and for Jack Hudson, there was only one response. "Fine. I'll take that risk." He paused for effect. "We'll all sleep a hell of a lot better at night if we take out Racheed."

"Hmmh," said Elliott with a hint of a chuckle as he hung up.

CHAPTER XXXVII

Less than fifteen minutes later, Hudson's phone vibrated in his shirt pocket. Elliott had moved faster than he thought.

"Go ahead and do it."

Hudson was not about to let anything vague slip through. "Go ahead and send the drone, then?"

"Yeah," replied Elliott. "Just don't screw it up. Make damn sure there are no innocent bystanders around."

"All right," said Hudson. "Thanks. I'll keep you posted."

"You'd better," snapped Elliott as he broke the connection.

Elliott's permission relieved the malaise that Hudson felt a few minutes before, and a bolt of energy charged through his system. "All right then," he announced to his crew. "We've got the drone."

The drone was stationed at Biggs Army Airfield, adjacent to Fort Bliss, a sprawling U.S. Army complex northeast of El Paso. Hudson contacted the base commander, and briefed him on the operation.

"I just talked to Glenn Elliott, the FBI Director in Washington," said Hudson. "We've got the go-ahead to send a drone with a missile after him."

The base commander never hesitated. “Okay. What is Racheed's position, as close as you can tell us?”

Hudson motioned to the agent watching that screen. He shoved the phone at him. “Here, tell the exact location.”

The information was relayed. A few minutes of work at Biggs was all that was needed to attach a rocket to the drone, the result of hours of intensive training. The military tech personnel were well-prepared for contingencies such as this, though they seldom expected to use a drone for this purpose. Though Hudson was in control of the operation, the drone would physically be operated by military authorities, working in conjunction with the FBI command center.

Shortly, the drone was whirring in the air, soaring east across the barren west Texas landscape. The closed-circuit camera fed video back to the command center, and the agents stared at the screen, straining to see how much progress was made and how much further was left to fly in the early morning darkness.

The drone did not follow the path of the plane along Interstate 10, but darted across the wilds, taking the shortest route possible. Forty-five minutes after takeoff, the drone's camera, equipped with state-of-the-art night vision capability, picked up a black Ford, cruising along Route 1111 at just under sixty-five miles per hour.

“Use the remote, up, up,” barked Hudson, wanting the agent in charge to pan the camera up. Wistert's plane then came into view. Like the drone, Wistert had the same night-vision technology.

“That's him,” said Hudson. “Now, let's see if there's anything around there...”

The camera swayed back and forth, surveying the surrounding landscape. A derelict house came into view, an unwelcome sight in the command center.

A split-second decision needed to be made. “Think anyone's living there?” asked one agent.

“Can't imagine it. That looks like a shack,” said another.

“Yeah, but we can't risk it,” decided Hudson, remembering Elliott's words. “If someone's in it, and we end up hitting it, it'll be hell to pay.”

In the SUV, Racheed Ul-Bashar was completely oblivious to the air traffic surrounding him. The airtight cabin of the vehicle prevented most outside noise, and the spartan lights of both the plane and the drone would have been visible only if the passengers had contorted themselves unnaturally. Time and again, he tried to contact the other terrorists, again to no avail. At the command center, the agents noted his repeated attempts.

"What is going on?" he asked Adeeb. "I'm not getting anything!"

"Try your personal cell phone," suggested Adeeb. "Maybe that will work better."

"Sure, why not?" agreed Racheed. The result was the same as before.

"Shit!" Racheed slammed his phone back into his pocket. He had not expected this problem, and simmered at the thought of his other men failing him. But there was nothing that could be done amid this desolation, hundreds of miles from anywhere important and cut off from communications. He leaned back in his seat and tried to calm himself, chanting Islamic music and passages.

The drone settled in behind the Ford at a lower altitude than the plane. "Fan out, fan out," Hudson screamed for the camera to scan the panorama.

Nothing showed up on the screen. "Turn it around," Hudson asked for a rear view. There were no headlights in sight.

"No sign of anything, Jack," offered one agent.

Hudson radioed the trail plane. "Wistert! Any sign of people out there, any cars around?"

"Nothing at all," said Wistert, voice crackling in static. His own night-vision technology turned up, as he called it, "pure wasteland out here."

"Make damn sure, once again. I don't want any other cars anywhere near him," Hudson replied. He watched the drone camera pan the landscape again. Several seconds passed, and the highway remained empty, except for the Ford. Wistert's voice broke the silence. "Still nothing, Jack. Haven't seen another car for miles. No houses in sight, either."

This was the moment, the best chance Hudson was going to get, and he knew it. "All right. Do it."

He called back to Wistert. "I'm launching it." He then remembered that the blast would temporarily blind Wistert if he were still wearing the night-vision glasses. "Get your glasses off, and get yourself out of the way."

"Got it," replied Wistert. "I'm gonna enjoy watching this one. Over." He ascended to over 10,000 feet, heights that protected the plane from any concussion or flying shrapnel.

The remote at Biggs ordered the launch of the rocket, which seared through the night sky, emitting a slight flame. The flash was barely discernible, but created just enough to reflect in Adeeb's outside rearview mirror. "What the...." he said, not loud enough to disturb Racheed, who continued his Islamic chants.

The rocket administered a near-perfect hit, slicing through the rear of the Ford, not far from the gas tank. The tank burst into flames, which in turn ignited the bomb. A massive fireball erupted, hundreds of feet high and thousands of degrees in intensity. The occupants in the front seat were annihilated and the vehicle disintegrated almost instantly, engulfed in white-hot flames that illuminated the landscape for miles and left a gaping depression in the pavement.

Racheed's dream was born on the desolate prairies of Seidu and Peshawar. It died on the equally lonesome plains of west Texas.

CHAPTER XXXVIII

At the command center, Jack Hudson waited for the drone to settle into place, having lifted away from the blast scene. As it did, the camera sent back video of the scene, but could not turn fast enough to provide a complete view of the inferno.

"Wistert! Did you see it?" he radioed to the plane.

"Sure did," said Wistert jauntily. "Great blast! Nothing left but burning wreckage."

"Did anyone get out?" Hudson asked cautiously.

"Not a chance," replied Wistert. "We watched the whole thing happen. There's nothing left of the vehicle. That thing's burning so hot that no one could make it."

As the drone camera settled, it sent back images of nothing but blinding, towering orange glow. The fireball dominated frame after frame, and Hudson sat back, awestruck at the magnitude of the blast.

"Geez," he said in a near-whisper, at a rare loss for words.

"Did you see the size of that thing?" said Wistert, almost breathlessly. "Holy crap, that thing was big!"

"Obviously that car had a bomb in it after all," replied Hudson, recalling Elliott's doubts. “I mean, how big that thing was...”

“Just damn glad it didn't go off in the middle of Nashville or somewhere,” observed Wistert.

Hudson's mind was racing too fast to offer a response, or a even sigh of relief. He hung up and called the Hudspeth County Police to secure the bomb scene. He then ordered several FBI agents and crime scene techs to that location.

The strain of the last several weeks had culminated in these last frantic hours, and the adrenaline rushed from Hudson's body. His legendary stamina, which had carried him to the heights of his career, could no longer hold up. The lives of thousands of Americans were saved, and this September 11 would not be a repeat of 2001. He dropped into a chair, his exhausted body limp as if no muscles could function. It took more strength than he could imagine just to raise his head and utter to his men, “it's over.”

Though they had seen the video feeds and heard Wistert's messages, the agents knew nothing was complete until Hudson gave the word. Then they stretched their arms over their heads, wiggling their backs and pushing their legs as far as they could reach, releasing the tension that had gripped them since the previous afternoon. Smiles broke across a few faces, while others shook their heads and raised their eyebrows, incredulous at what had just transpired.

Tony Martinez pulled his tired frame from his seat and stepped over to Hudson, slapping him on the shoulder. “Good work, my man,” he said. “That was some kind of a job.”

“Yeah. Thanks,” said Hudson, mustering a chuckle, thinking he had not slept in nearly forty-eight hours. He then excused himself from the command center and trudged outside to his vehicle. The center had been a pressure cooker for hours, and now it was over, he could not take another minute. There were still calls to make, and a little privacy was desperately needed.

The first call went to Glenn Elliott in Washington. “Jack Hudson here. We sent in the drone, and it did the job. Racheed and his partner were taken out.”

“You sure about that?” quizzed Elliott. “No chance they got out?”

“None. We annihilated them. The fireball was so big and hot, the vehicle disintegrated. There's a helluva crater in the roadway because of it.”

Elliott knew what that meant. “So there was a bomb, after all?”

Hudson was vindicated. “Yep. Sure was.”

“Hmmh,” A compliment would have brought Elliott down to Hudson's level, and that would not happen. “So, it's over.”

“Yeah. We got `em all. Everyone involved is dead, save for the informant.”

“The White House and State Department will be glad to know. We really did a job on this.”

Hudson knew that Elliott had never left his office in Washington since the tip came in. “Yeah. Right.”

He hung up and dialed District 6 headquarters of the Illinois State Police, where it had all begun weeks ago. His call went through to Lee Bickford, the commander.

“Jack Hudson here. I wanted to inform you that our operation was successful. The terrorist threat was eliminated, as were all of the participants.”

“Glad to hear it,” replied Bickford. “Congratulations on what you did.”

“Well, I'm calling to congratulate you as well,” said Hudson “You did a fine job in helping us, and thanks for your cooperation and advice. This country owes a great debt to you and your people, and particularly Trooper McCord. Without his professionalism, this plot may have never unraveled. I think a commendation is in order.”

“He's in line for one,” said Bickford. “We were happy to help. Good to hear it all turned out all right.”

“Sure did. Thanks again.” Hudson said his goodbyes, clicked off the phone, and leaned back against the head rest. He then dialed his wife for the first time in three days.

*****

There was still one matter to deal with. Hudson pulled himself back from his tepid celebratory call to his wife and climbed out of his car. He stalked back inside the command center and entered the room where Diego Garcia was being held.

Garcia's eyes were charged with anxiety, but Hudson was in no mood for soothing. “It's all over. You're safe.”

Garcia's life had been so tense over the last few weeks that his chest heaved downward in a deep sigh of relief. Then the conflicts in his mind arose once more. “What about Rodrequs?”

“Dead. The Mexican authorities raided the compound, and blew him away.”

The news pierced Garcia like a spear. He remembered his last conversation with Rodrequs, just earlier in the night. Images of their time as desperate, dirty little boys on the streets of Juarez, came immediately to mind. He thought of how they had risen to the top, side-by-side as friends, partners, brothers. The late-night beers, the bawdy jokes, Rodrequs' toothy smiles whenever a new deal was made, all flashed across his mind. So did the traffic stop in Illinois. His self-doubt at his chosen path, informant against his old friend, crept back in.

Finally, Garcia remembered his next question. “What about Rosa?”

“I'll call Springfield to release her. We'll fly her back to El Paso..”

That was all that Diego cared to hear. He wanted to be rid of Jack Hudson in the worst way. “Is there anything else, then?”

“Nope. You won't be charged with anything. You're done here.”

“Also, my children are still in Mexico,” said Garcia. “I want them sent over. Will you allow them to cross?”

“Yeah, sure,” said Hudson. “I'll call the border patrol and okay it. Have them sent someplace in El Paso that doesn't arouse suspicion.”

“I've got a friend there named Velandia. I visit him quite a bit. They won't suspect anything if I tell the babysitter to go there.”

Hudson hardly cared for the particulars. “Fine, whatever.”

Though his mind was still tortured with doubt, Garcia felt a pang of appreciation for Hudson. He mustered a measure of courtesy for the brusque commander who had given him and his wife a new opportunity. “Gracias, senor. For everything.”

“Yeah, see ya,” dismissed Hudson, turning on his heel and exiting the room.

Diego Garcia stepped toward the door and walked alongside his SWAT escort, who would drive him to Velandia's house. He proceeded outside into the early-morning darkness, lit only by curving sliver of the moon. As he boarded the FBI vehicle, his mind was a whirlpool of emotion, dominated by the repetitive images of the events of the last hours, since he had made the crossing with the terrorists into the United States.

EPILOGUE

Solomon Ul-Bashar had always loved the sunshine. As a boy, he had soaked up its rays on the sands of the beach in front of his family's home. As a man, he always rose before daybreak, true to his military training. As he prepared for the day, he always took a moment to watch the sun rise, reveling in its warm glow.

He still found solace in the sunlight, his only comfort in his ten-by-twelve cell in an Islamabad prison. The sunshine that penetrated the two-foot-square cell window was the only color amid the filthy gray walls and lifeless concrete. The late summer heat permeated the walls, leaving no respite for those trapped inside. For the last twelve months, he had languished in this animal's cage, convicted for providing his brother with the false military documents.

As he paced in his cramped space, he recalled how his nightmare began in mid-September last, sitting in his black swivel chair in his office at military headquarters across town. That September morning was no different than any other. He was going about his daily business, checking flight records, analyzing terror threats, and devising ways to penetrate the Taliban and other enemies within

Pakistani borders. His train of thought was interrupted by a pounding at his door.

As he cracked the door and peered into the hallway, a chill shot up his body, and his hairs stood on end. Several high-ranking officers were waiting with a detail of military police. The group brushed past Solomon, who stood at attention, and barged inside.

No words were wasted. "Mr. Ul-Bashar, it has been brought to our attention that you have aided in a major terrorist plot in the United States."

Solomon had tried to forget his exchanges with Racheed. He had feared that his provision of false military documents to his brother would be exposed, and had tucked his fright away, in a dark corner of his mind. In daytime, he was too busy to think of his indiscretions, though in recent weeks he had slept fitfully.

His first instinct was denial, but his remaining sense of honor would not allow it. He chose to question the accusation, hoping it was a mistake, or something he had overlooked. "What are these charges you say?"

"Silence!" The commander's directive was angry and foreboding. "Do not speak unless directed!" Solomon could only remain at attention.

"We have received information of a terrorist attack in the United States. The American embassy, and their State Department, have advised us that a man named Racheed Ul-Bashar, who is your brother, was the leader of the attack. His plan was to bomb major American cities. What do you have to say for this?"

Solomon could muster no words. "*Speak!*" barked the commander. His subject remained silent.

The interrogation continued. "We have also learned that it was *you* who aided in this plot. You supplied improper documents to your brother to help him with his attack. Again, what do you have to say?"

Solomon longed to beg forgiveness, and spew the sorrow that he had felt for his role. He wanted to remind his superiors of his dedication to his country since his induction twelve years before. His mind was a whirlwind, but his mouth was still. He was familiar with Pakistani military tribunals, where justice was an afterthought and innocence was rarely proven.

"Arrest this man!" screamed the commander. The military police stepped forth and jerked Solomon's arms behind his back, harshly clapping handcuffs on him. As the detail shoved him down the hall, Solomon struggled to maintain any semblance of the proud carriage he had worn for the duration of his military career, which was sure to end even if his life did not.

The tribunal was a sham, set on a guilty verdict. He was then escorted forcefully to his prison cell, sentenced to be his home for the next thirty-five years. By then, he would be an old man, likely living on the harsh streets. His parents would be gone by then, but in many ways, they had already died, outcasts from their privileged social position.

Mahammed had made the trip to visit Solomon once, and the despair in his face was too much for the son to bear. He hoped his father would never return. His mother did not even send her thoughts, mortified at her social shunning, mortified at death of one son and the disgrace of another. The sun then sank behind a dark cloud, leaving Solomon alone in his anguish.

*****

Across the world, Carlos Santos ignored the warmth of the September sun as he trudged up the flower-lined steps of his villa in his exclusive Mexico City neighborhood. The flowers were brown and dying as the summer turned to fall, and tiny weeds reached for the sky in their midst.

The rest of the villa was slipping into disrepair as well, as peeling paint and chipping stucco were gaining an increasing foothold. He saw the blemishes gaining on him, but was little concerned with their advance. He had painstakingly attended to his villa and gardens in the twenty-one years he had lived there, making it among the finest residences in Mexico City. Now, he had neither the pride nor the inspiration as he completed his first year after being pushed out of his position in the Mexican Army.

Burned in his mind was the shame of that day. He had been summoned to the commanding general's office and informed of the thwarted terror plot of Racheed, a man he had trusted implicitly. His superior was a longtime friend and ally, but on this day, he could do nothing. With a menacing glare, he simply asked Carlos for his security clearance and keys to both his office and the front door of headquarters. Tears of shock and embarrassment flowed down Santos' cheeks as the commander abruptly said, “you have disgraced your country.”

In the days that followed, word of his forced retirement leaked to the press, and soon Santos was splashed across the headlines, piling on his humiliation. No reason was given for his unexpected retirement, and many speculated that he had succumbed to the same corruption that riveted most Mexican authorities. He was in no position to rebut the claims. After all, it was his naivety that aided Racheed in his horrific intentions.

He exited the garden and passed through a sliding glass door, ignoring the light switch in his darkened parlor, and slumped into his favorite chair, still numbed from the recent past. From the next room, he could hear the whimpers of his sobbing wife, whose social position among the Mexico City elite was forsaken. He closed his eyes and hoped to drift off, escaping from the misery wrought by his precious daughter's boyfriend, a man he had wished for a son-in-law.

The day was far from over for the ex-general. He wearily rose from his chair, trudged to the garage, and climbed into his navy blue Mercedes, a car he once adored, but now seemed trivial. Trance-like, he spent the next twenty minutes navigating the bustling streets of Mexico City until he reached the gate of a campus of red brick buildings, each like the next.

He halted at the guard shack at the gate and informed the attendant who he was, and his purpose for being there. The guard allowed him to pass, and he strained his neck to avoid a glimpse of the subtly-placed sign that signified the campus as a mental institution.

Santos parked his car and walked, shoulders drooping and head bowed, across the lot and through the glass double doors into the lobby of Building D. Facing him across the lobby was an elevator with a silver door, shiny enough to pass for a mirror. He pushed the "Up" button and, once the elevator arrived, pushed "10" for the floor he needed.

The lights above his head lit, one after the other, from 1 upward, finally stopping at 10. The bell rang and the door slid open to reveal an endless hallway, with a nurse's station in the middle. The antiseptic smell familiar to hospitals wafted over him, and he proceeded down the hallway to Room 1087.

Maria was waiting for him as he stepped through the door. Dressed in a white terry robe, she interrupted her gaze out the window as she heard his footsteps. Her face was gaunt, her frame thinner, her eyes hollow, and he fought back the same tears as every other time his eyes now fell upon his little girl.

The sight of her took him back to the evening when he broke the news of Racheed to her. The fear that raced through his veins as he drove to her apartment that night, hours after his career had ended, exceeded anything he had felt in the army, fearful of her reaction upon knowing that her beloved Racheed was not only a terrorist, but dead.

He knew she would not believe him, and she did not. Her rage was uncontrollable, throwing everything she could find, physically attacking him, scratching his face and hands with her manicured nails. Finally, she was convinced of her father's sincerity and collapsed to the floor, uttering primal screams of anguish that still haunted his mind.

Her fragile psyche shattered, she now resided within these sterile walls, spending her days wandering the halls, singing to herself, and peering out the window with wide, glassy eyes. Those coal-black eyes, once vivacious and full of life, met his as he stood in the doorway.

"Father! Dear father! How are you today?" Maria said, a disturbed smile breaking across her face. He responded affirmatively and watched as she swayed across the floor past her bed, arms extended as if dancing. “What a beautiful day it is!”

She flitted about in the sunlight for several seconds, seemingly a child of four again, oblivious to the passing world. She then repeated the words that unfailingly struck terror in his soul. “Have you heard from Racheed? Oh my darling, Racheed! When will he come for me?”

Santos was now close enough to touch her, and he clasped his arms around her as she babbled, “Oh, my darling Racheed, my love! When will he come for me? When will he come?”

*****

The sun was also bright in the skies above Ciudad Juarez, where a secluded compound was tucked away on the outskirts of town. A sprawling hacienda, shops, and storage sheds lined the property, accessible only by a forgotten dirt road past the edge of the city.

Few residents of Juarez knew this compound existed, and Juan Rodrequs had wanted it that way. Now its new occupant, Diego Garcia, was glad of it. Years before, he had watched his old friend turn on his mentor, the former leader of the cartel, killing him and seizing control himself. Garcia had sat at Rodrequs' side ever since, and learned well. Now he had stepped in for Juan and was himself the kingpin in the cartel.

Shortly after his days as an informant against Racheed ended, Garcia moved his family from their previous comfortable surroundings into this masterpiece, a reflection of the unusually good taste exhibited by his old boss, who was otherwise a cur. His first order of business was to rip up the carpet in the parlors, removing any sign of the stains of blood that Rodrequs had spilled in his demise.

As the new leader of the cartel, his income was now among Mexico's richest, and he lived accordingly. Though the other cartel members were rattled at the loss of Rodrequs, they had no reason to suspect Garcia was behind it. His alibi that he was with his children on the night of the federalies' raid rang true with them.

They also had no idea that Garcia was once again an informant. As before, he was in close contact with the Americans, this time advising them of the operations of other cartels. Some of his calls went to Tony Martinez, who had transferred to a supervisory position within the DEA. Others went to his old nemesis, Hudson, whose success in shutting down Racheed earned a promotion to one of the highest-ranking men in the FBI's Washington headquarters.

Rosa also had no idea of his secret life. Their marriage had changed in the year since their ordeal, and they now slept in separate rooms. She refused to enter Rodrequs' old bedroom since, locking the door when she first arrived and never reaching for the key. A photo of her husband standing next to Juan Rodrequs was on Rosa's nightstand, much to her Diego's discomfort, who prayed the keepsake was a memento of him, not his late boss. But she clearly relished the upgrade in their lifestyle, and enjoyed all the luxuries that few other Mexican women could.

As he massaged a bottle of Corona and gazed out on the courtyard, he clutched the cross necklace that had given him strength through the past year. He knew this new life could not last. At some point, he would be exposed, or his inside work would hasten the demise of the cartel. Then he would have to flee, possibly back to America, hopefully with Rosa.

He reflected on the numerous crossings he had made through the tunnel, and his crossing back to Mexico to take over his old friend's cartel. Now as the late-summer sun set beyond his mansion, he wondered if another crossing was to come.

The End

And as you know, reviews are gold to authors....so, if you enjoyed this novel, please consider taking a moment to write an honest review. It is easy to post on Amazon or Goodreads.com, or simply email your comments to Publisher@oaktreebooks.com.

About the Author

C. Ed Traylor retired from the Illinois State Police with the rank of captain after 29 years of service. During that time, he served as patrolman, investigator, investigative supervisor, bureau chief, and staff officer. He subsequently served as police chief of a small central Illinois town before returning to the ISP with an assignment as investigator on the Federal Health Care Fraud Task Force.

Traylor earned a B.A. in social justice from the University of Illinois-Springfield and graduated from the F.B.I. National Academy in Quantico, Va. He lives with his wife, Pat, in rural Waggoner, Illinois. The couple has two daughters.

CPSIA information can be obtained at www.ICGtesting.com
Printed in the USA
LVOW11s2058190516

489052LV00002BA/352/P